Frank Meyer

America's Choice

Tragedy
or Triumph

CHARTER OAK
BOOKS

Published by
Charter Oak Books
P. O. Box 412
Olathe, Colorado 81425
www.freedom-loving-books.com

Copyright © 2007 by Charter Oak Books
Cover design by Aaron J. Meyer

Library of Congress Catalogue Card Number:

ISBN-13: 978-0-9785476-1-5
ISBN-10: 0-9785476-1-6

9 780978 547615

90000

Printed in the U.S.A.

Acknowledgements

I thank God for the privilege of being born in a nation where I had the freedom to explore many options in life.

When it comes to people to thank for help with this work, I have to start with my wife, Judith, who has been invaluable for her English skills and the love, patience, and encouragement she offered through trying times during the last four decades.

Then there are the members of my writer's critique group. An unlikely number of strangers working on different types of fiction, we came together with a common commitment to get published. Building a trust relationship, we learned to critique with honesty that encouraged us to press for excellence. John Craft, D'Ann Lincott-Dunham, Kim McKinnon, Gail Saunders, and, later, Mike and Vicki Ruchholft gave terrific feedback and plot suggestions that improved this book and the Clark Evans trilogy. Thanks also to Christine Allen for her work and encouragement.

I am thankful for the spiritual wisdom that comes from my relationship with the Lord Jesus Christ. He changed my life while serving as a young Air Force radio intercept operator in the Far East during the Korean War era.

After my discharge, I had the privilege of being discipled by Jim Downing, Hal Ward, and others while in training at Glen Eyrie, the Navigator headquarters in Colorado Springs. They laid a solid, Biblical foundation in my life that the Holy Spirit has used to keep me through the trials and tests that have come in later life.

I'm also thankful for the higher education I received at Whitworth College, Princeton Theological Seminary, and Regency University. The mentoring by men like Drs. Harry Dixon and David Dilworth was more important than knowledge gained from books.

Then there are far too many authors of great works to name who have informed me of America's awesome history, plus the harsh realities we now face because of our failures to maintain the greatness we once could claim. Joel Skousen's *Weekly World Affairs Brief* provided insights that shaped the plots in these novels. Thank God they all had the freedom to tell the truth.

It is my faith and trust in God's grace and mercy that gives me hope for the future. Jesus Christ is the King of all kings and the Lord of all lords. He will reign until all His enemies are put under His feet.

Comments from our readers about Frank's novel Gun Rites released in the fall of 2006.

"Frank, your book was fantastic! I sat up half the night because I could not put it down! A real winner!"
Jay Grimstead, Coordinator International Church Council Project and Coalition on Revival (CORE)

"Meyer has given us a novel which I thought was going to be a cheap (but cleaner!) knock-off of Unintended Consequences, but it took a surprising turn. And then another! It's not the most gripping thriller I've read (although it is quite a good read), but it is perhaps the most unusual one in that it presents an explanation that most novelists don't get, and don't care about. . . . When was the last time you read a novel that left you pondering world affairs, and their relevance to your life?"
Daniel New, former missionary, father of first US soldier, Michael New, to refuse to wear a U.N. beret

"Thank you so very much for your outstanding book GUN RITES. It's exciting and so very true. The cover design is fabulous. Who is Aaron J. Meyer? It deserves an award because it is captivating and full of life and message."
John Chalfant, author America: A Call To Greatness

"Your book is COMPELLING. I began yesterday and haven't been able to put it down. You have a real knack for storytelling while pointing to a moral. I will recommend your book to others.
Jack Monnet, PhD, author Awakening to our Awful Situation

America's Choice

Tragedy

Chapter One

The Beginning of the End

James Parr burst into his country home near Montrose, Colorado, slamming the door. His wife, Ann, frowned. She watched him slump into a chair, lean over the table, and clutch his head in frustration.

Placing a hand on her hip, she gave him a stern look. "Now what have you and General Leland been up to this time? You look like the world's coming to an end."

James, a former Army chaplain, shook his head. "It's enough to make a preacher cuss, so help me!"

"What?"

"I don't know how tell you."

"Oh come on, I doubt it can top all the gloom and doom you men have been conjuring up during the past weeks. Has there been another attempt on the general's life?"

"No--" James attempted to go on, but Ann cut him off.

"You went to console him while Florence visited her new grandson in the Springs."

"Yes, that's part of the problem." His hands chopped the air as he continued. "Mark is exasperated because he didn't convince Kenny to move his family here. Ken just can't

believe that Colorado Springs is Ground Zero, if and when
the Russians and Chinese launch their nuclear attack. Plus,
Mark couldn't keep Florence away from her new grandson.
She refuses to believe the strike could come within the next
twenty four hours."

"What? The strike might come tonight?" The color
drained from her face. She left the stove and sat down at
the kitchen table across from him. She had not wanted to
disagree with her husband whom she trusted and loved,
but she too found it difficult to believe such a disaster could
happen.

James shook his head. "Mark got an encrypted email
from General Brad Foster, Commander of the Mountain
Post at Fort Carson. Foster has begun dispersing his forces
into the mountains on an emergency training exercise. He's
doing it on his own initiative. His close friend, Air Force
General Robert Scott, has ordered the Stealth bombers
in his command on training missions that will take them
to isolated sites, along with their support crew and a full
compliment of weapons.

"Honey, these guys aren't noted for irrational actions.
They're among the few in command positions who don't
believe the propaganda coming out of Washington and
the administration. The word is that the leadership in
Washington has been called away on 'urgent personal
business.' Corporate jets are leaving the country in record
numbers. I'll lay odds that you'll see second-rate reporters
handling the national news tonight because the big boys will
be hiding in their prepared bunkers."

Ann scooted to the edge of her chair. "You mean this may
be the attack you've been warning everyone about? Tell me
that's not so."

James's look of despair gave her the answer. "God knows
we tried to warn the Christians and call them to repentance.
Mark's book, our Internet site, the radio talk shows we
spoke on, and holding all those meetings, which cost us a lot
of money, drew little response. Even knowledgeable people
think we're extremists for objecting to national identity
cards and roadblocks to catch terrorists."

He paused, rubbing his forehead before erupting in anger. "Roadblocks out here in the middle of nowhere, to catch terrorists no less. What a joke! I guess I might as well tell you I almost got in a shootout today coming home. I ran into Deputy Martinez and a National Guard trooper at a checkpoint east of town. Both of the idiots know me and know I have a permit to carry a concealed weapon. But still they demanded that I open my trunk. Plus, they wanted to confiscate my pistol. I swear, some day we'll probably have to fight those zombies."

"What did you do?"

"I put them on the spot and embarrassed them. I asked if they planned to shoot me if I didn't give them my weapon."

"You didn't!"

"Oh, yes. I looked them right in the eye and said, 'In Vietnam, I killed many a man braver than you'll ever be. You know I'm a law abiding citizen, so back off!' They knew I meant to draw."

"James!" Ann's voice had a scolding tone.

"Hey, if we give in to that kind of stupidity, where will it end? It all goes to show that our country has had it, and it's too late to do anything. Mark feels the same way. Tonight he's going to warn as many people as he can and tell them to 'get out of Dodge.' I've got Marcie sending emails to our supporters."

"So you think they'll strike tonight? What'll happen to Henry, Sarah, and the kids in Colorado Springs? We can't--"

"I'm going to call Henry as soon as he's home from work and plead with him to load the family in the SUV. They need to drive over here tonight. In fact, I'm going to order him to do it."

"But what about Florence? Is she coming home?"

"You know Florence. She loves the general, but they don't see eye to eye on this. She isn't about to leave that new baby. If the Russians had wind of her whereabouts and knew her, they'd think twice about nuking that place. If they send her to heaven, she'll probably toss thunder bolts at them."

"James, this is nothing to joke about!"

"It beats swearing."

"Oh," she gasped, wringing her hands, "what about Caleb?"

"Gunnison is not a target, but I called Russ on the way home. I told him he'd better get his firstborn home. If I know Caleb, he's in his Jeep with his weapons, planning to make it home in time for dinner. By the way, dear, you'd better check the frying pan. I don't want to be served a burned offering to celebrate our last meal as a free people."

Ann threw up her hands as she jumped out of her chair. "You men, joking when we should be praying."

James followed her to the stove. He put his arms around her as she turned the pieces of chicken in the skillet.

"We've done a lot a praying," he said, trying to comfort his faithful wife of nearly fifty years. "And we'll pray some more. But I believe God has heard and already decided what His answers are going to be. All we can do is accept the judgment we deserve as a nation."

Ann placed the lid on the pan, turned in his arms, and nestled her head against his chest. James held her close as tears streamed down his weathered face. For a moment, Ann felt safe.

•   For Jolene Howard, Secretary of Defense, it had been a long day. Attempting to balance the needs of America's worldwide military commitments was no small endeavor. With Captain Jarrell, her aid, she hurried into the Pentagon conference room for the military chiefs. Seeing only Admiral Earl O'Fallon, she asked, "Where are the others?"

"They've been called away."

Before he could explain, Jolene angrily threw her briefcase on the table. "What's going on? I've had meetings scheduled with several congressmen, but they canceled, because they've been called away on urgent business. How in God's name are we to get anything done if responsible people don't keep their appointments?"

The admiral started to speak just as Jolene's encrypted pager beeped.

"Now what?" Jolene read the message. " 'Red Dragon,'

what the--"

Captain Jarrell interrupted, "Ma'am, that's the code warning of an eminent nuclear attack on America. We've got to proceed right now to the FEMA bunker at Fort Weatherford."

She looked from the captain to the admiral, who showed no surprise. He said in a matter-of-fact tone, "That's what I was trying to tell you. I'm surprised you didn't receive the message sooner."

"Is this alert being sent to all our military units?" asked Jolene.

Admiral O'Fallon hesitated. "No, this is only for the command leadership. We can't send any alert until we know for certain that there is an actual attack. If this proves to be a false alarm, it will create chaos and throw kinks in our current operations."

Jolene's face revealed extreme shock. "But if our people are not notified until there's proof of launched missiles, they'll have no time to prepare or respond."

The admiral barked, "You are aware of the standing Presidential Executive Order that America is to absorb the first strike before we can retaliate."

"Retaliate with what?"

O'Fallon stood, gathering his materials. "This is no time to discuss possibilities. We have our orders and procedures. I suggest that we move to our destination. Then we can see if this is a real attack and decide how to respond. There's a chopper waiting for us."

Jolene knew he was right, yet something inside her resisted. Shocked upon hearing of the probable attack, she had an underlying feeling that something wasn't right. In the past, she attended a briefing on the possibility of why a strike might occur. She heard the plans to preserve national leadership if it did. However, the idea had been presented the way a life insurance salesman explained the buyer's policy. She knew she needed insurance, but she didn't plan to use it. With all her energy focused on the innumerable peacekeeping jobs of the military around the world, Jolene dismissed it. Now her mind whirled with conflicting thoughts. In the midst of disarray, the Russian military had maintained a large ICBM strike force. But would they be stupid enough to use them? She allowed her aid and Secret Service detail to hustle her to a waiting helicopter. It took off before she had even buckled her seatbelt.

Unmarried, Jolene had no immediate family to be concerned about, at least no one she could help at this point. Her parents lived in a retirement center in Florida, and a brother and his family, in California. Her career in the military had become her life. As the first black female with a Ph.D. to reach the rank of a four-star general, she held the honor of being the first female minority in the highest position of the military chain of command. If a real attack took place, what about the men and women in the Armed Services for whom she was ultimately responsible? How could she go to an underground facility with other top officials in the government and hope for a false alarm?

For the first time in years, not only did Jolene feel fear, but also a sense of helplessness. In the past, she questioned her boss, President Graham McCleen, as to why he had not rescinded President Clinton's long standing Executive Order, binding the military to absorb a preemptive nuclear strike before responding. He had convinced her that this was simply an assurance to Russia and China that America meant no harm to them. With all the treaties between America and Russia, it seemed a meaningless gesture. The anti-ballistic missile defense was insurance against an accidental missile launch by Russia or China or by a rogue nation. The main concern had to be terrorist attacks using nuclear weapons.

Only now, as the helicopter raced over the countryside, did Jolene begin to see the inconsistencies of these attitudes. If no one would ever use weapons of mass destruction, why did the American government build dozens of secret underground bunkers to ensure that its leadership survived such an attack? Suddenly questions she had suppressed came to mind with a vengeance. Had she been deceived? Was she being used?

Her face flushed. Did any of the men notice? The sense

of fear turned to anger. Her confidence of being in command changed to confusion. She needed honest answers before the day ended.

• Russian General Yakov Borisov could barely contain his excitement. His lifelong dream had presented itself. After decades of preparation, waiting, and questioning, he would unleash the greatest destructive onslaught possible on the world. Hundreds of missiles armed with nuclear warheads and launched from submarines, aircraft, and ground sites throughout Russia would hit America's worldwide military. Planes disguised as airliners had already taken to the air, winging their way toward targets. Alerted missile crews stood by, awaiting the final command to launch.

Russian President Ivan Solntsev took General Borisov's phone call. The men spoke in code since, in spite of all their encryption methods, the West might be able to monitor their call.

"General, I appreciate you checking in. All the final arrangements have been made for today's celebration, and our friends have agreed to join us. I trust that your staff is ready to do its part?"

"Yes, Comrade Solntsev. We are prepared to bring a full compliment of food to the table. I believe you will be pleased when you see how complete our preparations have been. Is everyone ready to gather for this grand event?"

"Yes, yes. Comrade Toschoff has prepared accommodations for all those invited to the festivities."

Leonardo Toschoff was the chief architect for a vast underground complex of bunkers and factories that would protect the Russian leaders and their ability to wage and survive a nuclear war. His favorite project had become a huge underground city known as Yamantau Mountain. Russia's political and military leaders would be protected from any nuclear counter attacks. Underground, fiber optics communication cables linked all the command centers. The production of vital war equipment would continue regardless of what happened above the ground.

"Very good, Comrade President. Is there any indication

that our special guests suspect anything?"

"None that we are aware of. Our tactics to keep them in the dark are working well. I look forward to their reactions once they realize the full extent of the surprise."

Borisov laughed. "Yes, I have also thought the same."

Russian and Chinese leaders secretly agreed to create a false threat of going to war against each other over a border dispute. This gave both nations the excuse needed to call up reservists and activate military assets that carried no threats to Western interests. The United Nations got the two countries to agree to withdraw their armies from mutual borders. However, each party used the six months of tension to prepare for war.

Only briefly had Borisov entertained thoughts of pity for those on the receiving end of the sudden attack. His entire life had been lived for this, to battle their greatest enemies. Not only did he have pride in the deceptions that he and the Russian leaders pulled off, but the fact that much of the firepower released had been paid for by America's taxpayers pleased him. As one of the former Soviet Union's past Presidents predicted, the Americans would hang themselves with the rope they sold the Russians.

Borisov concluded, "Then I will close our call so I can make final arrangements, and you will not be late to our appointment."

"We will drink a toast to your success, Comrade Borisov."

Placing the phone on its receiver, Borisov signed the final order that would be transmitted in code to all the armed forces headquarters. It ordered the full, preemptive nuclear strike against Western forces. No more waiting. No more fear of taking the risk. After handing the directive to his executive officer, he poured himself a generous glass of Vodka. Sitting back in his chair, he reflected on the fact that his name would be placed in the history books of all surviving nations as the commander who had prepared and carried out this unprecedented attack. More people would die in the next twenty-four hours than in any war ever fought on Earth.

•   Henry Parr saw his father's cell phone number on Caller ID.

"Hi, Dad. What's up?"

"Henry, you do know that I love you, don't you?"

"Yes, but that's the strangest greeting I've ever had."

"I wanted to make sure I had your attention."

"You've got it, at least for five minutes until Sarah has our dinner ready."

"I'll make it brief. I want you to pack up the family and drive over here tonight. Here's why." He covered the facts related to Ann earlier that indicated the strong possibility of World War III within the next twelve hours. A long pause ensued.

"You're serious?"

"Son, I know you've had your doubts, and I don't blame you. I'm also aware that I've not always been right with predictions about the future. But if I'm right about this and you don't come, you could all be vaporized -- with no second chances."

Henry sighed. James said nothing. He figured Henry's mind had flipped back to his father's scare over Y2K and the embarrassment when nothing happened. Henry continued to bring up the subject whenever friendly arguments occurred over various conspiracy theories. But in spite of disagreements, James knew his son's love for his family covered the differences.

"Wouldn't you know it?" Henry sounded tired. "The kids have a special youth program at church this evening, and Elizabeth has been invited to spend the night with a couple of her friends from school. You know how important that is to teenage girls."

James noticed that Henry wasn't arguing. He had begun to process the news. "All right, let me put it this way. If your mother and I ended up in the hospital and you were told we might not make it until morning, what would you do?"

"You know what we'd do."

"Okay, do it. Again, you know that General Mark Leland is no dummy. A radical? Yes. He's put his life on the line to fight for what he believes. Look, if I'm wrong, what will it cost you? A couple days pay and some discomfort. The kids can always go to church meetings. But, if I'm right and you don't come, you'll die with everyone else within twenty to fifty miles. There will be no reaction time once it begins. Most likely there will be no warning. And even if there is, the highways will be a big parking lot. Please, if for no other reason than to humor your old man, come tonight, now!"

"Let me talk to Sarah and the kids. I'll call you right back."

"No, I'll hold."

"Okay, you're paying."

James looked at Ann who had kneeled in front of an easy chair.

"He's talking to Sarah and the kids."

She nodded. James closed his eyes and bowed his head in a conscious act of submitting to God's will in the situation.

In no time, Sarah came on the line. "Dad, would you tell me what you told Henry?"

"Sure." James related the facts.

"Henry is switching through the news channels, and you're right. There are none of the regulars, but they're making it all sound normal. A Federal Reserve spokesman is promising to turn the economy around."

"That's because they don't know. They're cannon fodder, useful idiots, expendable troops in an all out war."

"But the United States has treaties with Russia. Their economy has been in shambles for years."

James detected hesitancy in her voice. He countered, "All the more reason why the leaders want war."

"But we're China's biggest trade partner. They've already conquered us economically. Isn't our main problem the threat of terrorism?"

"Do you suppose Russia and China have been building all those ICBMs to protect themselves against terrorists?"

"But they've been threatening to attack each other."

"And you, like most other Americans, believed them, right? Don't you suppose that could be an excuse for them to prepare for an all out war against us?"

Sarah's voice betrayed her doubts. "Well, yes."

"General Leland and I have proved, beyond a shadow of a doubt from a variety of sources, that, America's past administrations gave advanced military technology and money to the Russians and Chinese. This enabled them to build and perfect their intercontinental missiles. We know they have sophisticated, silent running, missile launching subs, which we can't detect. We also validated that the Russians lied when they claimed they had not placed those subs off our shores. We showed people the results of naval exercises that proved our carrier battle groups have no defense against the Russian supplied Sunburn and other anti-ship missiles. The fleets are disasters waiting to happen."

He paused. Hearing no objection he continued, "The media has turned the war on terrorism into a mantra to hypnotize the masses. We also proved that the last, so-called terrorist attacks had probably been set up by our own government agencies, or at least they allowed them to happen so they could institute stricter controls. And don't forget how the federal government used the hurricane disasters as an excuse to exert federal power over the states.

"But, Sarah, you know we love you and the kids. Please, if we're wrong, we can have a good time. The kids can play with the goats and see the baby chicks. Missing a few days of school won't hurt them. But if we're right and you don't come, it'll be over for you. That would break our hearts. Russ and his family are here, but we need all of you."

"If it's this bad, I don't want to leave all our pictures and-
-"

"Sarah, none of that is worth your lives. Bring sleeping bags, a few clothes, and your laptop with the picture CDs. Have Henry load his weapons and ammunition. Everything else can be replaced. We have plenty of room here for all of you. If this is the big event, we'll have to adjust to a new way of life. The important thing is that we prepare now to stay alive."

"This scares me. What about my family in Minnesota? Will they be safe?"

"Initially probably so. There are no military targets near

them. Where the fallout drifts depends on weather patterns. People will have time to prepare for that. For now, you've got to be concerned about your children."

There was a long pause. James heard conversation in the background.

"Are you sure we need to come tonight? Couldn't we wait until morning?"

"No! We don't know when the first strike will occur. At the latest, it will probably be early morning. From what we know, they're after the military, so we think they'll strike in the night. If they can wipe out our military, America will be no threat to them as they take over the rest of the world. With Cheyenne Mountain and the Satellite Command Center at Falcon, they'll have to take out the entire Colorado Springs area. You're living on top of the number one target for their missiles. So please, hurry with your supper, throw some stuff in the SUV, and come. Now! Phone us when you're in the mountains. We'll be up when you arrive."

"All right, we'll come. Do you want to talk to Henry?"

"No, just remind him to bring his weapons. Watch for deer on the highway, and come as soon as possible. One more thought. They might set off H Bombs high in the atmosphere to knock out communications. The Electro Magnetic Pulse, known as EMP, could take out electronic ignitions in vehicles. Pack your backpacks just in case. We'll pray that you reach here before that happens."

Ann heard the words she'd been praying for, "They're coming!"

•   Major Sasha Bagrii wiped the sweat from his brow. The dehumidifier was acting up again. He swore and muttered in frustration. This could interfere with his concerns for achieving a faultless launch sequence. There was the distinct possibility that humidity buildup in the cramped room could short circuit delicate electrical relays in the computers and their communication equipment.

The sequence for the launch of their massive intercontinental, nuclear armed, ballistic missile had already been programmed. The final launch order had set things in motion. He listened to the crew rehearsing the launch string. He had his best crew on duty. At last, the day they had trained for! There could be no foul up as with previous drills. Missile Launch Station #31 would launch and reload without flaws, or there would be hell to pay.

He could hear the tension in the crew's voices. Bagrii forced himself to stay in his chair. He knew that pacing behind them would increase their anxiety. His fingers drummed on the desk.

So far, the equipment was functioning in perfect order. Thanks to the American designed computer components manufactured in China, he had confidence that the computer hardware and software would function properly if Glukhov got the dehumidifier working. The irony of the situation did not escape him. Not only did they have American designed and paid for equipment in the launch mechanism, but vital parts of the giant, three-stage rocket had also been refined, thanks to American technology. The dehumidifier was Russian.

In various parts of the Motherland, mobile launchers stood ready with their SS-27 Topol-M missiles aimed at American facilities in Europe and the Middle East. The intercontinental missiles from hardened sites like his would travel across the North Pole to strike targets in the heartland of America while submarine launched missiles took out targets along the East Coast. Chinese missiles were to cover the West Coast. Planes giving the appearance of airliners would launch powerful cruise missiles almost on top of their intended targets. Nothing was to be left to chance. Several missiles had been targeted for each vital position.

One thing still puzzled Bagrii, the stupid Executive Order of the President of the United States that there would be no launch of the few missiles America still possessed until Russian and Chinese weapons had done their damage. Long ago, he gave up trying to understand the logic of such a suicidal order. The Americans had always been a mystery to him.

•   When Ann finished their supper preparations, she phoned James's faithful assistant, Marcie Wilden and invited her to join them. Earlier that afternoon when James returned from General Leland's house, he stopped at his office, a converted garage near his home. Relating to Marcie the evidence of an impending attack, he helped her draft an emergency message, which she sent by email to three thousand plus members on their newsletter subscriber list. It didn't mention the names of the military generals that Leland had received his alert from. It just told what General Mark Leland had learned from reliable sources. This might be D-Day. Everyone was advised to take appropriate precautions. Marcie also alerted the leaders of the prayer chain in their church's home fellowship groups. These individuals had been urged to phone people to pray as the Spirit of God led them.

Marcie helped James unplug the computers, printers, and fax machine. They placed the equipment in a Faraday room. The room had been encased in chicken wire and grounded by buried copper rods. This would protect electrical equipment from Electro Magnetic Pulses (EMP) created by nuclear blasts.

Marcie joined James and Ann for a quick meal. Afterwards, they spent the rest of the evening calling supporters of their ministry around the nation to give a "heads up" on the possibility of World War III. Beginning with the retired military personnel living near military bases, they urged them to pack and move themselves and their families as far away as possible. Many had already seen the email and were packing emergency kits and loading their vehicles.

Their subscribers were prepared for this possibility and needed no convincing. They just needed evidence of the moment to take action. James's trust level with them had been acquired over the years by writing to them about the ways their leaders were betraying America. Anyone not convinced had been dropped from the list long ago.

In a few cases, James contacted active duty military personnel. If those contacts considered themselves in eminent danger, they would put in for emergency leave due to unexpected family crises. It was better to suffer a reprimand for being late reporting for duty -- if it turned out to be a false alarm -- than to die in a nuclear blast. James agonized over the reality that, if the blast occurred, hundreds of thousands of men and women in uniform would stand before their Maker. It sickened him to think about it, but nothing more could be done. In recent years, he used every method possible and the limited means available to sound the alarm. The guilt now rested on those who had heard but never taken action.

By midnight, James, Ann, and Marcie had finished the list of names. Each of them felt a sense of dread. In prayer, they poured out their hearts with fervent requests to God, that He would spare His remnant and protect the righteous from imminent judgment.

The barking of their watchdog interrupted them. "Praise the Lord!" exclaimed James when he saw Henry's SUV appear in the driveway. The prayer warriors rushed outside. A flurry of greetings and hugs erupted. Ann lifted little Jason, the caboose of Henry's family, from his car seat.

"Oh, how he's grown!" she expressed with a great deal of enthusiasm. She hugged the sleeping two-year-old.

The women and children hurried into the house. James helped Henry untie the canvas tarp on the top of the vehicle that covered the sleeping bags and backpacks.

"Have you heard the late night talk shows?" asked Henry.

"No, we've been on the phones talking to our subscribers."

"Well, the word about a possible sneak attack is out. It's stirring up a lot of call-ins. They are all either quoting or cursing General Leland. A couple of them mentioned your email. But the mainline media is ignoring it. You do realize, if you're wrong, you're going to be the butt of jokes and ridicule in the media."

"It won't be the first time. I just hope and pray it isn't the last. This is one time I won't mind looking like a fool."

After they deposited their first load in the guest

bedrooms and hauled luggage from the back of the SUV, Henry looked up at the stars of the clear Colorado night.

"Dad, do you remember the first night we moved you here, how amazed we felt at the thousands of stars we could see? I can understand why you love it out here away from city lights and the noise. But, dang, it's such a long drive."

"Yes, I remember." He pulled his son into an embrace. "I'm glad you came. I couldn't bear the thought of losing you."

"Well, old man, I don't want to lose you either. Dads are kind of hard to replace, especially the weird ones." They laughed.

Henry's voice changed to a serious tone. "Do you really think we might be hit tonight?"

"Something tells me it's coming in about an hour."

•　　Deep inside Cheyenne Mountain, overlooking the sleeping city of Colorado Springs, Airman 1st Class Randy Page, a member of the night crew, stayed awake by double checking one of the special spy satellites. This particular satellite had the ability to lock on an airplane and provide a photo similar to an X-ray picture of the plane's insides. Page spent time focusing on a British Airline 747 packed with people. As he stared at the screen, he wondered what it would be like to be on the plane. He wished he could bring the picture in for a closer look at individual passengers, real close. The thought brought a sly smile to his face.

He widened the scope of his search. Noticing the call signs of a Russian airliner, he typed in the command, focusing the gaze of the satellite on the plane. It took a few seconds for the mechanism on the satellite platform to lock on to the moving aircraft so it could take a picture of the cargo in the plane. When the picture came up, it took another couple of seconds for Randy to understand. The model and call sign indicated a passenger plane. Yet long, cylindrical shaped objects appeared in the hold of the plane.

Something isn't right. This isn't supposed to be a cargo plane. Why is it posted as an airliner? Should I alert the duty officer or just log it as a question? Could I get in trouble for overusing the expensive satellite? What should I do? My activities are recorded on the hard drive. Better check it out.

"Captain Larson, would you come and take a look at this?"

While the captain approached, Page clicked on an icon giving him access to the schedule of incoming planes. He typed in the plane's number. The time of departure from Moscow appeared on the screen and also its declared destination, New York's Kennedy Airport.

"What you got, Page?"

"Sir, this is supposed to be a Russian airliner. But look at that cargo."

The captain bent over to peer at the screen. "Throw it up on the big screen."

They both looked at the large screen for a few seconds before the captain grabbed a phone and punched in numbers.

"This is Larson. I've got something here I'd like to look at, sir. Check on Channel 3."

Larson continued to watch the screen as he waited for Colonel Holman to make a determination. Page detected tension in Larson's posture.

The captain nodded and responded, "Yes, sir!" Directing his attention to Page, he ordered, "Plot the nearest intercept."

A few strokes of the keys brought to the screen an outline of North America.

"Bangor, Maine, sir."

Again Larson punched numbers into the phone. "This is Captain Larson, Cheyenne. Launch two interceptors. Priority alpha. We're sending the target co-ordinance."

Within seconds, the computer operator in Bangor acknowledged the receipt of the co-ordinance that would be automatically sent to the computers in the F-16 Interceptors.

Page worked his computer. "ETA contact eighteen minutes, twenty seconds."

Placing Bangor on hold, Larson again dialed the night commander. "Sir, we have two interceptors in the air, priority alpha, ETA eighteen minutes. Is there any other suspicious activity? None? Good. We'll stay on top of this situation."

Five minutes went by. Captain Larson paced behind the operator as they watched the plotted interceptors narrow the distance to the target.

A nearby computer operator called out, "Captain Larson, one of our undersea listening posts off Virginia is picking up a Russian missile sub opening its launch doors."

Before Larson could respond, Page shouted, "Sir, look! The Russian plane is launching some kind of missiles!"

"My god, what the hell--"

Larson's comment was cut short by an alert horn blaring through the room. All eyes focused on a large, central screen showing a map of the East Coast. The overlay revealed three glowing dots, indicating a launch of submarine based missiles.

Another operator spoke with tension in his voice, "There are live missiles launched from an aircraft over Wyoming. It appears they're headed our way."

Captain Larson grabbed another phone. As he did, he wondered if his alert would do any good. They could all see narrow lines fanning out from the submarines toward military bases, one, headed for Bangor, Maine.

•   Major Ron Gillespie and his wingman, Lieutenant Julian Lutz, reached cruising altitude coming out of Bangor Air Force Base. They had used after burners on their old F-16 fighter jets to gain altitude for their intercept of the Russian airline. Gillespie knew Lutz was as relieved as he was to have a break from the boredom of sitting in the ready room, waiting for something to happen. It was probably just a false alarm, but it got them in the air and gave them another opportunity to sharpen their skills.

Six minutes into the flight, Gillespie had finished a routine check of his instruments and the status of the two air-to-air missiles when the controller from the base burst into his headset. Instead of the calm professional voice, he heard an angry, frightened one.

"Air Force nine seven two niner, this is Bangor control. This is not a drill. Your target is launching cruise missiles. Close and destroy the target. I repeat, close and destroy the target ASAP."

Major Gillespie repeated the order.

"This is control, affirmative. It appears we're in on the beginning of World War III. Get the bastards."

Major Gillespie gave the standard "Roger, nine seven two niner, out." He switched to his wingman's frequency. "Let's go to afterburners and switch on forward radar. Arm your missiles. We may not be able to stop his launch, but we can sure as hell make sure he never returns home to brag about it."

Lutz answered, "Roger that. Radar on." There was a short pause. "See those missiles. It appears they are subsonic. Permission to break off and take out a couple of them with my missiles. You can handle the plane."

"Do it! I've got the target on my screen. He's dead but just doesn't know it yet."

Major Gillespie watched Lutz peal off and disappear into the blackness. He directed his focus on the supposed airliner that was making a turn after finishing the launch of its missiles. The minutes seemed like hours. He counted off the final seconds until he would be close enough to launch his missile, which was in a search mode. As soon as the missile sent a tone that indicated it had locked onto the target, the major punched the fire button and watched the missile drop from his wing, streaking out into the night. "Payback time, you sneaking SOB!"

He cut off the afterburner, edging his plane to the left to head off the slower moving target. He decided not to launch his other missile. This decision was confirmed when he saw a fireball light up the sky miles ahead of him. The target disappeared from his radar screen. He put the plane in a sharp, 180-degree turn and groaned when the G forces pulled him against the seat.

As he was coming out of the turn, he reported the kill to Gander control. Before he could receive an answer, Lutz's voice came through, "Congrats, Major! I got one and am about to launch on the second one. They are going slow enough. We should be able to knock down one or more with our cannons."

"Roger that, I've got the last one they launched on radar. I'll use my other missile on it and see if I can close on the next one."

Major Gillespie was so focused on losing altitude to close on the Russian cruise missile that he had no time to think about the larger picture.

Lt. Lutz came back on the air. "I got the second one! I'm closing on the next one. I'll use my cannon. Man this is like shootin' fish in a barrel!"

Major Gillespie's missile sent the tone showing it had locked on the target. He launched the missile and began to search for the next target. Suddenly the sky ahead of him lit up brighter than day. The light was so intense, it caused temporary blindness."

He called out, "Lutz, come in. What happened?"

There was no response. He repeated the call but didn't expect an answer. He assumed that Lutz's cannon fire had not only destroyed the cruise missile but somehow had set off the nuclear warhead. His wingman died with the missile. Seconds later, the missile he had targeted disappeared off the radar screen.

He switched to the Bangor frequency. "Air Force nine seven two niner requesting instructions. Original target destroyed along with four of the missiles they launched. It appears my wingman was lost in the action. Remaining enemy missiles are out of my range."

"Air Force nine seven two niner, this is Bangor control. Job well done. No further targets in your area. The entire United States is under nuclear attack. We suggest you go to the emergency field outside Seal Harbor as this base may be targeted for destruction. Bangor control out."

Major Gillespie acknowledged the message and switched on his ground radar to find his way to Seal Harbor. His mind was numb. He saw flashes of light far to the south. For now, all he could think about was getting his plane on the ground before his fuel was exhausted. He didn't want to deal with what might be happening to his family at Bangor. He could only hope and pray that he and Lt. Lutz had destroyed the missiles headed there. Neither did he want to think about the amount of radiation he'd been subjected to from the blast that killed Lutz.

•   Henry and Sarah joined the other three adults in the kitchen around the large table. Ann poured glasses of juice for everyone. They all felt exhausted, but had no interest in sleep.

Henry looked at his father and reported, "The children are in bed. Elizabeth and Chuck are asleep, but I think they'll want specific justification from Grandpa for missing the big deal at church."

James shrugged.

Sarah directed a question to her father-in-law. "If it happens, is it going to be the end of America?"

"As we've known it, yes. But life will go on, for some at least. Just how, that's a big question. Only time will tell."

"Henry told me you think they'll hit about 4:00 a.m., East Coast Time. If that's so, some of the missiles could be in the air now."

James nodded. "I wonder if they'll announce it via the early warning system."

He got up and turned on the radio to an all night station originating out of Chicago. The narrator's voice blared, "Slim Tone's magic will enable you to effortlessly lose those extra pounds without the sacrifice of all the good things you love to eat."

James couldn't resist a comment as he cut the volume. "By morning, that's gonna be about as useful as tits on a boar."

Ann rolled her eyes. "Dear, do you have to be so crude?"

Henry chuckled. "My dad, a farm boy to the last of his days."

The smiles left their faces when a beeping noise interrupted the program. James turned up the volume. An excited voice boomed from the speaker.

"This is the Emergency Broadcasting Network. This is

not a test. NORAD Command Center in Colorado Springs has announced the detection of incoming intercontinental missiles launched from submarines off the East Coast of the United States. I repeat. This is not a test. Should you lose this station, turn to the emergency numbers on your dial. You are advised to take precautionary actions."

Sarah's scream blocked the announcer's voice. James jumped up and headed for the door. Grabbing a pair of sunglasses from the counter, he shouted, "We've got the curtains pulled, but we need to stay away from all glass. I don't know where the missiles will land or explode."

As he spoke, the lights overhead flickered and went out. Seconds later they came back on.

"They've hit somewhere," James shouted.

The lights went out again. Sarah hid her face against Henry's chest. Ann grabbed a flashlight, located matches, and lit an old oil lamp. James hurried out the door. Suddenly the whole area lit up in a long flash.

They heard James yell, "Wow! That had to be a big one hitting the Front Range!"

Another flash of light followed that lingered a second or two. The windows of the house rattled as the ground shook the structure. Sarah screamed again.

James called out, "I'll bet a ground blast hit Cheyenne Mountain."

They saw him drop to his knees on the lawn in prayer. "Oh God, do not forsake us in this hour of testing. Receive into Your Presence those deceived souls who trusted in You but refused to accept Your challenge to repent. Forgive us for not heeding Your warnings. In this time of supreme judgment, have mercy on us, Lord God."

Sarah cried. Ann and Marcie fell to their knees to pray. James hurried back into the house where he placed his arms around Henry and Sarah.

"Thank You, Lord Jesus, for delivering our loved ones from the furnace of Your judgment, from the very jaws of the lion. Oh God, please deliver some of our servicemen and women from this terrible holocaust. Give them the will and knowledge to fight back against our enemies." After a time of silence, James groaned, "Oh, God, the pain!"

• Not one of the crew at Launch Station 31 had ever experienced the vibrations and muffled roar of an actual launch. With wide eyes, they focused on the black and white TV screen monitoring the rise of the rocket through the gapping blast doors. The screen went white when the flames of the exhaust became visible to the camera. The room stopped shaking, the roar subsided.

The crew held their collective breath, monitoring the critical seconds of the liftoff. A deep, unspoken fear filled the room that something might go wrong. If the rocket motors failed during the initial lift off, tons of explosive rocket fuel could be spilled above them. The oxygen would then be sucked out of their buried cave. The unthinkable filled their minds. Failsafe mechanisms would not arm the nuclear warhead until it was high in space. But no guarantee existed if the rocket motors failed. The missile would crash to the ground, and even if the warhead didn't explode, their underground command post would be turned into a tomb.

The crew began to breathe easier as the rocket rose higher and higher in space. They wished they could be outside to watch it disappear in the sky. Most of their families would experience the roar and watch the white exhaust tails of hundreds of missiles that filled the skies above Russia. Now the crew had to monitor the delicate maneuvers of the rocket, programmed to enter space at a precise angle that would guide it to an exact entry point. It would then take a pathway to the intended target.

Sergeant Gurianov, the first to notice something wrong, began to type instructions into his computer.

Major Bagrii jumped behind him, anxiety written all over his face. He peered over the sergeant's shoulder and shouted, "What's the matter?"

"The thrust of #2 engine is slightly off. It's causing the rocket to yaw."

His answer was in short bursts while he continued to concentrate on his computer. Flipping a large book open, the sergeant located the right page and ran his finger down a chart. Finding the precise number, he typed it into the computer. Both men watched the screen as data continued to come in from the missile.

Sasha could no longer remain quiet. "Did you correct it? You've only got a few more seconds until you lose control."

"No, it's not responding. There's nothing I can do. It has to be a flaw in the fuel or the lines feeding it to the engine."

"What does it mean?"

"I can't be sure. It'll be slightly off when it reenters the atmosphere. The internal guidance may be able to correct its path to the target. But then again, it may miss the NORAD headquarters."

The sergeant turned to look at the major. "Sir, this is not our fault. Our settings were precise. You know there have been problems in the fuel mixtures, causing an uneven feed in the tests of the engines."

"Yes, yes, I know. It is not your fault, Comrade. We can only hope that it will be able to readjust on reentry."

Major Bagrii put his hand on the sergeant's shoulder and looked at the other two operators.

"You did your tasks well. We have served our Motherland to the best of our abilities. We can take comfort that several other missiles are aimed at the important target, the NORAD Headquarters in Colorado. We can only hope some of them will hit their exact targets even if ours may fail. But wherever it lands, it will take out a sizeable piece of American landscape."

He fell silent for a moment. "All right, the crew that will help us be refitted with another missile will soon be here. We have much work to do to rearm. Let's be at it and hope that none of the American missiles launched in retaliation will break through our antimissile defenses."

His crew nodded agreement and returned to their duties.

Sasha could not help wondering where his errant missile would land.

Chapter Two

Terror Falls From the Sky

When Captain Larson sent the alert to the National Broadcasting System, Colonel Holman set off the alarm to prepare the underground complex for a nuclear attack. The massive outer and inner doors began closing while the guards on the outside scurried inside the mountain. A computer severed all the external power sources and electronic wires to the outside world. Communications arrived now via fiber optic cables that would not transmit EMP surges. Antennas on top of the mountain slid down steel pipes that closed over them.

Roused from his quarters inside the mountain, Air Force Brigadier General Lane Conley appraised the situation with the help of his aid. Within seconds, he ordered the alert status Def Con One broadcast to all command branches of the military worldwide.

Inside the command center, an atmosphere of controlled panic filled the air. Men who had spent years going through drills and endless hours of boredom found themselves electrified by the reality upon them. What they had dreamed of in the past and even hoped for, yet dreaded, rushed toward them. They responded mechanically with sweaty hands due to vast hours of training.

Continuing to monitor the Russian plane, Airman Page watched as it disappeared from the screen. He saw the computer project the missiles paths. They stretched toward targets all along the Eastern seaboard. The lines from the submarine launched missiles often headed for the same targets. Another overhead screen showed ICBM launches from the Soviet Union. It would take them as long as a half-hour to reach their targets. Perhaps those responsible for the American ABM defense would be able to take down some of them. But it soon became apparent that far too many existed. The missile defense system had been designed to take out one or two missiles either launched by mistake or by some rogue terrorist group.

The airman at a nearby console got everyone's attention. "The first of the missiles launched from Wyoming will impact here in one minute. There are at least six cruise missiles in the air. All are targeted for this area. Fifty seconds to impact."

Captain Larson reported to Colonel Holman, "All commanders have been alerted to the attack. FEMA is online. Omaha has launched the airborne command aircraft. Alert fighter aircraft are launched. We're buttoned up. Our anti-ballistic missiles are firing, but they'll be overwhelmed."

"Thank you, Captain." His voice choked when he added, "May God have mercy on us all."

Both men had wives and children in Colorado Springs. They steeled their minds against the incomprehensible as they referred to their checklists of precise duties to perform.

The airman near Page counted down the last seconds. "Five, four, three, two, one!"

There was a slight pause before they felt the vibration caused by a nuclear blast close enough to the mountain to cause the structure to shake. Their entire complex sat on massive springs designed to absorb the shock waves that came through the granite rock of the mountain. They couldn't hear the explosions or see the flashes. Deep pain surged through their minds because they knew that friends on a different shift, family members, and loved ones on the outside were being ushered into eternity. Most hadn't heard the alarms.

Captain Larsen's hands gripped the clipboard so tightly they turned white at the knuckles. Airman Page saw tears in the captain's eyes. He had met his attractive wife and two preschool daughters. Page didn't know how to respond, so he touched his leader's arm.

"I'm sorry, sir. Let's do what we can to pay them back."

Larson looked down. "Right. Thanks, Page."

The captain glanced at the overhead displays still

projecting the areas of attack. "The ICBMs will be hitting in about 20 minutes, and there's not a thing we can do about it but record it for history. My god, the inmates are in charge of the asylum!"

He turned and walked to his desk. He had seldom allowed himself to consider this possibility. Unthinkable! It seemed like a nightmare, but he knew he wouldn't be waking up in bed with his wife. His military training kicked in. He had to set aside his emotions and consider the next item on his checklist.

Young and inexperienced, Airman Page wondered aloud, "Why are we here to sound the alarm when there's nothing anyone can do to stop the holocaust? Something isn't right about this scenario."

. Secretary Jolene Howard and the military leaders gathered in the command center at the underground bunker. The Federal Emergency Management Agency had just received the Def Con One Alert when grim reports around the world began to come in. As Jolene predicted, most of the military was taken by surprise, and with such short notice, few had been able to prepare or launch counter attacks.

The coordination of the attack throughout the world occurred almost to the second. With international communications sent over fiber optic cable and through satellite, no possibility existed for part of the world to be forewarned by an attack on the other side of the globe.

After less than thirty minutes, one naval fleet still survived and fought back. Admiral Fredrick Markum, Commander of the 4th Fleet, headquartered on the Aircraft Carrier George Washington in the Indian Ocean, spoke with urgency to Admiral Earl O'Fallon in the Command Center.

"Our subs took out theirs before they could launch. We're arming our attack aircraft with nuclear weapons. We've launched cruise missiles at the bases where attacking aircraft came from. I need instructions. What targets are we to respond to with our remaining cruise missiles? I need this now! Our outer air defense ring has all but collapsed. The first wave of attackers, decoys, used up our planes'

long-range missiles. Their second wave has used up our
short-range missiles. It appears the third wave has launched
Yakhonts at maximum range. At Mach 2.9, they'll be here
in minutes. We can only pray our RAM defenses will protect
us. I've ordered my support fleet to scatter. Hold one."

Everyone in the control room stared at the equipment.
Jolene mentally searched for answers. What procedures
would be needed to respond to such a nuclear attack?

The mike on the carrier opened again. Admiral
Markum's voice came through clear with professional
calmness. "Our RAMs are firing. We're launching our
reserve aircraft."

Another pause occurred before his voice returned. "We'll
know . . ." His voice changed to static.

The operator looked up at Admiral O'Fallon who avoided
his gaze.

O'Fallon said, "See if you can raise their fleet air
controller."

The operator nodded.

"Command to GW3, request status report."

"There are . . . (static) . . . I count two, three . . . (static)
. . . yes, four mushroom clouds rising over the fleet. I
repeat, four nuclear explosions. We've lost contact with the
Washington. Woe! The shock waves are pounding us . . ."

Static remained on the channel.

Jolene motioned for Admiral O'Fallon to follow her into
the adjoining conference room. He closed the door behind
him.

"What about the rest of your forces?"

O'Fallon took a deep breath before answering. "Iran used
Russian made SS-NX-26 Yakhont, anti-ship missiles to take
out the naval task force in the Persian Gulf. The missiles
had been launched from ground stations in the desert. Our
ship's Rolling Action Missiles, RAMs, proved ineffective in
their attempt to defend the ships. Neither could the carrier's
planes mount a defense. A bloodbath ensued. Some of the
carrier planes survived and will recover on nearby bases or
in Israel, that is, if there's a base in Israel remaining intact.
The fleets in port in Virginia, North Carolina, and Florida

got hit by nukes from offshore submarines."

Jolene struggled to maintain control of her emotions. She sensed the admiral's fragility. He was on the edge of breaking too. "What about the Pacific fleets?" she asked.

"The Chinese launched Yakhonts and Sunburns from their destroyers and subs and even from patrol boats on the fleet near Taiwan. Those aimed at the carriers were nuclear. Others were conventional but deadly as well. Our RAM defenses failed there too. Our attack subs have neutralized their Navy. However, we've lost contact with the Seattle. We don't know if it's been sunk or if it's lying quiet until it retaliates. Our military on Hawaii took a hit by cruise missiles launched from a sub. An ICBM from China has also targeted Pearl Harbor. The same with the fleet off the Philippines."

"The bottom line, Admiral?"

"We no longer have a Navy in the Pacific or the Atlantic. North Korea has launched an all out attack on our forces there. So far they're using conventional weapons. Without backup, I doubt that South Korea can hold out. Our bases in Japan, Okinawa, and Guam have all been hit by nuclear weapons. Except for some of our subs and small units, our military has been decimated. Taiwan is under attack. Without our naval help, they won't be able to stand up to Mainland China."

• James led the adults in prayer. Later he phoned his other son who lived a quarter of a mile away. "Russ, I want to check to make sure you have all the shades drawn and have moved the children away from the windows. I don't expect any nearby blasts, but we can't be certain."

"Should we move to the basement?"

"That's a good idea. Then plan on having everyone over here at dawn with your survival gear. You did put all your electronic equipment in Faraday boxes, right?"

"Yep. We're as ready as we can be but finding it hard to believe this is really happening."

"I know what you mean. Pray with the children. I trust we'll see you in the morning."

"Okay, Dad."

While James was still on the phone, Henry and Sarah took a flashlight to check their three children.

James suddenly hollered, "Henry, wake the children and grab some blankets. Let's all hurry to the basement just in case there's a nearby blast."

Jason, the youngest, slept through the move, but the two older children were upset when they realized what was happening.

The family settled on the large sofa and easy chairs in the recreation room. As they waited, the enormity of the event hit sixteen-year-old Elizabeth. "Grandpa, has Colorado Springs all been destroyed?"

"Probably so, honey."

Frantically she blurted, "But what about my friends? Were they warned? Did they leave town?"

In the dim light, James shook his head and answered sorrowfully, "I doubt it."

Elizabeth began to cry. "But that's not fair! Why are the Russians doing this? It's so stupid."

"No, honey, it's not fair. Your friends' fathers and mothers were warned of the possibility, but like most people, they didn't believe it could happen. All we can hope now is that they died quickly and were ready to stand before God's judgment seat."

A sudden bright light invaded the room for seconds through the small windows in the sunken encasements on the north side of the basement.

James yelled, "Cover yourselves with blankets!"

When he saw his family freeze in fear, he jumped up, grabbed blankets, and flung them over everyone before collapsing on a loveseat next to Ann. They covered themselves, too. The women and children screamed when glass shattered into the room. The entire house shook. Ceiling tiles fell to the floor when a muffled boom reverberated through the valley. After it became quiet, James removed his blanket. Shards of glass fell to the floor as he did so. Again the room lit up, but not with the brightness this time. An eerie glow remained. Elizabeth cried loudly and then screamed. James ignored her.

"Henry, check the gas furnace. See if you can detect any gas leaks. Ann, put out the lamp just to be sure. I need to check things upstairs. The rest of you pray. There are no significant targets anywhere in this area, so that must have been a missile off course."

The skies lit up several more times. The family heard distant booms. It sounded like fireworks on the Fourth of July. By the time James returned, the cold spring air had cooled the room.

"I saw the top of a mushroom cloud off to the northeast. I turned the gas line off at the tank just to be safe. The blast shook the house badly."

Seeing the frightened look of Henry's son, thirteen-year-old Chuck, James sat down and put his arm around the youth. Chuck returned the hug.

"You will have to grow up fast. Grandpa's gonna need a lot of help in the morning when we all move into the barn."

Elizabeth asked through her tears, "Why do we have to move to the barn?"

"Dangerous fallout from nuclear blasts on the West Coast will be carried east by the winds and dropped here on the Rocky Mountains and all the way to the East Coast."

Chuck perked up. "I studied that in science. When nuclear energy is released, it creates radiation that can kill people and bring on a nuclear winter all over the world. Does this mean it will be winter instead of spring and summer?"

"No, I don't think so. It may cause bad weather, but the main thing to worry about is the radiation. We've got special potassium iodine pills for all of us to take that will help our bodies resist the harmful effects. We filled the loft of the barn with bales of hay to act as a barrier for the radiation falling on the roof. The animal pens on one side of the central structure and the equipment area on the other side will keep the radiation a distance from us if we stay in the center of the building. That's why we have to move into the barn. I've rigged up a generator to pump water from the well and spray it on the barn roof. That will wash the radioactive dust off into the gutters. The dust will then be carried away from the building.

"First thing in the morning, you'll have to help us clean out the tack room and where we keep the animal feed. We already have barrels filled with drinking water and emergency supplies. We'll move mattresses, sleeping bags, and camp gear for cooking into the rooms. When everything is moved in, we'll tape plastic sheets over areas where radioactive dust can drift into the living space. It's going to be cramped, because Russell and his family will be with us, too. But we can make do."

Elizabeth asked, "Will we have to stay there all summer? What about a bathroom?"

"We'll see how much fallout there is. I have an instrument to measure it. We'll probably have to stay in the barn for two weeks or--"

Chuck interrupted, "Don't you remember? There's a bathroom out there, right, Grandpa?"

"Yes, all the comforts of home. No stinky outhouses such as when we camp."

Elizabeth breathed a sigh of relief. A somber silence fell on the group. They were thinking about the grim implications of the present. The first stage of grief, shock, and denial was their defense against the incomprehensible.

•   Jolene had to fight to keep from vomiting as the magnitude of the catastrophe became more obvious by the minute. A haunting memory flashed through her mind. General Leland, a former commander, had tried to warn her of the sinister nature of international leaders. His description didn't fit with her plans at the time, so she ignored it. Now she realized she had been part of a gigantic deception. Tens, if not hundreds of thousands of dedicated men and women had been led to their deaths for a reason she couldn't fathom. The lack of a radio signal from the Command Center on the majestic aircraft carrier, named after the first President of the United States, was similar to a strobe light burning into her soul.

She turned to her wan looking assistant, Captain Jarrell.

"If you can't get through to the President, try to reach Vice President Lynch."

After several long minutes, Jarrell told her the vice president would soon arrive to see her. Jolene sat with a drained look on her face. When Vice President Lynch entered the room, she didn't rise from her chair. He sat across the table from her, sipping coffee from a mug with a FEMA logo on it. He motioned for the captain to leave. Jolene thought it odd that the sweater he wore gave him a casual look. No emotion whatever showed on his face when he looked at her.

"Mr. Vice President, I have questions that need answering. Why wasn't I informed of these possibilities?"

"Because you didn't need to know." His flat tone irritated her.

"But I had the responsibility for the use of our military to defend America. How is it that members of Congress and the administration had a twenty-four hour notice, but our military didn't receive an alert until the missiles were launched? Surely our intelligence knew this would be a real attack."

Again with no emotion, the vice president replied, "Yes, they knew."

Jolene felt such shock that she could hardly speak. She leaned forward and almost yelled, "Why wasn't our military alerted? I can't see how allowing our personnel and billions of dollars worth of equipment to be sacrificed is a wise thing to do."

The VP set his coffee cup down and leaned back in his chair. "You still have a great deal to learn about the way international politics work. I'll give you an example from history. In 1941, President Roosevelt set up the Japanese to go to war against us. He knew their fleet had headed for Pearl Harbor but didn't allow our military there to be warned. Why? Because he understood it would take that kind of shock, the destruction of the Pacific fleet, for the American people to be mobilized for an all out war. The approximate three thousand men who died proved to be a minor price compared to the half million Americans who eventually died in the subsequent war -- or the thirty plus million who died around the world. That war had been necessary to convince America to accept the United Nations. In like manner, the price to achieve lasting world peace will be initially higher with this nuclear strike. But it's a necessary price to pay for the final World War. And it's small in comparison to how many will die if we don't bring in the plan for an international government."

Jolene, stunned into silence, struggled to understand what she heard. Gathering her composure, she asked, "But who will keep the peace with our loss of the most advanced Navy, Air Force, and Army the world has ever seen? If our intelligence is right, we've lost all the major components of our naval task forces, every one. Our Army and Air Force have suffered similar fates here and abroad."

"Again, using the illustration of Pearl Harbor, when people heard that all the battleships of the Pacific fleet had been sunk or put out of commission, they thought our fleet was gutted. In reality, the Japanese did us a great favor. The loss of the battleships forced us to rely on the unproven use of the aircraft carrier. This turned out to be a great advance in weapons systems and the key to winning the war with Japan. The same is true of our current naval task forces. Those weapons systems have had their time in the sun. It's time to abolish them and move to more advanced weapons. But because military men and politicians are slow to change, it has been deemed by those with responsibility for world leadership that this is the best way to purge the old and make way for the new."

Jolene asked in alarm, "What new weapons are you talking about? I don't know of any better systems."

A condescending smile spread across the vice president's face. "The new systems require new leadership. The new leadership has to use drastic methods to condition the people of the world to go along with the changes that must take place. Unfortunately for many, they were beyond the ability to adapt. Americans have always been an independent lot, so it's better to simply take them out. Those who are allowed to survive will be too stunned to resist the changes required of them. Or, if they still refuse, we have camps prepared where their final days will be put to good use."

"Does the President agree with this? How can he agree when he professes to hold traditional Christian values? He, well, we all took oaths to uphold the Constitution, which means to defend the best interests of the American people."

Lynch cut her off. "Ms. Howard, I'm sure you realize the President takes his orders from others who hold the real power to make such momentous decisions. As a matter of fact, he argued against this plan. But he soon came to realize, as I've already explained, that we can't motivate the world to take the final plunge into global control without this type of war. We don't have the luxury of achieving what's best without paying a heavy price.

"You should understand this from your military training. In war, you don't have a choice as to whether some die or don't. It's a matter of the wisest use of the resources you have to achieve the ultimate victory. In the process, you endure losses. President McCleen understands that these are necessary losses. The fact that he is incommunicado is evidence of his emotional struggle to accept what's happening. But he'll get over it if he wants to stay in his privileged position."

Jolene slumped back in her chair, too staggered to respond. The vice president recognized this and shook his head. He stood to leave.

"As I said before, you have a lot to learn, so just settle down. You'll be told what to do when the time comes. In the meantime, 'go with the flow' and play the role you've been given. But don't question those with the real authority." He patted her shoulder and walked out.

Left alone, Jolene stared at the television monitors in the next room. Some had pictures of mushroom clouds. Most were blank because the sending stations had been vaporized. Tears filled her eyes. She remembered the words from the Bible, which she had not thought of in years: "Too whom much is given, much is required."

Did the warnings of preachers from my childhood actually come true? Is God punishing America? Am I being punished for sins I refused to face? What kind of evil have I allowed myself to be involved in?

Jolene closed her eyes and bowed her head. She had never given up prayer, but she realized it had been a mere religious formality. Now her heart cried out to God with a deep sense of shame and guilt. She remembered what General Leland had tried to warn her of years before, the corruption in high political offices. She now realized he had been right. However, it was too late to undo the past. For a moment, she wanted to die. She didn't deserve to live when so many who had looked to her for leadership were either dead or soon would be. She had trouble breathing. Her body trembled.

Then like a shaft of light bursting through the dark, a thought came to her. It was a memory of the book of Esther in the Old Testament. What if God has raised me up for this hour?

As one of the Jewish captives of the Persians, Esther had been chosen to be queen because of her beauty. Events she had no control over threatened the existence of her Hebrew race. Esther's uncle told her she had been exalted to a high position as part of God's plan. He therefore gave her a challenge. As a vessel in God's hands, God might work through her to save their people. Esther devised and executed a plan to defeat the enemy. It won her a place in the ranks of the great heroes of her people.

A grim purpose took root in Jolene's heart. Perhaps she could be a force to redeem good from this terrible loss. She had achieved her position because she learned how to play the military game. She used her minority race and femininity to the maximum advantage in a hostile, threatening environment. She knew her athletic figure and attractiveness had enabled her to win favor at key moments in the dominant male culture where she worked. A smile crossed her face.

All right, Mr. Vice President, so I have a great deal to learn. Very well, I will learn the rules of your game. But I will play to defeat your kind and all you represent. So help me God!

•   Comrade Toschoff prepared royal accommodations for those invited to the party in a massive, national command and control system dispersed in three underground locations. Besides Yamantau Mountain, there was the Yavinsky underground complex and the Sherapovo bunker site south of Moscow. Sherapovo had become the primary control center for Russia's civilian leaders. The Kremlin connected Sherapovo and other bunkers by a secret subway line. Once at Sherapovo, leaders would be able to conduct the war effort using a duplicate communication system that allowed the leaders to send orders and receive reports through the wartime management structure.

President Ivan Solntsev sat in an overstuffed chair with a command view of large television screens that displayed maps of North America, Europe, and the Far East. Computer screens revealed graphic overlays of the missile launches against land and sea targets. When each target had been hit, the indicator turned from red to green.

He had seen it all before in a mock, computerized battle that convinced political and military leaders of the readiness to strike. Now it was difficult to grasp the fact that each strike killed tens, maybe hundreds of thousands of human beings. It all appeared as a massive video game. He smiled at the reactions of the men at various stations in the room. They gestured thumbs up signals or gave high-fives to each other when reports of victory were received.

General Borisov watched a similar display in his Yavinsky underground bunker complex. A tense moment developed when the 4th Fleet in the Indian Ocean took out the Russian submarines before they had been able to launch even one missile. He had hoped to divert the air attack to other targets in Europe or the Middle East, but those could wait. The reserves to back up any such difficulty were doing their job. Relieved, the general watched the target designator turn green.

He picked up the phone and called the President.

Solntsev's voice sounded strong and confident. "General Borisov, your attack is proceeding magnificently."

"Yes, thanks to you and the leaders' excellent

preparations. The American's 4th Fleet had me concerned for a moment. One of our ICBMs aimed at NORAD went astray, but initial reports confirm heavy damage. I am concerned about our naval losses. We knew, however, that their submarines would fight back."

"Yes, Comrade, we have a worthy enemy, but I'm confident our second wave of attacks will be more than capable of mopping up what we missed on the first round. We will be toasting your continued success."

"Thank you, Mr. President."

Borisov sat back in his chair and watched his staff prepare an up-to-date report for him. He recalled that the American President, Franklin D. Roosevelt, had referred to the Japanese attack on Pearl Harbor that launched World War II as a "Day of Infamy." He wondered what terms the current American leader would use to describe this war. Whatever, it would go down in history as the greatest sneak attack ever carried out against a world-class power. His name, General Yakov D. Borisov, would be known as the mastermind who executed this military defeat of the greatest military power the world has ever seen.

While he acknowledged that it had been made possible by cooperation with American and world leadership, his pride did not allow it to become a predominate factor. In spite of the disarray of the overall military and the internal conflicts of Russian leadership, they had shocked the world. They would no longer have to play the role of being a second- or third-rate world power. They had the respect they deserved. Yes indeed, he would drink to their success.

•   Burt Wilson awoke to an early spring thunderstorm, or so he thought. It was not uncommon in Northern Illinois between Rockford and Chicago. But he didn't remember the thunder being so violent that windows rattled and the house shook.

He turned to look at the bedside clock radio. The power was off. This ratcheted up his concern. He got out of bed and opened the shades. Looking to the west, he saw an orange glow in the sky but no dark clouds. This puzzled him.

Wilson went back to his bed.

His wife of 46 years, Gloria, stirred. "Are you feeling okay?"

"Yes, but something weird is happening."

"Tell me about it in the morning." She rolled over and pulled the covers over her head.

Ignoring her, he found a flashlight and went to his study where he had a battery powered, shortwave radio along with his old but reliable Ham radio set. He took the radio out of its Faraday box, turned it on, and began to search the AM dial. Hearing static, he punched the button for shortwave and turned the dial to HCJB out of South America. Occasionally Wilson listened to the Christian missionary station where he heard the international perspective on news.

An American pastor was teaching on the book of Revelation when a brilliant flash of light lit Wilson's study. As his eyes readjusted, he peered out the window to a starlit heaven. "What in the world is happening?" he muttered.

Just then an excited voice broke into the radio program. "We interrupt this scheduled program to bring an urgent news bulletin. We have just learned that North America is under attack. Russia and China have launched a preemptive nuclear strike against American targets. We do not have any specifics at this time. Our original source was knocked off the air by a massive power outage across North America. We are seeking confirmation from other sources." The announcer began to repeat the message.

"Oh my god! That's where the light . . ." Wilson shouted, "Gloria, get up! Get in here! Now!"

A retired autoworker, Wilson was different than his neighbors because he was into preparation for hard times. He had a small, gas driven generator in the garage. In case of a natural disaster when power went off, he had a plan to be able to operate his Ham radio and keep food in their freezer from spoiling. Unlike most of his neighbors in their suburban community, he didn't like being dependent on the local grocery stores for food.

He met Gloria in the hallway and blurted out the news.

Sensing her skepticism, he added, "Listen to the news. I'm gonna fire up the generator so I can get on the Ham radio network."

On the second pull, the generator started. He threw a switch on the junction box that directed the electricity into the house. Returning to his study, he was relieved to find that EMP from the nuclear explosions had not damaged his old, vacuum tube transmitter and receiver.

When the unit warmed up, the airwaves were full of excited voices. Much of the traffic was concerned parents or grandparents wanting information from areas where their loved ones lived. By listening to the responses, Wilson was able to piece together what had happened. The large cities had not been targeted, but there were enough major transmission lines destroyed to bring down the entire power grid.

When Gloria finally accepted the reality of what was happening, she was amazed to find that the phone system still worked. Wilson phoned their son Jerry in Rockford who was unaware of the chaos. They had to let him listen to news coming over the shortwave station before he believed it was nothing more than a power outage.

Throughout the night, the Wilsons' emotions were jarred as they listened to tragic reports from around the world. The damage and loss of life were massive.

At first light, someone pounded on the front door. Before Gloria could reach it, Ralph Leonard, a neighbor, shouted, "Burt, are you up yet? What the hell's going on? How come we're having a power outage? I can't even get my SUV started."

Gloria opened the door. "Haven't you heard? America's been hit by nuclear weapons, we think from Russia and China. The power is off all across the nation."

Ralph's mouth dropped open. "Huh? You kiddin' me?"

"No, Ralph, I'm not joking. Burt's been talking to people on his Ham set all across the nation. It looks like we're in World War III."

Before she could elaborate, Ralph moaned, "Oh my god, what're we gonna do? Is this for real?"

"Come in and listen." Gloria directed him to the room where her husband was writing on a note pad. He nodded to Ralph and continued to write. Ralph listened, shaking his head.

When a burst of static blotted out the transmission, Wilson turned the volume down.

Normally loud mouthed, Ralph spoke as if in a trance, "My oldest boy is stationed at an immense air base in Germany near Wiesbaden. Have you heard anything about that area?"

Wilson shrugged and gave Ralph a weary look. "From what I've heard, all major military bases have been nuked. The strike was against military targets, not just in America but around the world." Noting Ralph's face, he added, "I'm sorry."

Ralph looked at the floor. Tears filled in his eyes. Glancing up at his neighbors, he blurted loudly, "My god, what're we gonna do? I just can't believe it!"

This was the remark heard everywhere that morning. Most of the neighbors were like Ralph. They hadn't known what was happening. Once the news broke to a few, it spread rapidly. Ear-piercing screams were heard throughout the neighborhood. Small groups gathered on lawns to exchange news. Neighbor after neighbor couldn't start his vehicle because EMP had fried computer circuits. Only a few old pickups started. Several neighbors piled into them and drove to the nearest grocery store. It didn't take long for the basics of life, food and water, to take first place in their concerns.

Panic set in when someone noticed ashes falling from the sky. They weren't sure why, but they knew this wasn't a good sign.

•   Dawn brought a flurry of activity. Russell, his wife, Hannah, and their four children arrived at James and Ann's home with a pickup load of survival equipment. As James had predicted, his oldest grandson Caleb showed up with his jeep full of gear. Ann directed the clearing of the barn where family members placed their sleeping provisions and cooking supplies.

While the family moved into the barn, James took a battery operated, two-way radio from the Faraday box, installed the battery, and called the leaders of his local congregation. The first man to respond was Richard Hampton, the head elder in James's scattered group of house churches.

"Rich, how's your family? What's happening in your neighborhood?"

"In spite of our preparations, everyone's in shock. I've got neighbors busy sealing their houses, preparing for the fallout. With so many windows out, it's a gigantic task. We're taking in the Clarks and Mrs. Peabody, but I'm concerned about those who are totally unprepared. I'm afraid there will be ugly reactions when the truth of this is revealed to the masses."

"Right."

Rich continued before James could comment further. "Tom told me City Market and Safeway have both been cleaned out by mobs, along with the liquor stores. He said the rumors of what happened range from a space alien attack to Russians landing at the airport and the rest of the nation being wiped out by nukes. A few people think Jesus returned, and they got left. It's a mess!"

"Where are people acquiring their news?"

"A certain number of cell phones and part of the phone system are still working. A few have battery operated, shortwave radios. The sheriff has deputies with loud speakers driving around telling people to prepare for fallout. The EMP didn't knock out all their vehicles."

Another man joined the conversation. "Hi, this is Boyd. I just tuned in. The EMP got my new pickup, but my old one is running fine. My boys are loading buckets of emergency supplies that we prepared in the past. We plan to drive around and give them to people in the neighborhood who didn't prepare. We'll also take along the printout of instructions that tells how to survive the fallout. Then we're planning to come back to button down. Did you guys lose the glass in your houses?"

James and Rich responded in the affirmative. James added, "Thanks for the report, Boyd. I trust you're going to be armed when you distribute those supplies. We may have to use deadly force to protect our families from people out of control."

"Yeh, I told my boys to lock and load. I sure hate to see this, but darn, we tried to warn them. Now they're going to have to get along the best they can with what they have."

Rich agreed. James suggested, "If you talk to any of the other elders or deacons, tell them to call me. I'll leave my radio on standby. Let's follow the procedure we agreed on to report at 6 p.m. In the meantime, my boy, Russ, will set up a Ham radio to learn what's happening all over the country. Until later, let's sign off."

He put in a call on a separate channel to Major General Leland's home. Leland had been his commanding officer in Vietnam where James served as an Army chaplain and helped the general make a commitment to Christ. Later he educated his former commander on the true history of America and how leaders in the 20th century had sold the nation out to the New World Order elitists. Leland remained in the Army long enough to earn his 2nd star and also acquire inside information, while attempting to save the integrity of the military. Finally, however, the powers-that-be wouldn't put up with his attitude. Leland was forced into retirement. Due to his friendship with James, he moved to Western Colorado and became a member of James's congregation.

The husky voice of Sergeant Ball came on the line. "Ball here. Over."

"Sergeant Ball, this is Chaplain Parr checking in with you to see how you are."

"We came through fine, sir. Lost a lot of glass, but no structural damage. I'm guessing you know what's troubling the general."

"Yes, is he available?"

"No, sir. He's putting the horses away so we can hurry inside as soon as we detect fallout. He isn't in the mood to talk now. You know how he bottles things up until he has time to work everything out. He's a tough one, sir, but this is a pretty deep wound."

"Right." James hesitated. "I want to express my sympathy to you, Sarge. I know your fiancée was with Florence and her son's family. These things are impossible for us to figure out, but we know they're all with the Lord now. We can't stop trusting in God's mercy."

Ball's voice faltered. "Thanks for your concern, Chaplain. Our loss is pretty small when we think of all the good men and women in uniform who met the Lord last night before many of them were ready. It makes me extremely angry."

"All the more reason we need to fight to survive so we can lead in the recovery. We're going to need the general more than ever now. You tell him I'm praying for him and all of you over there. When he's ready, we can begin planning our counterattacks."

"I'll tell him, sir. How's your family?"

"Thank the Lord, my son Henry and his family made it out of Colorado Springs. We all came through last night shook up but safe."

"That's good news. I'm glad to hear your family is with you. One more thing I think you'll want to know. We got a quick message from General Foster. He got most of his division out before the strike. He's putting his men up in some mine shafts to keep them out of the fallout. He had to leave quite a bit of his heavy equipment. He also got most of the Green Beret command out. So we have some forces that can fight back. I thought you'd want to know."

"I appreciate that. We'll remember his men in our prayers. Contact you later. Out."

James's entire body trembled. Thoughts of his close friends and their personal losses filled him with grief. He reminded himself that millions of people were experiencing the same gut wrenching sorrow on top of the shock of their lives.

To work out the distress, James put his mind to the tasks at hand for his family. He supervised the relocation of the chickens to a large horse stall. The hens would be content with their new home, but the rooster would probably crow at odd hours, disturbing everyone's sleep. At first, his family would think it was funny, but then various ones would become irritated and want to butcher the fine-feathered creature. James would have to educate them. The rooster was needed to be able to hatch eggs in order to have more chickens.

The milk goats were nervous when placed in their pen. Ann would teach the older children how to milk them. He knew Elizabeth might resist at first but then change her mind. She would enjoy the attention the goats gave her. They'd help take her mind off her friends who had died in the destruction of Colorado Springs.

Chuck helped his grandfather take care of the horses. The large animals would become a vital part of their transportation since fuel for vehicles was in short supply even though James had large tanks of diesel and gasoline stored.

The Parr families had settled in the barn by the time the first radiation appeared. The adults worked hard to remain calm in front of the children. They tried to make it out to be an enjoyable camping experience. However, the cramped space along with the lack of privacy and the comfort of their electronic devices soon put everyone's nerves on edge as the initial shock wore off. They missed being able to turn on the television to find out what was occurring around the world. Knowing that terrible events had taken place, but not having the details, bothered everyone.

Russ had brought along a portable Ham radio setup. When he attached it to the already positioned antenna, he searched the dial to learn about other parts of the nation.

Taking notes, he called to James and Henry, "The nuclear explosion that took out our windows happened east of here about thirty, maybe forty miles as the crow flies near Crested Butte. The shockwave flowed down the valley and virtually leveled Gunnison. Dad, I'm sure glad you phoned me in time to be able to have Caleb come home. He'll be upset when he learns that many of his friends at school are probably dead or injured."

James cautioned, "I think we'd better keep the grim news from the younger children. I'm sure Caleb will want to know. As an Army reservist, he won't wait for them to call him up."

Throughout the night, the men took turns standing guard in case desperate neighbors tried to take advantage of their preparations. The women kept the children busy with games, studies, meal preparation, and cleanup duties.

During the next few days, Russ continued to receive reports from fellow Ham operators around the nation. Using their battery powered shortwave radios, news from other parts of the world also became available. No accurate count of the people lost in the initial attacks could be given. Estimates ran in the millions. Hospitals in those areas not hit by direct blasts had been overwhelmed. People suffering from shock or victims of the devastated areas became their patients.

The tens of thousands of people not killed by the blasts were left in desperate straits from injuries or lethal doses of radiation. Millions more would suffer terribly, and many would die during the next weeks and months from the effects of radiation. Few had potassium iodine pills, which would have enabled their bodies to resist the fallout. Neither could most people seclude themselves where the fallout would not harm them. Most normal supports for life depended on electricity. It was nonexistent except in a few areas where small generation stations had disengaged from the national power grid and provided electricity to limited areas. As word spread about the location of those areas, an influx of refuges from communities living in the dark joined the more fortunate.

Russ reported that food riots in major cities turned vicious. Government efforts to provide emergency aids had been hindered by the lack of electricity and transportation, which depended on petroleum. Refineries could not function. Filling stations had no electricity to pump fuel from storage tanks. As a result, all social order in many parts of the country had begun to break down. The police, who in the past relied on help from National Guard units, now had to be on their own. In most cases, they didn't have the manpower to handle the crises.

It soon became apparent that the end of the world had not occurred as some had predicted since the beginning of the nuclear age. Many parts of the world were unaffected by nuclear fallout. Other areas would receive enough fallout to negatively affect the health of those with poor immune systems. But life would continue for most people, only with the new reality that Russian or Chinese armies had invaded nations throughout the Eurasian continent. No longer did American armed forces protect Europe or Asian Rim countries. The few elements of the American military that survived outside America were either overwhelmed or struggling to exist without the constant flow of supplies from the USA. Yet they had no plan to give up the fight, especially soldiers inside the United States.

The Parrs, like millions of other survivors, set about adjusting to the realities of life in a post nuclear world. Better prepared than many for their tasks, they determined to carry on. They had stored a variety of foods and essential survival supplies. Some of their cache would be shared with neighbors who had not prepared. James's foresight to store seeds enabled him to distribute a portion to others. Spring gardens would be a reality. Life had been pared down to the basics -- food, water, and shelter. Surviving Americans struggled to adapt to the new existence.

The sudden attack would be called many names, most of which could not be said in polite company. Everyone knew the meaning of the numbers 911. James and the members of his congregation referred to the catastrophic event as "Doomsday." Later it became simply "D-Day."

•   Some people living in America had felt no dismay when the nuclear attack occurred. Surprised and shocked? Yes. But disappointed only by the fact that it added to their problems. The plan had been to prepare a surprise of their own that would go down in history as a clever, devastating attack against the unbelievers.

Sam Kirkland, a light skinned Middle Eastern transplant, had taken an American name to draw attention from his Iranian background. Sam's Islamic Imman taught

him to hate America. But instead of being urged to train
as a soldier, he'd been challenged to infiltrate the enemy's
camp and strike within the system. By being patient and
persistent, he would be able to achieve results and earn a
greater reward from Allah.

After acquiring a university degree in Tehran, he trained
in biochemistry at New York University where he also
attended a Muslim mosque. Openly a member of the Muslim
community, he never became involved in political issues.
Fellow students and workers viewed him as a progressive
Muslim interested in one thing, acquiring and enjoying
wealth. If the subject of terrorism came up, he would be one
of the first to criticize those of his faith who supported the
concept.

Because of his high paying job as a chemist for a perfume
company, Sam purchased a house on Long Island in an
upscale suburban community. Other nationalities settled
in the area and also enjoyed the American dream. It didn't
disturb Sam's neighbors when three men moved into his
large home. No one knew that they had crossed the border
between Mexico and Arizona and driven to the New York
area in a rented car. They used international credit cards
and drivers licenses to acquire their car. The men arrived
only days before the surprise attack by Russian missiles.

Sam's houseguests had been watching television when
the newsflash appeared on the screen about the nuclear
attack. At first they thought it was a strange advertisement.
Soon, however, it became apparent that it was real, and it
frightened them.

They got Sam out of bed and began to pummel him with
questions. "What do we do? We don't have enough biological
agents to make an impact. We have no way to spread the
small amount that we have."

The leader of the three new members of the team, Calieb,
tried to interrupt Sam as he watched the television news.
"What about the team with the nuclear device?"

Sam ignored the men and watched the news until the
power failed.

Lighting a candle, he motioned for them to calm down

while he gathered his thoughts. "We can't strike now because we're not prepared. If the other team struck, their small blast would be seen as part of the attack. After all the years of preparation, I am not going to sell my life cheap."

He paced the floor. The others waited. Trained as a scientist, he weighed the pros and cons of the possibilities. After several minutes, he stopped, made eye contact with each man, and then spoke. "We need to settle down like everyone else and survive as best we can until we are able to strike. If they had intended to take out New York City, we would have already been hit. I know how to seal the house against the fallout that will come. I'll take Calieb, and we'll buy as many food supplies as possible. While we're gone, I want you men to fill the bathtub with water and every bottle in the house you can find. Let's get to work!"

By the time the two men arrived at the nearest all night grocery store that was operating on an emergency generator, other people were filling their baskets with bottled water and canned goods. Sam and Calieb each loaded a grocery cart with sacks of flour, beans, rice, and other staples along with canned foods. Before they got to the cash register, the generator failed. The emergency exit lights enabled Sam to lead the way out of the store as crowds of people fought to rush inside. By the time they'd loaded their supplies into Sam's van, the store was mobbed with frantic people.

Back at their house, Sam hurried to his laptop computer and made a list of things to do to prepare to survive the fallout. He had purchased a generator to provide a steady source of electrical supply when they would build their cultures in his basement laboratory. Now they had power, one of the few houses in the area. As copies came off the printer, Sam explained to the men that, as soon as dawn appeared, they would distribute the flyers to homes in the neighborhood.

Calieb asked, "Why are we doing this? What do we care about them? Let them die."

Sam made sure the men were paying attention. "I've lived here long enough to understand this culture. It will put us in good stead with our neighbors. This is the way

Americans act. We may need their help in the future. It will help remove us from suspicion. Trust me.

"We'll have to wait for the right time to carry out the attack we've been given. When we do, the entire world will know who did it and why. We will use this time to prepare. Somehow many will survive this attack. Just when they think they are again safe, they will experience terror as great or even greater than what they are now experiencing. But to accomplish our mission, we must survive. By the will of Allah, we will do this."

D-Day Minus Three Days

The six o'clock radio reports from church leaders were bleak. Mike Moore, a compassionate deacon, served his fellow man with dedication.

He poured out his heart to the others, "Pastor, it's grim here in town. Armed gangs of people are roaming the streets, breaking into people's homes, and looking for food or booze. There are reports of those resisting being shot. The police are overwhelmed. They're staying home to protect their own families and stay clear of the fallout. We gave out all the extra food and supplies we had. But you'll not believe this. A father we know with a large family came by, and when I offered them rice and beans, he cursed me. He said they wanted food their kids would eat. Man, what are we supposed to do to--"

Rich interrupted, "Mike, we heard that the sheriff arranged for a truckload of beans to be brought in from the warehouse in Olathe and corn, from a local farmer. They're cooking it in the cafeteria for the people taking refuge in the gym. The water system is still working by gravity, so people should be able to prepare it even if they have to build a fire outside."

"I heard the same thing, Rich. But didn't you get the point? People are so spoiled they want cold cereal, pizza, or hamburgers and ice cream. Their kids won't eat real food."

"Then let them go hungry. Given enough time, they'll

change their minds," someone chimed in.

"In the meantime, their parents will become desperate. Don't the people in the streets know they're being radiated by the fallout?" James asked.

"They're not concerned about the future. All they're thinking about is the here and now," said Mike.

"Nothing new about that, right, Pastor?"

"You're right about that, Tom. But what is new is the fact that the judgment of God is literally driving some people insane. But the question is, what can we do for them, if anything?"

"This is Boyd. We have to protect our families however the situation requires. If some of you need an extra man to help stand guard, my oldest, Bradley, is willing to help. He's well armed and not afraid to shoot to kill, if necessary."

"Oh god, I hate to think that it's come to this," Mike lamented. "We've been praying that the Lord's angels will protect us and scare them away. So far, we've not been threatened."

"This is Rich. Mike, I know your heart, and I certainly affirm the need for prayer and trusting in the Lord's protection. But, brother, what about our neighbors who don't have the faith to trust God? Are we to stand by and let the wicked abuse or kill them? Maybe God means for us to be the instruments of justice since most lawful, civil authority has failed in the community."

The network was silent for a while. James waited to see what Mike's response would be. It was a long time before Mike answered Rich's challenge. "I never thought of it that way. I'll pray about it."

James affirmed, "You're both right. We need to pray for God's protection as well as His justice to be given out to those who are abusive. But we also need to be ready to take action, regardless of how repulsive it may be. I suspect it will only be a matter of time until those of us living in the country will have to face the gangs. They'll come looking for our animals, so keep a sharp lookout. And be careful about letting anyone come into your homes because they can bring in radioactive dust.

"I encourage all of you to celebrate the Lord's Supper every day at one of your meals. Even in this time of seeming defeat, we need to hold up the victory of the Lord Jesus over all our enemies. This is our nuclear counter attack in the spiritual realm." Several "Amens" followed their pastor's admonition.

"If anyone wants to take Boyd up on his offer, he can keep his radio turned on for a little while. You can talk privately with him. The rest of us should sign off and save our batteries. God bless and keep you all in His loving care."

D-Day Plus One Week

•   Mother Nature appeared to weep over suffering humanity. Western Colorado received a great deal of rain during a twenty-four hour period in the lower elevations and snow in the mountains. James used a Geiger counter to measure radioactivity in the first rains. Later in the day, the water was clean. Like tears washing the soul, the rains washed most of the radiation from the land and housetops into the rivers.

The following night Russ nudged his father awake. "Annie's growling, and the goats are spooked. I think someone's outside."

James threw his blanket back and sat up. Already dressed, he slipped his feet into his boots. Picking up his short barrel, 12-gage shotgun, he followed Russ to the front of the barn. The soft glow from a nightlight enabled James to find a battery powered, infrared flashlight and red goggles. Russ turned the nightlight off.

James pulled the curtain from a window covered with clear plastic. Putting on the goggles, he shined the infrared beam toward the house. Three armed men stood next to an open window. It appeared they were watching someone who had climbed into the house.

James whispered to Russ what he had seen. Then he said, "Go back and wake everyone. Tell them to hide behind the barrels in the storage room. Bring Henry, Caleb, and my rifle with the night scope." Russ moved off in the dark. James turned his attention to the intruders once more and listened to his family members waking up and moving about. The strangers outside didn't appear to hear anything.

Caleb was the first to hurry to his grandfather's side. "What's up, Grandpa?"

"Take a look." James gave him the goggles. "How many do you see?"

"Three. No, there's another one climbing out the window. Wait, two have come out of the house. They're pointing this direction."

Russ and Henry walked up and heard Caleb's whispered report.

James handed Henry the shotgun, taking his rifle from him. "I'm going to climb up to the shooting position in the loft. Henry, take the position in the machine shed. Russ, sneak out to the goat pen. Caleb, take the front entrance. Don't shoot to kill unless they fight back. Wait for my lead. Go!"

Before James left, Caleb confirmed that the strangers were moving toward the barn. James slung his weapon over his shoulder, climbed to the loft, and opened a small shooting hole. Easing his rifle into a firing position, his eyes adjusted to the dark. He could see five figures moving toward the barn.

Downstairs Annie began to bark. James threw a light switch, illuminating the area in front of the barn.

"Don't move, or we'll shoot to kill!" yelled James.

The men froze. One started to raise his weapon.

"Don't move! There are four guns on you!"

"We're just looking for something to feed our families!" a man called out.

"You're going about it in the wrong way! Drop your guns! You can come back tomorrow in the light and explain your needs! We'll share some food with you. And if you're legit, we'll return your weapons."

The spokesman looked the barn over and replied, "We need our guns for protection."

"Tough! It's your choice. Put your guns down or die!"

James hoped his voice didn't betray the tension he felt. The prospect of shooting another human being didn't make him happy. Decades before, he'd killed enemy soldiers in Vietnam and still suffered from gut wrenching nightmares that left him at the point of vomiting when he awakened. He knew his sons and grandson were sweating it out, wondering if they could actually pull the trigger. James mentally voiced a prayer that the strangers would obey. All the while he steeled himself to do what had to be done in order to protect his family.

"Hey, I heard you was a preacher."

"You heard right. But I'm no fool, and neither are my three sons." His voice grew strong as he sensed the men's fear. "This is your last warning. Put your weapons down and leave! Now!"

The gaunt looking man held up one hand and began to lay his weapon down. "Okay, don't shoot." He turned to the others. "Do as the man insists." He looked up toward the loft. "How'd you know we was out here?"

"God told me!" His conscience rebuked him. But at the same time he inwardly chuckled observing the man's reaction.

The man began to back up.

James called out, "What's your name?"

"Uh, Smith."

"We bid you good night, Mr. Smith. Don't forget to announce your presence tomorrow when you come through the gate -- unarmed."

The man nodded. He and the others turned and ran into the darkness. James watched until he could no longer see them before switching off the light. He climbed from the loft and instructed Caleb to collect the weapons.

"Do you think Smith will be back?" asked Russ.

James shrugged. "I doubt it. Huh, Smith. How original!" The younger men responded with nervous laughter.

Ann called to them, "Is everything all right?"

"Yes. They left. Put the kids back to bed." Turning to his sons, James added, "We'd better have a double guard the rest of the night. I'll take the next watch with Caleb. You guys comfort your wives and children. Don't forget to thank the Lord. The next time it might not end so easily."

The rest of the night was uneventful, but gunshots were heard in the distance.

Chapter Three

Up From the Ashes

D-Day Plus Three Weeks

The weather beaten, battle scarred, Blackhawk helicopter descended from the Rocky Mountain foothills and flew toward the charred remains of the former bustling city, Colorado Springs. Highways and streets with rusting skeletons of cars and trucks revealed the outlines of the city. As far as the eye could see, gutted foundations of homes and businesses marked the area.

In the downtown area, hulks of concrete buildings still stood, especially parking garages. The lower decks had withstood the nuclear tipped missiles. One could only imagine the fiery hell that erupted around those caught there at the time of the first blasts. After three weeks, smoke still rose from the pile of coal next to the remains of the city's power plant.

Retired Army Major General Mark Leland released his seatbelt to kneel between the two pilots. He looked out the front of the chopper. He wore headsets and a mike that enabled him to talk to the pilots without shouting above the noise of the chopper. But no one felt like talking. Crossing over the last of the foothills that gave way to the expansive prairie, the remains of the city and military bases came into full view.

The older man, forced out of retirement by the preemptive nuclear strike, pointed to the left, directing the pilots to a specific area. "See the remains of the golf course just beyond the ruins of those large buildings? It's a couple of blocks to the left of the center of the golf course."

With a "Roger," the head pilot altered his course and allowed the craft to settle toward the earth. They flew over a scene of total devastation.

"Okay, see that traffic circle? It's straight ahead and to the left three blocks beyond. After a short block, turn right and then an immediate left. It'll be the house at the top of the ridge on the right side."

"Got it, sir. I'll make a slow pass over it."

The alert general suddenly exclaimed, "That's it with the little flowering tree stub out front. My god, something actually lived through it all! Amazing!"

Only a couple of hundred feet above the ground, the downdraft of the chopper stirred ashes and dust from a former asphalt street. The heat of the nuclear blasts had melted it, burning the tar and leaving pulverized gravel.

"Sir, I can hover for a few minutes if you'd like."

"Thanks, Colonel. I'd appreciate that."

Sergeant Ball joined the general at the door of the chopper. They checked to make sure they had the right location. The sergeant had been there before D-Day, so he remembered enough of the features to recognize the place.

Like a hawk looking for its prey, an advanced Apache attack helicopter gunship circled. Major Tim Sparks, the pilot, didn't expect to find any resistance but remained alert for signs of threats to the general. Sparks had first put his life on the line to protect the commander during a terrorist attack on his superior's headquarters while stationed in the Balkans. Since then, he had been available to the general to risk his life to save the man he had come to respect and cherish as an American hero. He not only felt this way due to the general's leadership abilities, but also because he considered Leland a trusted friend.

Sergeant Ball remained silent as they looked at the remains of a beautiful home in an upscale, middle class suburb. It was the home of General Leland's stepson, Kenny, the only son of his second wife, Florence.

The general broke the silence, speaking to the sergeant through the chopper's radio system, "This must have been near the epicenter of the blast that took out the area. Look how the cars are flattened. Blasted Russians! They probably aimed for Cheyenne Mountain but hit here, ten miles northeast."

"Well, sir, it looks as if they were able to make a direct hit on the mountain. You can see the crater better from here."

They looked to the south at the imposing outline of Cheyenne Mountain and beyond at the majesty of Pikes Peak with its snowcap. The general remembered how much Kenny had loved its beauty. Leland tried to persuade him to move to the Western Slope where he and his wife had their retirement home. But Ken's work with satellites, which the young man had been trained for and loved, was located in Colorado Springs. In spite of the threats of this possibility, they, along with millions of other Americans, continued to believe such a thing could never happen in America.

"Bastards! I still can't believe we trusted their phony treaties. I don't know who was more stupid. We Americans for believing our political leaders or them for making such an outrageous move to allow our military to be taken out."

The general took a deep breath and felt sick as he looked into the basement. There he saw the rusted remains of metal objects that had been vital parts of the home.

"I guess there's no way we can climb down there. It's not logical, but I wish I could look around."

The sergeant turned and shook his head. "It's still too hot to be safe, sir. We can't let you become exposed to any more radiation."

For the first time, the general smiled. "Sergeant, you never cease to amaze me. I believe I'm going to keep you around. By the time you're through training me, you'll be ready for your promotion to general."

The sergeant's black face lit up with a smile. He knew as well as the general that he would never leave the commander's side, if ordered. The sergeant had chosen to retire and live near the general even though they were in different social circles. Ever since the general had intervened in a critical situation to save the sergeant's life during the last days of the first Gulf War, they'd been close friends. The appreciation and respect each had for the other bridged their differences in race, rank, and social class. Since Doomsday, the sergeant had seldom been more than a few yards from the general. He considered it a rare privilege to be able to serve such a leader at a time when America desperately needed true patriots to lead the country out of its dilemma.

Before D-Day, the general spoke with force against disarming America in the face of the ever more powerful Russian and Chinese militaries. As a result, threats came against his life. Close friends knew the powers-that-be would not hesitate to have the general involved in a fatal accident to silence him. The sergeant provided protection, hiring, and the supervision of a private security detail for the general and his wife.

The sergeant's wife had left him years earlier. Months before D-Day, at the general's insistence, he considered remarriage. The young woman who caught his eye was a member of the security detail guarding the general's wife. Linda had driven to Colorado Springs with Florence. There was no way to know whether she had been at the house or nearby when the bombs hit. Neither woman had been heard from since. Both men suffered the uncertainty in silence.

The general shook his head in disbelief and anguish. For a few minutes, he seemed lost in thought. The pilot raised the chopper into the sky. General Leland had lost both of his wives as the direct result of rogue governments. The loss of Sharon, his first wife, who was killed in a terrorist attack while they were on duty in the Middle East, caused the general to struggle with bitterness. Now those feelings returned with vengeance. He felt helpless because he had not been able to prevent either loss. The sergeant, knowing him well, called him back to the present.

"Sir, when the radiation cools some, would you like me to send a medical team here to see what remains might be collected for a proper burial?"

The general turned to the sergeant. "No, since we can't do it for everyone, we won't do it for anyone. Anyhow, they're not here, thank God."

"Yes, sir. I think we've confirmed what we knew to be true. There's no kidding ourselves anymore. We know they were here. Someday, God willing, when we've got peace in

this country again, maybe we'll be alive to come back and
raise a memorial."

"Good thought, Sergeant."

They continued to look around, lost in a host of
memories.

"I imagine little Andrew slept in the same room with
Kenny and Laura. They were so enthused about him. Kenny
was a proud father. My god, Sarge, what a waste! What
a stupid, idiotic waste! It's hard not to be bitter and want
revenge on the whole damn nation."

"I know how you feel, General. But like you asked
earlier, who is ultimately at fault? Those who attacked or
those who allowed themselves to be deceived into lowering
their guard?"

"Yes. You'd think we'd learn not to trust anyone with
absolute power. But here we are, two old soldiers turned out
to pasture. Now we're expected to pull miracles out of an
empty hat so the ones fortunate enough to survive can have
their country back. If I didn't have faith in a just, sovereign
God, I'd have gone mad a long time ago."

The general realized he didn't need anything from this
place. He had his memories. He had snapshots and videos
back at his retirement home where he could watch lost
family members. But he was glad to have been able to come
and put the ghosts of uncertainty to rest.

"Well, Sarge, we've got lots of work to do. Sparks will be
running low on fuel if we don't move out. Colonel, let's get on
down to Cheyenne Mountain and see what we can salvage,
okay?"

"Yes, sir."

•   General Leland's Blackhawk landed on a cleared spot
on the side of Cheyenne Mountain. An electric powered golf
cart transported him and the sergeant. The chopper with its
crew lifted off to a makeshift airport to refuel, along with the
major's Apache.

The golf cart made its way through rubble to a tunnel
that opened into the underground complex. In front of a
security station, the cart came to a halt. Brigadier General

Brad Foster, Commander of the Mountain Post, waited.

After the proper acknowledgements, General Foster brought Leland up to date on the situation while they rode into the Command Center. "You can see that the complex has lived up to its original purposes, at least in terms of its survivability. Most of the equipment is intact, but the ability to communicate with the outside world is hindered by the loss of our antenna field and the destruction of other U.S. bases and many of our satellites.

"However, our operators have been able to tap into a couple of satellites which survived. Elements of the remaining Air Force used fighter-launched rockets to take out the key Russian satellites, so they're greatly restricted in their ability to monitor what's happening in the states. The East Coast FEMA Command Center at Fort Weatherford is in charge of coordinating the response of our surviving missile submarine force and some super secret weapons from Area 51. They didn't take out Washington, D. C., because they wanted a government left with the authority to surrender.

"However, our leaders have not officially capitulated. Our attack subs got most of the Russian and Chinese subs and surface fleet but not before they used nuclear equipped, Russian-made Sunburn missiles to take out all our carrier battle groups and most of the support ships. Our losses have been staggering. But so were those of the Russian and Chinese Navies. We don't have a complete picture. However, the nukes launched by our subs have done significant damage to both the Chinese and Russian, land based militaries. The Russians used nukes with warheads that had armored noses and delayed trigger fuses to take out the control centers of our land based missile launchers. So virtually all those missiles never got used."

Leland answered, "I'm glad to see we're fighting back. But I suppose our glorious government leaders still refuse to admit they cooperated with the destruction of our own military."

Foster shook his head and sighed. "They know that we know how they sold us out to the world leaders pushing for the grand New World Order. But they're not about to admit it."

"I got the same feeling when Jolene Howard phoned and asked me to take this command. You know, she was on my staff in the Middle East. Back then, I tried to clue her in as to what was going on politically, but she didn't want to hear it. Obsessed with rising to the top, she never listened to me. I think she knows now that she was deceived and being used. But as a good military mind, she's trying to pick up the pieces and make the best of the hand she's been dealt. She let me know she had stuck her neck out, insisting that I be given the command out here. So I think we can trust her to be honest with us and give us all the help she can."

Foster summarized, "What it comes down to is this, they're allowing us to take over the defense of the Western United States with what little forces we still control. They'll direct the worldwide resistance, which at this point the Russians and Chinese don't seem concerned about. Frankly, I think you and I will have our hands full with our assignment. My suggestion is that we concentrate on solidifying our section of the country. When we've done that, we can worry about the next phase. For now, we're in a fight for survival, which doesn't mean we don't take steps to prepare ourselves for the next phase of action that might be against some of our supposed allies. Does this make sense?"

Leland nodded. "Give me an overview of what we're faced with here in the West."

Foster pointed to a captain standing next to a computer operator. "Captain Larson will bring you up to date on what we know."

A map of North and Central America appeared on a large screen in front of them.

The captain began his presentation sober faced. "Here's what we've learned from our intelligence at this point. We don't think the Russians will be making any advances against North America. They're concentrating their efforts in Europe and the Middle East while keeping a wary eye on their partners in crime to the East. The Cubans infiltrated some trained troops into Florida, but the Americanized

Cubans are dealing with them. However, the Chinese
are definitely planning to place and keep armies on the
continent. Some of the Marxist South American countries
are lending support. The Chinese already have a sizeable
force in Mexico with support units moving up from the
Panama Canal. We think this army will attempt to take
control of the Rocky Mountain passes first, to cut the
country in half.

"Another major Chinese force has landed in Alaska to
capture the oil from the North Slope. They came in on ships
disguised as tankers. But the Alaskans have blown up
portions of the pipeline to keep them from obtaining the oil.
We think their army will come down the Alaska Highway.
They infiltrated special commando units into Vancouver,
British Columbia and the Seattle area disguised as students,
businessmen, and tourists. They're softening any resistance
that survived the nuclear attack.

"They also had a division on ships that landed at their
seaport in San Diego shortly after the nuking of the El
Mira and Camp Pendleton Marine Bases. They already
had stockpiled support equipment and supplies in their
warehouses. We believe they'll be moving up the California
coast to take over the food sources of the San Joaquin
Valley. Both of these western armies are counting on being
able to live off the land for the most part.

"The Mexicans are cooperating with them under the
assumption that they'll eventually be able to repossess the
Southwestern United States while the Chinese settle for
the Northwest, the Rocky Mountains, and as far into the
Midwest as they're able to conquer. The force coming up
through Mexico has jet aircraft and helicopters to support
their heavy armor. Fortunately for us, the super highway to
be built as part of the planned merger of the United States
with Canada and Mexico never got built. It would have
enabled them to move into the heartland of America much
quicker. We'll provide you with estimates of their men and
weapon systems." The captain paused.

"What do we have to oppose them?" asked the general.

"All the major military bases were destroyed in the

nuclear attack. Most National Guard units had been poorly manned and equipped to begin with. Many were on duty in the Middle East. Our strongest forces are those General Foster ordered out on maneuvers before the nuclear strike. However, we are dangerously limited on fuel and munitions. But the morale of the men is high.

"We also have large numbers of former military men we can count on as armed civilians to develop county and state militias. We are calling up reservists and volunteers to join the 4th Infantry Division. We're gathering data on Green Beret trained personnel who can form teams to be sent into key areas to organize local resistance. They'll be effective wherever we have to fight guerilla warfare." The captain stopped, waiting for questions.

Looking at the map, Leland rubbed his chin. "Not the best position to be in, but the thing we have going for us is that we'll be fighting on our home territory against an invading force. There's no question what we're fighting for this time. Our enemy's primary disadvantage is his long supply lines. A small force can bug the hell out of the attackers coming through Alaska with hit and run tactics. We need men who are trained to live off the wilderness areas in Canada and Alaska. They should be able to re-supply their needs by taking military stores from the enemy forces.

"The enemy troops in Southern California are going to have their hands full trying to control the local population there and coping with harassment from guerilla forces in the cities. The gang members make up a good-sized army, and they're well armed. But, the question is, with whom are they going to side? We need to see if we can find help from surviving naval forces to deal with the Chinese supply ships. As to the force coming up through Mexico, we'll suck them into the mountains while we pester their supply lines. We'll have to take out their air cover first and then deal with the land forces. We'll trade territory for time. Plus, we can't centralize our forces to tempt them to use nukes. But let's see if we can scare up a couple of nukes to use against them. They started it, so I see no reason why we can't use the same when it's to our advantage."

Foster shrugged. "The word I got from headquarters is that they're working on a gentleman's agreement for all combatants to go conventional from this point on."

Leland sighed and shook his head in disgust. "Great, now that it's to the enemy's advantage to do so!"

Foster continued, "That's not all. Since much of our military in the states has been wiped out, our wise leaders from the East have asked the United Nations to send in troops from neutral nations to assist us in keeping internal order."

Leland dropped his head and muttered a silent curse. An audible sigh followed. "Nothing like knowing who your real enemy is. But American troops have had their backs against the wall before and rallied, pushing their enemies back to achieve great victories. So however we have to do it, we will. We'll take on the first threat and neutralize them, and then deal with our backstabbing friends."

Foster smiled. "Sounds good. Let's go to lunch where I'll introduce you to your support staff we've assembled. I'm sure you'll want to get right to work."

General Leland turned and looked into Captain Larson's eyes. He sensed the pain in the young man's face. "Captain, thank you for the presentation and the work you've done here. Would you please convey my appreciation to your staff? No doubt you've all suffered losses, so I want you to know, I am deeply grateful for your devotion to duty. Be assured I'll do all in my power to see that those who perpetrated this crime against humanity will pay for it. We're American warriors with a proud history. We will rise from the ashes of this initial defeat."

The captain came to attention and snapped a sharp salute. "Thank you, sir. You can depend on us."

Leland returned the salute and then followed General Foster. It would be a long day, but already the excitement was building in the old general. A gauntlet had been thrown down, and he wasn't about to let the challenge go unanswered. He was not in a mindset to plan on anything but eventual victory. He had a personal score to settle.

•   Members of the Parr families still appeared in shock three weeks after the nuclear attack. They had been fortunate. James and Ann's time, money, and effort to prepare for this possibility had paid off. The word must have spread among the scavengers to avoid their place because they didn't have any more night visitors. Others in the valley were not so fortunate.

The people in their church fellowship had also prepared for this possibility. However, many in the community had been left on their own. Reports from leaders in the congregation revealed that the elderly and those in poor health were the first to succumb to shock, the lack of food, and damaging effects of the radiation fallout. Some chose not to endure and took their own lives or gave up, willing themselves to die.

James sent Caleb to use the Geiger counter to check for pockets of radiation. Finding low levels, James spread the word that it was safe for people to come out of their shelters. Henry and Russ helped James saddle two horses. He and Caleb visited neighbors to check on them and share iodine potassium pills for those suffering from radiation sickness. The men also took small bags of ground grain and beans to families in need.

The white bearded pastor, easily recognized by everyone, was welcomed into the homes he visited. James realized most were still in shock, even those who had accepted his warnings that this kind of disaster might occur. His prayers and challenges helped many come out of their dark moods.

The next day James's grandchildren worked with him to sweep up broken glass throughout the house. Henry and Caleb cut pieces of plywood and stretched heavy strips of plastic over window frames to replace the shattered windows. Everyone was happy to be out of the barn, doing something constructive. Physical fatigue would help alleviate the shock and despair.

Caleb called into the house, "Grandpa, do you hear that?"

James motioned to the children to be quiet. He heard the distinct sound of an approaching helicopter. Joining the men outside, they watched an Army Blackhawk helicopter come into view. It flew directly to their farmstead, circling once before setting down in a pasture. The horses there galloped to the opposite corner. The goats and chickens, obviously afraid of the noise, hurried to the barn.

Caleb retrieved his M15 rifle and moved behind a large tree. James told the grandchildren to go in the house. The men watched someone in uniform dismount and walk toward them. James met the stranger at the fence.

"Chaplain Parr, I'm Major Hank Johnson, a member of General Leland's staff. He wants to confer with you. We've got a secure feed in the chopper. But before you speak, he asked me to give you a brief overview of the situation he's faced with so you'll understand what he's asking of you. May I join you now?"

James nodded and shook the major's hand. "Hop over the fence. We'll sit on the porch. Is this something my sons can listen in on?"

"No problem. We don't want to talk about it on the air in case the wrong people are able to break our encryption."

James led the major to chairs on the porch and introduced his sons.

The major inquired, "Don't you and the general go back a long way?"

"Yes, I was a chaplain serving under his command in Vietnam. I had the privilege of introducing him to Christ, so we've been close friends since. We are neighbors here because I was able to talk him into moving to this area when he was forced into retirement."

"That's good. The general has great respect for your spiritual maturity. He, well, we are going to need all the help we can acquire from the Lord."

The major gave an overview similar to what General Leland had heard from Captain Larson at Cheyenne Mountain. When he was finished, James walked with him to the chopper where he was given a set of earphones and a mike. The radio operator made the connections.

"Mark, James here." There was a smile in his voice when he asked, "How in the world did they con you into taking this job?"

"I made them promise to stop trying to kill me and give me another star if I succeeded. Besides, old soldiers like us never back down from a good fight."

"I figured. The major filled me in on the big picture, but how are you doing?"

"Sergeant Ball is taking good care of me. We'll make it." Pausing briefly, he went on, "I need to run some things by you and ask for prayer and help recruiting special troops in the valley."

"Fire away."

"First of all, how is your family?"

"Everyone is still in shock, so I have them all working, cleaning up, and trying to experience some sense of a normal life. I've also had them on a few missions to help people in town. The children see how well off we are compared to those who made no preparations."

"Sounds good. Tell them to thank God you're not in one of the big cities. We understand things are going from bad to worse for survivors. We're placing some of our military in Denver to help restore order and move in food. A lot of the elderly are dying. But here is the main reason I'm calling. The major will give you a list of specially trained men we're looking for to fill holes in our ranks. We will accept women who can fill support roles, but they will not serve in combat units. The Russians and Israelis learned a long time ago not to try that. Since we don't have to worry about the feminists, we'll get back to the way it ought to be. Now when it comes to defending their homes, give them all the weapons they can handle.

"Those men and women who can't come with us need to be formed into local militia units under their county sheriffs. Depending on our need, where we can, we'll leave National Guard units to support the local needs. I would appreciate your being a go-between for the major and the community. Then I want you to encourage the pastors to come together and light a fire under them to have their people back us in prayer. Have you been able to find out how people are responding spiritually to the attack?"

"Somewhat. They're still in total shock. The main

problem is that all most Christians talk about is the soon return of Jesus. Just hang on, and we'll be 'raptured.' And sure enough, some of them are meeting Jesus, but not by rapture. I don't see a repentant attitude among the survivors, which amazes me. What's God got to do to get us on our knees?"

"I don't know, James. Our back is against the wall. But one thing is certain. If we lose, we'll go down fighting. You might pass the word on that, from the intelligence reports I've seen, Israel took one hell of a pounding. I don't think they'll be in any shape to rebuild their temple in this century even if they survive as a nation. Fortunately for them, the Muslims are so busy fighting each other, they haven't been able to unite and take on what's left of the Israelis' military."

"That's interesting, but I'll bet most preachers will use this same information as another sure sign that Jesus is coming soon. Of course, if He does, I'll be the first to praise Him. But I'm sure as shootin' not going to encourage my people to put on white robes and wait on a hilltop. The Bible tells me to occupy until He returns. Anything else?"

"Yes, if you or any of your people get special dreams or words from the Lord, don't hesitate to let me know. I'm looking to Jesus as the Commander and Chief of this operation. I recall your teachings that we have to win the spiritual battles before fighting in the physical realm."

James nodded to the radio and gave a thumbs up signal to the major. "Will do, brother. Keep your powder dry, and stay in touch."

"One other thing. Tell your grandson, Caleb, that he and all reservists are being activated as soon as communications are restored. If he'll come back with the major, I'll see that he gets placed in a good outfit. I've sent word to my grandson, Joshua, to come on in too. My daughter is not happy, but we've all got to be ready to pay a price."

After signing off, James conferred with Major Johnson and made plans. They flew into Montrose, landing near the sheriff's office to explain the plan to him. The sheriff agreed to pass the word around the area. Men with military experience were to come to the airport the next morning.

James used his congregation's radio network. He called men to report to the Montrose County Airport where they would hear what Major Johnston had to relate.

When all that was accomplished, they flew twenty miles north and repeated the same process with the sheriff of Delta County. Afterwards, James invited the major and his crew to spend the night with the Parr family. They gladly accepted the invitation.

As the women were cleaning up after the meal, James noticed that Elizabeth responded favorably when the young radio operator paid special attention to her and asked her to show him how to milk goats. He told her he had a ranch background and liked farm animals, but had never been around goats. James noticed that Henry was uptight and placed his arm around his son's shoulders as Elizabeth led the soldier toward the barn.

"Don't worry, Son. She's just being herself, exploring her feminine nature. That poor young man is like a lamb being led to slaughter."

Henry shrugged. "Yes, but I know what's on the young man's mind, and that's my daughter. That makes a lot of difference from my perspective."

"Oh, I understand. But give puppy love a chance. It'll help take her mind off the friends she's lost."

"Okay, but I'm still going to keep an eye on things."

•   James traveled the next week throughout the valley with Major Johnson, recruiting men for duty with the 4th Infantry Division. They suggested how the county sheriffs could organize militias to maintain order and begin preparing to defend the valley from outside aggressors. No longer was it just a matter of physical survival. They had to prepare to survive as a free people. Daily a foreign army moved toward them. The war would be fought on American soil, and they would soon be near it or on the front line.

The Parr family rose early to prepare a final breakfast for Major Johnson and his crew. Not just new friends would be leaving. Caleb had packed his old army uniforms and would depart with the crew, along with his friend, Joshua. James led the group in prayer before the men climbed aboard the chopper. Everyone had tear-filled eyes when the machine rose and flew toward the east.

In the coming weeks, many homes in the valley would have tearful farewells as sons, daughters, brothers and sisters, and husbands and uncles left to become part of the 4th Infantry Division now disbursed in small units in Southwestern Colorado and parts of New Mexico. They prepared to meet the Chinese/Mexican Army that made its way toward the Rio Grande. For the first time in over a century, a foreign army would place soldiers on American soil. Only this time, America was in no condition to adequately defend herself.

• Sam Kirkland and his guests made a big hit in the community. Like their neighbors, they had been part of the huge group of people who descended on the Super Wal-Mart and other food and hardware stores in the area. Their practical, handout instructions telling how to seal homes from radiation fallout and make good use of water and food supplies gained them the appreciation of their neighbors. Sam even included suggestions on the value of fasting and how to get through the first few days of the body's adjustment to the absence of food.

Once the Muslims were sealed in their own two-story home, they retreated to the basement to remove themselves as far as possible from radiation dust. This fit well with their plans. Sam had been collecting lab equipment needed for the production of biological cultures. He brought home the used equipment that had been discarded by the company he worked for. He also paid cash for new items so that nothing could be traced to him. One of his new co-workers, Calieb Ashwah, had brought the starter cultures hidden in a thermos bottle. Together they set up the equipment, tested it to make sure the deadly toxins could be isolated, and then began to produce a variety of biological agents, which they would some day release onto the survivors of the nuclear holocaust.

As they adjusted to the new environment, they realized this could prove to be a blessing in disguise. They would not have to worry about neighbors or Homeland Security agents barging in on them. Everyone concentrated on surviving. They would have to bide their time, but the longer they had, the more biological agents they could produce. The larger the cache, the greater the death toll would be when their time came. Truly Allah was watching out for their best interests. Thoughts of revenge for real or imagined offenses would carry them through the difficult times ahead.

Chapter Four

Ambush in the Rockies

In the weeks following D-Day, the Chinese/Mexican Army moved up Mexican Highway 45 and crossed the border at El Paso, Texas. Their goal was to progress along the ridge of the Rocky Mountains to gain control of the East/West Interstate Highways 40, 70, and 80. If successful, this would divide the West from the rest of the United States.

The pass east of Albuquerque would make a logical place to cut Highway 40. Eisenhower Tunnel at the top of the Rocky Mountains could be blown in order to halt traffic on 70, and the pass west of Laramie, Wyoming, would then be easily defended. If these areas were secured, their forces could move north to block Interstate 90 in Montana.

The Americans offered little resistance at El Paso. Chinese MIG jet fighters tangled with jets of the Texas Air National Guard that produced mixed results for both sides. Two full squadrons of Chinese jet fighters along with Mexican aircraft took charge of the El Paso airport. Anti-aircraft missile units were set up around it.

Their tanks and heavy artillery were hauled north into New Mexico on flatbed trucks. The wheeled personnel carriers ran on their own power. They interspersed mobile anti-aircraft vehicles along the column to protect against air attacks. Attack helicopters ranged out several miles on each side of the head of the column looking for opposing forces. Most civilians in small towns or along the Interstate fled with what they had been able to load into cars or pickups. When the army camped for the night, they set up ground-to-air missile defenses. During the day, this meant that their column of vehicles stretched out over thirty miles except when they moved up an Interstate and used both lanes.

General Leland kept the armor of Fort Carson in

Colorado. He sent a small force down I-25 to form a
defensive position north of Santa Fe. When Caleb reported
to Leland, he carried a report from James of a vision he
had while in prayer. He saw a major Chinese army coming
into Durango, Colorado, destroying much of the town as
people fled north. Then a powerful light descended over the
mountains. He heard a commanding voice proclaim, "This
far and no further."

Leland was encouraged. He planned to coax the invaders
into the mountains where he could use his sparse forces
to the best advantage. Setting up extra radio traffic north
of Santa Fe would make it appear that he was preparing
to meet the invading army there. He wanted to turn them
toward the western part of Colorado. His intelligence
sources indicated they would not risk a head on fight if
possible. Being at the end of a long supply line, they had to
conserve their supplies. Modern warfare tended to consume
huge amounts of ammunition quickly.

The Chinese Army took the bait and turned north on
Highway 44. They left a small force to fight off any counter
attack by Leland's forces north of Santa Fe. The Mexican
Army was moving west into Arizona along Interstate 10.
The Americans only had enough forces to harass them when
they moved to link up with the Chinese forces in Southern
California.

As a result, Leland ordered limited night attacks on the
Chinese column by helicopter gun ships. The jet fighters
he was able to put together were ordered to take on the
air cover and whittle it down. He also located two cruise
missiles loaded with small explosive devices that would be
scattered from the missile as it flew over the El Paso airport.
The explosives were powerful enough to destroy any nearby
aircraft. This was followed with a ground level attack by
jet fighter bombers. The combined attack destroyed most
of the invading planes and helicopters along with several
transports that were unloading critically needed cargo flown
in from China. By the time the Chinese army reached the
Colorado border, it would only have a few helicopters for its
air support.

• Caleb Parr had joined the Army Reserves when he turned eighteen. Home schooled, he wanted experience out in the world before going to college. He trained as a long-range scout. This required going stealth in occupied territory and gathering information that required on-sight eyes and ears to interpret what was going on. The army depended on satellites and a sophisticated array of small drone aircraft to give the big picture of the battlefield and potential of the enemy forces. But the enemy learned to camouflage and deceive. Thus, it was important to send in small teams of specially trained men to sniff out what high tech cameras could not discern.

General Leland had 20-year-old Caleb assigned to a commander known for his skills in recon and also training young men. The general knew that Caleb had the potential of being a leader. He had observed Caleb's character from early childhood and watched as his grandfather tutored him in leadership skills. Not only had the young man excelled in sports and big game hunting, he received top marks in his army training before returning to acquire his college education. Six-foot-two, he kept his body in lean condition and developed an outgoing personality that gave him a good rapport with members of both sexes. All these qualities would serve Caleb well in service to his country.

When a Special Forces crew used a high-flying, small drone to monitor the enemy's column, it spotted a motor home with extra guard units around it. They assumed the Chinese general was using it as their mobile command center. The Chinese column had camped half way between Albuquerque and Durango. Their army had to wait while a bridge was repaired. An American team had blown it the day before. Caleb's squad was dispatched as a recon unit to check out the motor home. They were dropped off on a butte overlooking the camp.

The unit on top of the butte erected a canvas tent that, from the air, looked just like a large rock. From it, they used powerful night scopes to monitor the activities in the camp. It became obvious that the motor home was indeed their command center. Guards were positioned all around the vehicle. Next to it was a van with satellite dishes and a large antenna field.

The radio operator used a small satellite dish to make contact with General Foster's headquarters. Caleb was assigned the task of using a laser to direct a beam on the Chinese general's motor home. A lone F117 Stealth bomber flew over that night and dropped a laser-guided bomb. The team was alerted and turned off their night scopes so the flash would not blind them. The bomb hit seconds later causing a reverberating roar that bounced off the canyon walls. When the team turned their night scopes back on, they observed the ruined vehicles. Intercepted radio transmissions later confirmed that the Chinese general and his command staff had been killed.

The army didn't move for several days until a replacement command staff arrived from China. No sooner had the army moved out than Bradley Fighting Vehicles attacked the back of the column that was not as heavily guarded, destroying fuel, ammo, and supply trucks. They retreated into the desert canyons before the Chinese could rally a strong counterattack.

Individual snipers attacked the column, using long-range, 50-caliber sniping rifles. A well-placed shot could disable a key vehicle or kill a high-ranking officer. When Russian made Hind helicopters moved against the suspected snipers, Stinger missiles rose to take out the Hinds. Their air cover was slowly worn down. The resistance eased up as the Chinese army moved into Durango, Colorado, a deserted, ghost town. The troops were hard to control, looting stores and homes. There was little food, so the army moved up the Million Dollar Highway, headed for the fertile Grand Valley on the other side of the San Juan Mountains. It seemed they were in easy reach of their goals to take and control the mountain passes of the two major freeways, Interstates 70 and 80, and rail lines that connected the East to the Western part of the U.S. The American forces had other plans.

D-Day Minus Six Weeks and Three Days

• James and his sons, Henry and Russell, were part of two hundred men traveling from Grand Junction to the Montrose area to join units from Fort Carson, which General Leland marshaled north of the mountain town, Silverton. The Parr men were moved with the others in a large, double deck trailer normally used to transport cattle. They sat on sleeping bags or boxes of supplies and protected their rifles during the jostling whenever the trucks maneuvered sharp turns. Some of the men tried to sleep. Others kept up nervous chatter with their friends.

Russ tapped his father's arm. "Dad, remember Burt Wilson, the contact I had in the Chicago area?"

"Yes, what about him?"

"He sent his last report before we left. He's out of fuel for his generator. The worst of it is that they are also out of food, and he and his wife are both sick from radiation. There's cannibalism in his neighborhood. Many of the elderly have already died. The authorities gave up trying to bury them all, so they're stacking the dead in an abandoned house. The next time it rains, they're going to set it on fire to dispose of the bodies."

James shook his head.

Russ went on, "Some of the people managed to plant gardens, but most are so weak they can't keep the weeds down or prevent others from coming in and stealing anything edible. The problem is, most people don't know what's ready to eat until they pull up the plants. So it's an enormous mess. I'm sure glad we got out of the city. It must be a living hell."

James used his free arm to hold Russ against the side of the truck as it took a sharp turn. "Yes, those things are happening all over the nation. General Leland told me that city people are streaming into the country looking for food. At first, the farmers tried to share and help until they got overrun. It turned into open warfare in places. In Eastern states, troops are being used to keep people in the cities so farmers have a chance to care for their crops and animals.

That way they'll have produce and meat to ship into the cities. But now there's so little fuel that farmers can't care for the crops or transport their produce to the cities. Most of it is rotting in the fields. It's one gigantic, ongoing tragedy. We're fortunate here in the valley that we have so many horses we can put to work and use for transportation."

"And some of you had the foresight to store large tanks of fuel," Russ added.

Men seated nearby added bits of news they had picked up from relatives or friends in other parts of the nation. These facts, along with the reason they were being transported to another area, gave them a growing sense of anxiety by the time they arrived at their destination.

General Leland had requested that James stay at the mountain cabin, the headquarters for their forces, which had been set up for the ambush. The structure, one of several used during the summer by out-of-state vacationers, was located at a wide spot in the road called Chattanooga. Such summer places were located north of another small town, Silverton, off Highway 550 in the San Juan Mountains north of Durango. The ambush would be their main effort to destroy the advancing Chinese army.

James accompanied the general as he discretely toured their forces with General Foster. Three weeks before, eighteen M1A Abram tanks and two-dozen Bradley Fighting Vehicles had been dug into positions camouflaged with webbing and tree branches. Several had walls and roofs of old cabins to disguise them. Their positions would give them direct firing lanes on all segments of the twelve miles of highway winding up the mountainside. Soldiers and civilians used rakes and shovels to cover the tracks made by the tanks while getting into position. They also dug firing pits for the infantry and civilian militia to provide rifle and machine gun fire on trucks and enemy personnel. These were also carefully camouflaged.

Most of the helicopters in the Chinese forces had been destroyed. However, it was likely that an air recon would be sent by them to check for any kind of resisting force. Days before, the Americans flew a camera equipped, reconnaissance aircraft over the area to make sure their positions were well hidden. The soldiers were housed in homes and businesses in Silverton while they worked on the ambush project. During the final nights, reinforcements were trucked into the area and quartered in heavy stands of timber.

To make it appear that there was only minor resistance, two checkpoints were set up on highway passes leading to the area. The people manning them prepared to fire a few shots and retreat at the first sign of the invading force. Silverton had been evacuated, but the surrounding hills had become an array of carefully concealed weapons pointed at the deserted valley below. General Leland anticipated that the Chinese would set up their mobile artillery to provide support for the armored columns moving up to the next pass.

After returning from the inspection, James ate with the two generals and key members of their staff. Later, Henry and Russell joined their father outside the cabin as the sun settled over the mountains. The two younger men were part of an infantry force dug in a quarter of a mile from headquarters near the horseshoe turn where the highway grade steepened before reaching Red Mountain Pass. James was scheduled to join them before the fighting began. But now they were faced with what soldiers throughout the centuries hated, the boring but terrifying lull before the battle.

They exchanged small talk about their positions. Henry indicated he had serious questions to discuss. "I still don't understand how the Russians were able to mount an attack when they have been a basket case economically. Everything I read said corruption dominated the nation. Their infrastructure had collapsed, much of their military was in a shambles, and most people lived in poverty. Criminal elements ran the country."

James agreed, "Yes, that's true. It may have been to make us lower our guard, or it was the leaders' way of putting their emphasis on the ultimate goal. No one really knows what happened in Russia."

"What bothers me," Russ added, "is why leaders commit such evil to become big shots. God knows men like that have more money than they can spend and all the luxuries possible. Why do they want power over others when it comes at such great cost in lives and destruction of property?"

James said, "Americans have had centuries of strong Christian influence which affected even the secular areas of our society. We were conditioned to be good people. We all knew that politicians and big businesses pulled shady deals, from local to national levels. Yet overall, we expected people to do what was right.

"We paid taxes to set up a welfare system because we wanted to help those less fortunate. People believed every child should be educated and have a decent place to live and good food. It was commonly accepted that anyone who worked hard could become rich. To make this possible, we needed roads, rural electricity, clean water in homes, and 'a chicken in every pot.' This all seemed the norm.

"But the reality is that, down through the centuries and in most areas of the world today, these attitudes are rare. Look at third world nations. Whoever acquires power to lead such a country uses his authority to accumulate wealth and makes off with literally millions of dollars. Using the people to his own advantage, such a leader gets by with atrocities unknown to the world perhaps for years because the nation accepts it. In the meantime, dictators allow their people to live in total poverty, and then they abscond when found out. Such leaders do only what is necessary to stay in power. Without the influence of Christ and the Bible, men don't have the ability to care about others."

Henry asked, "Is that what happened in Russia and China?"

"In Russia more than China. The Chinese leaders realized they would get more out of their people if they allowed enough freedom for them to prosper. The massive population was able to improve their living standards through a form of free enterprise. Their leaders maintained control while providing limited freedom. As they raised their standard of living, it brought the foreign exchange, making it possible to build their military to its extraordinary strength.

"In both cases, the people have been propagandized. They believe this war is justified. Our corrupt leaders helped them by turning America into a worldwide empire. In the process, virtually everyone in the world has reason to hate us due to the way we've thrown our weight around. So the Russians, the Chinese, and especially the Muslims believe we're getting what we deserve. In some ways, they're right. We turned away from God and high moral standards, especially many of those who profess to be Christians. As a result, God has allowed judgment to fall on us."

Russ countered, "I see your point, Dad, but it's a bit severe. Can our nation ever recover? How does it honor God around the world when the most noted Christian nation of modern times is reduced to ashes and chaos?"

Henry also voiced what was troubling him. "I don't understand either. Most of the nation is in shambles. Electricity hasn't been restored, commerce is dead, and people are starving and dying from radiation sickness. The war around the world is still going against us. We've heard about some 'whiz bang' weapons that came out of Area 51 in Nevada, but we don't have any of them here. We're outnumbered, outgunned, and fighting for our lives. I want to know why."

James answered, "The bottom line is we're paying the penalty for forgetting God. America was established as a Christian nation, ruled essentially by God's laws. But we turned from those laws. We threw them out of the schools, removed them from our courthouses, and substituted a million manmade rules and regulations.

"Therefore, just like God's chosen people of Israel in the Old Testament, God warned us through many prophets. But Americans refused to listen and turn from their sins. We murdered tens of millions of babies in their mothers' wombs. God's ancient laws included 'an eye for an eye, a tooth for a tooth.' In other words, like for like. Now tens of millions of Americans have died or will die equally horrible deaths. It's simply the justice of a righteous, holy God."

Henry leaned forward and with a raised voice countered, "But, Dad, we didn't abort babies or abuse our neighbors! Granted, Russ and I haven't been the most fervent Christians. But when you compare our nation to the rest of the world, America has been a great place to live and work. Like you said, as a nation, we helped a lot of people all around the world. Not only did we send missionaries who built schools and hospitals, we also sent billions of dollars worth of aid. Whenever there was a disaster, Americans sent the most help. That ought to count for something."

"I'm sure it did figure in God's justice, but we, the members of the body of Christ, knew all the time that gross corruption was going on. Yet we didn't use every effort to stop it. How many times did you picket an abortion clinic or get in the face of your representative in Congress? What did you do to influence the voters in your precinct?"

Henry sighed. "Yeah, not much, but would that have made any difference? You and the general stuck your necks out, got beat up by the media, and were made to look like fools over and over. Did it change anything?"

"No, it obviously didn't turn the tide, but I'm confident we were obedient to God. In spite of what we did or didn't do, we all share the guilt. Thus, we all have to share the punishment. It's only by His grace that we're not consumed by His wrath."

Henry shrugged. "If we can't stop this invading army, we may all be consumed, as you put it. What will they do to our families if we don't stop them here?"

James didn't hesitate. "Rape the women, let the old people and the youngest die, and enslave the rest. It's happened many times throughout history. We can't assume it won't happen to us."

He saw his sons wince. "I know the thought hurts, but we've got to face facts. The Chinese want our land to grow food for their people, so they're risking it all. The Mexicans believe we stole this land from their ancestors. They plan to reclaim it. But, we're not defeated yet. We need to be in prayer, pleading with God for His mighty help even though we don't deserve it. That's the essence of grace."

Henry admitted, "I wish I had your optimism. I just hope our tanks have enough shells to take out all their tanks, armored weapons, and personnel carriers. I don't feel confident facing all that fire power with nothing but my rifle."

Russ reasoned, "Our generals know what they're doing. Caleb got a couple of messages to us. He said they've been wearing the Chinese forces down little by little while sucking them into a trap. This is going to be their Waterloo. In some ways, I feel sorry for them. By this time tomorrow, I suspect most of them will be dead. Don't you think so, Dad?"

James's eyes filled with tears. Memories flooded his mind of a time when the boys had been small. The family sat around a campfire in the mountains. He was the center and star in their world. They trusted him. Now they were grown men, and he desperately wanted to be able to protect them. But he knew it was out of his hands. The realization shook him to the core of his being. He forced himself to put a positive twist on Russ's question.

"Yes. The general said we've tapped into their radio network, and they've left Durango. Plus, he's got scouts like Caleb's outfit shadowing their every move. So we know what they have and where they are all the time. True, they still have many more tanks and men than we do. That's why the general has avoided direct contact with them by our main force. He's picked this spot as the best place to hit them. If God wills, we'll wipe out their main force tomorrow. Then we can counterattack and push the rest out of the country.

"Of course, if they spot us or smell the trap, we might have to fall back. That would make us all vulnerable. In any case, tomorrow is going to be a big day. Get some rest now. I'll try to have something hot for your breakfast. I'm going to accept the general's hospitality and sleep in one of the bunk beds. I hope my roommates don't snore.

"One added thought, don't be surprised if you are almost paralyzed with fear right before or when the shooting starts. You won't be the only one. It's a natural reaction to the terror of the unknown and the threat to our lives. Pray and quote Scripture. That will help. If things don't work out as

planned, there's no shame in retreating to fight another day.
Work your way back north over the high passes, and join the
families that will flee to the mountains if the enemy's army
makes it into our home valley. If one of us is badly wounded,
don't let that stop you from leaving. Understood?"

His sons nodded. The darkness hid their tears. As they
hugged their father, he sensed their anxiety.

James blessed them before they moved out to find their
sleeping bags. "The Lord bless you and keep you; the Lord
make His face shine upon you, and be gracious to you; the
Lord lift up His countenance upon you and give you peace."

•   Awaking from a nightmare, Airman Randy Page threw
back his blanket and sat bolt upright on the edge of his cot.
Slowly his mind returned to reality. The days confined in
Cheyenne Mountain's tomb had merged into weeks. What
had at first been an exciting, though terrifying adventure
now alternated between a grinding nightmare and boring
routine.

Stumbling to the bathroom, he realized he had to talk
to someone about his inner turmoil before he cracked, just
as a couple of the other crew had. After showering, he put
on his uniform and headed for the kitchen where he got a
mug of coffee. Then he walked down the corridor toward the
operations center.

Upon entering operations, he saw Captain Larson at his
desk. "You're kinda early for your duty, aren't you?"

Page stopped in front of the captain, avoiding his eyes.
"Sir, I was wondering, if we could have a talk." He made eye
contact and continued, "Like, man to man. You know what I
mean?"

The captain motioned for him to take a seat. "Sure,
what's on your mind?"

Page sat down, placed his coffee mug the desk, and
looked around to see if any of the men at the consoles were
listening. Since they were not paying any attention, he
looked at the captain and leaned forward.

"Well, sir, I don't know how to express this, but I've
had trouble sleeping. Except when I'm on duty, then it's so

boring it's hard to stay awake. But when I'm off duty, well . . ."

Page struggled for words, so the captain asked, "Are you sure I'm the one you should be talking to? Have you talked to the chaplain?"

"Yes, sir, I have, but he's older. He seems so solid in his faith. You're more my age. We went through those first hours together. I know you've lost your family, and it hurt like hell. Yet you've stuck to your job. I respect that, sir."

"Thanks." The captain hesitated due to the intense sorrow that surfaced by Page's words. "It's been the hardest thing I've ever had to do in my life. I'm not ashamed to admit I've prayed more since then than I did all the rest of my life. But it's a day-to-day struggle." He refocused on the face of the younger airman. "You haven't heard any word about your family, have you?"

Page bit his lip and shook his head, fighting tears. "Nothing. But I'm hearing that part of Indiana is where there's been lots of rioting, looting, and deaths from radiation sickness. My folks were like most people, just living from paycheck to paycheck. Mom wasn't in good health. My younger sister, well, she's a real beauty. I wish I was there to protect her."

Larson nodded. "You feel helpless, right?"

"That's it, sir. I feel so helpless. Not just for my family, but everything. Our job was to warn the men and women in the armed services around the world of an impending attack. We had all the sophisticated satellites, listening devices, and instant communication with the whole world, but when it came crunch time, we didn't make an iota of difference. Millions died. All we could do was confirm what happened. Our military got massacred, including the other crews that worked this station. We could do nothing."

He shook his head. "Now the Chinese and Mexicans are closing in on us. You've seen the size of their armies. They've got zillions of tanks. Most of ours are burned hulks that never made it out of Fort Carson. What'll we do if they show up here? What good is the information we're giving General Foster's troops if they don't have the tanks to stop the Chinks?"

Captain Larson made no comment.

Page lifted his hands in a gesture of helplessness and mumbled, "What are we going to do?"

Larsen remained silent. He wondered if all the men had such doubts. Had their personal losses caused them to feel such hopelessness, too?

Finally he asserted, "We're not totally powerless. We're making a contribution to our forces. We are providing vital intelligence to the units out West and our few assets still at sea. If you think we have it bad, what about the guys on the attack subs? They are out numbered and alone with virtually no hope of being re-supplied."

Page snapped, "Yes, but at least they have a way to fight back. But what can we do? We can't even go off the mountain because the radiation is so high. God, I don't know if it's day or night, not that it makes any difference." Looking beaten, he put his questions before the captain. "Can we really make a contribution? Is there any hope?"

Larsen tried to reassure him. "My faith has taught me that, as long as there's life, there's hope. There's no question, the military and all America has its back against the wall. But times like these test our fiber as men. I told General Leland we'd do our part. Our shift is doing the work of four, so what you're experiencing is burnout."

He leaned toward the younger airman who shifted in his seat. "Remember what you said to me that first night when we realized what was coming down on us?"

Page shook his head.

"You said, 'Let's repay the bastards with all we've got.' Your support meant a lot to me because I realized my wife and daughters would die. Talk about feeling helpless! Fear gripped my total being as it never had before. Had it not been for the demands of the moment, I would have been immobilized. Later, I determined not to give in to the bitterness of my loss. I'm a warrior. I took an oath before God and man to defend my country, and with God's help, I'm going to do that until my last breath. You're part of our team. We need you. Your country needs you.

"Ours is not an exciting, easily identified part of the battle. But the right bit of intelligence at a critical moment can do more to win a major battle than a boatload of weapons. The big boys back East are relying on some new, sophisticated weapons system so secret they won't even tell us anything. I hope it works. But as far as I know, here in the West, we're relying on riflemen, tankers, and a few airmen who still have choppers or fighters to fly and the civilian militia. They need us for communications and intelligence. We can't let them down."

Page sat taller in his chair. "No, we can't, sir. Thank you. I think I'll go work out and get a bite to eat before it's my time to report for duty."

"Sounds good. Nothing like physical exercise to clear some cobwebs."

Page stood to attention and saluted the captain. Larson returned the salute. Page grabbed his coffee mug and headed for the door where he paused and looked back at the array of computers and large screens. Then he walked out with a spring to his walk.

• Heavy tanks, supported by armored personnel carriers, led the Chinese army out of Durango. Only token resistance was met as they crossed the first pass and dropped down into Silverton. To the invaders, it appeared to be just another deserted mountain town. The main force began moving up the next section of the winding mountain road while the mobile artillery set up a support firebase in the valley outside Silverton. Chinese air recon spotted light fortified defenses being built at Red Mountain Pass. The artillery would pound it if verified that it was a major point of resistance.

The long stretch of highway wound up the side of the next range of mountains from Silverton. A lightly armed recon unit had gone ahead and ran into light resistance that fled after firing on the unit. The recon team proceeded down the other side of the pass. Trucks loaded with infantry were interspersed with heavy tanks and armored personnel carriers, which ground their way up the horseshoe. All the while, hundreds of eyes peered through sighting scopes or tree branches. The roar of motors and clanking of tank treads heightened tensions for those waiting to spring the ambush. Diesel smoke drifted through the clear mountain air. Officers and sergeants watched their men and whispered encouragement as they admonished them to keep their fingers off triggers.

Just as the lead tanks approached the top of the pass, an explosion brought large boulders rolling onto the highway. A single sniper fired at the column. The lead Chinese units returned fire, spraying the area from which the shot originated with machine gun fire. No more return fire occurred. The commander in the lead tank called for a bulldozer.

While the large dozer was transported on a trailer and unloaded, convoy vehicles slowly compacted on the highway. Stopping, many of their men dismounted to relieve themselves along the road. Just as the bulldozer was about to clear the obstruction, rifle fire and a lone machine gun opened up on the column, taking down several of the men caught outside their vehicles.

The Chinese commander didn't know that the sniper fire had taken down most of his battalion level commanders. The men in the column scrambled to the protection of their tanks and armored vehicles. Spotters tried to get a fix on the location of the guns bearing down on them so they could call in artillery support. Suddenly all hell broke loose.

From carefully hidden positions on opposite hillsides, Abram tanks opened fire on the stalled Chinese tanks and methodically began to destroy them. The Bradley Fighting Vehicles at the same time used their 30mm rapid firing cannons to take out the personnel carriers. Every three to five seconds, eighteen Chinese tanks became scrap metal and deathtraps for their crews.

A few of the Chinese tanks returned fire before being consumed, but their targets, the exposed turrets of the Abrams, were small and heavily armored. Most of the rounds were absorbed by the rock in front of American tanks or bounced harmlessly off the sloped armor.

For two or three miles on the road leading from
Silverton, the Chinese tanks were able to leave the
deathtrap highway at various places and roar through brush
toward their ambushers. They took out two of the Bradleys
before being knocked out by methodical fire from American
armor and infantry launched anti-tank rockets.

As soon as the battle began along the forward highways,
the ambush was also engaged against the artillery and
supply units set up in the valley around Silverton. From
the surrounding hills came a rain of tank, mortar, machine
gun, and sniper fire. Within minutes, the areas around
the small town had become a blazing infernal of death and
destruction. Exploding ammunition and fuel sent thick
columns of black smoke into the air.

The troop carrying trucks in the middle of the column
were blown up by cannon fire. They were hit with 30mm
rounds from the concealed Bradleys or sprayed with
machine gun fire of 50-caliber or small caliber fire from
closer positions. Every portion of the highway was covered
from the exposed side.

For miles along the hills, civilians had been placed with
the military in concealed bunkers and foxholes. They were
mostly hunters who had a variety of heavy caliber rifles
previously used to shoot large game animals at ranges
up to four and five hundred yards. Their rifles were used
with deadly accuracy to take down individual soldiers who
escaped explosions or machine gun fire.

A half dozen Chinese attack helicopters that tried to
come to the rescue were quickly blown from the sky by
Stinger missiles or 30mm fire from the Bradleys. Within
fifteen minutes, most of the Chinese army had been put
out of action. For another ten minutes, individual rounds
were fired to pick off the isolated tank or vehicle that had
somehow escaped.

For twelve miles, the mountain highway was a
continuous line of fires. The mountains reverberated with
the explosions of munitions and the rattle of small caliber
munitions burning off in the destroyed vehicles. Thick black
smoke drifted east. All along the road, fires began to spread

into surrounding timber or brush. It was still wet enough
that, in most cases, the fires didn't burn far.

Some soldiers escaped the infernal and were hunted on
both sides of the highway by troops and civilian militia. A
few prisoners would be taken.

•   James remained in the vicinity of his sons during the
battle. A series of foxholes concealed them on top of a ridge
that looked out over a valley toward a bend in the highway,
two to three hundred yards from their position. The men
held their fire until the tanks opened up. James crawled
along the line to encourage his soldiers and make sure
they stayed down, resisting the urge to fire before ordered.
He understood the tension the young men felt. Cold sweat
covered his brow when he recalled his baptism of fire in
Vietnam.

What surprised James was the fear of dying that hit
him in the pit of his stomach. Before going to sleep the night
before, he had logically reasoned away this fear because he
had lived a full life. His faith was solid. If he caught a bullet,
he would immediately be in the presence of God. His prayers
had been for his sons and the other men he knew. But as
enemy vehicles roared by, his heart began to race, and he
breathed with quick gulps. He needed his own reassuring
words to the other men as much as they did.

He knew his sons wanted to be near him but denied the
urge for a practical reason. If they received return fire, he
didn't want one well-placed artillery shell to take out the
entire family.

When the firing began, a truckload of Chinese troops
disembarked and made an attempt to hide behind their
truck. Evidently an officer commanded the survivors to
attack down the bush-covered slope toward the trenches.
These soldiers were easy targets for hunting rifles with
scopes. James dropped two of the men with his rifle. His first
rounds took out machine gunners on two of the trucks before
they could adjust their fire against the trenches. In minutes,
there were no more targets. Some men in the trenches
continued firing into the burning wreckage.

James shouted, "Cease fire!" His hands shook. Breathing deeply, he made an attempt to calm his nerves. The ambush had been successful, and so the men exchanged congratulations.

Only one man had been injured in the trenches. He caught a bullet in his arm that shattered the bone. A first aid team quickly took him to the field hospital.

James crawled from his trench and ran to Henry who sat staring at the wreckage. Henry didn't look at his father or speak. Shock registered on the younger man's face. James rubbed his son's back.

Henry uttered in remorse, "I understand now what you told us about Vietnam. I was so scared I almost wet my pants. It was exciting seeing what the tanks were doing. Just like the movies, except for the noise. My god, I thought my eardrums would burst! They're still ringing. I fired several shots into the truck right in front of us, but it wasn't until they came out and charged down the hill that I had to pick out an individual soldier in my scope. I only shot one of them. I couldn't bring myself to do it again." He dropped his head and glanced around to see if anyone else was listening.

James hugged him. "It's okay. I pray you'll never have to do that again. But remember, if we hadn't killed them, they would have gone over the mountains and probably raped our wives and your daughter. This is the hell of war. Killing is something we can't avoid.

"Why don't you stay here?" James suggested. "Let the regular troops take care of the wounded and see if there are any prisoners to round up. Use your scope to cover them, okay? I'm going to check on Russ."

Henry nodded. James moved down the ridge, noting that most of the men had begun walking across the narrow valley between them and the highway. He spotted Russ in the trench looking through his riflescope to cover the men walking toward the highway.

"Are you okay, Son?"

Russ glanced up. "A little shaky, but I'm all right. I'm glad it's over. Is Henry okay?"

"Yes, but a little shook."

A shot rang out in front of them. They both ducked and scanned their front.

Someone yelled, "Just finishing off a gook."

James saw the pain on Russ's face as he heard the word gook. "I know what you're thinking. He was a man. But to last as a soldier, that is, as a killing machine, you have to depersonalize the enemy. They become Nazis, gooks, chinks, or just targets. Most of us can't see ourselves killing other humans."

Russ nodded.

James kneeled and positioned his weapon to be ready to cover the men in front. Neither of them said anything as they watched the soldiers check enemy bodies and search wreckage on the road. When there was no more danger, James motioned to Russ to sit with him in the trench.

He asked, "You okay?"

"Yes, but it's strange. In a short time, I've had a whole range of emotions. Gut wrenching fear, dread, excitement, and even pleasure. But wow! We beat them, and we lived through it." He took a deep breath. "And now I feel sick." Russ swallowed to keep from vomiting.

James put his arm around his son's shoulders. "Welcome to reality."

Machine gun and rifle fire echoed in the valley, followed by a loud explosion, and then only the crackling of fire in the vehicles. They didn't speak for a time. The trembling in Russ's body subsided.

James rose to his feet. "I'm going to check in with General Leland. Why don't you get Henry and some of the boys from the valley and start collecting the Chinese weapons and ammunition? We need to take as much as we can back for the militias. I suspect this won't be the last battle we'll have to fight."

Observing his son, he suggested, "You'll probably lose your breakfast, but you'd better get used to seeing and smelling dead bodies and what war does to them."

"Okay, Dad."

James headed for the command bunker.

· General Leland had watched live video feeds of the battle in a hidden bunker where he also received reports from commanders down the line. It soon became evident that the Chinese army had been destroyed. He looked over the shoulder of a soldier receiving live video on a laptop from a drone high above the ambush site. James waited while the general ordered troops to go after a contingent of Chinese soldiers retreating up a small valley. An officer got on the radio and gave instructions. Leland turned, motioning to James to take a seat. The general sank wearily into his chair behind a small desk and breathed a sigh of relief. He smiled at James.

"The boys did a good job. It was a massacre. They walked right into our trap. Their commander got used to us sniping at him with no major follow up. It's amazing how quickly a habit can develop." Noticing James's rapt attention, he asked, "Are your sons okay?"

"Yes, it was a good baptism of fire. Both are sobered. Only one man was wounded in our section."

The general stretched. "We only took a few casualties, thank God. We may take a few more mopping up the survivors. With so many of our soldiers having lost their families on D-Day, I doubt if they'll be in a mood to take many prisoners. I don't blame them." He was silent.

The computer operator held up his laptop so he could see a shot of the wrecked artillery pieces in the Silverton valley. Leland gave the soldier a thumbs up and returned his attention to James.

"There's real satisfaction from a well laid plan that defeats the enemy with virtually no loss of our own troops and equipment. But what a dreadful waste of life! Yeah, they were the enemy, but they only served the real enemy. Given other circumstances, the men killed might have been fellow workers and companions in the legitimate pursuits of life. Dang, what a waste!"

James asked, "What now?"

"The army units will move against the elements left as a reserve in Durango, Santa Fe, and eventually El Paso. If they put up much resistance, we'll surround them and cut them off from any re-supply so they won't be able to hold out long. I've got to conserve our men and supplies to take on the larger forces in Arizona and California. The Green Beret we sent up the Alaska Highway is drawing blood every few miles. I don't think the Chinese will have much of an army left by the time they reach our border. We'll send most civilians home with you. I want you to work with the sheriffs and continue training the home militias."

"Where are you going to set up your headquarters?"

"I may stay on the Western Slope and let Foster lead the 4th while I organize to take back the Western states. My main job will be rustling up supplies for our forces. We'll see each other now and then."

D-Day Minus Eight Weeks

•   Just when things looked hopeless, the power came on. The initial nuclear attack had downed major power lines. Another problem occurred with the burned relay stations that shorted out the system. The power at first remained on for minutes at a time, then hours. Several days passed, however, before utility companies were able to keep the power on full time. A nuclear generating plant south of Rockford had been put back on line. It was connected with others in Northern Illinois and Wisconsin and brought electricity to Burt Wilson's neighborhood.

Radio and television stations that had their staffs began functioning. As a result, people throughout the country learned they were not the only ones suffering. Though bleak, the news at least let people know they weren't alone. Many realized that the silence had only increased their suffering. It was a new experience for the young people.

With power, fuel was available for the trucks that had not stopped functioning due to EMP. Bulk grain and meat distribution were under the protection of National Guard troops and police. If people threatened to riot, troops opened fire. Many died. Word got around that, starving or not, food distribution would be orderly.

A serious danger surfaced when people received their food allotments. While returning home, those without threatened to steal their food or shoot them. They learned to travel in armed groups to solve much of the problem.

Ralph Leonard, working with Burt, had built respect in their neighborhood when they helped others deal with radiation fallout. They had given out information about sealing houses. The elderly, those who were sick, or individuals living in one-story homes that provided little shelter from radiation exposure were the first to have died. A few committed suicide. Burt's wife, Gloria, was one who succumbed to a stress caused heart attack.

The next danger, fire, had come from a totally unexpected source. Without electricity, people used their fireplaces or propane grills to cook. In order to keep neighbors from knowing they were cooking, many lit fires indoors. Houses caught fire. Without fire departments or water pressure, entire blocks of homes downwind burned. This created a new group of homeless people.

Burt and Ralph took turns going door to door in their subdivision. They cautioned people to be careful with their fires and warned of the danger of burning propane stoves without proper ventilation.

The next critical issues were food and water. Most homes had little food. Although people complained bitterly about lack, the reality was that the average person could live weeks before death occurred by starvation. But the human body could not sustain itself long without water. Again, Burt and Ralph took the leadership, telling everyone how to collect safe water after a rainstorm.

They organized men to go into a low valley and dig a shallow well to collect drinking water that had not been contaminated by fallout. Soon after the power returned, the waterlines filled with treated water. People were relieved to find they could flush their toilets. Some took showers even though the water was cold.

With electricity, Burt "fired up" his Ham radio and began exchanging news and reports, but with fewer operators than before. One of his favorite contacts was the Parr family in

Western Colorado. Burt was able to pass on the news that
the army and local people in Colorado had stopped the
invading Chinese army.

As Burt and Ralph compared what they were hearing
through the mass media, they realized the word coming out
of the administration in Washington didn't match what they
were hearing over the Ham network. Like their neighbors,
the overarching demand was keeping body and soul together
in their struggle to return to some kind of normalcy.

Chapter Five

The Peacekeepers Arrive

Airman Page stretched his muscles as he went over details of his shift with his relief operator. After a thumbs up from his relief, he took his coffee cup and headed for the exit.

Captain Larson motioned to Page. When he stopped next to Larson's desk, the captain asked, "How would you like some sunshine and fresh air?"

Page's face lit up. "Great!"

"Colonel Holman has arranged for a couple of officers and enlisted men to visit our former homes to see if there's anything we can salvage. Radiation specialists have determined if we stay away from large metal objects, we'll be safe. The weather is warm, so we're going in an open truck. I'd appreciate if you'd go with me."

Without stopping to consider what this might entail, Page accepted the invitation. He got something to eat and went outside with the other men. They assembled at the rebuilt entrance of their underground base. It took a few minutes for their eyes to adjust to the bright sunshine. A clear blue sky reigned overhead, typical of Colorado.

Allowed outside for brief periods after the nuclear attack, the men appeared eager. This was the first time any of them had been permitted to descend into "the Valley of Death." Previously they used binoculars to view the destruction, but this seemed different. The road descending the mountain had been cleared of debris and graded. The driver used an older map to take the men within a block of their former homes. The closer they got, the quieter the men became. Page sensed they were steeling themselves for what they had to face.

Captain Larson signaled for Page to join him when the

truck stopped. They saw burned out basements, partial remains of fireplaces and tree trunks, and hulks of vehicles. The asphalt had burned, leaving gravel streets. Yet in yards here and there, green plants pushed through the horror. Life was determined to overcome death and destruction.

Page followed the captain up a side street while the truck continued on. All they could hear was the crunch of their steps in the gravel. Page, concerned, watched the captain whose jaw quivered. His normally erect bearing resembled that of a much older man. His shoulders slumped.

Page had been to the captain's house once before but couldn't remember anything about it. Larson turned into a driveway where he stopped and looked. The only thing above ground was the hulk of a burned vehicle. After an agonizing moment, the captain turned to Page and pointed to the wreck.

"I guess there's always a bright side. I had four more years of payments to GMAC on the Suburban. They're free to repossess it."

His attempt to smile faded. He wept and wiped his face while continuing to look at the destruction.

Page stepped close and placed his hand on the captain's shoulder. "Go ahead and let it out, sir. My dad taught me that's it okay for men to cry."

The captain fell to his knees and expressed his pain in groans. He sounded like a wounded animal. Page's cheeks were tear streaked, too, not just for the captain's loss but also for his teen sister who had disappeared in the chaos after the attack. Two communications had come from his parents struggling to survive. He fought blaming himself for not being able to protect his little sister.

He kneeled next to the captain. Slowly composure returned to the men. The captain pulled a handkerchief from his pocket and grasped Page's arm. With a lowered voice, the captain said, "Thanks for being here with me. I didn't want to face this alone."

Page nodded and helped him to his feet.

With a deep sigh, Larson shook his head. "I don't know what to do. I don't want to leave, but I don't want to face what I might find."

Page spoke softly, "My dad said it's best to face your fears and not hide from pain or bury it. You were a church going family, right?"

Larson nodded his head.

"As I understand the Bible, your family members aren't dead. They're alive and in a much better place. Instead of seeing all this wreckage, let it remind you of what used to be. Remember what the chaplain said last Sunday, we still have our memories."

The captain affirmed, "You're wise for your age."

Page felt close to Larson, something he'd never experienced before with anyone in the military. He hoped it would last since he admired and respected his superior.

"Well, let's take a look," said Larson. "The blast seems to have shoved everything into the basement, toward the back of the house, or out into the yard."

They walked across a concrete slab and looked into the hole. The burned kitchen stove, refrigerator, washer and dryer, and water heater were the only items easily identified.

The captain pointed to the far corner. "Look, there's the antique iron bedstead Sherry inherited from her grandmother. She loved it. I had it repaired and refinished as a birthday gift to her."

Larson's mood changed quickly. "Oh god, we had it so good. The girls were so beautiful. What insanity caused this? God, why have You forsaken us?"

He turned and walked away. "I can't do it. I can't go any further. Not now. Maybe later. Like you said, they aren't here. They're gone."

Randy followed trying to imagine Larson's pain. His own thoughts rocketed back and forth in his mind. He hated the people who had done this. Yet he did not want to give into bitterness. How could he ease the suffering of his friend? Maybe just being here was enough.

As they walked, Page looked specifically at each ruin on both sides of the street. Who lived there? What had been their hopes and dreams? Was the entire family together when it happened? Were some of the men in New Mexico or California with the army units?

The silence was broken by the sound of a large plane. They looked up and watched a C5 transport come from the east, circle, and settle toward the Colorado Springs airport. It had been a long time since they had seen a plane. This one's tail was painted blue with two large letters in white on it, UN.

Page wasn't sure why, but he knew he didn't like what he saw. UN troops were being stationed all over the East and Midwest. Would this mean he'd have to work with their personnel in the mountain? The men there had become a tight knit group. Even though bringing the UN in meant he wouldn't have to work such long hours, he didn't look forward to the changes.

When the plane was lost from sight, they walked on to the pickup point. It would be an hour or so before the truck was scheduled to return to pick them up. Perhaps the captain would open up while they waited. Page was concerned about his mental stability. He sensed that his commander had been bottling up his feelings and putting on a brave front as an example for the men. He said a silent prayer that this would be a healing experience.

• Russian President Ivan Solntsev asked General Yakov Borisov and his trusted friend, F. B. Markov, the head of the Counter Intelligence Agency, to join him for a private meeting after their conference with high-level Russian commissioners and military leaders.

Markov poured drinks for everyone as they sat down and waited for Solntsev to reveal why he had brought them together. Solntsev sipped his drink in deep thought. Then he spoke reflectively, "It's up to us to make the final decision, is it not? Do we wait for the Chinese to make a move, or do we hit them first?"

Markov glanced at Borisov before commenting. "We all know the problems of a two front war, but at the same time, we realize the danger of being hit when we least expect it. My question is should we consult with our financial backers in the West first?"

Solntsev retorted, "Why do we need to ask those backstabbing bastards anything? You know as well as I do that they have set us up for this. They are playing both sides of the fence. They want us to exhaust ourselves in a war against China so they can move in and finish off the survivor."

General Borisov blurted, "But isn't that exactly why we should not attack China until we've solidified our positions in Europe and the Middle East?"

"General, we don't have that luxury. If the Chinese hit us first, they could cripple us so we couldn't fight back without pulling most of our resources out of Europe."

His comeback silenced the other men, so the President spoke again, "Okay, let's review the key facts. The news of the defeat of one of China's armies in North America is only one of the setbacks they have experienced. Their attack on Taiwan consumed more men and high tech resources than expected. Even without the support of the American Seventh Fleet, the Taiwanese put up a fierce fight, and only the threat of using nuclear weapons against them brought their surrender.

"Their capture of the nations of Southeast Asia, including Australia and New Zealand, was a breeze for them except for their traditional enemies in Vietnam. The nuking of Hanoi and old Saigon brought down the formal government, but the fighting forces have simply retreated to the jungles and mountains and are taking a terrible toll on China's men and equipment. Yet they will be too proud to pull back. They are also in a standoff with India and Pakistan, both of whom have their trigger fingers on their nuclear weapons waiting for China to make a wrong move. Which presents a wonderful opportunity for us, right?

"Let us talk the leaders of India and Pakistan into joining us in attacking the Chinese and get them off both our backs once and for all. With our combined nuclear attacks, we can take out not only most of their military forces, but their ability to produce replacement equipment. With our control of the Middle East, we'll let them have what they can keep in Southeast Asia. The forces that will control those nations can't bother us.

"Now let us be brutally honest about our situation. After our initial success of the preemptive nuclear strikes against American and Western European military forces, our efforts have been inadequate in our follow through on the ground. The years of neglect of the Army and Air Force have enabled our foes' surviving armed forces to raise stiff resistance. While those who rolled over and played dead are no immediate threat, we know they hate and mistrust us. Also, our efforts to reassert control over our former Soviet Union Republics and especially the Muslim nations in the Middle East are not going well.

The Muslims hate us as much as they hate the Americans, because they know we want their oil. The weapons we sold to those nations could easily be turned against us, unless we can show them we are the power to be reckoned with. How do we do that? By blasting China back into the Stone Age with the one thing we have that they don't, excess nuclear weapons."

The other men sat in silence, digesting the proposal.

Markov was the first to speak. "But again, what about our financial backers? Can we dismiss them? Do we not need their past experience and their wealth? Can we dismiss America? Whatever hit our anti-missile defense system has all the markings of a new weapons system developed by the Americans."

General Borisov muttered, "Too little, too late. I'm not concerned about America. We will be long gone before they can do more than battle with the stupid United Nations."

The President smiled and nodded in agreement. "As far as the so called elite of the world, screw them. When we have knocked out the Chinese, we will be in a much stronger position to negotiate. We can bow and scrape and pretend to go along with them to acquire more loans, and when we've rebuilt, we will turn on them, right?"

The other two men raised their glasses and replied in unison, "We will drink to that!"

D-Day Minus Five Months and One Week

•   James stood in the cramped communications trailer
waiting for General Leland to finish a phone call. His friend
was agitated while trying to be diplomatic. James felt
uncomfortable listening to the conversation but dismissed
his feelings as he too became upset at what he was hearing.
Finally, the general promised to consider a request and
broke off the call. He shook his head and looked at his
friend.

James asked, "Mark, why in God's Name do they think
the United Nations' so-called peacekeepers will help our
situation? The troops are coming from communist countries
in South America. We might as well invite the Chinese to
help us maintain order while we fight their army on the
West Coast. Besides that, we've got no security problems
here on the Western Slope or in Denver. If the clowns back
East really want to help, why not send troops to clean up the
final resistance in California or up in the Northwest?"

The general slumped in his chair and held up his hand.
"Look, James, you know I don't trust our glorious leaders
or the UN anymore than you do. But my back is against
the wall. I need supplies and munitions for our troops on
the West Coast. We used up most of our supplies taking out
the forces that came up through Mexico to push them back
across the Rio Grand. But I don't need more men, especially
foreign troops. The powers-that-be have a limited supply of
what I desperately need, and these are the conditions I've
got to meet to obtain them."

James answered through gritted teeth, "Come on,
brother, you know what they're after. They want to tighten
the noose on us before we have a chance to recover and
take control of our own situation. It's been their plan all
along to bring in foreign troops who won't hesitate to fire on
Americans like us who refuse to go along with their ultimate
goal of setting up a one-world government. And besides, we
don't need more mouths to feed. We're having a hard enough
time taking care of the people we already have. If the people
on the Front Range would come across the mountains, we'd

be swamped."

"I know that, but they claim they'll bring their own supplies and support personnel, so they won't be a burden to the local situation. They tell me they'll be able to reign in the rogue elements that aren't willing to pay taxes and go along with restoring political order to the region. That's all bogus. We know it. But again, I need the help they can give in order to boot the Chinese off our continent. I'm in a Catch 22. Foster's forces are out of fuel, ammo, medical supplies, and spare parts. Jolene Howard is doing what she can to back us. She thinks the powers in Washington will assure me that I'll have all we need and more if I agree to their bringing in the provisional UN peacekeepers. So I'm sorry, buddy, but you're going to have to put up with them, at least for the time being."

James protested, "Wait a minute, what do you mean, I'll have to put up with them? Where are you going to be?"

"I've got to move my headquarters closer to the action on the West Coast. Foster warned me not to go back to Cheyenne Mountain, at least for the time being. He thinks I might have a fatal accident that wouldn't be accidental. They need me but--"

James interrupted, pointing his finger at Mark for emphasis, "I agree with him. I don't trust those snakes on the East Coast even though it does seem that Howard is pulling for us. I think the President is a spineless wimp, and I wouldn't trust the vice president if he swore on a stack of Bibles. That's why I don't want them sending us their UN stooges."

Leland held up his hands in a gesture of surrender. "Okay, we agree. I'm appointing you as my military liaison for this region. The sheriffs will be responsible for the county militias to help them maintain law and order. The military has to turn these matters back to the elected political leaders at some point, the sooner, the better. But I'll let them know, if they can't handle any situation that arises, the military will step in and restore order according to constitutional provisions.

"For you to have clout, I'm giving you an official

commission as a full bird colonel in the regular army. You can appoint yourself a staff. This will give you the authority to call on the county militia units to protect the safety and welfare of the general population. I can't leave you any military. I've got to have them and their equipment out West."

James smiled. "Does that mean I get a raise?"

Laughing, the general said, "Sure, we'll double your pay. But of course with deductions, you'll get exactly what we've been getting, nothing."

"Such a deal. Maybe when the powers-that-be send in the peacekeepers, they'll also restore Social Security. Then we can go back to our former high lifestyle."

"And restore my retirement pay. Ha, that'll be the day." The general began looking through the papers on his desk. "I need to change the subject. Here's a report I got from the new captain, Caleb Parr."

"Captain!" James exclaimed.

"Yes, Foster gave him another field promotion. He's now in charge of a reinforced recon company. It seems Caleb got hold of two of the special built dune buggies used by the Delta Force boys. He put his platoon on them and some dirt bikes. Then he used a Pioneer drone to show him where the Chinese were guarding the roads and sneaked around them. They circled behind the main command post in Western Arizona. He captured supply trucks and used them as cover to drive his men right into the command post. They destroyed the whole complex and took the Chinese general and two members of his staff prisoners. This whole Chinese army pulled back into California. The boy has a good combination of guts and brains to use all that high tech stuff and then go in as infantry and fight man to man."

"With the protection of the Lord," James added. "His guardian angels probably have gray hair by now."

"Agreed. I thought you'd like to pass that on to Ann and his parents. I'm sure they're praying. Of course, ask them to keep praying for my grandson, Joshua. He's a tank commander now. The last I heard from him was that their cannon is so worn it throws shots all over the place when they do have the ammo to shoot. He uses his Abrams A1 more as a moving machine gun bunker than a tank killer. Fortunately, the Apache choppers have taken out most of the Chinese tanks." Leland yawned and shook his head.

"But anyhow, this is how I know it's not just Foster's opinion that we need spare parts and supplies so desperately. Joshua tells me the tanks' treads literally fall apart. Their electronics have worn out, and they have to scrounge fuel from old filling stations. So please, James, try to keep the peace with the UN boys as long as possible. I need the spare parts, fuel, and ammo I can obtain from back east. When I clean out the Chinese and push the Mexicans across the border, we can come back and send the UN troops home. Okay?"

James gave him a thumbs up as the general tossed him a set of bird colonel emblems. One of the enlisted men held up a phone, signaling the general. Another call waited. Leland picked up the phone on his desk and returned James's salute. James climbed out of the van and headed for his horse. He had a lot to think about.

Although he had not been looking for more responsibilities, he had to admit he liked the promotion. He knew by the men's reactions to him that, being a military chaplain and pastor didn't carry respect outside the local men who knew him. It made his blood boil every time he sensed men thinking of him as a softy or effeminate because he was a man of the cloth. There was no conflict in his mind about being a man of God and a warrior. You did what was required by the situation. He had proved his metal as a warrior in Vietnam and also in the ambush at Silverton. Yet with UN troops coming, he shuttered to think what this might entail.

He would have time to mull it over as he rode the five miles back to his place. What little fuel they still had was reserved for farm tractors used to grow food or to keep the irrigation canals in repair. The farmers would have to scramble to be able to bring in their fall crops.

•　　Russian Major Sasha Bagrii sat quietly in a state of

exhaustion. He felt like a zombie behind his desk where he reviewed recent events. He had only been able to snatch a few minutes of sleep in the last two days. Or had it been longer? When the order came to reprogram the ICBM in his launch station, it required a task he felt incompetent to carry out. His team had to open the warhead on the missile and hook up a computer to the guidance mechanism. The new program was all computerized. Maybe that was why he had sweat over it so much. He could not be sure what one computer told the other's memory bank.

Then came the endless checking and double-checking to make sure the new target had been programmed with precision. All his training in the past covered targets in North America. Now the missile, aimed at a target in China, caused extreme frustration because he knew nothing about it. It could be dangerous to question his leaders, but what the hell had they been thinking? They had cooperated with China to defeat the most powerful military in the world, and both embraced communism. Why had these allies turned on each other?

Yeah sure, he heard the line coming out of Moscow. China had secretly turned on them. Strange how it's always the other guy's fault. The masses of little yellow men meant to take the oil in Eurasia and the minerals in Siberia. They had to be stopped. Yet he, a mere major, knew that fighting a war on two fronts would never be a good idea. Especially when the war with the West was not going as expected even after smashing their military.

The Americans had fought back in ways unexpected by the Russian leadership. A secret weapon took out the early warning radar while anti-missile defense batteries exploded on their launching pads. No one said how the West did it, but fear existed that a new kind of laser or giant, magnetic rays had been projected from stealth aircraft. Whatever, Bagrii detected extreme fear in his leaders.

Then the Chinese had turned on them, the double-crossing bastards. But that should not have surprised anyone. Was it not their nature? The animosity between the Russians and Mongols went back centuries. Thus, the missile that had been loaded in the major's silo and not used in a follow up attack on the West was ready to be used to incinerate a million or so Chinese.

But what if they could not stop the Chinese hordes? There were no more missiles to reload into their silo. Would that mean he and his men would be put into the meat grinder of the ground troops? He was too old for that, too soft from sitting around in his underground hole for too many years. He directed some choice swear words at his glorious leaders. He had been set to retire in just five years.

The major tried to force his mind to think of nothing while he watched his crew go through another practice launch sequence. At least Glukhov had the dehumidifier working. He must have found some parts made in America.

D-Day Minus Seven Months and Two Weeks

•   UN troops had landed at the Montrose airport in a C-130. They took over the terminal building as their headquarters and bedded their troops in a nearby hanger. Their American officer and his mixed national staff took up residence in the nearby Hampton Inn. The local militiamen felt no surge of enthusiasm when the unit was reinforced with two Abram tanks, several armored personnel carriers, and a company of troops from South America. The equipment seemed in good repair, so they wondered why it had not been sent to the front in the West where it could be put to good use.

The townspeople gave the peacekeeping soldiers a friendly welcome. All had been invited to attend local churches. The few who did were shown every courtesy. However, the militiamen had a healthy distrust for the supposed peacekeepers especially when they heard that in their neighboring community, Grand Junction, another similar unit had also been established. That force would control the traffic, what little there was, of the East-West Interstate, Highway 70.

The first sign of the intentions of the new forces came when the commander, Lt. Colonel Bruce Wiles, explained to James and Sheriff Black that they would need to begin the process of collecting all military weapons in the hands of the militia and private citizens. Since the UN troops had come to maintain law and order, there would be no need for weapons in the community, because they could be used by unlawful elements.

James looked at the sheriff and then, the commander. "What unlawful elements are you referring to? Granted, we've had a few incidents when hungry people used their weapons to steal food or fuel, but as the crops were harvested this fall, we've had no more problems. How do you propose to police the outlying areas when we're all desperately short on fuel?"

"Well, Colonel Parr, these are my orders. It's part of the whole process of restoring harmony to society and bringing the people under the control of the regional and national government authorities. The higher authorities have their reasons for setting such standards."

"What standards are you thinking of?"

"There's the matter of collecting taxes and the assignment of vital resources as well as the wise use of manpower. They're not just concerned about this area of the country, which happens to be blessed with an ample supply of food. They must look out for the welfare and just distribution of resources throughout the whole country."

James glanced at the sheriff as he spoke. "Okay, I'm impressed with their concern. I appreciate that they have some big issues to deal with, but what does that have to do with the effort to collect weapons from people in this region? Do they have a shortage of weapons in other parts of the country?"

Wiles hesitated. "No, I don't think that's the reason."

James persisted, "We've heard via our contacts through Ham radio that a lot of weapons have been collected from people in the eastern part of the country. The people there aren't too happy with the results. In fact, we've heard that some have been forcefully moved into labor camps. Others seem to be in trouble with the government because they didn't go along with the orders restricting the activity of the

Christians. To be blunt, we've heard that UN peacekeepers are acting more like a conquering army, and the civil government is taking on the character of a dictator."

"Colonel," the commander exclaimed, rolling his eyes, "I don't think I need to remind you that these have been very unsettling times which have called for drastic actions to maintain the peace and security of the people! The nation is under martial law. Recovering from the breakdown of law and order requires strong-armed tactics until the infrastructure of our society can be rebuilt. The purpose of government is to assure that law and order is restored."

James raised his eyebrows. "Wonderful, I agree. But law and order have been restored here. If it's such a problem in other areas, I suggest you take your troops and go to those areas where your services are needed. We don't want or need that kind of enforcement in this state. Which brings up another point. I noticed you referred to our region and nation but made no mention of the state of Colorado."

The commander's expression showed that he thought James's point was totally insignificant. "I'm sure you're aware of this, the emergency required that regional governments be established because the states were not able to deal with the demands placed on them."

James turned to the sheriff and inquired, "Sheriff, do you recall the people being asked to vote on that?"

Sheriff Black shook his head.

The commander stiffened as he snapped, "Gentleman, I have my orders! We are under martial law! Such decisions are made at the top!"

James leaned forward pointing his finger in the face of Wiles. "Commander, let's get one thing straight. You can take that order and stick it in a dark hole where the sun doesn't shine, okay? As I've tried to tell you and your higher command structure, the people in this part of the country are Americans who still live by the law of the land. Our law is first of all the Bible. Second, we have the American Constitution supported by the Colorado Constitution. We don't cotton to any UN version. We relish the old original Constitution of these United States of America.

"You may recall, the Second Amendment of that Constitution guarantees the right of all citizens to bear arms. So you send word back to your authorities that we aren't about to give up any of our personal weapons or any of the military arms that will remain under the control of the local militia. And if they're dumb enough to order you to try to collect them from us, I assure you, we will resist with deadly force."

The UN commander's face flushed in anger.

Sheriff Black shifted uncomfortably in his chair. "Pastor, I think you're being a little hasty and overstepping your authority here. If the UN troops can take over some of our duties to assure that we have law and order, why do members of our militia need heavy weapons? After all, there is little indication that the Chinese or Mexicans are any future threat to us or anyone else here in the Rocky Mountain region."

James turned to look into Black's eyes. "Sheriff, I'm sure you've noticed that the UN troops are not Americans." To Wiles he asserted, "And, Commander, I don't know how you understood the oath you took when you became an officer. But I swore allegiance to the Constitution of the United States of America. Until we the people approve by our free vote a change in our ultimate laws, the Constitution is the law I'm going to obey, emergency or no emergency. And I'm quite sure I speak for the majority of the people in the community. I also speak as the appointed military commander in this valley."

The commander attempted to regain his position of authority. "Colonel, that America died with the destruction of the nuclear attack. We are living under a new reality that requires a different set of rules, if we are to survive as a nation in a radically changed world situation. Our leaders have achieved some semblance of world stability. With the Russians and Chinese fighting each other, this gives the formerly free nations of the world an opportunity to stabilize our situations and--"

"That's fine," interrupted James. "I'm all for a more stable world situation. But I assure you, our citizens

having the ability to protect themselves is no threat to
anyone any place." He raised his forefinger and resumed,
"Unless outsiders want to disarm us so they can force their
standards on us and turn us into their docile slaves. If that's
the real aim of your masters, you're going to have to bring a
hell of a lot more firepower against us than what your puny
force represents locally.

"We were duped once by these so-called world leaders,
but our eyes are open now. We're not about to give in to
their brand of slavery, call it what you will. We don't intend
to end up as a formerly free nation. We shed our blood to
throw off the Chinese threat. Our sons are still putting
their lives on the line to drive out the last of the invaders.
So the minute your United Nations peacekeepers begin to
look like another force to push someone else's agenda on us,
we will again put our lives on the line to maintain our God
given, lawfully guaranteed rights! Not government granted
privileges, but constitutional rights!" James sat back and
stared at the commander.

The commander shuffled papers before announcing in a
huffy manner, "I think we can end this meeting. I'll report
back to my chain of command and relay their response.
Until then, you are dismissed."

James stood and turned to Sheriff Black. "Did you notice
that, Sheriff? Our new 'massa' has dismissed us. We is
now free to shuffle off to our cotton patch so's we can work
hard to pay our taxes to da new 'massa.'" Looking into the
commander's eyes, he leaned forward, put his left hand
on the desk, and lowered his voice as he placed his other
hand on the butt of his sidearm. "This boy and the people
I represent ain't gonna put up with no outside 'massas.'"
Then he straightened. His left hand drew a small radio from
a side pocket. "I've got armed men outside in case you've got
any ideas of doing something irrational."

A look of guilt flickered across the commander's face. He
removed his hand from the phone. James backed toward the
door and motioned for the sheriff to leave ahead of him.

•   Lt. Colonel Sasha Bagrii's earlier fears had been

confirmed. After launching their missile against the
Chinese, it had taken his command structure less than
forty-eight hours to issue new orders. Since there were no
more missiles to load into their launchers, he had been
given a promotion and command of all the guards, crew, and
maintenance personnel in the squadron. They were ordered
to report to the 92nd Infantry Division somewhere on the
Eastern Front.

Four old trucks had been given to the soldiers to haul
kitchen equipment, a few old tents, and meager food
supplies. But the men would have to march, carrying their
weapons and personal items. As the news spread, some of
the men simply disappeared. While Bagrii issued severe
warnings on the penalties for desertion, he secretly didn't
blame his men for leaving. Though they had all been
through combat training, the reality was that most were not
in physical shape to endure the rigors of infantrymen.

He said goodbye to his wife and children, appearing
confident. However, he did not expect to see them again. The
few reports from the battlefront were not encouraging. The
Russian army was taking a terrible beating by the masses of
Chinese troops pouring into the "Motherland." It appeared
to be a repeat of what he had read about the early years of
World War II when the German armies pushed into Russia.
But he reminded the men that Russia was a vast country.
Eventually they would drive the invaders back just as their
ancestors had.

He hoped he would live to see that day. Now he had
to worry about moving his men to the front where they
could make a difference. He was not sure how many weeks
it would take them or what kind of dangers they might
encounter along the way. He had heard that biological
weapons were being used. The threat of attacks from the air
was also a concern. What had often been life in a tomb now
became "the good old days."

•   James awoke with a start. Due to the faint light coming
through the bedroom window, he knew it was still a half
hour before dawn. Easing out of bed, he began to thank the

Lord for the night of rest. A thought entered his mind like a shaft of light in a dark room. Take the women and children to the mountains.

He had heard the voice of God enough to know that this was not his own mind. A chill ran down his spine. He sensed this message was for Ann and also Sarah and her children. To be sure, he asked, "Lord, does this include Russ's family?" He sensed, "No."

"Is this in relation to the UN and their intentions?" A clear yes echoed in his mind. Again he thanked the Lord and promised obedience as he proceeded to the bathroom.

After breakfast, James asked Elizabeth and Chuck to do the dishes. When they were out of hearing distance, he relayed the early morning message to Ann, Henry, and Sarah. "Take a week's supply of food and your backpacks. If it's not too cold at night, maybe the kids can set up a tent and--"

Henry broke in, "I'll drive them up, Dad, but I'm coming back. If the UN comes, I don't intend to leave you here by yourself."

"Thanks, Henry, but I'm going to have the neighbors on high alert. I've already set up a plan for Rich and Tom to bring in a rapid response team. Unless the UN brings their entire force, we'll have enough firepower to drive them off. I hope the commander isn't stupid enough to try anything. We'll be ready if he does."

Henry wasn't convinced. "With two of us, one can stand guard while the other sleeps. There are enough men in the area of the cabin to watch things up there. Besides, no one needs to know the women and children are there."

Ann looked at the two men she loved and assured them she would be covering them with prayer.

James was not able to convince Marcie to leave. She lived in a small apartment above his office and said she had too much work to do. She was prepared to add her weapon to the fray if needed.

Henry returned by mid afternoon. From that time on, they would remain fully dressed with their weapons and ammunition in easy reach.

Chapter Six

The UN Attack

D-Day Minus Eleven Months

In the cool of the night, blood oozed from the dead. Faint columns of steam rose from the still forms scattered near the farm buildings. A raging fire in the demolished Parr home cast eerie shadows over the remains of an intense battle that had ended just minutes before.

James dropped to a knee and leaned his rifle against the tree. Blood ran from a face wound on to his white beard. He took the hand of the younger man whose body laid next to the tree. Marcie disheveled and already on her knees next to the body, looked up and slowly shook her head. Tears washed smoky grime from her cheeks.

"I'm sorry, James. There was nothing we could do to save him. He didn't suffer long. His last words were concern for your welfare."

James's heart still pounded in his chest from the shock of the brutal fight. In an attempt to respond, he shuddered. Sobs erupted from his chest. His body shook, and his words were choked. Gently he patted his dead son's cheek, trying to ignore the blood soaked shirt where the bullet exited.

Two men approached still holding their weapons at ready. They stood silently for a moment. One kneeled next to the older man and placed an arm around his shoulders.

"I'm so sorry, Pastor. If only we could've gotten here sooner, maybe--"

Raising a hand in protest, James grasped the man's arm and spoke softly, "No, you did what you could. I prayed it wouldn't come to this. I tried to reason with their commander and the sheriff. But I guess we all knew it would lead to violence." Overwhelming grief made it impossible to continue for a few moments. At last he asked, "Did you see

Russ?"

"Yes, sir. He's all right. He's helping to move some of the supplies out of the garage and your office. I don't know if they'll be able to save your office. They're taking your computers and the files out just in case. Marcie, you may want to go to your apartment and retrieve a few things."

She waved off the suggestion. James showed obvious relief that his younger son was safe. "Did we lose any others?"

"Yes, sir, Boyd Thompson. A sniper got him. Thompson's son was slightly wounded. We got the sniper before he could take out anyone else. We had the advantage of cover and catching the rest of them in a crossfire."

"Then Boyd and Henry were the only casualties on our side?"

"Yes, sir."

Bullets began to cook off in the burning building. The men ducked and looked around. When they realized the cause, they relaxed.

The other man standing over them spoke, "What do you think we should do now, Pastor? Don't you think they'll know this raid went bad and send more UN peacekeepers from the base at the airport?"

James sat down with great effort, leaning against the tree next to the body of his firstborn. He removed his own hat. Then he reached up to feel the bloody spot on his forehead where shrapnel had broken the skin. Resting against the tree, he closed his eyes.

He thought for a moment before speaking. "You're probably right, Rich. Why don't you and Tom gather their weapons? I'd suggest you take the machine gun and set up an ambush down near the river. Let's plan on hitting them hard. Then before they bring in air support or tanks, we'll head for the hills. We'll use up whatever firepower we can't take with us and destroy the rest. Does that sound like a good plan?"

The two men nodded in agreement.

"What should we do with the prisoners and their wounded?" asked Rich.

"Let them take care of their own wounded. Hold them in the shop until we leave. Then turn them loose. If they speak English, let them know we'll accept their surrender, but if they come against us in battle, we'll kill them." James said all this through gritted teeth.

Before leaving, Rich knelt in front of his beloved pastor and shined his flashlight on the wound. "Pastor, you'd better have Marcie clean that wound. We don't want to lose you too. And, brother, we feel bad about losing Henry. He was a fine man. We'll all miss him somethin' terrible. I can't imagine how it must hurt you."

"Thank you, brother." James squeezed his arm and looked into his face. Remembering Rich's Vietnam experiences, he asked, "You doin' okay?"

Rich hesitated before he spoke. "Yeah. Things ole Mad Dog learned in combat came back quick. I've often prayed I'd never have to return to this again, but, hey, you gotta do what you gotta do. I've got the Lord now. He'll take me through this."

James reached up and patted his shoulder. "You're a good brother. Would you let Russ know where we are? Ask him to come as soon as he has things in hand."

The two men simply nodded and moved out.

Marcie began to wipe the blood from James's face. "I have to find some gauze and tape. I'll be right back."

Her husband had returned from the first Gulf War a sick man. James ministered to them frequently. When Jack died after suffering terribly from Gulf War Syndrome, Marcie became the personal secretary to James. She was a devout co-laborer in their ministry to veterans, their families, and a local congregation of home-based fellowship groups.

After she left, he reached down to straighten his son's hair and held his hand. Quietly he began to quote Scripture. "The Lord giveth and the Lord taketh away, blessed be the name of the Lord. God so loved the world, He gave His only begotten Son . . ."

Lost in thought, he didn't realize how long it was before his younger son, Russell, was kneeling next to him. Russ buried his face in his father's chest and sobbed.

James stroked his Russ's head. Both were speechless, grappling with their sorrow.

Finally the older man was able to verbalize his comfort for his son. "He's at peace with Jesus now, Son. We've got to hold on to that truth. His fighting days are over. Ours are going to become worse. I'm not sure whom we should feel the most sorrow for. That's logic speaking, not my heart."

Russ straightened. In the flickering light, he looked at the still form of his only brother and inquired, "Did he suffer much?"

"I don't think so. The wound created a lot of shock. I wasn't able to stay with him, but Marcie helped him right away. She said he didn't last long. Two of the men carried him out here away from the fire." He hesitated, and then his voice hardened. "I at least had the satisfaction of sending the bastard who shot him in the back straight to hell along with several others. I don't think they expected us to fight back so strongly. Nor did they anticipate you and the others arriving here so quickly. Serves them right for siding with the devil. May they all rot in hell!"

"What do we do now, Dad?"

"We take the fight to them, an eye for an eye. No more talk. No compromise." His anger welled up. "They've revealed their true purpose and nature. With God as my witness, I will not stop until every foreign troop is pushed off our land, or I'll die trying."

"No, I mean with Henry."

"Oh. I don't know. We can't leave him here. No telling what the S O Bs would do with him. Your mother and Sarah and the kids need to see him so they can grieve. It's going to be hard on them."

"Yeah. Even with all the death and suffering we've seen this past year, it's hard to believe it's hit our family." Russell looked at his brother. "Where will we bury him?"

"We'll take him up in the mountains near the cabin where your mom and his family are. We'll do the same with Boyd. Tom and Rich are gathering up the weapons and plan to set up an ambush for the relief force our enemies will send out. Why don't you go home and help your family prepare to head for the retreat cabin? Then come back with your pickup. I'll wait here. I need some time alone after Marcie patches me up."

He put his hand on his son's shoulder and rubbed the back of his neck. "We've tried to prepare ourselves for such possibilities. I know you and many of the others didn't believe that the powers-that-be would take this type of action to seize our guns after all we've been through. I'm not admonishing you with 'I told you so.' I'm just grieved that it's come to this. But, we're not beaten. We've taken some heavy blows as a community. There's probably many more coming. We've got to believe fighting for our freedom, and, if need be, dying is better than giving in to their using United Nations troops to enslave us, okay?"

"You're the general now, Dad."

"Let's be more humble. I'm content to be a colonel under General Leland's authority."

"All right."

"You'd better leave now."

Russ glanced again at the still figure. Reaching over, he squeezed his brother's arm. Then he grabbed his semiautomatic M-16 and moved in the direction of the lane that led to his house. He had a lot to do before the sun rose.

Meanwhile, James continued to sit next to the still form of his firstborn. Alone, he allowed the tears to fall. The stark reality of death had claimed Henry's bodily presence, but it could not remove memories of the many years of life with this son.

Henry had been born while James served as an Army chaplain in Vietnam. When the family finally reunited, as a new father, he grew close to his baby son quickly. Three years later, Russell arrived when James was burdened with pastoral duties. There was so much to remember. His heart swelled with love and admiration for Henry, which he had often felt but not expressed. Why was it so hard for a man to express his deep love for his own sons?

Both Henry and Russell had difficulty understanding his fight against the growth of big government and the whittling away of the cherished freedoms he had shed his blood for

in Vietnam. He always knew the boys loved him even while
finding it hard to accept the struggle his calling had placed
on their home life. When they accompanied him on a return
trip to Vietnam, a new closeness developed with them. There
they met the wife and son of one of the Viet Cong whom
James killed in the heat of battle twenty-five years earlier.
James had returned a picture of the soldier with his young
wife and baby that had been found in some gear he brought
home from the war. The trip gave his sons a deeper insight
into the trauma of the war that had shaped their father's
life.

James's mind bounced between logic and raw emotion.
The question of why his son had died and not him kept
forcing itself into his mind. He quoted Scripture to remind
himself of the great promises of God. Gradually, he came to
the conclusion that this was not a time to question the God
Who had sustained him for well over fifty years of his adult
life.

•   UN Commander Bruce Wiles listened to the stressed
voice of the raid captain reporting the fierce resistance
encountered at the Parr home. When he heard gunfire and
the scream of the captain before the radio went dead, he
pounded his fist on the table and cursed.

Shouting his frustrations to the lieutenant in charge of
the night shift, he yelled, "Those idiots! They were supposed
to be in his house before he knew they were there. How in
the hell did one old man and a civilian son put up such a
resistance?"

The young, South American officer wisely kept his mouth
shut. Wiles got up and paced the floor muttering.

The small observation helicopter he had ordered to the
scene of the raid reported in on the radio. "The house is on
fire. I see bodies on the ground. It looks like some of our
troops have surrendered. What are your orders?"

Wiles grabbed the microphone from the operator. "Can
you see how many men the resistance force has there?"

"I'll have to move closer. Wait, we're receiving ground
fire!"

Wiles yelled, "Get out of there! Return to base! Out."

He slammed the microphone stand on the desk, sat down at the table, and opened a map of the area.

After studying it for several minutes, he addressed the lieutenant, "Okay, the gunfire, explosions, and fire have been seen and heard over much of that part of the valley. So the militia has been alerted. Our next move must be stronger."

He stopped to think. Suddenly he shook his finger at the junior officer and growled, "I underestimated the resistance. I thought we had placated Colonel Parr by assuring him that we only wanted to send the heavy military arms to the forces fighting in California. I hoped this would cause him to let down his guard. And by waiting through the winter, I thought he'd believe we were backing down. Then we could capture him with a night raid. Without their leader, the militiamen would buckle. Obviously, I misjudged my opponent. So we learn from this."

The lieutenant swallowed hard and acknowledged, "Yes, sir."

Wiles mused, "They'll either turn tail and run for the hills, or they'll stand and make an attempt to take out our relief force. So, if they stay, we've got to hit them hard. We can use this as an opportunity to show them who's in charge here and probably take out some of their leaders. We'll use them as an example for the rest of the militias in the valley.

"Call out the company. We'll lead with a tank and the personnel carriers. They'll wet their pants when they see an Abram coming at them. But leave one here with a squad on full alert because they just might try to hit our headquarters while we're out there. I'll be in the command chopper. Any questions?"

The lieutenant straightened. "No, sir."

"Good." Wiles slammed his fist on the desk. "We'll hit them at dawn. Send one of the Blackhawks ahead of the column to check for an ambush. Get the other one from Grand Junction and hold it in reserve. Let's show these country bumpkins what military men can do!"

The lieutenant jumped up, saluted, and gave the

expected response, "Yes, sir!"

•   The James Parr home had been reduced to ashes by
the time Russ returned. He wrapped his brother's body in
a blanket, placing him in the back of a 4X4 pickup along
with Boyd Thompson. There were also boxes of supplies,
sleeping bags, and other items that would be taken into the
mountains.

James decided to stay to direct the ambush of the UN
relief force and rally the militia he had organized for just
this possibility. Through cell phones and radios, he sent the
alert that was passed around the valley to all militiamen.
Those who could leave their wives and younger children
with family members headed for their prearranged meeting
places. Then they faded into the surrounding mountains
with their weapons and emergency supplies.

By the time James had walked down the road toward
the draw leading to the small river, a half dozen other men
joined the ambush team. Tom and Rich used a pickup to
bring the weapons gathered from the slain strike force.
When the other men arrived, they picked out a 30-caliber
machine gun that had been mounted on the disabled
Humvee, two portable rockets, and a SAW machine gun to
be used in the ambush.

The rest of the weapons and ammunition would be
taken with them as they retreated into the mountains. One
weapon was the 50-caliber sniper rifle used to kill Boyd
Thompson. Craig Dawson asked for permission to take
charge of it. He was a large construction worker. The extra
fifty pounds of weapons and ammunition made his load
heavy, but manageable.

Tom met James and explained their planned ambush.
"I've arranged for a pickup to be parked along the road
where it can be seen from the bridge. If the relief force sends
a lone vehicle to scout the area, Len Hamilton will shine a
light and fire a warning shot to stop them. Then he'll drive
away as if it was the only resistance being offered.

"If the vehicle follows him, Len will drive to your place
and engage the UN troops. Those of us in ambush will lie

low and wait until the main force arrives. If they bring a tank or heavy tracked vehicle, we'll wait for it to reach a large explosive device we've planted under the cattle guard this side of the river bridge. When I blow it, that will be the signal for the others to open fire."

"What about any armored personnel carriers?"

Pointing toward the valley, Tom assured, "I've got Daniels with two handheld rockets where the stream makes that sharp turn before the bridge. Craig might be able to disable them with the 50-caliber rifle. So one way or the other, we can deal with them. All the men have either horses or motorcycles to escape on if we can't stop their attack."

James squeezed Tom's arm. "Sounds good. Where do you want me and my trusty 308?"

"Why don't you go over behind the big tree? I've got my ATV parked just over the ridge so you can ride out with me. Or if I'm hit, the keys are in it. Take it and go out on the old logging road. The men are all instructed to meet at Flosin's Mine."

"Okay, Tom. Has anyone been listening to the sheriff's channel?"

"Yes. The word got back that the strike force was having the stuffing kicked out of 'em, and the UN boys are putting together a backup force. So they should be here anytime. Why don't you go get set up? I'll do one last check with the boys to make sure everyone is ready and their positions are well camouflaged in case the cowards wait until daylight to attack. I'll tell the men to stay deep in their holes until the mine is set off in case they use thermal detection devices."

James made his way over to the spot suggested by Tom. By the time he returned, the colonel had moved rocks to form a protected position from which he could fire at any spot on the road, the bridge, or beyond. His night scope would not pick up anything further than the river unless there was the light from burning vehicles.

•   Tom called to Len Hamilton as dawn approached. He ordered him to park the pickup under trees near the farmstead and cover it with brush to hide it from the air.

He told another man to go with him. If the chopper came
back to check things out, they were to fire on it from one of
the barns to make it appear that a force was defending the
farmstead. The men obeyed and had barely set up when an
observation chopper flew over, following the road toward the
Parr home.

Seconds after it crossed over the ridge, the ambush team
heard the automatic fire of Len and Sam's AK47s. It would
take a lucky hit to bring the chopper down, but for now,
they didn't really care. They would be able to hide behind
concrete walls if the chopper attacked them with its light
machine gun or rockets. The chopper returned machine gun
fire, circled, and flew over the area where the ambush was
set. Then it flew on out to Highway 550.

James and his men stayed beneath their camouflaged
positions. They heard the rumble of heavy trucks and the
squeaking tracks of a tank. While none of the men voiced
concern, this struck fear in their hearts. The light rockets
they had were no match for an M1A tank. If the mine didn't
take out the tank, it would be a lopsided battle with their
light weapons against the 105-millimeter cannon.

All the men were alert. Most of them emptied their
bladders, not disturbing their camouflage. Afterwards, they
rechecked their weapons and the extra ammunition they
had laid out. Finally, they "hunkered down" in their holes.

Tom double-checked the wires leading to the detonator
that sat next to his right hand. The tank would slow down
for the bridge and then make a turn to cross the cattle
guard. If they sent a team ahead to check for mines, the
metal of the cattle guard would interfere with the metal
detector. Leaves and dirt hid the mine from view.

It was getting light enough to see a Humvee in front of
an M1A tank as they moved around the curve in the road
leading to the bridge. Behind the tank were two armored
personnel carriers followed by three trucks loaded with
troops. To James, it appeared the UN commander was not
taking any chances. He would assume the locals were well
armed, but only with light weapons.

Tom whispered a short prayer, asking the Lord to give

him wisdom as to when to set off the tank mine. James was also praying, just loud enough that Tom could hear him quote the Psalms that asked God to enable them to triumph over their enemies.

The Humvee stopped short of the bridge. Two soldiers leaped from the back, ran to the side of the bridge, and shined flashlights underneath to make sure there were no explosives. Satisfied, they returned to the vehicle and gave a thumbs up to the commander of the tank who was using his binoculars to scan the road ahead.

A small herd of cows grazed in the field across the river from the approaching vehicles. The animals had stopped eating and watched the noisy, strange looking vehicles. The turret of the tank moved slowly from right-to-left as instruments in the tank scanned for hot spots. The men in the ambush team ducked behind the earthen wall of a deep irrigation ditch where they had dug foxholes.

Tom watched through a narrow crack. He almost stopped breathing as the Humvee and the tank began to move across the bridge. His thumb was poised over the button. The Humvee rattled across the cattle guard, and the personnel carriers and trucks followed the lead vehicles.

Only three of the men in the ambush squad had ever killed in the heat of battle. The fight at James's house just hours before was the second time Tom had killed. He had fought in the ambush of the Chinese and Mexican army at Silverton. But now it was even more personal. He felt a certain joyful anticipation in what was about to be released upon the attacking force. These enemies had been ordered to attack and kill people he loved. They threatened the future of his family. Then too, they were not a faceless enemy. He had seen them up close in town.

An Irish company handled the helicopters and tanks. The infantry were Argentinean troops who had been brought in to recruit Spanish-speaking citizens. But now in Tom's mind and the minds of the other men, they were simply the enemy. The foreign troops were personal enemies and foes of everything valued in America.

When the tracks of the tank dropped on the bars of the

cattle guard, Tom waited a fraction of a second before his thumb drove the plunger down to send an electronic signal to the detonator in the mine. There was a flash under the tank before it disappeared in the dust thrown up by the powerful explosion.

The tank commander's body emerged from the top of the debris like a rag doll. He landed on the back corner of the tank and fell to the ground.

James watched the explosion. Before the shock rolled across their position, he squeezed his trigger. The machine gunner in the Humvee was the next man to die. The driver hit the brakes. He was looking wildly around when a bullet hit him in the head.

A cascade of bullets burst from the hillside into the vehicles behind the burning tank. Craig's sniper rifle roared, sending an armor piercing, 50-caliber bullet crashing through the armor of the lead personnel carrier. The bullet did terrible damage to the soft bodies as the missile bounced around inside the chamber. By the time the men had dropped the rear doors and begun to pile out of the deathtrap, several were either dead or mortally wounded.

Tom's man, hidden in a small ditch next to the river, sent one of the rockets into the second armored personnel before the rear door could be dropped. Either the concussion or flying shrapnel killed the men inside. The machine guns on the trucks began to rake the hillsides in an attempt to seek out the flashes of light from concealed positions. But before they could do any damage, James and another shooter with telescopic sights eliminated them from the battle.

The M-60 machine gun and the SAW raked the trucks and the men piling out of the first armored personnel carrier. The stream of bullets took a large toll on the closely packed soldiers who tried desperately to leave the trucks to find shelter along the road or under the trucks.

No one in the ambush team noticed the Blackhawk helicopter until several rockets swooshed in, exploding near one of the dugouts across from James and Tom. Immediately the fire from the ambush team shifted from the ground to the air as the helicopter rushed over them. The door gunner put out a stream of tracers that cascaded into one of the dugouts. Lance Boone, a farm boy who had been born and raised less than two miles from the site, was instantly killed when three of the bullets nearly severed his head from his body.

Craig had just put a fresh magazine in the 50 and was able to get one shot off before the helicopter flew over his position, veering to the left. He picked up the heavy rifle and swung it around, following the movement of the chopper. Just before it disappeared over the ridge, he fired a shot and watched the tracer go up the exhaust of the left motor. Other bullets had found their mark. The chopper did not return to threaten them. Later the men would come across it where it had been forced to land in an open field. They made sure it never flew again.

By the time the men returned their fire to the vehicles on the road, there were not many targets left to shoot. A soldier in the lead Humvee had survived. He fired back at the hill as he ran for the bridge. One shot dropped him just before he made it to the first personnel carrier. The ammunition in the burning tank began to cook off, pushing flames and smoke up through the opening at the top of the gun turret.

The few men alive and unwounded in the attack force were in no mood to play hero and draw the fire of the ambushing party. They either played dead or hid behind the vehicles and in the ditch. Tom looked at James who was watching for another target through his scope.

"Pastor, I think we've whipped 'em. We'd better pull back and let 'em lick their wounds. They may have some heavy mortars to back 'em up."

The older man nodded in agreement. "Had we best stay and cover the others while they pull back?" he asked.

"Right." Tom pulled a whistle from his pocket and blew three sharp bursts. He yelled to Craig, ordering him to put a bullet in every motor and take a position to fire on the troops on the road. James looked across the road. He saw the men come out of their firing positions. Two carried the body of young Boone. They would tie him on his skittish horse to take him back into the hills for a proper burial.

Craig's 50 roared several times while James and Tom looked for any sign of resistance. There was none. The observation helicopter appeared about a mile away from them. Craig fired a 50-caliber tracer that drew near it, causing it to beat a hasty retreat.

James and Tom could hear the cries of the wounded, calling for help. They felt no pity for them. Their hearts were already hardened to the deadly task that had been forced upon them, that of killing other men.

•   Weary, the group met Russ and the others later that morning at their mountain retreat. They had inflicted a major defeat on the local UN forces. But their excitement was quelled as they went about the task of laying three bodies to rest. Russ and another man had already dug two graves.

James rode the last few miles in the pickup with the weapons. Russ approached him as he climbed out of the vehicle. James's face was stained with tears.

"Mom's waiting for you out on the point. She said she wanted to be alone for a while.

James said nothing.

"I hear you guys really clobbered the UN relief force."

"Yes, it was a turkey shoot. I hope they figure it out that we're not going to give in to their demands. Is someone with Sarah and the kids?"

"A lot of our friends are in the house with them."

"Okay, I'd better go comfort your mom." There was a terrible sadness in his voice.

When he approached Ann and saw her tear-streaked face, he couldn't hold back his own grief.

"Why? I want to know why?" Ann blurted out. "What has all your preaching and protesting gotten us? My son is dead! My home is ashes. We're fugitives in our own land, and the whole country's in turmoil. So what good was all your work? Where is God in all this?"

She backed away when James tried to embrace her. He stopped trying to reach for her and wept.

She wailed, "Oh I know, you'll quote Job or some other

noble sounding Bible verses. But will it bring my boy back to me? Will it?"

When she didn't receive an answer, she stepped forward and pounded her fists against his chest before collapsing in his arms. James stroked her hair. His body rocked with sobs that matched hers.

Finally she pulled away, looked into his face, and whispered, "Why, why?"

"I don't know, Hon, but Job was right. The Lord gives, and the Lord takes away. Our only response must be, 'Blessed be the name of the Lord.' "

Ann turned and looked at the beautiful mountain range in the distance, trying to gain her composure. She wiped the tears away and stood in silence.

James spoke with caution, "Let's sit down over here."

She followed his lead and took his hands in hers. "I know I'm being selfish. So many around the nation have lost entire families. My brother and sister are probably dead, along with most of their children. But I can't help it. It's so painful."

"I know, dear. In our hearts, he's still our little boy. My argument with God is why not me instead of him. I've had a full life. He still had so much ahead of him, and his children need him." He couldn't go on.

They sat in silence for a long while before James whispered, "I love you. I know it hurts unbearably, but we've got to remember where Henry is. He's in the presence of the Lord Jesus. We've got to hold on to this, because, if it's not true, we're truly lost, with no hope."

Ann snuggled into his arms, and they became lost in a flood of memories.

Later, James wept with Sarah and the children as they struggled to deal with the loss of their beloved Henry. After the men had fashioned a crude casket from plywood and laid Henry's body in it, the family gathered around for one last goodbye. Ann related the events of Henry's birth and told about the joys of his childhood. As the first waves of grief subsided, James asked the children to tell some of their cherished memories of their father. Their stories brought more tears, interspersed with laughter, which at first seemed inappropriate until James assured them it was part of the grieving process.

After a long time with the family, James assumed the role of pastor and led the committal service. The sun was setting in the west as Henry's body was lowered into his grave. Two men watched at a nearby high point for a possible attack from the air by the UN forces' remaining helicopters.

James reminded everyone gathered that death for those in Christ was a glorious entrance into life without end. He spoke with a gentle voice, "Christ promised a resurrection to a new life. Those who die in the cause of freedom give hope to those of us who survive, hope that our nation will also rise from its current death throes."

There would be more time to grieve during the days between attacks or counter attacks. But now, James had to meet with militia leaders to plan. They would not hide and wait for the enemy to find them. The battle would be taken to the enemy to either drive them from the valley or die trying.

• Secretary of Defense Jolene Howard was preparing for a meeting with the President's Cabinet. She had received a report of the UN battle in Colorado. It was becoming a pattern, and she wasn't sure what she could do about it. Secretly, she felt delighted to hear that the local militia had fought back and dealt the UN force a crippling blow. In too many cases in other parts of the nation, it was the opposite. The resistance was poorly armed and led. UN troops had massacred American civilians.

Sitting through the Cabinet meeting, she half listened to the issues being discussed. She mechanically breezed through the report prepared for her by her staff that updated military situations around the globe and in America. She requested more supplies and equipment and also better medical care for members of the armed services who had been wounded while performing their duties.

After the meeting, Jolene waited for an opportunity to

approach the President. When he looked toward her, she smiled. "Mr. President, could I have a private word with you?"

He nodded and motioned to chairs while making his final remarks to other Cabinet members. As she waited for him to join her, she noticed how he had aged in the past year. A once handsome man, he now appeared hollow and pale. It gave him a perpetually sad look.

He dropped into the chair next to her. "What can I do for you, Jolene?"

She appreciated his air of informality but chose to address him in a formal manner. "Mr. President, I'm concerned about the reports I'm receiving regarding the actions of UN troops here in our nation. I knew it would cause a fuss if I brought up my objections in the meeting, but I need to let you know where I stand."

"What's your concern?"

"First of all, the incident in Western Colorado indicates that there is an increasing resistance by our citizens which I fear could lead to an all out civil war. This could cause great consternation by our troops overseas when they hear what's happening back home. Therefore, again I suggest that, instead of sending foreign troops here, we should bring our troops home and let the foreign troops fight the battles overseas. Doesn't that make sense?"

"Jolene, we've been over this before. In situations where internal force needs to be applied, our own troops often side with the local people and are hesitant to fire on them."

Sensing her need to respond, the President raised his hand and pursued his line of thinking. "You've got to remember, we're going through a very unpleasant time, and often we have to accept second best. Our allies have learned that it's best to have outside troops in the nation to control local populations--"

"But Americans are different. Our people are used to governing themselves or at least being able to help in making decisions about social and political policies. Using outside troops to force a new way of life on them only causes them to be more determined to fight back."

President McCleen sighed and shook his head. "Jolene, you just don't understand. The old America is dead. It no longer exists. It died along with the millions that were killed on D-Day. Like it or not, we're in a new reality, and the fact is, we're not in charge of our destiny. Those who went before us made that decision. We have to live with it and make the best of it."

"But we don't have to accept it," she retorted. "All those buried in Arlington are a witness to the fact that, with sacrifice and determination, we can fight back and reclaim what was once ours."

Again the President shook his head. "I'm sorry, but I no longer believe that." He glanced around the room. Seeing no one within earshot, he spoke in a lowered voice. "If I had known it would come to this, I would never have agreed to it. I hate myself that my name will go down in history as the President who sold out our great nation. But now it's too late to do anything about it." He shrugged. "I can only hope to preserve some freedoms and comforts for my children and grandchildren and seek God's forgiveness and mercy, not that I deserve it."

Jolene didn't know how to answer. She wanted to lash out at him, but at the same time, she felt pity for the man. She would have no support from this defeated, enslaved leader. She smiled and then felt extreme disgust, for she was falling back into the politically correct mode by uttering platitudes she inwardly hated but knew he wanted to hear. She would have to find her own ways to fight back.

Chapter Seven

Battling the UN Forces

James didn't know how long it had been since the last shots were fired. He just knew there were no other targets or threats. His ears rang from the explosions. Slowly he released his grip on the rifle, leaned back, and closed his eyes. The pain came, a burning, throbbing annoyance in his left leg. He remembered feeling it during his rush to this position when an explosion knocked his legs out from under him. There had been no time to pay attention to it. He had rolled into the ditch, brought his rifle up, and kept firing. It was kill or be killed. Rage and the fear of death blocked the abuse his body took.

As the adrenaline rush subsided, his body began to protest in earnest. Utter exhaustion joined in. He was aware of his need to pay attention to the pain, but another part of him simply wanted to shut it off. He wanted to sleep, to somehow forget it or, better yet, to wake up and find that this had all been a terrible dream.

"Oh, God!" he groaned. "Let it just be another nightmare. Rich can't be gone. First my son and, now, one of my closest brothers in Christ."

He had led Richard Hampton to Christ in Vietnam and guided his transformation from a hateful, savage killer called Mad Dog by fellow airborne troopers to a gentle, compassionate warrior for Christ. Rich hadn't wanted to take up physical arms again, but when he did, he was determined to do what had to be done to protect his family and others in the community.

This had to be a cruel joke, seeing his friend's body blown into shapeless bits of flesh and blood. Part of James wanted to pull himself out of the ditch to confirm his fears. No, I'm too tired. It was just a bad dream. I'll wake up soon.

A familiar voice registered in his conscious mind. "Sir, are you all right?"

His eyes focused on Tom Medine's face. James's response was mechanical. "I'm okay. How about you?"

"Just a couple of flesh wounds," Tom noted. With enthusiasm, he added, "We licked 'em, sir. The few survivors have retreated. Man, there for a while, I never thought we'd do it, but we did. We cleaned up real good. And a lot of it was your doing, Pastor. When you charged, I think it scared the hell out of 'em, and you gave us courage. When they ran, we cut 'em down. We sure did. I don't think they'll be coming this way for some time."

Noticing only a slight nod, Tom slid into the ditch next to James. "You sure you're okay? Looks like your leg is bleeding. Want me to take a look at it?"

James coughed before speaking. "If you would. I'm kind of zonked. I'm too old for this."

"You'd never know it by the way you fought." Tom took out a knife to slit James's pant leg and removed a first aid kit from his web belt. He wiped off blood to see where a bandage was needed.

"Here's what's causing the problem, a piece of shrapnel." He pulled it free, causing James to flinch. "That should stop the bleeding. I don't think it hit any arteries." He poured peroxide on the wound and secured a bandage to James's leg.

"Thanks."

"Have you seen Rich?" asked Tom.

James's voice broke as he pointed. "What's left of him is over by that big rock."

"Oh no! Not Rich!" Tom remained silent for a while. "Weber was also hit bad. I don't think he'll make it." Tears began coursing down his cheeks. "It's hard to believe Rich is gone. What should we do now?"

James's leadership presence returned. "Go tend to ours and their wounded. Collect their weapons and anything else we can use. If any of their vehicles are still working, load the stuff on them. We'd better fall back, and head for the ranch. They might send in aircraft to strafe us, so have the guys hurry. If we can, let's take our dead with us to give them a decent burial."

"Yes, sir. I'll have the men on it right away. We're sure going to miss Rich."

"Yes. Thanks for your help."

After Tom left, James used the scope of his rifle to scan the ambush site. He needed to be certain there were no enemy soldiers ready to pick up the fight. Seeing no indication of resistance, he crawled from the ditch and limped toward the abandoned trucks of the UN convoy. The armored personnel carrier was engulfed in flames, so he assumed any explosives or ammunition in it had already cooked off.

Other men from the ambush forces approached the vehicles, holding their weapons at ready. Whenever they approached a body, the weapons were kicked away. Then the soldier was checked to make certain he was dead.

Suddenly all the men ducked and turned their weapons toward a shout. A white rag on the end of a stick appeared, waving over a large rock. In broken English, cries resounded. "Don't shoot! Don't shoot! We surrender."

"Okay, come on out with your hands up!"

Three pairs of arms rose above the rock, followed by the UN soldiers.

James shouted, "Ask if they speak English."

One of the soldiers nodded vigorously. "Yes, I speak little."

Again James commanded, "Frisk them, and put them to work taking care of their wounded. The rest of you collect weapons and ammo. Load it on any of the vehicles fit for the road. Let's make it quick. We need to clear the area as soon as possible. They may have sent a radio message of the ambush."

As the men hurried through their duties, James made it a point to go to the body of the commander of the UN relief force who was lying in the roadside ditch. James was confident his own bullets had brought the man down. He rolled the body over and was dismayed to see the uniform of a United States army major. This was the uniform he himself had been so proud to wear during his tour in Vietnam. Now he was torn with anger and grief that he and his friends were being forced to fight against other Americans. He started to reach for the dead man's dog tags, but decided against it. It was better not to know the man's name.

James heard a truck being revved, so he reached down to unfasten the man's pistol belt. Someone could use the weapon. James slung his rifle over his shoulder, picked up the major's M-16, and walked to the pavement to wait for the truck. He became conscious of the odor of burning flesh from the personnel carrier. The smell of death was nothing new, yet it was as repulsive as ever.

As the adrenaline continued to wear off, his mind reviewed events leading up to the ambush. During the raid on his home after the destruction of over half the local UN detachment, a member of the sheriff's department tipped James off to the date that replacements were arriving from Denver. James then led a group to this canyon thirty miles east of Montrose where they spent the night and early morning preparing an ambush.

The UN force was larger and better armed than expected with two grenade launchers on Humvees and an armored personnel carrier. A shoulder-fired rocket took out the personnel carrier, but UN grenade launchers sprayed the hillsides with their deadly fire before they could be silenced.

Rich had exposed himself in order to have a better position to fire on the convoy. One or more grenades hit him when James yelled for him to get down. The shock of seeing his friend's body disintegrate was almost more than he could bear. That's when he became irrational and charged the enemy. It had been a dumb thing to do, but perhaps God used it to give the others courage to stick with the battle. One thing was now clear. The UN troops would not reach their base.

The truck stopped for James. The driver grinned as his commander climbed into the cab. "She needs a new windshield, but it's running fine. Wait 'til you see the stuff in the back. It looks like we'll have the heavy weapons we've needed to hit their headquarters. Now we can be the peacekeeping force, right?"

James nodded. The driver accelerated and drove around the burning personnel carrier. It was time to begin planning the next engagement.

•   Thirty-six hours had passed since the men who participated in the ambush had slept. They arrived at their camp near Silver Jack Lake with all the captured vehicles and materials.

Several wives and children hurried from the ranch house to greet them as they drove up. James experienced more agony when he saw Rich's wife looking over the trucks. Ann spotted James and the bloody bandage on his leg when he climbed out of his truck. She rushed to hug him.

"It's not bad. Help me walk over to Kate. You're going to have to help her."

Ann gasped and whispered, "Rich is dead?"

"Yes," he uttered in distress.

Ann helped him limp toward Rich's wife. When they got close to her, Kate began to shake her head. James couldn't hold back the tears. He held out his hands toward her and spoke with great compassion, "I'm so sorry, Kate."

She dropped to her knees, burying her face in her hands. James and Ann kneeled and placed their arms around her. The three wept together for a long time. Tom, along with several women, formed a circle around them and bowed their heads in prayer.

Finally, Kate raised her head and asked, "How did it happen?"

"The enemy had more fire power than we expected. They fought back and sprayed the hillside with grenade launchers. Rich rose from behind some rocks for a better shot. I yelled at him to get down, but one or more grenades hit him. He died instantly." James could barely finish. "The boys had to bury him there."

Her body began shaking. Tom kneeled and put an arm around her. She accepted his hug. James prayed, watching the shock settle over this strong woman who had already

lost a number of family members in other parts of the
nation.

Kate looked at Ann and then bowed her head in silent
prayer. She raised her head and with a surge of energy,
declared, "I'm sure the men are hungry. We'd better put
lunch together."

Ann offered her hand, pulling Kate to her feet. Others
hugged Kate while the group walked toward the ranch
house. Ann steered James to the porch where she made him
sit down, and there she began to take care of his wound.
Marcie brought warm water and first aid supplies. By the
time the women had his leg bandaged, James was eating
a plate of food. Other men settled on the expansive porch,
enjoying their first hot meal in a couple of days.

A dirt bike tore up to the ranch buildings. It braked to a
stop in front of James, and the rider ripped off his goggles.

"Colonel, bad news. While you guys were out on the
ambush, some local Mexicans raided three homes on Spring
Creek. They raped the women and killed old man Riley and
the Harveys' two boys. We think old lady Watson burned up
in her house. When Swanson and me came after them, they
pinned us down and then took off with a bunch of the loot in
a couple of pickups. We killed one and wounded two others. I
thought you ought to know."

James shook his head in disgust. "Are the women being
taken care of?"

"Yes, my wife and Lila Swanson have taken them home.
It ain't a pretty sight." He began to reveal more but stopped
when he realized women were listening.

One of the men on the porch swore and exclaimed, "I
think we need to go kill every damn Chicano in the valley."

Tom retorted, "Oh come on, Clint. What about Louis
here? His family is Chicano. Are you gonna shoot him after
he's fought with us?"

"Well, no, he's okay. He's part white and knows what it
means to be an American."

"Then who are you gonna shoot? What kind of name do
you think Medine is? You gonna kill me and anyone who's
just a third white or a tenth? Are you gonna include their

wives and kids?"

Clint threw his hands up. "I don't know, but we gotta do something. How are we going to know who's with us and who ain't?"

James raised his hand for their attention. "This is the problem when ethnic groups start fighting each other. Rational thinking goes out the door, and pretty soon you have a blood bath on your hands. It's been happening all around the world for a long time. Here in America, we were set up when the federal government allowed a flood of illegal immigrants to invade our nation after 9/11. It was part of the plan of the New World Order elitists. They knew our nation couldn't hold together with several different language groups who have different ethical standards. If the illegals were allowed to keep their culture and not required to become Americans, it would add to the turmoil. Now we've got to live with the problem, and it isn't going to be easy to solve. It'll probably mean that, what was once the United States of America will be a confederation of different nation states."

"But who's going to decide who takes over any given region?" asked Tom.

James shrugged. "The way it's always been settled. The groups fight it out. The winner takes all. The winner can then decide whether to drive out all those who are different, enslave them, or allow them to stay as second-class citizens. In any case, it's not going to be pretty." He exhaled deeply. "It means we aren't anywhere near the end of the bloodshed."

Everyone was quiet. Luis, an older Chicano, broke the silence. "I'm old enough to know what made America great. Regardless of your race, religion, or education, if you wanted to be an American, it meant speaking English and living by the law, law that applied to everyone. My forefathers came to this country without any money in their pockets. They were willing to work at jobs others didn't want. They worked hard, learned the language, and sent their kids to school so they could acquire an education and melt into society. Some of the old people went back and forth to Mexico, but the next generation didn't want anything to do with the old country. It couldn't compare with what we found here in America.

"The problem with the flood of illegals who came into our country during the last decade or so is that they weren't required to learn the language. The government took care of them whether they worked or not. They were encouraged to hate everyone who was already here and established. They're stupid but deceived, so it isn't all their fault, not that I agree with what they're doing. They're simply doing what they did before they came because they never had any good laws. As the colonel knows, they didn't have true Christianity. That's the real issue."

James responded, "You are absolutely right, Luis. But I don't know if, in the midst of all the turmoil, we'll be able to reach them with the message of the Lord Jesus. I'm afraid many will have to die before others wake up. I'm open to extend the hand of peace and fellowship to anyone. But I'm not about to lie down and let anyone take what our forefathers gave us. I've put my life on the line several times to preserve America. While we can no longer save the entire nation, I'm not about to give up trying to preserve a portion of it for the high ideals found in the Bible and the original Constitution."

The others murmured in agreement. James persisted, "What we're going to have to do is require every man to swear an oath to the Constitution of the United States of America as the law of the land."

Tom spoke enthusiastically, "Right, Pastor, and they'll have to place their right hands on the Bible."

A look of concern showed on James's face. "I'm not sure we can do that, at least not if it's an indication of a forced conversion. But, on the other hand, whether they are professing Christians or not, if by placing their hands on the Bible, they are agreeing that the Christian faith is the basis for our social order and they agree to live in peace with this philosophy, then that would be okay."

Tom nodded. "We've allowed people of other faiths to live in peace in our midst, but the laws of the land have always originated from the Bible. That's basic to Christianity. If people refuse to support these concepts, they'll have to move out of the country. They can't stay here and fight what the majority agrees on."

The rest of the men showed their approval by nodding their heads.

James asked, "All well and good, but how do we fight off the UN troops and clean up our own backyard at the same time?"

"We'll do what you've taught us," answered Tom. "Take one step at a time. Let's give the UN commander an ultimatum to leave while he can or else we'll use their own weapons to take him out."

"Okay, you have a crew trained on the TOW anti-tank missiles, and find someone who knows how to use the mortars we captured. Ask Juan to see if we can raise the commander on one of their radios. His wounded troops should have arrived by this time. I'll take the radio up on the high ground and see if I can talk some sense into his head."

The men returned to their meal. The biker was led into the house to be given food.

• Sam Kirkland and his three houseguests survived the radiation fallout with few negative physical effects. It had been a struggle to keep body and soul together during the long months. On this particular evening, they were celebrating their first meal with meat in a long time. Sam had traded a gun on the black market for a lamb, olive oil, fresh onions, and assorted greens. Since electricity had been restored, they were roasting the lamb in the oven. Sam brought everyone up to date about their plans while they waited for their dinner to finish cooking.

"When I was in the market, I spoke briefly to Masha. He assured me the two Cessna 182s we purchased before D-Day are still in the hangers. He and the other pilot are ready whenever we give the word and provide the biological agents."

Calieb inquired, "Has he heard any more news from the team with the suitcase weapon?"

Sam shook his head. "They were killed in the early rioting, and the weapon was destroyed when their apartment complex burned. There were efforts to bring more weapons in, but we have no way of knowing if they did and where those weapons are. So we've altered our plans to make sure we strike the leaders in New York and Washington, D.C. Masha and I agreed on the change after I told him the good news."

He smiled and looked around the room from man to man, which seemed to take forever. The others suddenly lost their interest in food.

Calieb, irritated at having to wait, asked, "What good news?"

Sam laughed and gestured with his hands for patience, allowing the suspense to build.

"Well, come on," urged Calieb, "what have you heard? Tell us."

Sam reached into his shirt pocket and pulled out a folded piece of paper. It was a computer printout. He straightened it and held it up for everyone to see. "The year of silence has been broken. Our overseas backers sent this through a courier who gave it to me in the marketplace just this morning. Next week there is going to be a meeting of world leaders in Europe. It will be held at the same time of a UN meeting in New York and a special meeting of the U.S. Congress in Washington, D.C. We have been given the privilege of bringing vengeance against the leaders of the UN and Washington."

The men jumped up laughing, almost out of control. They gave each other high fives and shouted praises to Allah. After a considerable amount of backslapping, Calieb asked the question in all their minds, "But how? Without the nuclear weapon, how can we be sure we will take out the leaders?"

Sam motioned for the men to be seated. "We have used our time well to produce additional biological agents and prepare the two vans in the garage for disbursing the toxins. The plan remains for one van to circle the New York City area. If you can get past roadblocks, head for Boston. The other van will go south to Washington where it will drive around the beltway. With electrical power on in the major cities and the increase in fuel being made available, there will be more vehicles on the road. The van will spread viruses and bacterial agents all along the way. These will drift with the wind and be breathed by anyone downwind. Once these people are infected, they in turn will infect others as the various diseases develop. Am I right, Calieb?"

Calieb, the chief biologist, was responsible for bringing in the cultures and multiplying them. He answered, "But these are general viruses that drift with the wind. How can we be certain we will hit the most important targets?"

"Remember, we are not the only ones spreading the biological agents. Masha's team plans to use the airplanes to drop vials of toxic agents in lakes and rivers to infect water supplies for the target cities. By flying low, they will stay off the military radar. The planes are also equipped similarly to the vans so that, as they fly upwind from the cities, they will disperse deadly germs into the air to settle over the cities, especially over the Capitol and the UN building. Their final mission will be to move in as close to their target building as possible where the leaders will be gathered.

"If they are shot down near the buildings, the explosion will scatter the toxins. If they are able to crash into the Capitol or the UN building, it's doubtful the authorities will suspect biological agents because they will be thinking of explosives. By the time they figure out what the real purpose of the attack has been, it will be too late. The toxins will be drifting into all the surrounding areas. If one agent in our soup does not reach them, another one will."

The men exchanged glances and smiled enthusiastically to show their satisfaction.

Sam resumed, "We have become angry and frustrated, hearing the news on shortwave radio of how the Russians have taken over where the Americans left off oppressing our people. But remember, it was the Americans who were the first to corrupt us. They enabled the Russians to rise to power. Allah has rewarded our patience. Now we will strike and take revenge on our enemies in a way that will shock

them and bring great rejoicing to our oppressed peoples. So
let us celebrate with this meal, renewing our pledge to give
our lives for the glory of Allah."

Again the men jumped to their feet with a great deal of
exuberance. They began to sing in their native tongues and
danced, congratulating each other for their good fortune.
The fact that it had been the generosity of Americans that
enabled them to survive after the holocaust had not changed
their desire for revenge.

•   Juan Juarez drove James to the top of Cimarron Ridge
where they looked down into the Montrose valley. The sun
was just setting so the view was incredibly beautiful. Juan
turned the radio on to call the UN commander. He spoke
in both Spanish and English. After several attempts, an
operator acknowledged his call in English and asked him
to wait. James admired the red clouds in the west as he
waited.

The radio broke the stillness. "This is Commander
Wiles."

"Colonel Parr here. I assume your reinforcements have
arrived. We did what we could for your wounded."

"Yes, they are here. You have made a grave mistake. I've
spoken with my high command. They're threatening to nuke
this whole damn valley if you don't immediately surrender
the weapons you took and turn yourself in for disciplinary
action. This is no idle threat."

"Oh, so this is how they want to bring peace and
prosperity to our nation. Accept their brand of slavery or
be nuked. I thought the nukes were to be used against
America's enemies, not our own people. But then again,
since they allowed the Russians and Chinese to nuke us, I
suppose they wouldn't mind killing off more thousands. Are
they going to allow you to leave before they nuke us?"

There was a long pause before Wiles answered. "I'm
ordered to give you twenty four hours to bring in your arms
and turn yourself in."

"All right, I'm going to give you the same amount of time
to agree to leave, or we take you out. By the way, have you

caught and punished the Mexicans who raided the homes at Spring Creek?"

"That is none of your concern."

"Oh but it is. Your lack of action shows me you are one big bluff. You're not doing your job. Neither is the sheriff. You might pass this on to him that we're not pleased with his inability to protect our women and children."

"He's not obligated to protect criminals."

"Good night, Commander. Remember, twenty-four hours or you and your men are fair game. By now, you ought to be figuring it out that we're pretty good hunters."

James motioned for Juan to throw the switch. "Let's hurry back to the ranch."

•   Feeling a great heaviness, James gave the squad leaders the news. It brought mixed reactions.

Tom spoke first. "Do you think they'd use a small nuke on us?"

James shrugged. "I'm not sure they have any nukes or even if they have a way to deliver them. They agreed with the Russians and Chinese not to use nukes anymore. If the word gets out that they are nuking our own people, it would really stir up the Rednecks. But if that's the only choice we have, we might as well go out in a flash. I'd rather do that than live under the kind of freedom they're proposing."

The other men agreed.

James noted, "General Leland and I talked about this possibility. He told me nuclear devises aren't effective in the mountains. Besides, with a westerly wind, they'd lose more people from fallout than they'd kill here. It sure wouldn't make them look like peace loving leaders. But two can play the game. I'll go back up on the hill in the morning and talk to the commander again. I'll make a counter offer and tell him we found some nasty biological stuff the Chinese brought in. We don't know how bad it is, but they sure as hell had it protected. The diagrams on how to use it are pretty simple."

Tom looked startled. "I haven't heard of that before. Is it safe to have around?"

James laughed. "I hadn't heard about it before either, but they won't know that, will they?"

Tom breathed a sigh of relief. "You had me worried for a minute."

"I hope we don't get General Leland in trouble for the hell we're raising here. He needs the big boys believing he's working with them. However, he thinks Southern California is a lost cause. By the way, it looks like the Chinese are going to be satisfied with controlling the Asian Rim. Even if they decide to pull out, it won't be worth trying to control the battle between the American Orientals and the Hispanics. The general believes the only peaceful solution is to give most of Northern California to the Orientals and Whites, the Northwest to the Whites, and Southern California and part of Arizona to the Mexicans. Then he's planning to come back here and throw the UN out of the mountains as far as the Mississippi.

"So, Tom, spend tomorrow training on the heavy weapons. Plan on moving out for Montrose after dark. You've got to take out their tank and helicopter and be ready to reduce the terminal to rubble. Mike, you take your snipers in small groups and infiltrate around the airport.

Harry, your men will provide protection for Tom and Mike's teams and be prepared to mop up. You guys put your heads together. Work up your plans on a map so we all know who's doing what. I don't expect the commander to respond to reason. But I do expect Sheriff Black to see the light and get his men on duty out of town until the attack is over."

As James was finishing, a young boy hurried from the house and handed him a piece of paper. The men watched as he read it.

He looked up, explaining, "You'll be interested in this. It's a message from General Leland. Our forces have driven the Chinese and Mexican forces out of Arizona. But California is a big mess. Everyone is fighting everybody else of a different culture or nationality. He's about ready to pull his forces back and let the different groups fight it out, including the Chinese force that's there. He doesn't think they'll be able to muster up a threat to the rest of the country. Plus, he's proud of how we took on the UN force. He's getting ready to turn his forces against the UN and drive them out of the Western half of the U.S."

The men shouted with a great fervor. James waited for them to quiet before going on. "The news from around the nation remains grim. There are reports of many ethnic fights, especially in the big cities where UN peacekeepers are siding with the largest group of the area. So much for their peacekeeping role."

The men groaned. James sensed their deep hatred for the peacekeepers.

"But, the general has also sent word that electrical power is being restored to major parts of the country, especially to the remaining refineries. This will help us get back to a more normal lifestyle. So it's not all bad news. He again compliments us for our efforts." James put the paper down and looked from man to man. "I don't think there's any doubt he'll be behind what we're going to do. So let's make sure we do it right and set an example for others around the nation. Let's close with prayer."

•   As James had expected, Commander Wiles refused to respond to reason when he contacted him the next day. Wiles had his orders and continued to threaten with the most serious retaliation by UN forces. James could tell by the tone of the commander's voice that he believed the report on captured biological weapons. If he believed it, so would the men in the higher chain of command. James reissued his conditions and threatened an eminent attack. He was confident the commander believed him.

After returning to the ranch, he decided to hold the attack off for another twenty-four hours. Instead, he sent Mike and two sniper teams to harass the UN troops throughout the night. He'd have two other teams do the same throughout the following day so none of the enemy troops would be able to sleep. Tom felt pleased to have another day to train his crew on the TOW missile and mortars.

Kate and her friend Barbara agreed to go into town to

pass the word among faithful members of the underground who would be ready to support the attack and pick up helpful, last minute information. By late afternoon, they learned that two squads of UN troops had arrived from Grand Junction. They also heard that one of the sniper teams had put an attack helicopter out of commission with a well placed 50-caliber round. This was one less factor to worry about.

By midnight, all the forces had bypassed the lightly manned roadblocks. They gathered in positions around the airport where the UN troops had retreated. The M1 Abrams tank had been positioned in the empty parking lot in the front of the terminal. Tom set up the TOW anti-tank missile launcher less than three hundred yards away, behind a board fence. When ready to launch, all they'd have to do was remove one wide board. A side shot at the tank would then be available.

Half a mile away near the north end of the runway, the mortar crew set up in the parking lot of an abandoned warehouse. Using a laser beam, they measured the exact distance to the terminal. Their first rounds would be close, if not right on target. The first targets were the sandbag, machine gun nests on the four corners of the terminal building. A contest would ensue between the mortar crew and the snipers as to who could take their enemies out first. One of the Humvees with a mounted grenade launcher was to be driven up as soon the battle engaged to spray the terminal building and the nearby hanger used by the UN troops as a barracks. Through their night scopes, the attackers watched as the UN troops fought sleep.

At 3:30 a.m., the TOW missile was launched, followed immediately by a dozen rifles that dropped a dozen or more UN soldiers. On their journey to hell, the tank crew joined them. Within seconds, the mortar shells began to land from the two tubes. By the time four mortar shells hit near the terminal, the Humvee's grenade launcher was taking out what was left of the machine gun crews and punching holes in the terminal building. When men scurried from the makeshift barracks, the grenade launcher shifted its aim to them and their barracks. The grenades went through the thin metal walls before exploding and creating mass carnage among those still putting on their battle gear.

Within five minutes, James passed the word by radio and cell phones, "Cease fire!"

There was no longer any resistance from the United Nations forces. An eerie silence fell over the area except for the rounds still popping off on the machine gun on top the burning tank. Those close to the terminal heard the cries of the wounded.

James raised a megaphone to his mouth. "We will accept your surrender. You are beaten. If Commander Wiles is alive, I'm willing to talk terms."

He handed the megaphone to Juan who repeated the offer in Spanish.

The area rocked from an explosion in the tank that blew the gun mount off and threw it more than twenty feet from the body of the vehicle. Flames shot high into the air, lighting the entire area. Those in the vicinity of the blast felt the shockwave. Windows in nearby buildings shattered.

James's voice boomed. "Put down your weapons! Help your wounded move away from the fires, and come out with your hands up! You will be treated well and allowed to leave the area."

Juan repeated the order in Spanish. They were amazed at the large number who survived the onslaught. The battle was over. The only casualty among the attackers occurred when a stray bullet from one of their own machine guns hit a rifleman in his leg. UN troops were less fortunate. Many would never return to their homelands.

•   Burt Wilson looked out the window of his home and saw his friend. He raised the window, whistled to get Ralph's attention, and motioned for him to come inside. He had a cup of tea waiting by the time Ralph had walked around the house to the kitchen door.

Burt handed Ralph the tea and said, "Have a seat. I've got some hot news."

Ralph yawned wearily.

"First, how are things going at the plant?" asked Burt.

"Well, if we could obtain the extra parts needed, we'd be able to turn out plenty of the fix-it kits and have more vehicles up and running. The engineers have figured out how to bypass what the EMP burned out. But with fuel still being rationed, I don't know how much demand there'll be for our kits. Okay, what's the big news?"

Burt winked and unconsciously glanced around as if he expected someone to be listening. "I just talked to my contact in Western Colorado. The local militia there not only wiped out the UN's relief force, but last night they attacked the UN headquarters and hit them hard. He said he's got it on good authority that the Army of the West is leaving California and will push the UN out of all the Western states."

Ralph perked up, exclaiming, "Wow, I wish we had that kind of organization and leadership here!"

"I'm no military leader, but if anyone calls for volunteers, I'm going to respond. Ever since they rounded up my boy and sent him off to a work camp, I've known those skunks weren't here for our good."

"Yes, but what are you going to fight with? They collected all our guns."

Burt grinned. "No, they didn't. I did what a Vietnam vet friend suggested. I gave them an old 22 and a single barrel shotgun. I hid a pump 12-gage and a 38-caliber revolver with plenty of ammo. Darned if I'm going be defenseless with all the lawless gangs around."

Ralph raised his finger as if to scold him. "But if you use them, they'll figure out you've got guns. Then they'll throw you in a prison work camp."

"Fine. I will have saved myself and other folks here in the community at least for the time being. I just might shoot the UN troops when they come to investigate. Since Gloria died, I'm to the point where I'm ready to go. But with God as my witness, I'll take a few of them with me."

Ralph shook his head. "I don't know. You've told me the Rednecks in the South are fighting back against the UN occupiers, but I think the old politicians and criminal elements in Chicago are working hand in hand with them. I don't see much hope for us here."

Now it was Burt's turn to point a finger in his friend's face. "Listen, we aren't beat yet. I'll bet there are plenty of hunters up in Wisconsin that didn't turn in all their guns. In fact, the impression I had is that there are lots of people who think it's time we kick the traitors out who betrayed us and work at being what America always was, a free people."

"I'm all for it. But since things are beginning to return to some semblance of normality, I'd hate to end up in more fighting and turmoil. It's hard enough trying to get any business going as it is. God is going to have to do something about the leadership in Washington. There isn't a lot we can do at this point."

Chapter Eight

Hope for the Future

After the United Nation's troops left the valley and
Sheriff Black resumed his responsibilities, James and Ann
moved back to their farmstead. A neighbor had previously
taken their animals to care for them. The emergency
supplies that James had not been able to take to the
mountain cabin were confiscated by UN troops. With the
help of church members, they set up living quarters in the
barn. Marcie moved into a neighbor's house to help take care
of orphaned children.

Russ returned to his home with his family and asked
Sarah and her children to move in with them. Young Chuck
volunteered to stay with his grandparents to care for the
goats and chickens, which the neighbors had returned. The
other grandchildren helped plant a garden.

One day as James sat reading his Bible, Rebecca, his
oldest granddaughter, burst into his study out of breath. Her
faced was stained with tears. "Grandpa, you've got to come!
Daddy just got word that Caleb's been wounded. We're all
scared."

James hugged her. "Did the message say what was
wrong?"

"Yes, he's lost an arm and has other injuries. That's all
we know."

"Honey, let's pray right now."

"Sure, Grandpa."

James raised his face toward heaven. "Lord Jesus
Christ, we've committed Caleb into Your hands. Therefore,
we continue to trust Your mercy and love. Give those who
are ministering to him wisdom. Provide whatever medical
supplies they need to ward off infections and do what they
can to bring healing to his body. May his body respond to

Your mercy so we can receive him back into our fellowship. Comfort all those who love him as we continue to place him in Your loving hands. Amen."

"Thanks, Grandpa."

"Okay, let's go talk to your parents and see if we can get more details. If need be, I'll pull strings through General Leland's office."

•   Caleb returned after two agonizing months. General Leland sent an aged C-130 transport plane to make several stops in Utah and along the Western Slope to drop off men whose injuries had not allowed them to stay on active duty. The plane also picked up mail, items of clothing, bandages, and other items for troops still fighting in California. James and Russ had a team of horses and a rubber tired wagon at the airport to pick up Caleb and two other men they would drop off on their way home.

The plane only stopped long enough to discharge the men and accept a limited number of boxes and bags that were quickly loaded on board. Fuel was scarce, so within minutes the plane taxied away. Russ and James met Caleb with hugs. Caleb wore a long sleeved shirt; the left sleeve was pinned to his shoulder. There were two men on crutches, each, missing part of one leg. James and Russ grabbed their personal bags, carrying them to the wagon where a guard stood holding the nervous team of horses.

Caleb stared for a moment at the wreckage of the terminal and the hangers nearby. "It looks like you guys had to do some heavy persuading to move the UN out of here."

James responded, "Yes, it ruined a fine terminal building. But we don't have much use for it any more. For the time being, we keep guards here round the clock just in case they try to come back."

Caleb nodded. James put his arm around his grandson's waist to help him toward the wagon. "There's a bunch of people waiting at home to give you a big welcome. With our current mode of transportation, it's going to be late by the time we arrive."

The conversation was light on the way through town and

on out into the country. The detour to drop off the other two men took an extra hour. There was a great deal of weeping and giving thanks as their families and friends greeted the soldiers.

The wagon crossed the river and made its way around the burned out tank still blocking the road to the Parr farm. The cousins had come down the lane to welcome the returning hero. After many hugs, Caleb elected to walk the rest of the way. He joked with the siblings he hadn't seen for well over a year. They all wanted to talk at the same time. James and Russ rode on ahead to give them time to catch up with each other.

Hannah walked out to meet James and Russ. "Is he all right?" she asked.

Russ jumped off the wagon and kissed her. "He's doing fine. The kids are all talking at once. Let's go meet him. Dad can take the horses on to the barn."

When they were within a hundred feet of their children, Hannah ran to Caleb. He grabbed her with his good arm and swung her around before allowing her to rain kisses on his face. Everyone formed a circle and joined the hugging.

Finally Hannah pulled away. "We have a feast waiting, and your grandma is anxious to see you, too."

They proceeded to the porch where Ann and Sarah waited. Caleb embraced his grandmother in a long, tender hug and thanked her for her prayers. Then he turned to Sarah. "I was sorry to hear about Uncle Henry." They too embraced.

It was almost dark by time the whole family gathered at the table heaped with fried chicken, roast beef, and an assortment of dishes filled with foods Caleb had not seen in months.

James led them in a prayer of thanksgiving to God for having spared Caleb's life and bringing him home. He also prayed for General Leland and the troops still fighting on the West Coast. When he said, "Amen," Hannah took a plate and led Caleb around the table, filling the plate while the children followed. There was great joy in the Parr home that night. A heavy burden had been lifted.

The next morning as James fixed a hole in the fence of the goat pen, Caleb walked up the lane toward him. James tightened a couple of wires before putting his tools down. His grandson wore blue jeans and a short-sleeved shirt, revealing the stub of his arm that ended just above his left elbow. James couldn't help but notice how much older Caleb looked as he greeted him.

"Did you sleep well last night?"

"Not really. I ate too much. It was all so good."

"I remember when I came home from the Korean War. I had Mom fry a dozen eggs for breakfast. I ate them all, along with toast and bacon. It was so good to be home!"

Caleb looked at the burned remains of his grandfather's house and the bullet holes in the trees and buildings. "This is where Uncle Henry died?" he asked.

James nodded.

"Could we take a walk?" asked Caleb.

"Sure, I think I've foiled those pesky escape artists for the time being."

The men walked down the lane and up a wooded hill until they came to a large rock where the family had created a rough picnic area. James often came here to pray over the valley that stretched out to the north and south. He waited, keenly aware that this was not the teen he'd known before. They stood looking out over the valley. Finally Caleb sat down on the large rock, lowered his head in his one good hand, and began to cry. James sat next to him, placing his arm around his shoulder. Deep sobs shook Caleb's body. James prayed silently and continued to wait.

Between the deep breaths and sobs, Caleb spoke falteringly, "Grandpa, I wanted to talk to you because I know you will understand. I love Dad, but I don't think he could feel the pain." He looked at his grandfather who nodded and squeezed his shoulder.

Caleb looked across the valley. "At first, it was scary but exciting. I felt we were doing what had to be done to protect those we loved and the country we believed in, at least what was left of it. I prayed a lot like you taught me. I know it was only by God's grace that we got out of situations where we should have been killed. We were so outnumbered and outgunned at times. Then when we stopped the Chinese at Silverton, it felt so good. I couldn't believe it when I was given a commission and put in charge of one of the scout platoons.

"It made me want to prove myself. I had guys under my command that had lost their entire families on D-Day. They had nothing to go home to so they wanted revenge and were willing to risk it all because they didn't care if they lived or died. They just wanted to take as many with them as they could. So we took risks, and we didn't take prisoners unless we needed to gather intelligence. The more we saw what the 'Chinks' did to our people and also what the Mexicans did who were fighting with them, the more determined we were to drive them out of the country. I have nightmares remembering some of the carnage we saw."

He wiped his eyes to brush away the tears but also to try to end the memories. "What they did to the women and even children was barbaric. Why do men do that?" He looked intently at his grandfather.

"When law and order breaks down, men without God revert to something that is subhuman, demonic. It's happened throughout history. It's a shock to us because, for the most part, Americans had risen above that. At least, we haven't been exposed to it. We've been a blessed nation."

Caleb looked into his grandfather's eyes with a painful expression. "Grandpa, I can understand doing what you have to in order to defeat other soldiers. But to torture and do what they did to women and children doesn't make sense."

James rubbed his grandson's shoulder and waited.

Caleb continued after a long time, "We killed so many, we lost count. Then one day we were about to spring an ambush on a small Chinese patrol when they stopped, formed a circle, took out books, and began to sing and lift their hands in prayer." His voice broke as more tears fell. Again James waited.

"A couple of the men stood separately, not taking part. At first I thought they were standing guard, but after awhile, two of the men in the circle got up and went and spoke to them, obviously urging them to join in. After some persuasion, they did, and the others gathered around them. After more prayer, the two must have given their lives to the Lord because the others shook their hands and embraced them. They sat down in a circle again, got out some bread and a cup, and celebrated the Lord's Supper."

He looked into James's eyes. His sentences were emotional bursts. "Grandpa, I wasn't more than a couple hundred feet from them. I could feel the presence of God. It took all my will power not to join them. By this time, I wasn't doing much praying. It didn't seem to fit with the killing we were doing. Half of the guys in my group were not Christians. Some were bitter at God for what had happened. I tried to talk to them and urged them to not be angry with God. But we were constantly on the move, so this was a new experience for me. As the enemy troops got up to leave, out of the corner of my eye I could see one of my guys ready to blast them. He was waiting for my orders, so I was able to stop him. We let them go. Some of my men were ticked."

James patted his shoulder. "You did the right thing."

"Yes, but a few days later, we ambushed a retreating column of troops. We had claymores set up and a cross fire of machine guns. They never had a chance. When we moved in to finish off survivors and salvage gear we needed, I came across the same squad of men. One of their Bibles had been riddled with bullets. One man was still alive. He was trying to pull something from his pocket. I kneeled and helped him. It was his Bible. He kissed it and looked into my eyes. Then he smiled and tried to give me the Bible as he kept repeating, "Jesus, Jesus." He died with a smile on his face."

Caleb struggled to go on. "Something in me snapped. All the killing, the destruction, I couldn't take it anymore." His chest heaved with sobs.

James's strong presence affirmed Caleb.

"My first sergeant was an older veteran. He saw what was happening to me. He pulled the outfit together and took us to an abandoned resort. We were all exhausted. So we forgot the war for a few days. The men found a stash of booze. They got me drunk for the first time in my life, but it didn't help.

"A couple of days later, a company sized Mexican group stumbled on us. We reacted out of instinct. They must have been mostly greenhorns because we slaughtered them. That's when I got hit. One round was a big one. It practically tore my arm off. If I'd been able to get to a good hospital, they probably could have saved it, but our medic knew he couldn't. So to lower the chance of infection, he had to take it off. I also picked up some shrapnel in my leg. Some of it's still there. A doctor said it might work its way out."

"That's what they told me in Vietnam, but it used to set off alarms at the airports. I practically had to strip naked to prove what it was."

Caleb looked into his grandfather's eyes again and gripped his arm. "Grandpa, I want to apologize for the way Dad and some of us complained when you tried to warn the country that all this hell would happen if Christians didn't repent. We didn't understand. Now I do. I can appreciate the hell you went through in Vietnam and how you didn't want it to happen here. I'm really sorry."

"It's okay. I regret that you had to learn it the hard way."

"Does the pain ever go away?"

"No, not completely. But what you're going to have to decide is, are you going to let it bring you closer to God, or will you let the devil use it to torment you until life becomes a living hell? This is where I can help you make the right decision."

"I've been hoping you would. But what do I do now?" He dropped his head. "I'm a cripple."

James hugged him. "No you're not. You've lost an arm, and your emotions are shot to hell. But lots of people with two arms don't use them for anything meaningful. Like the physical body, emotions heal. I guess you didn't lose your manhood, right?"

"No." Caleb looked puzzled.

"Well then, one of the first things you need to do is marry and raise a half dozen disciples of Jesus. The first commandment in the Bible is for man to multiply."

"Who'll have me?"

James answered with a chuckle in his voice, "Oh, you might be surprised. Remember Rich and Kate's daughter, Anna Lee?"

"Yes, she was a skinny teen the last time I saw her. She was cute, but--

"She's all grown up now and filled out in places that catches a man's eyes. She reminds me of your grandmother when I first met her. Anna Lee has been eyeing you since you first came home in uniform, and she always asks about you. If you'll give her half a chance, she'll fuss over you as only a woman can that loves you. There's nothing like the love of God and the love of a good woman to help you heal the scars you're bearing."

James saw a flicker of hope in Caleb's eyes. "You remember that King David was a man of war. He killed his share of men. But the Bible also says he was a man after God's own heart. So having been a killing machine does not disqualify you from becoming a man of God. There's no limit to God's mercy or His forgiveness.

"Now don't get me wrong. I know it's not going to be easy. You'll have nightmares. Oh God, how you'll have nightmares now and then for the rest of your life! And there's no guarantee we won't have to shed more blood to keep our freedom. What was once America is no more and probably never will be. The way we'll go as a political unit is still up for grabs. But as I keep telling the people here, life goes on. Couples will fall in love. Babies will be born. Old people will die. So we've got to take it a day at a time."

James watched Caleb reflect on his comments. The older man went on, "It's easy in times like these to only see the problems. We have to work at being thankful. As uncertain and difficult as life is, it's still good. As long as we have life, there's hope."

Caleb nodded in agreement, clearing his nose and drying his eyes.

James encouraged him, "You may not want to do this right away, but the reality is that we need men with your experience to train the young men coming to fighting age

here in the valley. For the foreseeable future, we're all
citizen soldiers, like it or not. I never go anywhere without
my side arm. When I leave the place, I take my rifle. We're
at war. So the challenge to all of us is how do we rebuild
our part of the world? How do we begin to set up trade and
eliminate the nuts that think this is an opportunity for them
to become little dictators? I don't think you're going to be
unable to find work. The only downside is that for some time
in the future, your pay will be mostly in barter items."

"But, Grandpa, how are we going to rebuild? We're
practically back to horse and buggy days. In some parts of
the country, it's chaos with virtually no law and order."

"Yes, we've lost a lot. But some of us have been talking
about it. Again, we can look at what we've lost and don't
have, or we can look at the possibilities. The breakdown
of federal and state authority has some benefits especially
in areas like this where we've got a hand on general
social order. One is that we're free to invent and try new
things without politicians or powerful, rich people being
threatened.

"Remember how we used to talk about the free energy
machines that were suppressed? Well, a few of the guys
have been working in their shops using parts from old cars
and electrical transformers and have come up with some
pretty exciting ways of generating electrical power. We're
praying that God is going to show us how to enable every
home, business, and farm to be energy independent. Plus,
others are learning how to work stills to make a grade of
alcohol that can serve as gasoline and turn plant oils into
diesel fuel. A company in town is experimenting with ways
to produce inexpensive hydrogen. Necessity is the mother of
invention."

They sat lost in thought.

Finally, James continued, "I'm still the military
commander in this area, so you rightfully fall under my
jurisdiction. Captain, I'm in need of an assistant who can
help me care for the widows and the families of the men who
died in service to their country. I'm giving you a direct order
to report to my office after lunch. Be prepared to make a call

on a certain widow and her daughter who live within easy riding distance."

Caleb smiled. "Yes, sir, Colonel. It will be my pleasure to serve under your command."

"By the way, do you have a Class A uniform?"

"Yes, sir. General Leland even gave me some medals."

"Wear it and the medals." James smiled and winked. "It'll make a good first impression."

Ann would be pleased to see her crusty old husband play cupid.

•   Wisps of smoke trailed from the left inboard engine of an old Hercules transport as it settled on the Montrose runway. James and an assortment of people from the valley stood near the ruins of the airport terminal waiting for the plane to taxi toward them.

While the turbines wound down, the ramp lowered and a steady stream of men in various kinds of uniforms began to depart the plane. Some were on crutches. Others were carried on stretchers. In one case, men with only one arm helped with a stretcher. The wounded from the Army of the West were the first to return home.

James stood with a somber appearance as he watched neighbors and friends rush to meet the soldiers. Mothers, wives, and children embraced their loved ones. Other men relieved those carrying stretchers. A few remained with James. They wore faces of stone. Others wept because their loved ones had not returned. They were there to support their neighbors.

General Mark Leland was one of the last to descend from the plane. Across the tarmac, he caught the eye of James who straightened and touched his hand to his forehead. Mark returned the salute before stepping off the ramp to make his way through the crowd. Many went out of their way to greet him.

James met the general and shook the hand of his friend. A firm embrace followed. "Welcome home, Mark."

Mark looked at the crowd helping the wounded move toward waiting wagons and a few pickups that had been returned to service. "Not exactly a victory procession. It's one hell of a way to end a campaign."

James took his arm and directed him toward Russ's pickup that was running on homemade diesel. "Don't be too hard on yourself. At least this phase is ended, and you brought some of the boys home. It could have been a lot worse."

He noted tears in the eyes of his old friend.

James asked, "With that smoking engine, can I assume you'll be staying longer than you had planned?"

"Yes, I talked to the crew chief after we landed. He said he'd have to wait for things to cool down before he could determine the extent of the problems. If need be, we can fly on into Colorado Springs on three engines. We're used to taking risks to get by."

"Good. Then we'll have time to talk some things over. Let's go down to the old truck stop restaurant. The cook there has come up with a reasonable substitute for coffee."

After greeting others who had stopped for a snack, James and Mark settled in a booth in a private corner. Mark sipped at his cup before giving a long sigh. "I guess you're waiting for an assessment of the situation."

"Yes," said James, nodding his head.

The general relaxed his large frame against the back of the booth and let out a breath in resignation. "Foster and I decided that the best thing we could do was pull our troops out and let the factions in California fight it out. With the irrigation and water systems damaged and the fighting keeping fuel supplies from getting to the farmers, there's little hope of any rebuilding until the fight has gone out of all the contending parties. In the meantime, there's no use our boys dying while trying to keep an impossible peace.

"With your forces here kicking the UN out, we'll bring the units we have left to clean them out of the Western states. We're in contact with another major organized resistance in the South that's doing the same thing there. I've asked for a meeting with Jolene Howard to see if we can negotiate some kind of agreement with the rats in D.C."

"Humph! Good luck!"

Mark gestured, implying that it was the best he could do.

James raised his hands in frustration. "Nah, I don't mean what I just said. Luck has nothing to do with it. This is what I've wanted to talk to you about. First, I agree with your decisions. But I want to lay a challenge on you, or at least talk out what I've been wrestling with."

Mark leaned forward and sipped his drink. "Fire away."

"I hate to admit it but losing my son, Henry, and then Rich, one of my closest brothers in the Lord, has shaken my faith like nothing else."

He couldn't speak for several moments. Wiping tears from his eyes, he shared, "I came across a couple of verses in Psalms 44 that stopped me dead in my tracks. David wrote, 'Through You, Lord, we will push down our enemies; through Your name we will trample those who rise up against us. I will not trust in my bow, nor shall my sword save me.'

"Brother, I know there's a place for using weapons to resist and put down evil. I know there's a balance between spiritual and physical warfare. I hate to admit it, but it seems we're too quick to use our physical weapons and not willing to pay the price of fasting and praying. We don't have the guts to wait on the Lord and radically trust Him."

Mark answered, with a look of impatience, "But, brother, we've been praying. I've prayed more in the last year than all the rest of my life. I believe God answered our prayers. It's the only reason we're sitting here with some degree of freedom."

"Yes, I acknowledge that. I'm not criticizing you or condemning anyone. Maybe I just need to tell you what I've been doing. God used that Scripture passage to drive me deeper into prayer and spending time with Him. I've gathered a small group of others who feel called to intercession. Most are widows who have lost everything and have nothing but the Lord Jesus to lean on.

"Ann and I have been meeting with them. We've literally been crying out to God day and night. We're finally doing in a much deeper way what you and I were calling Christians to do before D-Day. What's encouraging is that God is raising up other groups like ours in different parts of the nation."

Mark nodded and asked, "Are you suggesting that this is something I should do instead of guiding the physical warfare?"

"No, no. I just want you to know about my struggles. Well no, it's more than that. As your spiritual leader, I'm confessing my sin, my failures of the past. I thought I knew what prayer was. I thought I was doing all God required, but now He's taking me a lot deeper. Does this make sense?"

Mark nodded. "Yes, you're letting me know that it's taken tragedy to draw you into a deeper relationship with God. I can identify with that. Those of us whose business is to kill and destroy the enemy are caught in a dilemma. The horror of what we do conflicts with the love of doing it. As we grow older and more mature, we not only come to hate it, but we end up hating ourselves for doing what we do. Yet I despise the alternatives worse. That's the only thing that keeps me going. I want my grandchildren to live in freedom, and if this is the price I've got to pay to achieve that, then so be it."

Sergeant Ball interrupted the men. "Sir, the crew will have the plane ready by the time we return. There's a front moving in, so we need to take off now if we're going to make it over the mountains with only three engines."

"Thank you, Sergeant. I'll be right with you."

Ball nodded to the general and glanced at James who gave him a friendly smile and also thumps up before he turned and walked away.

The general took a final drink from his cup. "Well, brother, we'll have to continue this another day. In the meantime, I'll give added attention to my prayer time and will be anxious to see what God does in answer to the earnest prayers of His people. But don't be too hard on yourself. I remind you of God's forgiveness and grace. Nothing would please me more than God intervening in this war in some dramatic way to shorten and lessen the conflict."

The two men stood and headed for the airport.

Chapter Nine

The Final Judgment

•   James was not easily shocked, but the reports on
shortwave radio from a station in South America left his
entire family traumatized. He sat in silence, staring into
space.

The reporter's voice sounded strained. "Reports are
sketchy, but an enormous tragedy is taking place along the
East Coast of the United States. Hundreds of thousands of
people have acquired a variety of illnesses due to a terrorist
biological attack. While sections of North America were
returning to order following the chaos of the nuclear strike,
panic has been spreading again.

"It appears that biological agents were dispersed by
vehicles along the major freeway system from Washington,
D.C., all the way up the coast to New York and beyond.
More evidence has come to light that one or more small
aircraft were also used to spread toxins. A ground to air
missile shot down a private plane upwind from the U.S.
Capitol. It is feared that this act distributed deadly viruses
around the Capitol building. Members of Congress and other
government leaders were meeting at the time of the incident
and reportedly became infected before they could be taken to
safety.

"Reports are that there has also been a deliberate
attempt to infect delegates meeting at the UN building in
New York at the same time that the U.S. Congress was in
session. A small plane flew around the UN building several
times before crashing into the main structure. It's not
known if biological agents were spread by the crash or by
members of UN staff gathered from around the world. All
that is known is that shortly afterward, people throughout
the UN building and surrounding areas had respiratory

problems, followed by internal bleeding, which led to their deaths. The hospitals in the New York area have been overwhelmed. Medical staffs themselves are becoming ill with deadly symptoms. Officials have been unable to identify all the viruses.

"It is feared that people fleeing infected areas will spread these viruses to other parts of the nation. All airports are denying landing rights to planes coming from the affected coastal areas. Neighboring states have set up roadblocks. This part of the nation has one of the heaviest concentrations of population in North America. There are no cures or known methods to help people already infected. We will bring more news on this as it becomes available."

Another reporter came on the air. "Meanwhile, reports from Europe tell of a terrorist act against international leaders meeting near Paris. A plane carrying a nuclear weapon crashed into the hotel complex housing delegates of world leaders. The leaders had been meeting with delegates from Russia and China in an attempt to work out a peaceful settlement for all parties. The explosion leveled the entire complex and created severe damage for several miles. An Islamic terrorist group is claiming responsibility. Other reports suggest it may have been a Russian or Chinese cruise missile. Leaders from both nations deny this. Earlier stories of the meeting revealed that members of the most wealthy and influential leaders in Europe, America, and Japan were attending the global summit. Stay tuned for the latest report." The station returned to its previously scheduled program. Russ turned the volume down.

James buried his face in his hands. The rest of the family sat in stunned silence.

Russ was the first to voice his concern. "I can see why the American radio and TV news has blocked this out or downplayed reports of the biological attack on the East Coast. They don't want the panic to spread. FEMA officials are probably working hard to keep it from spreading west or south."

James looked up and nodded.

"Dad, why is God bringing more judgment on America?

Wasn't the nuclear destruction enough?"

James straightened and thought for a moment. "I don't know, Son. From General Leland's reports and those of his contacts, I've learned there has not been widespread repentance and turning to God by people in the Northeast, especially around New York and Washington, D.C. I'll have to check with Leland, but I suspect this attack is aimed at the leadership and power centers more than the general population. Yet many innocent people are going to suffer, as happened in the nuclear attack."

Ann put her arms around Elizabeth and Sarah. Then she spoke to her grandchildren. "Your grandfather tried to get a message out to America for years. If the nation didn't turn back to God's law as revealed in the Bible and expressed by our federal Constitution, he said God would bring terrible judgment to the nation. We did all we could to warn people, but few listened. So what we see is God's anger being expressed for our nation's sins. We can't understand all God's ways, but historically when God judges, He doesn't play games."

James agreed with an "Amen" and added, "This doesn't mean there isn't hope for us and for those who survive. God always preserves a remnant for a reason. His remnant is to rebuild. He's placing a grave responsibility on the younger generation. We don't need to fear that the biological agents will come here. Most have a short life and are not spread from person to person. Those that are can be contained by quarantine. However, we do need to take to heart the lessons we learn from this so God doesn't have to judge us to capture our attention."

The grandchildren were quiet, but it appeared to James the experience was making a strong impression on them.

• Staff Sergeant Randy Page, newly promoted, sat in shock as he listened to the chaplain's message following a bombshell announcement by Colonel Holman. Page's commanding officer, Major Jack Francis Larson, had taken his life. Larson had been promoted from captain to major at the same time of Page's promotion.

Details were sparse. Finishing his midnight to 8:00
a.m. shift, Larson changed into his Class A uniform and
caught a bus taking personnel to the airport. He asked the
driver to drop him off at the bottom of the hill. The major
was last seen walking toward his former home on the
outskirts of Colorado Springs. When he didn't report back,
a search party found his body where his wife and two young
daughters had died in the initial attack. Death occurred due
to a self-inflicted gunshot.

Page tuned out the chaplain's remarks, trying to
figure out why his friend had snapped. Larson became
withdrawn following their traumatic visit to his home. He
was devastated by the nuclear attack on Colorado Springs.
However, his work at Cheyenne Mountain continued to be
a meticulous performance. In fact, Page recalled having
boasted to others about the captain's sterling, unwavering
leadership.

In the stress and demands of their duties, rank had often
been ignored. They were a team doing what had to be done
to accomplish their mission. The addition of UN personnel
to the staff placed an added strain on the old hands, but
again Captain Larson worked hard to keep their section
functioning efficiently.

As Page pieced together the puzzle of the last months,
he remembered how the captain had slacked off physically.
Larson stopped caring about staying in shape. His excuses
for not playing a game of handball or working out in the gym
seemed justified at the time. Page wondered why he had not
been able to see what was happening. He knew he would be
haunted by such thoughts long into the future.

Suddenly Page became aware of the chaplain closing the
meeting in prayer. He hadn't heard anything prior to that as
he was only going through the motions with his colleagues.
The group filed out of the room and went their separate
ways.

Page wandered down the hallway that took him by the
mailroom. He looked forward to the weekly letter from his
parents since periodic mail delivery had been restored.
Praying always for a miracle, he hoped a letter would arrive

from his sister or word of her.

His heart leaped in his chest when he saw an envelope in his box. He dialed his code and removed the letter. Its origination was inside the Cheyenne Mountain complex. He drew a sharp breath when he recognized the captain's handwriting. Ripping the envelope open, he began to read. The note was handwritten, short, and too the point.

> *"Dear Randy,*
>
> *Please forgive me for letting you, the USAF, and my country down.*
>
> *Now that I see strong indications that things are turning around for America, I can no longer resist the temptation to join my loved ones and stop the unending, unbearable pain. I only pray that God will forgive me for my cowardly action.*
>
> *You have been a faithful friend to me in spite of the military rank that strained personal relationships. I would never have made it this far had it not been for your strength and support.*
>
> *Please do not allow my poor example to deter you from faithfully carrying out your duties. I hope you will apply for officer training, as you will make an excellent leader of men. Check your personnel file. I have added a detailed report on your performance during this trying time of duty. I trust that my actions will not soil my recommendations for your advancements in rank.*
>
> *Again, I ask for your forgiveness and pray that the Lord Jesus will forgive me so that someday we'll meet again in an existence where there will be no tears, no pain, or sorrow."*

The note was signed, "Your friend, Jack Larson." Page stood for a long time looking at it. Slowly he stuffed the note back in its envelope and walked to the chapel. He was relieved to find the place empty. Before he reached the altar and kneeled at the kneeling bench, deep, agonizing sobs erupted from him. His handkerchief was wet by the time he gained control. He rose and sat in a pew, staring at the communion table and cross.

The echo of the shift-changing bell brought him back to the present. Glancing at his watch, he realized he was due at his station. Hurrying toward the command center, his mind wrestled with the contents of the note. He would have to turn it over to Colonel Holman. He decided to make an appointment with the chaplain, too. Talking out his feelings would hopefully have some theological questions answered.

By the time Page took his chair behind his assigned computer, he was ready to focus on the task at hand. He had heard through the grapevine that General Leland was in a high level meeting at the facility. As he listened to the operator he replaced, another shock riveted through him. The terrorist attack on the East Coast had been much worse than initial reports suggested.

He let out an audible groan. "Oh great! Here's another tragedy, and all we can do is sit and record the facts." Typing in his personal code, he made a silent resolution. Someday I'm going to be in a position where I can either prevent such things or actively help to resolve them.

• The Secretary of Defense Jolene Howard had just entered the Cheyenne Mountain complex when her assistant alerted her to an urgent message. After perfunctory introductions and greetings in the conference room, she asked if she could take an important email. She read the report with a somber face. Events at the Capitol were magnifying. She turned her laptop screen, enabling Generals Leland and Foster to read it. They shook their heads. Jolene thanked her assistant and dismissed him. He closed the door to the conference room as he left.

General Leland was the first to speak. "Jolene, we

appreciate you coming to meet with us. It looks as if you got out of Washington just in time."

"It has to be God's mercy, because I don't think anyone saw this coming."

Leland spoke again, "I need to ask a personal question to begin our meeting. I never felt free to ask you this openly while you were in Washington. But now that you're here in Colorado, I trust we can speak freely. Did the President or any other Cabinet member inform you in advance about the preemptive nuclear strike to take out our military?"

Jolene shook her head before he finished his question. "I had no idea it was planned. There was nothing I could do once it started. It was the darkest day of my life."

"I thought that's probably the way it was."

Foster's face revealed his amazement.

Jolene said with conviction, "General Leland, I remember you tried to warn me about the shadow government and what was going on in our nation's Capitol and financial centers of the world."

Turning to Foster, she added, "At that time, I was on his staff in the Middle East." Looking into Leland's eyes, Jolene spoke with conviction, "I'm sorry I wasn't able to see it, but my pride and ambition blinded me. Then that night when I realized what was happening, your words made sense. I decided to bring you back into uniform. I knew you could be trusted to do what was right for America. The others didn't trust you, for good reason from their perspective, but they admitted they needed you and knew you'd do a good job. However, I think they were planning to get rid of you as soon as they had things under control."

"Yes, we figured that. But we believe God had other plans, and we felt we could trust you. This leads to my next question. What did they tell you about their long range plans?"

Jolene rolled her eyes. "I was informed early on by the vice president that I had a great deal to learn about who was actually running the global scene but that I would be told only what I needed to know for my job. My assignment was to carry out orders from the exalted ones." The last was said with sarcasm.

"I decided to play the game and go along with them
but look for ways to throw some sand in critical gears. It
actually became fun. I discovered that the President and
most members of Congress were wimps or just plain actors
playing parts they'd been given. The vice president, with the
help of his handpicked cronies, was the real leader at the
Cabinet level."

"What about the global/international elitists? What did
you learn about them?" asked Foster.

"Not much. Every time I probed, I was told I didn't need
to know, that it would only confuse me. Ha! That was close
to the truth because I got the impression there was a great
deal of confusion in the higher echelons of authority. There
was so much international backstabbing and jockeying for
power that it was driving the vice president nuts. Also,
in many nations, the top dogs were frustrated that they
had to rely on their bureaucrats, some of whom resented
being used. So a lot of grandiose schemes never worked out
because a few underlings sabotaged their plans."

"Do you think this is partly what's going on now with the
attacks against the leaders?" inquired Leland.

"I don't know what to think," said Jolene. "It's all
staggering. These attacks are too great a project for mid
level managers. It is either Islamic terrorists or perhaps
Russian and/or Chinese leaders striking back at the
globalists, because they know they have been used. Yet I
don't know how they were able to set up the attack in this
country and hit the world leaders at the same time. It's
hard to know. It could be a combination of factors, although
it appears these attacks were all carefully planned to
simultaneously take out the key world leaders."

Leland leaned forward and spoke earnestly, "I had
a phone conversation right before the meeting with my
pastor, former Army Chaplain James Parr, whom I think
I mentioned to you before. I respect his keen spiritual
insights. He feels, and I agree, that what has happened to
our leaders is the judgment of God. It really doesn't matter
who is being used to carry out the destruction. The Bible

is full of examples of God using wicked men against other evil men and women to bring His wrath. The end result was that the godly remnant He preserved had an opportunity to regroup and rebuild under His leadership. The same is true today.

"Foster and I believe it's a sign of God's grace that you're here to escape the terrible wrath of God. It's also an indication of His leading for the future as well as an awesome responsibility being placed on our shoulders. We must seek His guidance as to how to put this country back together again, at least those parts that we can salvage."

The Secretary of Defense and General Foster nodded approval and accepted the challenge General Leland laid before them. Theirs was an awesome responsibility.

Tears coursed down Jolene's face when she read additional news reports at her computer. Massive deaths on the East Coast, particularly in New York City and the Washington areas, were ongoing. While she knew that many leaders deserved what happened to them, she also recalled numbers of good people who had served in the Capitol. Because of their ignorance about the true designs of their leaders, the innocent also were suffering. It was the result of their service to 'the beast.'

• James jumped in surprise when the phone on his desk rang. Picking it up, he was pleased to hear General Leland's voice.

"James, this is Mark. How are you doing?"

"The phone startled me. I have to become reacquainted with these devices since we were without them so long. Thanks for asking. We're doing well. But we continue to be staggered by the news from the East Coast. I'm no longer hesitant to speak out, that it's the judgment of God falling on our federal leadership and their supporters. I pray this will finally move the survivors to repentance."

"I assumed you'd heard the news from shortwave radio. What you probably didn't hear was that Jolene Howard, Secretary of Defense, has been conferring with Foster and me at Cheyenne Mountain. As near as we can tell, she's the only Cabinet member to survive, which makes her the ranking federal leader at this point. Both houses of Congress have all died. With few exceptions, I don't think we've lost much. I'm sorry to have to bring you this word."

"How did your time with Miss Howard go?"

"There's no question in my mind that she's with us and was even before the terrorist attacks. She has been skating on thin ice with the powers that be because she sided with our concerns. But since they needed her, they tolerated it. Now we've got to start all over and reevaluate where to go. That's one reason I'm calling. I would appreciate your input on what this means for the future, from a spiritual standpoint."

"Did she have evidence that the people in the East have had their eyes opened as to the real intent of the UN forces being brought in to control the population and not merely to restore order?"

"Yes, the Rednecks in the South have been giving them fits. Even the liberals in the Northeast didn't relish foreign troops telling them what to do."

"That's good. Maybe now they'll see that they put their trust in human leaders whose goal was to enslave them. If they can understand that, perhaps they will discern that it's God's mercy He allowed the terrorists to take them out. Just as Satan's followers thought they had overcome God when they crucified Christ, so the terrorists thought they were dealing a terrible blow against Christianity by taking out our leaders. In reality, they were carrying out God's overarching plan to bring judgment on the elected leadership in D.C. and also the world elitists."

Leland interrupted asking, "Do you think the message of repentance will sweep the nation?"

"I think so. I hope so. But what's going to happen in the political realm?"

"From what Jolene, Foster and I can see, there's no way to hold the old union together at this point. Washington is going to remain a ghost town for months, if not years, because we don't have the manpower or means to remove all the dead bodies and clear out the deadly biological spores, bacteria, and such that remain. The buildings, records, and files will be there for the most part, but it can no longer be the focus of a federal government. We think this is going to result in the nation being broken up into regional units where the states will be the main focus of civil government.

"Do you remember the idea from the Civil War era about saving Confederate money because the South would rise again? There's a strong move to resurrect a confederation of southern states. However, due to the nature of the highway system, communications, and power networks, these economic realities will be a strong push for cooperation between the regions of the nation. The fact is if we're going to revive economically, we need each other. But it's going to be a rough, unpredictable ride and a long time before America returns to normal. You and I certainly won't live to see it, but, hopefully, our grandchildren will."

"There's no question whatever, Mark, the kids are our best hope for the future. Caleb is out in the valley exerting leadership. He was delighted to see Joshua return. Josh is going to be the best man in Caleb's marriage to Rich and Kate's daughter, Anna Lee. I can see them rising in the ranks and eventually in political leadership. Their physical and emotional scars will be powerful forces to keep them on the right track with the Lord."

"I agree, James. You and I will have to stick around as long as they will tolerate us and pass on the lessons we've learned. I'll turn my command over to Foster. He and Howard are going to work together to remove the UN from the Continent and help the states cooperate for their mutual benefit. With the UN leadership gone and all the chaos in their home countries, the nations that sent troops are calling home their survivors. Also, with the cream of the so-called elite taken out, the Europeans are going to have their hands full just keeping their own little fiefdoms under control. With more Muslims in most of the European nations than nationals, we think Old Europe is gone forever.

"You'll want to hear the latest intelligence. When the North Korean troops saw the prosperity of the South, they knew they'd been deceived by their leaders. There has been a military coup, and the North's new leaders are looking favorably at the Christians in the South. The same has happened all over Southeast Asia. Many Chinese Christians volunteered for duty in the Asian Rim countries. This has resulted in powerful moves of the Spirit wherever they have gone. So with the breakup of the central government as a result of the war with Russia, there is a whole reconfiguration of Asian nations.

As far as the Russians are concerned, they're bogged down with what's left of the Chinese army, rebellions by Muslim factors in the former republics, and uprisings in the Middle Eastern nations. The Islamic leaders now hate them as much as they hated us. So the Russians are no threat to us. Again we see God using the turmoil to bring His people into positions of leadership. So not all is bad news."

James responded with a strong "Praise the Lord!" Then he changed the subject. "Well, brother, you must return to Western Colorado. Your garlic patch needs some tender loving care. I'm teaching Henry's boy, Chuck, to become a master gardener, but I've told him you're the specialist when it comes to garlic and herbs."

Leland laughed. "Sergeant Ball was commenting on how he missed our fresh garlic. That's added motivation for us to come home. Tell Chuck, come fall, I'll give him some good growing stock for his garden."

The friends said goodbye. Both were weary yet invigorated with a sense of hope.

Epilogue

As elderly gentlemen, James and General Leland eventually died in their sleep. Their families and friends who appreciated their leadership laid them to rest.

James, Mark, and others like them failed to prevent the judgment of God from falling on America, but they were a strong force in helping the people raise from the ashes of defeat.

The American dream lived on and provided a powerful stimulus for the rebuilding that took place. It could have been different had the people responded to God's gracious call to repent.

The tragedy could have been avoided.

Author's note

"I call heaven and earth as witnesses today against you, that I have set before you life and death, blessing and cursing; therefore choose life, that both you and your descendants may live." Deuteronomy 30:19, NKJV

". . . if My people who are called by My name will humble themselves, and pray and seek My face, and turn from their wicked ways, then I will hear from heaven, and will forgive their sin and heal their land." 2 Chronicles 7:14

Some readers may question whether God would work in such miraculous ways in the 21st century as the following novel suggests.

If you doubt these possibilities, consider this. All depictions are foreshadowed in Scripture. The God Who created billions of galaxies and the minute complexities of the cells of your body is quite able to destroy entire armies and humble the mightiest of nations and/or men. He has done it before many times in the past. So is there any reason to believe He cannot or will not do it *if* we meet His preordained conditions?

The fate of America or any civilization does not rest in the hands of the wicked. God is in control of His creation and works in and through His Body, the Church of the Lord Jesus Christ, to accomplish His ultimate goals for the Bride of Christ. But He binds Himself to the conditions of His covenant as expressed in the above Scriptures.

After reading this special two-in-one book, you will have a better understanding of the choices before us all. In the process, I trust, you will also experience a reading adventure.

"History fails to record a single precedent in which nations subject to moral decay have not passed into political and economic decline. There has been either a spiritual awakening to overcome the moral lapse, or a progressive deterioration leading to ultimate national disaster."
General Douglas MacArthur

Frank Meyer, November 7, 2006

America's Choice

Triumph

Please note:

In this scenario, you will see many of the same characters that are in *Tragedy*. However, keep in mind, this is an alternate possibility for them.

Chapter One

The Message Delivered

James Parr, a retired pastor and former army chaplain, heard a clear command in his mind: "Stand!" He stood to attention, waiting for the President of the United States to recognize him.

James, seated toward the back of the group of America's Christian leaders, had been invited to the White House luncheon. Two other leaders started to rise to add their responses to the President's speech. The President fixed his eyes on James and nodded in recognition.

"Sir, I have a question and a statement," said James with authority. "The Almighty God, whom you profess to know and serve, wants to know how you can stand here pretending to want our counsel when, on your desk, is an executive order that you were discussing with your advisors this very morning. The top secret document deals with the use of secret prison camps already built for some of the people in this room and many of their followers."

The smile on the President's face vanished. The attention of those in the room was divided. Some stared at James in utter contempt for his gall to question their

"Christian" President. Others were amazed to see the shock of recognition spread across the faces of those seated at the head table.

James's voice boomed on. "Do you think, sir, that the God of our Lord Jesus Christ did not know you were discussing the demise of millions of His servants last night with select members of your Cabinet? Do you think He does not care when you treat the subject of a preemptive nuclear strike by Russia and China as a mere unfortunate price to be paid for the supposed good of the New World Order? Do you think He approves of you and your elitist friends riding out the attack in the safety of prepared bunkers while our military is wiped out and the fallout condemns millions of people to sickness or death?"

The mouths of those at the front table fell open in astonishment. Fear showed in the rapid movement of their eyes. They leaned back in their chairs as the voice of James, the prophet, came forth with even greater force.

"You may play the hypocrite with these deceived sheep seated before you. You may make fools of God's people and the people of America, but God Almighty will not be mocked. He has heard the cries of His remnant across this land which once honored the Lord Jesus Christ, His Church, and His Word of truth. Although the land is cursed, because of the shedding of innocent blood, which you and those before you have not tried to stop, God is willing to show mercy. Because of the memory of the godly founders of this nation, some who occupied the office you now hold, and for the sake of many in our land who have not bowed their knees to false gods, God is willing to forgive.

"However, He demands the repentance of leaders as well as the people. Thus sayeth Yahweh God, Creator of the heavens and earth. He will give you, Mr. President, and your administration seven days from this hour to come clean with the American people and validate this prophetic word. Each day you delay telling the truth about your evil plans, every day you hesitate taking steps to turn from that wickedness, you, Mr. President, will pay with the loss of a member of your immediate family or your administration by the hand of Almighty God. You will start by telling the truth to the Church leaders gathered here today. Reveal the plans to use United Nations troops to imprison all those who oppose the implementation of the New World Order. If you do not, the judgment spoken here will begin immediately, in this hour."

The face of the President was ashen. He stood transfixed. James did not give him an opportunity to interrupt. His outstretched arm swept across the entire audience as he continued. "Furthermore, hear the Word of God, for you who have eaten the delicacies of the king without inquiring of the cost. The Lord Jesus Christ is dismayed at how you have allowed yourselves to be deceived. We who know Him have been weighed in the balance of God's justice and found seriously wanting. If there is not widespread repentance, Yahweh God will bring on this nation the evil these leaders have devised for us. But if there is a deep sorrow and complete turning from your sin, He will spare America of His wrath.

"So you will know that Yahweh has spoken, the two leaders here who spoke deceptive words out of their pride and ignorance will be mute for twenty four hours. Repent or God's pronounced judgments will fall. I wipe the dust from my feet as a final witness."

James wiped his feet on the carpet, turned, and walked toward the door. A Secret Service agent opened it. Before leaving, James faced those at the head table who were still shocked into silence.

"Mr. President, you have seven days for a full disclosure to the nation. Do not wait, or the price will be high for you and all those siding with you in these sins against God and His people. Begin to speak the truth now, or the wrath of God will immediately fall upon your family."

As the door closed behind him, James took a deep breath and smiled at the Secret Service agent who walked out with him. He asked, "What's the procedure for getting a cab to the airport?"

Agent Daniel Barnes stated matter-of-factly, "I think they're going to want to talk with you after that message."

James grinned. "I've had higher orders that I'm to leave after delivering the message. I wasn't sent by God to argue the points."

Raising his eyebrows, Barnes said nothing.

"If your bosses want to talk to me later, they'll know how to find me, okay?" James added.

The agent gestured to move down the hallway. "Come with me. I'll see that it's arranged."

As they walked, James touched the man's arm. "The Lord Jesus sees the heart of love you have for your little girl and wants you to know His power. After you have released me, call your wife and confirm the good news. Emily will be out of bed, dancing around the house."

The man stopped and faced him. "The doctors said she'd never walk--"

James held up his hand. "God's Word supercedes the doctors' good intentions. Do as I say. When you get the confirmation, the Lord will give you an opportunity to share the good news with the President. Be sure you tell him exactly how it came to be."

Barnes hesitated. Seeing the older gray haired gentleman radiate confidence, he replied, "Yes, sir."

They continued walking down the long hallway. James had a smile on his face. This was definitely scary. Walking in the Spirit is fun. But I give all the praise to You, Father. I could never have done this on my own.

The agent interrupted his thoughts, "Are you sure you want to leave? I heard what you had to say. Again, there will be people who will want to speak to you."

"You're probably right about that, but I've said all that I was sent to say. Besides, I have strict instructions to not stick around, so please get me a cab. I don't intend to be mauled by a bear."

The agent had a puzzled look on his face. "But there are no . . ." Noting the smile on James's face, he said, "Okay."

Instructions were given to another agent who moved James through security. When his laptop and travel bag were retrieved, he was escorted to a cab.

He wondered what was happening back in the large meeting room. He was curious about what would follow. As the cab made its way through heavy traffic, the gravity of the message he, too, had heard for the first time began to boggle his mind. Preparing his laptop to take notes, he recalled how this had come about.

He and his wife Ann had been impressed by the embossed invitation to attend a special luncheon at the White House for a select group of America's Christian leaders. That someone in the administration had noticed his ministry to veterans in the mountains of Colorado was cause for surprise. His first reaction was to turn it down. Not only would it strain his budget to travel from Colorado, there was the matter of placing his stamp of approval on a President and his administration. James had serious doubts about his leaders, in spite of the President's enthusiastic support from Evangelical Christians and political conservatives.

Knowing that God works in mysterious ways to achieve His ends, James took the invitation to his prayer warriors, asking them to pray with him about what he was to do. They agreed and to a person came back with positive impressions that he was to go to Washington. They believed he should prepare by prayer and fasting. Each of them promised to do the same.

The week before the trip, James juice fasted and spent most of his time at his isolated mountain cabin. He read the Bible, seeking wisdom from God as to what the Lord expected of him. He was both disturbed and encouraged by the Scriptures that the Spirit of God impressed on him. They dealt with being unafraid, not intimidated by those in high positions. As a chaplain in Vietnam and later with his ministry to veterans stateside, James had considerable experience in dealing with a variety of political leaders. Strong examples came to James from the Bible of prophets who warned the leaders of their day, calling them to repentance in the Name of Yahweh, the God of the Hebrews.

Returning home, he asked Ann, "Is this the Spirit of God, or is it my vanity speaking? I don't think I'm afraid as I much as I'm asking, 'Why me?' I'm just a little guy from nowhere."

Ann turned the heat down on the stove and sat next to him at the kitchen table. "It's good to see your humility, dear, but look at the emails you've received from your prayer group. They're all listing the same Scriptures you were given. There's no indication that they had talked to each other previously about their impressions."

"I've noticed that. But I asked the Lord to give me specifics. So far there's been nothing. Not that there aren't issues I'd like to challenge this administration about. For example, there are plenty of ways the veterans are being neglected and mistreated. They've given their lives to carry out questionable tasks in the name of American justice. But these are my concerns. If I'm to be a true prophet of God, I'll have to speak His Words, not my own. Frankly, this is not something I've had that much experience with other than in my private counseling."

Ann patted his hand, smiling. "Dear, you've always been impatient. You're just going to have to trust the Lord."

"Right. Waiting has not been one of my virtues."

The matter was settled the night before James was to catch an early morning flight to Washington's Dulles Airport. Within an hour, five members of his prayer team phoned to give him the same Scripture they felt applied to his situation. "You will be brought before kings to bear witness of me, but do not worry about what you will speak. It will be given to you in that hour." This was specific enough, but, at the same time, it frightened James worse than any fear he'd faced in combat when his life was on the line.

Three from the prayer group met James when he changed planes at Denver International Airport to lay hands on him and pray. Peace filled his spirit by the time he boarded the plane. It was clear. God had spoken, confirming His message. All James had to do was walk it out. Deep in his heart he hoped there would be silence during the luncheon. After all, how would he know if it was himself or the Spirit of God?

The dining room in the White House held seventy pastors and ministry leaders from across America. Not all were from large ministries or churches. There were men and women, conservatives and liberals, and a generous sprinkling of minorities. The President had been introduced to each guest, greeting everyone by name. They all felt special, that the President of the United States sincerely appreciated each ministry.

Stewards escorted the guests to prepared tables.
After they were seated, the official chaplain of the Senate
gave thanks for the food and asked God's blessing on
the gathering. President Graham Nelson McCleen, Vice
President Harold B. Lynch, and select members of the
Cabinet were seated at the head table. During the meal, two
popular Christian musicians entertained the group. Each
guest had been able to choose from a generous menu when
accepting the President's invitation.

While some finished their desserts, the President stood
to make his remarks. He praised the Christian leaders for
their contributions to the spiritual welfare of the nation. He
especially wanted them to know that their efforts to help the
poor during the current economic stress were appreciated
by the administration. He explained that he was struggling
to balance the needs of people throughout America as
well as the suffering around the world. America's armed
forces needed prayer as they labored to free nations from
oppressive dictators and guard our nation against terrorist
attacks.

The guests interrupted the President enthusiastically
with applause from time to time. He acknowledged their
positive response. However, James's countenance was not as
radiant as the expressions of others. As he listened, an inner
voice spoke to him. It seemed that a Power Point display
began to appear in his mind, interspersed with video clips.
He heard the President, but the mental presentation had
vivid clarity. His heart beat faster, yet a calm settled over
him, enabling him to relax.

His eyes drifted to a nationally known, highly regarded
pastor who rose to compliment the President on the fine
job his administration was doing. James heard the words.
Immediately a sense of deep sorrow filled him. In his mind
a devilish voice laughed hysterically at the hypocrisy of the
remarks. James knew the man was deceived and suspected
that he spoke from his own vanity. The knowledge did not
move James to be critical. Instead he wanted to weep. When
the leader finished, the room erupted in applause. Those at
the head table beamed.

An equally famous lady who led a nationwide organization of conservative Christian women rose to speak. Her remarks were generous, but she also talked about the abortion issue and the negative effect the economy was having on families, especially children. The President thanked her, promising that his administration was equally concerned. He said they would do all they could to improve the economy.

James recalled that the lady had an angry look on her face as she listened to his prophetic message. He typed the message God had given him into his laptop. Now that there was time to think about the gravity of the message, it made a deep impression on him. He wondered how the announcement would be received.

Chapter Two

The First Shoe Falls

A stunned silence hung over the room after the door
closed behind James. The two Christian leaders who had
earlier praised the President had terrified looks on their
faces. Most of the guests watched the head table. If the
moment had not been so serious, the confusion of the
nation's leaders would have seemed hilarious.

The President attempted to speak, glancing first at his
advisors and then at his audience. "I'm frankly shocked, as
I suspect many of you are. Someone in our group has leaked
extremely sensitive information about national security
issues. While we were dealing with the general areas,
nevertheless--"

The vice president jumped to his feet, interrupting, "Mr.
President, I don't believe this is the place to comment on
these subjects. We need time to discuss this in private."

The others at the table murmured and nodded in
agreement. The President hesitated. He was struggling
to know how to deal with the men and women before him
whose attention was fixed on him.

"I think the vice president is right." His political
instincts had returned. "Let me express again my
appreciation for you good people coming today. Allow me to
apologize for the rudeness of one of our guests."

Before he could continue, an elderly black pastor,
Jefferson Boyd, jumped up with energy inconsistent with his
age and robust size. "Mr. President, with all due respect, sir,
I admonish you not to think of this as a rude interruption.
After over fifty years of ministry, the word given today has
all the marks of the Holy Spirit of God. I beg you, sir, take

this seriously. I for one earnestly request that you explain to us now the details of the truth or falsehood of the matters our brother spoke about. I caution you, this is no time to mince words because we are in the Presence of Almighty God."

Turning to the woman next to him, he asked, "Sister Hobbs, can you speak to us?"

She shook her head. Her body shook with emotion as she wept.

"You're not playin' games with us, are you, Sister?"

Again she shook her head. Her mouth moved, but no sound came forth. She dropped her head in her hands, and her sobbing continued.

The elderly gentleman turned and pointed across the room, shouting a command, "Brother Hanson, speak to us."

The Reverend Doctor Clifford Lansford Hanson also shook his head in despair. He rubbed his forehead, all the while trying to control his emotions.

Softly spoken prayers broke out in the room. Several guests slid from their chairs to kneel. They buried their faces in their hands. Others lifted their hands, praying quietly in strange tongues.

Pastor Boyd extended his hands toward the President and lowered his voice in a pleading tone. "Mr. President, I feel the Spirit here. We are in the presence of Almighty God. I beseech you to tell us the truth lest you fall under the judgment that has been spoken. Tell us the truth. Now!"

Several "amens" and affirmations emerged from the guests. By now, hardened looks covered the faces of Vice President Lynch and the Secretary of State, Richard Languard. The President seemed confused. The vice president grabbed his arm and began to pull him to one side, pointing to a cell phone in his hand and whispering something in his ear. The President nodded. Pastor Boyd was dismayed as he heard the President regain his composure and speak himself into judgment.

"Something urgent has come up. If you all want to stay, you may use the room as long as you need it. Our staff will assist you when you are ready to leave."

The President and everyone at his table began to head

for the door. Secret Service agents positioned themselves
between the political leaders and their guests. However,
there was no threat from the guests who were either in
prayer or reaching out with gestures of supplication to the
President in a final effort to urge him to reconsider. As the
administration filed out, Pastor Boyd raised his arms to
heaven and spoke loudly to the group.

"We needs to pray, brothers and sisters. We needs
to pray real hard. We needs to get honest with God right
now. We have heard the word of the Lord and a great
responsibility has fallen on us." His whole body shook from
the intensity of his supplications to God.

A few in the group cried, "Amen!" Their chorus of voices,
raised in prayer, grew in volume as some of the guests
watched looking uncomfortable.

•   Vice President Lynch was the first to speak when the
door to the dining room closed behind them. "Who was that
radical freak, and how in the hell did he know all that? We
need answers, and we need them now!"

An uneasy chatter broke out in the group as they walked
toward the Oval Office.

Jolene Howard, the first female, African American
to become a four star general in the army and then be
promoted to Secretary of Defense, was the only woman
in the President's group that day. Growing up in a home
where her parents took her to Pentecostal Holiness revival
meetings, she was subdued by the happenings at the
luncheon. While she had long ago abandoned her childhood
church practices except when needed for political reasons,
she had enough spiritual discernment to recognize what had
happened. She spoke quietly but with conviction when the
group gathered in the oval office.

"Mr. Vice President, I understand how you think that
person was a religious radical. However, I want to caution
you, there has been no security leak. It's doubtful the
gentleman had any foreknowledge of what he was talking
about. I think you need to consider what we just witnessed.
It was something beyond our understanding."

"What?" There was disgust in the vice president's voice.

He turned on the younger woman, venting his anger with sarcasm. "Do you believe that religious hocus-pocus was real? You think those pious fakes didn't set this up?" Making an ugly face, he grabbed his throat and acted like he couldn't speak. "If it wasn't set up, it was psychosomatic. No, we have a mole in our midst, and we'd better find him." He squinted his eyes and looked directly at Jolene, adding, "Or her before more damaging information is spread!"

The secretary of state, a tall, slender man with dark rimmed glasses lending him the look of a college professor, was already using his legal training to tackle the problem. Ignoring the underhanded remark by the vice president, Languard raised his hand to get attention. "Okay, there are a lot of people who know about the camps, but only a few know they were being discussed this morning. But, my god, only top administrative people attended last night's meeting. How could anyone have talked to that crackpot between then and now?" Not expecting an answer, he continued, "We should be able to track everyone's activities in the hours between our meeting last night and the luncheon today. We can start with phone records. No one is excluded."

The vice president dropped into an easy chair and took out his cell phone. Jolene rolled her eyes, shaking her head in dismay. The others seemed lost in thought.

President McCleen raised his hand to speak. But suddenly the door burst open. His personal secretary shouted, "Mr. President, your mother's on the line. It's an emergency!"

The President hit the speaker button on his phone without thinking. "Mother, what's up?"

"Your father is having a stroke or something. Dr. Horn is here, but he can't seem to do anything. We've called an ambulance. Your father has a terrified look on his face. Please pray. Oh god, Son, I'm afraid, I'm so afraid."

No one in the room moved. The President asked, "Mother, when did this happen?"

"Just minutes ago. We had finished lunch and were visiting with Dr. Horn and his wife. Suddenly your father gasped and fell off his chair."

Color, which only moments before had returned to

the President's face, drained from it. He looked confused and struggled for words. "Mother, we'll get the best help available. Call your pastor. Tell Father we'll be praying for him. I'll meet you at the hospital."

His mother whispered an affirmative and hung up.

Jolene could not resist. "The man at the luncheon said if you didn't tell the truth, judgment would fall on your family immediately."

The vice president jumped to his feet and slammed his fist on the desk. "Oh for God's sake, it's just a coincidence! That's all it is. Let's forget the religious mumbo-jumbo. We've got to deal with reality. We have a snitch in our midst, a serious security breach."

Jolene raised her eyebrows. She moved toward the President who was visibly shaken.

The vice president took the lead. "Okay, the first thing we've got to do is impress on that religious bunch that what they heard today involves sensitive matters related to national security. Therefore, they are not to speak to anyone about it. If they breathe a word, we'll close down their ministries or churches, fine them, and send their butts to prison."

His eyes searched those of the others. Sensing no opposition, he persisted. "Also, we've got to rein in that so-called prophet. Get him in custody now. Put the pressure on him to reveal who his sources are. Then put a gag order on him, or put him away under some part of the Patriot Act."

As an afterthought, he added, "Mr. President, you'd better go to the hospital to check on your father. We'll take care of business here. Keep us informed. We're sorry this has been added to your pressure, but you know we have the best medical care here in Washington."

The others murmured their support. They scattered to take care of urgent matters commanded of them by the vice president. Jolene comforted the President. His secretary, with a bewildered look on her face, waited for instructions.

•   As James sat in the airport, he was not surprised to see two well-dressed men approach and ask, "Are you Chaplain James Parr?"

"I'm the man," he answered with a smile.

Flashing their badges, they introduced themselves. "I'm Agent Thomas. This is Agent MacAlroy. We're with the FBI. Would you please come with us? There are people who want to ask you some questions."

"Do I have a choice?" asked James.

"No, sir."

The agents weren't smiling. James noticed two other similarly dressed men observing him. He shrugged, closed his laptop, and placed it in the carryon case before getting up to follow the agents through the terminal. He noticed that several people seated around him were watching with interest. He wanted to assure them he was not a terrorist but thought better of it under the circumstances. Suddenly the adventure didn't seem pleasant.

• The President's press agent, Jordan Miles, was sent to speak to the luncheon guests. He regretted coming to the event, and yet he had an intense curiosity about what had just taken place. Upon entering the dining room, Miles had difficulty getting the attention of the group. They had taken the President at his word and were using the time to pray and talk to each other in small groups. A few were eager to tell others, who were less informed, about some of the harsher realities such as the existing prison camps in isolated sections of the country. They made it known that the prophet's words did not surprise them. This shocked the others. Yet no one was prepared for the message from the President's press secretary.

"I've been sent by President McCleen to ask your forgiveness. The photo opportunity we promised for a picture of you with him has been canceled. Also, he asked me to tell you that what you heard today is a matter of grave national security. Because the facts were distorted, you are not to speak of them to anyone, including your spouses, when you leave here. What you heard is to remain in this room until you are cleared by direct communication from the President's office."

Pastor Boyd was the first to speak. "And if we choose not to?"

"You will be subject to arrest, confinement, and severe fines to you personally and your ministries."

Before the press secretary could continue, the black brother blurted, "Oh, then we'll be the first of the Christians thrown into the lion's den already prepared for us. Young man, is that how you treat honored guests of the President who were invited to a meal in his own home?"

This rattled the press secretary. He was used to being asked pointed questions by the press but nothing as direct and personal by a respected member of the nation's clergy.

Miles raised his hands in a pleading gesture. "Look, we just want you to know that, if this inaccurate information were to be spread widely, it could cause a great deal of confusion among the populace and bring about unnecessary trouble while the leadership has other urgent matters to deal with."

Boyd pointed his finger at Miles and countered, "Sir, I believe that a national concentration camp system and a preemptive nuclear strike are *urgent* matters for consideration. So is the threat to take away our rights as citizens to speak our minds and our rights as men and women of God, leaders in the Church of the Lord Jesus Christ, to declare the Word of the Lord and the truth to God's people." His voice rose in intensity with each word. Pointing directly at the press secretary, he asserted loudly, "Young man, if you don't want to experience the direct and severe judgment of God, you had best watch what you say and whom you threaten."

Miles's face reddened, but his training in public relations came to the front. He raised his hands again in a pleading gesture. "Please, I am representing the President of the United States who needs your support now. You heard him express his appreciation to you for your work on behalf of the American people. Is it not in your hearts to support him as he faces some very tough issues? And besides, he needs your personal prayers. He's just received word that his father, whom I know you all respect as a great American and world leader, has just suffered either a serious stroke or a heart attack."

Due to a lack of spiritual discernment, the press

secretary was confused by the immediate outcries of prayer and supplications to God from the assembled leaders. Here was confirmation that God had begun to fulfill the prophecy. The first of the warnings had been verified. The President had not told the truth, and as prophesied, a member of his family was stricken. The fear of God swept forcefully through the ones being brought into a deeper walk with their Lord. They forgot about Miles and lifted their attention to heaven.

The press secretary retreated. He realized he was totally out of his element. He gave the secret service instructions to not allow anyone to leave the room until different orders came from the President's office.

• Dealing with the Christians in the dining room created an argument in the vice president's office that was increasing in volume. The vice president exerted his authority. "Before they leave, they *must* sign a statement not to disclose any of the information they heard or, so help me, they will go straight to jail! It's that simple."

Jordan exclaimed, "Oh great! And what would you have me explain to the press when several thousand phone calls start coming from people wanting to know what happened to seventy of America's most widely known and respected religious leaders? Oh sure, I know. We'll tell everyone that they were stealing the White House silverware. Or we discovered they were plotting to assassinate the President and his Cabinet in an attempt to take control of the national government and set up a theocracy. Therefore, we've arrested them and denied them all their liberties provided by the First Amendment to the Constitution."

The press secretary paced the floor, his words dripping with sarcasm. "No, I've got it. We'll accuse them of being terrorists. That's it. Under the Patriot Act, we don't have to tell anybody anything. Seventy religious leaders just disappear into the federal prison system after having lunch at the White House, and we take the fifth. Now that's the best idea yet. I need a fifth of the best from the liquor room." He dropped into a chair.

Secretary Languard rolled his eyes. Shaking his head,

he spoke directly to the vice president. "I agree with Miles. For God's sake, we can't arrest these people, and we can't enforce a gag order on them either."

The vice president was about to tie into the press secretary when the head of the White House Secret Service, Agent Barnes, interrupted them. "Sirs, we have a situation developing in the dining room. Some of the guests are upset. They want to leave now. They're on their cell phones and sound angry, very angry."

Everyone looked at the vice president who asked the press secretary, "Was there a recording of the meeting?"

"Yes, there's usually a master recording."

"Okay, see to it that it's lost permanently. Then call a press conference in time to make the evening news. We'll beat them to the punch with our version of what happened. We'll make them look like the fools they are. So, Barnes, let them go. Tell them there were some security matters outside. In order to protect their welfare, we had to delay their departure." He motioned for Barnes to leave and focused his attention on the small group.

"Okay, gentleman, let's put together our version of what happened. We'll sell it to the news people. We'll see who the public will believe."

The body language of the others spoke volumes about their discomfort. But unable to come up with a better plan, they began to brainstorm the new approach.

• Press Secretary Jordan Miles walked to the podium in the White House conference room. The news reporters gave him their attention as the cameramen zoomed in to get a good head shot.

"Thank you for assembling on such a short notice. There was a confusing, unfortunate event at the luncheon here in the White House earlier today, held for seventy religious leaders from throughout the nation. President McCleen wanted to personally thank them for the fine work they are doing to help the nation during this time of economic and international challenges. However, one guest accused the President and the administration of grievous charges that got confused in the minds of those attending the luncheon.

Members of the President's Cabinet felt we needed this
press conference to be sure that the correct interpretation of
what happened is told to the public.

"The guest who spoke somehow heard about a morning
discussion the President had with several members of his
Cabinet. They were talking about the need to review a
longstanding policy to have holding areas around the nation
in case of a major terrorist disruption. In such an event,
there could be a need for detaining large numbers of people
until it is assured that they are no threat to the populace. I
remind you of the government's decision at the beginning of
World War II to incarcerate individuals of Japanese descent.
While it was an unpleasant task, and, in hindsight, perhaps
not needed, at the time responsible leaders felt it had to be
done for the safety of the American people.

"Somehow a few of the leaders at the luncheon got the
impression that these camps are intended for Christians
and regular American citizens. Of course nothing could be
further from the truth. Why would the administration want
to imprison some of our most loyal, respected citizens? The
idea is absurd.

"The second area of misunderstanding concerns another
meeting of Cabinet leaders last evening wherein they
discussed the remote possibility of a preemptive nuclear
strike by Russian or Chinese forces. It is the responsibility
of the administration to consider all possible threats to
America and the steps needed to protect our leadership
should such an unlikely event occur in the future. To that
end, there have been provisions laid out guaranteeing the
safety of government leaders from such a remote possibility.

"Again, there was a misunderstanding by those at the
luncheon after the accusations of one guest. They thought
our administration was knowledgeable of an actual planned
attack against America in the near future. Of course this
is nothing but fear mongering. We can't judge the person's
motives, but it seemed to be an attempt to get attention
and discredit the political leaders of the nation. You all
know there are religious elements that are in disagreement
with some of our foreign policies. This of course is their
guaranteed right according to the Constitution. However,

the attempt to draw attention is not something we want to encourage. Therefore, we won't release the name of the person bringing these unfounded, misinformed accusations.

"President McCleen asked that I conduct this session to clear up these misunderstandings. He regrets that he wasn't able to be here to personally answer questions, but by now the nation knows he has suffered a terrible personal loss. Since you have information on the death of his father, I'll take a couple of questions. Rod."

"It sounds like some conspiracy nut was invited to the luncheon."

"You're probably right although we don't want to mischaracterize the fine people who attended. However, we all know there is a small segment of our society that understands everything in terms of conspiracies and a mystical shadow government that's responsible for the evil in the world. Of course there are wealthy people who exert great power and influence over business, and, thus, the economy and politics. This no doubt influences a few government leaders to some degree.

"Today we had another example of well meaning people jumping to wild conclusions that don't fit the facts. Again, that's why we called this impromptu press conference so you'll have the opportunity to get the facts to the American public before unnecessary harm is done. Yes, Marilyn."

"Is the guest who caused these misunderstandings being charged?"

"No, he hasn't broken any law. He was just rude and misinformed. But perhaps we should charge him for the fine lunch he enjoyed." Receiving only snickers from a few reporters, he took the next question. "Tom."

"Will more details be released concerning the two subjects you mentioned, the holding areas and a preemptive nuclear strike?"

Jordan raised his eyebrows, clearly disgusted at such a thought. "No, these are matters of national security. We don't feel there's a need for further discussion beyond what is already known about these vague possibilities. One of our greatest concerns for the safety of the American citizens is the threat of terrorism. If you want more news to cover, I'd suggest you report on that subject."

The press secretary held up his hand to indicate that there would be no further questions. He finished, saying, "This covers the issue well enough. We hope you'll get this on the evening news. I'm calling the press conference to a close so you have time to make your deadlines. Thank you again for coming."

The media personnel rushed out to faithfully parrot what they had just been given.

•   Christine Fleming and her husband Erich were like many awakening Christians across the country. They sensed in their spirits that something threatened the very existence of America as a free nation. There had been many prophetic words given on the Internet to warn people not to take it for granted that the only enemies of America were rogue terrorists. A growing awareness emerged to an even greater threat. It existed in the deceptive leadership of the government in Washington and its relationship with other world powers.

When Erich returned home from work, he was not surprised to find Christine on the phone in a deep conversation with her friend Laura. She lowered the phone to return Erich's kiss and whispered, "I'll be off in a minute."

Erich went to the family room where their three young children were watching a video. Four-year-old Lucy leaped up, jumped into her daddy's arms, and gave him a kiss as he swung her around. The oldest, Bobby, hit the pause button so he and his brother, Jonathan, could give their father hugs. Sensing they were absorbed in the plot of the video, Erich returned to the kitchen. Christine was off the phone, preparing a dish for the oven. She handed him a hot drink. "How did work go today?"

He shrugged and sat down at the table. "Thank God it's a job. After six months of being unemployed, I'm happy to be doing something. But it's quite a different caliber of people I'm working with now, compared to those at the investment firm. You wouldn't believe the foul language. Most of them can't complete a sentence without swearing or using the 'f' word. Plus, there's the usual hassle from the contractors.

We're either too early or too late on the delivery, or the
slump isn't right. Or we don't dump it at the right speed.
I didn't know there was so much to learn about pouring
concrete."

"You'll do fine, honey. You know I'm proud of you for
taking a job that's beneath your skills. It puts food on the
table until you can get back to helping people with their
investments. And, honey, I doubt it's less humiliating than
having to stand in lines at the welfare office." She noted his
smile before continuing. "Did you hear the news about the
prophecy at the White House luncheon today?"

"Yes, something about prison camps and a preemptive
nuclear strike. I wouldn't have paid much attention to it if
the President's father hadn't dropped dead as soon as the
leaders rejected God's command. Wow! It sounds kind of
scary."

"It's awesome. Of course the White House and secular
media are playing it down. They're telling an entirely
different story than those who were at the luncheon. The
thought that our Christian President could even consider
such things is blowing the minds of most conservative
Christians, even those who don't believe God speaks through
prophetic words. All kinds of reports are on the Internet
from those who attended the luncheon. The mainline media
isn't giving them any exposure, except the liberals who think
that people who believe like we do are a bunch of dummies.

"Some conservatives at the luncheon are still skeptical.
But most agree this is a time for serious prayer. If you don't
mind watching the children, Laura and a few others and
I are going to get together to pray and wait on the Lord. I
don't want to exclude you, but I know you're tired and need
your rest. We may want to spend the whole night in prayer.
Is that all right?"

Erich thought for a moment, realizing he would have to
put the children to bed. "Sure, I'd like to be part of it, but I
don't think I can pray all night even if I didn't have to drive
that concrete truck tomorrow. But I agree. This needs to be
taken before the Lord. I've read about those prison facilities
in isolated areas of the country, so it doesn't surprise me
that our leaders have plans to use them. If they aren't

stopped, they'll be sending Christians to such places just as Hitler sent Jews and Christians to Germany's concentration camps. I'm convinced there are no political solutions to the problems we face, so go for it. God promises to answer the prayers of His people."

"Thanks. I'm putting this in the oven for you and children. Bobby needs some help on his math, and Jon wants to quote his Scripture memory for you. They all worked hard on their studies today. We had a great time. I'm sure Lucy will want you to read her favorite stories. I just wish I'd started home schooling sooner. It's such a blessing that we haven't been able to afford the private school."

"Good. The kids seem much happier. Greet the others for me. I'll pray with you until I fall asleep."

• James was driven to a large parking garage and escorted from the car to an elevator that ascended several floors. Taken to a room, he was told to wait. One of the men stayed with him.

After only a few minutes, another man, dressed in suit and tie, entered the room. "Chaplain Parr, I'm Agent Dale Brock. I've been asked to question you about some sensitive matters you brought up at the luncheon with the President."

James nodded. "Am I under arrest?"

Brock shook his head. "Not at this point. We don't know if any crime has been committed."

"So this is a fishing expedition?"

"Well, it's--"

James cut him off. "What I'm asking is whether or not what I say here can be used against me in a court of law. If so, I need legal representation. At least my assumption is that's still my right according to the law."

Brock was obviously uncomfortable. "Let me put it this way. I've never been confronted with this type of a situation. The White House asked us to find out how you learned about the information you revealed to President McCleen and his guests at the luncheon. They didn't even tell us what the information was, just that it deals with national security issues. From my understanding of the situation, if anyone has broken the law, it would be the person who revealed the information to you. Unless that person informed you that this was classified information, I don't think you could possibly be charged for having revealed it."

"You would have a difficult time charging my source with a crime, or at least making it stick."

"That's not for us to decide."

James shrugged. "You're probably right about that."

"Then would you please tell me who the person was and how he conveyed this information to you?"

James rubbed his chin for a moment. "Have you ever read the Bible?"

"The Bible?"

"Yes."

"Well, yes, but not for some time." Brock struggled for words. "But what has that got to do with this?"

James leaned forward and lowered his voice. "You want to know who revealed the sensitive information, right?"

"Yes." Brock raised his eyebrows, and he too lowered his voice.

"Okay, the Bible has many historical accounts of how God revealed secrets through His prophets. So guess what? God is still God. He still works the same way from time to time, and this was one of those times."

James could hardly keep from laughing at the look on the younger man's face. He went on, "Did I know about the prison camps built in out of the way places across America? Yes. Did I know about the possibility of the Russians being set up to launch a preemptive strike against America? Why not? It's common knowledge for those who want to speculate about such things. A number of people have posted these predictions on the Internet."

James raised his forefinger for emphasis. "But I didn't know that the President had discussed these two issues with his Cabinet last night and this morning until moments before I declared it to the group at the luncheon. That's why I said you'll have trouble trying to serve a warrant on the Holy Spirit of God for revealing state secrets."

Brock fidgeted with his tie. "So you're saying . . ." He coughed nervously. "You're saying it wasn't someone from the White House staff or one of the Cabinet members?"

"Yes, sir. That's what I'm saying. Think about it. Part of the prophesy God spoke through me was that if President McCleen didn't tell the truth, the wrath of God would *immediately* fall upon his family and eventually his administration. Right before your friends picked me up at the airport, I saw a newsflash that the President's father has dropped dead. I didn't get the exact time, but I suspect it'll be confirmed that it was right after the President refused to come clean with those at the luncheon. Do you think I could have caused that?"

"Uh, no."

"Do you think God may have had something to do with the timing of this death?"

"Well, I don't know--"

James interrupted, "Just an amazing coincidence, huh?" Seeing a confused look on the agent's face, James continued. "Son, you're in way over your head in matters you don't know anything about. Neither does the leadership in the White House. Otherwise they would not have shown such astonishment at God's Word to them. It must have hit real close to the truth or they wouldn't be so shook."

"You're right, this is not something I'm trained to handle. I think I'd better check with my supervisor as to how to proceed from here."

"Good decision. Ask them to explain this to me. Since I'm a retired, commissioned officer in the United States Army and an ordained, old, white guy minister, I don't fit the profile of a terrorist. And since I haven't been charged with a crime, there's a limit on how long you can detain me. I have a plane to catch and a life to return to, okay?"

Agent Brock rose from his chair. He responded with respect. "Yes, sir, I'll convey this information."

The next hours proved to be a confirmation of James's observation. The agents were over their heads in matters they didn't understand. He had an enjoyable exchange with the agents, helping them grow in areas of the Spirit of God. He forgot about legal matters and turned the session into an old fashioned Bible teaching and witness.

As the afternoon wore on, several agents willingly identified themselves as Bible believing Christians. They explained to the others the legitimacy of the chaplain's claims. While waiting for permission from the White House to release James, the men enjoyed a meal at the cafeteria. The Christian agents were fascinated by the chaplain's experience at the luncheon earlier in the day.

The permission to release James enabled him to catch the last red eye flight out of Dulles for Denver. The delay turned out to be a spiritually invigorating experience for him.

Chapter Three

The Circle of Judgment Widens

Vice President Lynch began the early morning meeting before all the council members were able to take their seats. "Look, people, we've got to get a better handle on this crisis. We all know that, with President McCleen's loss of his father, he's preoccupied with personal matters at this time. It's up to us to carry the ball. My phone lines have been jammed with senators and corporate leaders wanting to know what the hell's going on. The ones I've talked to are pushing the panic button. They don't know what to believe. So, Miles, what's the latest on our media blitz to counter the religious nuts?"

Before the press secretary was able to answer, the door of the room opened. A secretary spoke directly to the vice president. "Sir, your wife is on the phone."

The vice president growled, "I said I wasn't to be interrupted!"

"But, sir, it's an emergency! It's your son!"

The vice president punched the blinking button on the phone console in front of him and lifted the headpiece. "What's up?" He felt the blood drain from his face as he listened. "Wait a minute. The new drug was supposed to prevent that." He listened again for a couple of seconds. Angrily he countered, "But, he was doing fine." Then more softly he said, "Okay, I'll meet you at the hospital just as soon as I take care of a couple of things here."

Slamming the receiver down, he looked visibly shaken and had to work hard to control his emotions. His eyes appeared blank for a moment. When he finally spoke, it was through gritted teeth. His anger increased at every word.

"Someone get that blasted prophet on the phone. I want to talk with him now!"

Richard Languard asked, "What happened?"

"My son, Tommy, is having another seizure, a bad one. My wife just phoned 911. She's taking him to the hospital. He hasn't had a seizure in months because he's been doing great. We thought we had it under control."

Jolene suggested warily, "You'd better go to the hospital, sir. We'll discuss the issues and give you a report."

"No, we've got to get to the bottom of this nonsense now!" Looking at his assistant who was working at the phone, he asked, "Have you got him yet?"

The man held up his hand. He spoke quietly into the phone and wrote a number. He began dialing. "Just a minute, sir."

The vice president drummed his fingers on the table in obvious agitation as he waited for the assistant to connect the call. The others in the room expressed nervous uncertainty with glances to each other or by fingering their pens.

"Chaplain Parr, the vice president would like to speak to you."

The vice president punched the lit button. "Prophet, or whoever the hell you are, I want this nonsense stopped right now! I don't know and don't care how you're doing it, but I want it stopped, or there will be hell to pay by you!"

He listened. Then he yelled, "Don't give me your religious mumbo-jumbo!"

Languard interrupted, "Harry, put it on speaker so we can all hear."

The vice president hesitated a moment and angrily punched another button on the phone.

James's voice was audible through the speaker. "I don't think I'm being unreasonable to ask specifically what you're referring to."

The vice president leaned forward, shouting into the phone again. "You know darn good and well what I'm referring to! You and your bunch are trying to manipulate President McCleen and now my family. We're not going to put up with it! You're messing with the wrong people, you hear?"

"Mr. Vice President, I will tell you what I told your men who interviewed me before allowing me to return home late last night. I am merely a messenger for Almighty God. I do not know what actions will fall nor do I have anything to do with carrying out the specific judgments that He pronounced on you. Nor do I have any idea how or on whom they will fall. If you want that stopped, you must comply with God's demands which were--"

The vice president angrily clenched his hands. He felt a blood vessel of his forehead beating hard. Before James could finish, he shot back, "That's a bunch of crap! The only god is what we make of ourselves or what weaklings like you invent to con equally weak and stupid people who don't want to take responsibility for their own actions."

"Then why are you complaining to me? Why are you asking me to do something about *your* problem? If you're so almighty powerful, you stop what you don't like, Mr. God!"

The vice president was taken back. Not only did the logic of James's comment make sense, the fact that someone dared to speak to him with such boldness surprised him. He was ready to lose control when Jolene spoke with urgency in her voice. "Mr. Vice President, please let me say something."

Realizing that he was losing control, he nodded and leaned back in his chair.

"Chaplain Parr, this is Jolene Howard, Secretary of Defense. Please don't be angry with the vice president. He just heard that his son is having a major seizure. His wife is rushing the boy to the hospital. This is coming on top of the President losing his father. Plus, you've probably seen the news reports this morning. This has all of us deeply concerned. Surely you can understand."

"I understand your concern. I'm sorry to hear of the President's loss. But they were warned by God and told what they must do to avoid further judgment. My understanding was that none of you or your families are exempt--"

The vice president shouted, "He's threatening us!"

There was anger in James's voice as he retorted, "No, Mr. Vice President, I am not threatening anyone. I am simply telling you the facts. It is your hardness of heart and your spiritual blindness that is threatening you and your families."

The vice president slammed the headset down. The people around the table sat in stunned silence before Jolene spoke. "Mr. Vice President, may I attempt to clarify this?"

He appeared too angry to speak. With a sneer on his face, he motioned to Jolene.

"I have a religious background that gives me insight into what is happening. I trust the President chose me for this position because I could add to the counsel of this group."

Lynch rolled his eyes. With sarcasm he blurted, "You were chosen because you're an attractive female with an impressive military background who can be controlled. With you as a part of our Cabinet, we can make the public believe our administration is doing something new and innovative in our relations to the military and the women of color."

Jolene hesitated a moment. When she spoke, it was with firmness. "I choose to ignore your remark. I'll share my counsel since you seem to have lost all objectivity and the ability to understand the true nature of this problem."

Lynch, in a sarcastic gesture, bowed his head toward Jolene and motioned for her to continue.

She made eye contact with the others around the table. "When I was growing up, my parents took me to churches where the type of religious expression we experienced at the luncheon was accepted as normal. I saw people instantly healed and others freed from what they claimed were evil spirits. I also heard many similar types of prophetic messages. Most were vague. Generally nothing specific happened to validate them. When I finished college and entered the military, I set that kind of faith aside because I saw that it would hinder my desire to rise in the ranks. I played the political game well in order to achieve this position but . . ." She was silent for a brief moment. "I never gave up my faith in God. What I have seen happening during these last hours has shaken but also strengthened me."

The vice president interrupted, sarcasm dripping from every word. "Oh, I suppose you're going to tell us you've met Jeeessus?"

Jolene didn't hesitate. Staring at him, she answered, "No, I've simply reintroduced myself to Him. Therefore, I understand what is happening and why it is happening. It's not psychology or mind over matter or some kind of witchcraft. What we are experiencing is the direct intervention of the Creator God into our affairs whether we like it or not." She leaned forward and looked directly into the vice president's eyes. "Or whether we agree with it."

This was too much for him. He pounded both fists on the table so hard the glasses and cups rattled. He then began a swearing streak that would shock old sailors. The group of Cabinet leaders sat in stunned silence, listening to him curse God.

Jolene jumped up, angrily shaking her finger at him. "This is uncalled for! I'll not put up with this childish, uncouth behavior!"

Lynch continued his outburst, pounding both fists on the table. Finally, he pointed a finger at Jolene. "Shut up and sit down! I'm in charge here! I'm god in this situation, so you'll do what I say. Got it?"

The eyes of those in the room flitted from the vice president to Jolene who stood her ground, glaring at him. The group gasped in unison when he opened his mouth to draw a deep breath. His hands rose in the air as if trying to protect himself. He lurched back in his chair so forcefully that it threatened to topple backwards. For a second, everyone froze. Those nearby jumped up and grabbed him. Languard's assistant dialed the phone to alert Secret Service to call an emergency medical team to the room.

The vice president's eyes were wide open staring at something evidently so terrifying that he could only blurt, "No, no, nooooo!" This was spoken with great intensity until a scream erupted that sent chills down everyone's spine. His head fell against the chair, and his arms dropped to his lap. His mouth opened wide, and his eyes stared unseeing toward the ceiling. They heard a rush of air from his mouth but saw no evidence that it was followed by an intake.

No one breathed for what seemed a long moment before a medical team burst into the room. Utter chaos erupted. Some scrambled to get out of the way of the medical

personnel as others tried to leave the room in panic or stood
frozen in fear not knowing what to do. The medical team
laid Lynch's body on the floor and loosened his tie and shirt
collar. Next, they cleared his throat. An attempt was begun
to resuscitate him.

Languard looked at Jolene who had collapsed in her
chair breathing deeply. When their eyes met, she spoke just
loud enough for him to hear. "We've just seen someone who
deserved it enter hell. I don't think he'll be coming back."

He physically recoiled and then sat in the chair next to
her where he placed his head in his hands. She leaned over,
whispering, "Did you hear about the Secret Service Agent's
daughter being miraculously healed yesterday?"

Languard glanced up. "No, what happened?"

"As Agent Barnes was escorting the chaplain out, the
chaplain told him to call home. He would be informed that
their daughter, Emily, whose back had been broken in a car
accident, would be healed. When he phoned home, his wife
was screaming with joy. Their daughter was jumping and
running around the house. Now get this. The doctors said
her spinal cord had been severed, that she would never walk
again."

"This has been confirmed?" He looked intently into
Jolene's eyes.

"Yes. Barnes told the President, and the President told
me. I had my secretary check with the doctors. They have no
explanation. They've never seen anything like it. Never!"

He put his hand to his mouth. "I'm scared, Jolene. I've
not been confronted with this kind of power before."

"You should be frightened!"

He ignored the others in the room and reached to take
her hand. "I want your counsel. I'm serious."

They watched the White House doctor prepare to give
the vice president a shock to his heart. It didn't work. A
medic worked on his chest in an attempt to keep the dead
man's heart pushing blood to his brain. Jolene sensed that
it was futile. God had acted, and man's actions were now
useless. A new kind of fear gripped her as the medical team
placed the vice president's body on a gurney and rushed him
from the room.

• Calieb Ashwah walked across the border of Mexico and Arizona with the help of a Mexican "coyote," a man trafficking in human cargo. Two other Middle Easterners accompanied him. They hiked in the dark through the desert for several miles until they came to a dirt road. A nine-passenger van waited for them and the five Mexicans that had come with them. They were each given a bottle of fresh water and a candy bar. Just before dawn, Calieb and his two friends were dropped off on a street corner in Tucson. He made a phone call and waited until a car arrived to pick them up. They were taken to a safe house.

After several hours of sleep, they were fed and given packets with green cards, cash, and a credit card to rent a car. There was also a map of the United States with their route to New York City clearly marked. They were headed for the home of Sam Kirkland on Long Island. Sam was a sleeper agent who had prepared a cover for them to do their work. Calieb held a graduate degree in biochemistry from the University of Cairo. His two companions were trained in the use of biological agents but were primarily along to carry out the actual distribution of the toxins when the time came to strike.

His most precious possession was a metal thermos bottle, which he kept in a small satchel along with a shaving kit, personal items, and snacks. Even his companions didn't know that, while the thermos contained coffee, the part of the thermos normally used for insulation was stuffed with small vials of deadly toxic biological agents. These were cultures that would produce larger quantities. When released properly later on, they would result in the death of hundreds of thousands and possibility millions of people. His host in America had a lab fully equipped, ready for him to prepare a large batch of toxins.

Calieb had been to America years before as a college student, so the size and wealth of America was not new to him. However, his two companions had only seen America from the viewpoint of Hollywood movies and television. As a result, they were in constant awe as they drove across the country. His attention was drawn to the tension in news reports about religious issues raised at the White House. When they stopped for the night at a motel, he watched the news and began to understand the reason for such turmoil.

It amused him. Christian leaders were accusing their government of grievous wrongs. This had created panic in the stock market and an even sharper division of opinion among the population. He saw this as providential. Allah, Calieb believed, was producing a climate wherein his mission would be less likely exposed because everyone's attention was focused on the problem with leaders.

When his team did strike in the future with biological agents and the suitcase nuclear device smuggled in by another team, the current problems of the American people would pale in significance. After years of preparation, the time to take vengeance for past wrongs was upon them.

•   Top members of the Cabinet were ushered into the Oval Office while the President was still on the phone. He motioned for them to sit down, all the while speaking into the phone. His voice revealed deep sorrow.

"That was Patricia Lynch. She's in shock over the loss of the vice president but says their son's condition has stabilized. He's still in intensive care at Walter Reed. I promised I'd go by as soon as I can." He could barely control his emotions.

Jolene's voice was full of compassion. "Mr. President, we're concerned about you. We've heard rumors about your grandson."

A look of anguish darkened his face. "My son called about an hour ago. His wife put little Jared down for a late morning nap. When she checked on him an hour later, he was already gone. She called 911, but the medics couldn't bring him back. They think it was crib death. The whole family is devastated."

Jolene was crying by the time the President finished. "I'm so sorry. This must tear you apart."

The President nodded grimly. "It's been just 24 hours since my father's death." He hesitated. "Jolene, tell me, do you think . . . " He couldn't finish.

"Yes, I think it has to do with the prophecy. Mr.

Languard and I have come with a plea. We feel it's time for you to consider meeting the conditions of the prophecy before worse judgment falls on your family or the rest of the staff."

President McCleen dropped his head into his hands and rubbed his forehead. "I don't think you understand. I can't tell the truth. It's not my decision. Jack, you know that."

Jack Warren, head of the treasury, nodded solemnly and said, "He can't tell the truth. We all know it would create further chaos in the markets. The DOW took a terrific hit today from the word the preachers are spreading on their radio and television shows. Computer and phone lines to Congress have been jammed. There's even a threat of a run on the banks."

Languard ignored Warren and spoke with conviction to the President. "But, sir, that's the point. The news is already out. People are not buying the lame version put out by the press secretary."

Warren shot back, "Yes, but the majority of the people don't believe the religious leaders. They're just reacting out of fear. If we give the media another day or two, they'll make them look like a bunch of fools. Don't you think so?" His question lacked conviction. Jolene and Languard shook their heads.

Jolene ignored Warren and leaned forward to ask, "But, Mr. President, who else will fall to God's judgment? Don't you believe we're dealing with Almighty God? If you doubt it, I urge you to view the video recording of the meeting in which the vice president was taken."

President McCleen spoke softly, "But, Jolene, he's had a weak heart. Everyone knew he was at risk. He got too worked up."

"No! The timing was no accident. He was cursing God and challenging His authority. It was as if he saw something that had nothing to do with his heart. In fact, I'll be surprised if the autopsy confirms it was a heart attack--"

Languard interrupted, "Mr. President, you know I've not been even mildly religious like you and your wife. Most people don't expect an eastern liberal Unitarian to believe much of anything. But this has shaken me to the core.

It's my opinion that we are dealing with a power beyond ourselves. Frankly, I'm scared. I was going to say scared as hell because for the first time in my life I'm afraid there is a hell. If so, I'm pretty sure that's where I'm headed if I don't make changes. I'm with Jolene. I think it's time you square with the people and get this off our backs. Then we'll worry about the next steps--"

Warren interrupted, shaking his finger at the other two Cabinet members. "Can't you get the facts through your heads? He can't admit anything."

The President slumped in his chair, running his hands nervously through his hair. "I spoke to Mr. Stafford last night. He promised that their spiritual resources are going to be used to counter this attack. You know he's one of the guardians of the Bohemian Grove and high up in several international fraternal groups. He admitted it's a spiritual battle. There was no question in his mind. But he was confident that his contacts are going to be able to counter it. They represent powerful spiritual forces."

The President was silent for a few moments before proceeding. "Personally, I've never taken all that occult stuff seriously. I pretty much left it behind when I graduated from the university. So if they want to believe it and practice it, it's not my place to tell them what to do."

Languard and Jolene exchanged glances before Jolene asked, "Didn't you read your briefing this morning?"

"No, I was helping Mother prepare for the funeral, so I didn't take the time. I glanced at it. I thought you'd alert me if any critical actions are needed."

Jolene said, "Mr. Stafford died last night. His maid found him this morning lying under his pyramid device."

The President reacted as though someone had slapped him in the face. He gasped and covered his face with his hands. "Oh, god. Oh my god!" For several moments he looked like a beaten man. Then he cried out, "He's the most powerful man I know. He and my father go way back. He's my connection with Europe and the real world leaders. Are you sure?"

"Yes," Jolene responded. "We're well aware of the world leaders and their immense power. But I want to remind you, Mr. President, in the eyes of the American people you are the most powerful person in the world. In their understanding, the office you hold is the most powerful human position in the entire world." She stopped and looked at Languard who nodded his approval at her tact.

By now, Warren was on his feet waving his hands and pointing his finger at the other two Cabinet members. "We don't give a tinker's damn what the American people believe. America is part of a delicate global economy where no one person or group rules. It's not in our prerogative to act independently. We must go along with others who have a much greater say and control than we do. We can act independently only when it does not interfere with global plans."

Jolene gestured with her hand to stop Warren. "Mr. President, the removal of Mr. Stafford may be God's way of showing you that you need to exercise the authority the American people have given you. Whatever power his group represents is nothing compared to the power of God. I lay no claims to understanding the complex economic makeup of the global situation. That's not my area of concern. But they are in no position to stand against the will of God."

Warren shook his head in disgust as he droped back into his seat.

There was a sad urgency in the President's voice. "But you're asking me to admit to the American people that we've committed treason. We've betrayed them. Do you want me to admit that we've cowed before world leaders who are out to destroy America, the America our citizens have known, loved, and trusted us to defend? How do you think they'll respond? What do you think the world leaders will do to us?"

President McCleen became more animated with each sentence.

"Do you think the people will say, 'Oh how nice of you to tell us the truth! We'll forgive you and elect you to another four years.' No! They'll charge us all with treason. If Congress doesn't deal with us, they'll throw out Congress as well. The streets will run with blood -- and some of it will be ours. So what it comes down to is this: We're damned if we do and damned if we don't." He slumped low in his chair.

Jolene glanced at Languard who motioned for her to speak. "Mr. President, we've taken the initiative to ask the chaplain who brought the prophecy at the luncheon to meet with you with the hope that he can help you make a decision. He was hesitant to come. In fact, he insisted that his coming be kept from the press. We've sent a military plane to pick him up. He should be here by morning. Would you please meet with him?"

Warren challenged in anger, "You don't have the authority to--"

"Hush!" Jolene spoke like a mother to a naughty child. "We're not asking your opinion."

Seeing the President hesitate, she shifted in her chair. "Sir, since God used him to bring the original message, we feel that God may continue to use him to provide wise counsel. This is not a time to look for a political consensus. This is the time to get directions from God. Who better to trust than one proven to be a reliable messenger?"

They remained silent. The President stared into space. After a minute, he responded, barely audible, "All right, schedule a meeting with my secretary. Tell her to clear as much time as you think we'll need."

Warren scowled from his chair but said nothing. The other two Cabinet members stared him down.

•   Men whose names were seldom associated with political affairs hastily put together an international phone conference. The wealth they controlled and their family heritage gave them powerful authority with national leaders. Their phones used the most sophisticated encryption available.

Sir Robert Lanford Davies initiated the conversation. "I received a call from our contact in D.C., which validates our concern about the events taking place in America. He confirmed that the deaths of the vice president and the President's grandson, coming on the heel of the loss of the President's father, are causing him to falter. He may give in to the demands of the so-called prophetic message delivered at the White House luncheon."

Baron Rudolph Steinberg, with a heavy German accent,

added, "We must also consider the impact of our loss of Mr. Stafford. The enemy is raising the stakes. Perhaps we need to gather the whole council to join us to fight this attack."

Another man said, "I think that's a bit premature. What's needed is for someone to impress on the American President that he must find a way to calm the waters of dissent without revealing our plans."

"Do we need to do more than simply warn him?" asked Davies. "Maybe it's time he's replaced. We have sleeper agents who could do this for us. Since there is already considerable chaos in the American public, perhaps the solution would be to add fuel to it in order to draw attention away from the original focus."

Steinberg affirmed the suggestion. "Yes, we can send a strong reminder to the President and his administration. They need to know who's in charge. If he survives, he'll get the message. If he doesn't, we accomplish what you suggested."

"I agree with these ideas," Davies stated. "As an added backup, one of us needs to talk to the Russian leaders to see if they can move up their time table."

"Could you take care of that?" Steinberg asked.

"Yes."

"Good. I will set in motion our message to President McCleen. In the meantime, I'll put a team together to come up with suggestions as to how to honor the memory of Mr. Stafford."

Davies proposed, "May I recommend that we combine the event with a gathering of the leadership for a full consideration of these matters after we see how the Americans respond and what the Russian and Chinese report? This may turn out to be for our long term good as it draws those of like mind to a mutually agreed upon solution."

"A very good proposal," Steinberg concluded. "I will run this by some of the others and get back to you. Let me remind everyone that we have suffered set backs as did our fathers before us. But we will continue to overcome as we press for the higher goals. Also, we each need to call upon our respective spirit guides to counter the religious aspects of this attack."

The others agreed. This ended the conference call.

•   Russia's President Ivan Solntsev placed a call to Comrade Leanardo Toschoff, the chief architect and engineer of the Yamantau Mountain project. "Comrade Toschoff, I am calling to congratulate you on the excellent progress you and your team are making on the total underground complex. The Politburo asked me to convey our appreciation for the fine work you are doing."

"Thank you, Comrade President. It is my privilege to serve the Motherland in this great endeavor."

"We have one question concerning your last report. Is there any possibility, if an emergency situation were to occur, that the completion date could be moved forward? Or maybe I should express it this way. Since the power plant is up and running and some of the factories are already functioning, would it be possible to consider the main complex fully operational, say in three to six months?"

Beyond the clever deception of the fall of the Soviet Union in the last decade of the 20th century, one of the great achievements made by the Russians since their supposed demise was the construction of a huge military underground complex. The bunkers were to enable Soviet leaders and key personnel to endure counter attacks after a preemptive nuclear strike against the West. The underground cities and factories would also make possible the continued production of vital war material, free from the effects of radiation fallout or missile attacks.

Toschoff's office was in the underground city at Yamantau Mountain. The secret complex was being built in the heart of a granite mountain. It was to serve as a bunker and factory complex where missiles could be manufactured without Western interference or knowledge. It reflected their pride in the progress being made to deceive the West about their ultimate intentions to launch a preemptive nuclear attack in order to destroy America's military might.

There was a short pause as Toschoff gathered his thoughts. "Yes, we can accomplish most of the goals set for the project by then, but we will not have all the life support systems in place for optimal comfort of the entire population. Some of the housing projects will not be finished. Nor will all the systems for production of the comfort foods from the dairy be fully operational."

"So, some of the people will have to make sacrifices in order to carry out the mission which the project is designed for. But it will function as planned."

"In an emergency, yes. But given another full year, as we originally planned, the project will be totally functional. At that point nothing can interfere with our ability to meet the goals established for the undertaking."

"Thank you, Comrade Toschoff. At this point, I fully anticipate that you will have the full year. However, given the political situation developing in the West, some in leadership believe we may be required to act sooner than planned. Therefore, we wanted to hear from you as to how ready you will be if the need arises. Again, we have great confidence in your abilities to meet the goals we have agreed upon. If there is any way I can assist you, as I have stated before, please do not hesitate to let me know."

"Very well, Mr. President. I will do that."

The Russian President hung up and took an expensive cigar from his pocket. Now was the time to savor a bit of fleshly pleasure as he mulled over tantalizing thoughts. He loved the international power plays he was part of. It was similar to a game of chess, but the stakes were infinitely higher than any played before.

Ivan Solntsev had learned how to give a few of his pawns, even major pieces in the game, in order to reach his exalted position in Russia. There was no doubt in his mind that he was playing against men on the international scene who had vast amounts of personal wealth and the inheritance of impressive names of centuries past. Solntsev had neither. But the ultimate power to reach the top of the heap, to pull off a global checkmate would come to the man willing to risk it all with nothing to lose. This was his one opportunity, and he intended to beat all the players in this game for mastery of the entire earth. He would be the first man to achieve this age-old goal.

Chapter Four

Answering the Call to Duty

James had been in the Denver airport when the call from the vice president came on his cell phone. In no mood to mince words with the number two man in Washington, it still bothered him that the VP had cut him off. However, at the time, he dismissed it. When his shuttle flight landed at Montrose, the first thing he saw on the television in the lounge area of the airport was news of the vice president's death. It stopped him short.

He watched with a crowd of travelers as the reporter related the details. Those around him expressed their thoughts with no hesitation. He murmured, "Wow, Lord, you're taking this serious!" Noticing that a TV crew was watching the passengers who waited for their baggage, he decided to collect his suitcase later. He ducked out a side door and headed for his car.

After bringing Ann up to date, he made a conference call to his prayer group to give them a firsthand report. He also contacted three of the group who were unable to be in on it. Then phone calls from the media began. Several religious leaders had publicly identified James as the one bringing the prophecy. He told them he had no comment. There were plenty of other people at the luncheon who could give them all the information they needed.

Because of the insistent attention from the media, he almost missed the phone call that came from Washington. The telephone company interrupted a conversation to inform James that the White House was phoning. Jolene Howard persuaded him to accept their invitation. A military plane had been scheduled to pick him up and fly him directly to Washington for an early morning meeting with the President. After the call, he looked through a couple of newspapers, logged onto the Internet, and caught up on what was happening throughout the nation. He had seen and read enough to know that all the religious leaders who attended the luncheon were spreading the message of the prophecy.

It didn't surprise him that the media was playing up the extremes on both sides of the issue. They had ridiculed him and his close friend, retired Major General Mark Leland, before. He prayed that the Christians would get the message: This was a time to pray, not an opportunity to get into theological arguments over how God manifested His will.

James struggled with the request from the two Cabinet members to counsel the President. He sensed that his part in the whole affair was to deliver the message and fade into the background. Given the realities of the modern media, that proved to be a naïve assumption. He didn't trust the urge to get involved yet reason demanded that something had to be done. The news media made it sound as though the nation would be torn apart by the tension and turmoil. The ACLU was threatening lawsuits and screaming about the separation of church and state. He turned to his trusted friend, General Leland.

"Mark, you've been in the Washington scene. Do you think I should counsel the President?"

"Unless you've had a direct word from the Lord not to, I'd say yes. But don't let the Oval Office scare you. He's a man who puts his pants on one leg at a time just like us."

"Yes, but the pants he fills happen to be those of the man in the most influential position in the world."

"So? He's still a man. More importantly, God is the One Who set this up."

"But I thought my job was only to deliver the message."

"That's all you needed to know at the time. How many times have you pointed out that, if we knew the full plans of the Lord ahead of time, we'd either do nothing or we'd wet our pants? However, I think your request to keep it from the press is correct. That protects the President as much as it does you."

With no response from James, the general continued, "You see how the press and the markets are in a panic. Something has to give. Let the Lord work through you. We'll cover you with heavy artillery and air strikes, through prayer of course."

James acknowledged good naturedly, "Yes, sir, general, sir. I'll take that as an order."

After the conversation with Mark, James gave Marcie, his personal secretary and ministry co-laborer, orders to contact a list of people he didn't have time to talk to. His prayer partners were not to share the information with anyone. When Marcie understood what James wanted, he went home to shower, repack, and nap.

Ann already had fresh clothing laid out for him. He asked her for a back rub and prayer to help him place the whole matter in God's hands. He accepted her assurances and was soon asleep.

•   Media trucks and vans, sent to interview James, were stopped at the edge of his property. He would have privacy at his house. General Leland arranged for him to be picked up by Sergeant Ball after he walked across a field at the back of his property to avoid the media.

James arrived at the Montrose terminal around 5:00 p.m., and noticed that the jet, an Air Force Gulfstream, had already landed and taxied up to the terminal. While an Air Force captain escorted him to the aircraft, he became aware of the speculation among the local people. He was sure Ann would receive a number of calls from friends trying to find out what was going on. He chuckled as he boarded the lavish plane. Besides the captain and crew, he was the only passenger. After a delicious meal, an attendant folded his seat into a bed and gave him a blanket. James woke up just as the jet was touching down.

By midnight, he was in a guestroom at the White House. As exhausted as he was, James was too pent up to sleep. He read his Bible, prayed, and slept a couple of hours before a porter brought him breakfast at 6:00 a.m. An hour later, Agent Barnes arrived to escort him to the Oval Office.

Outside the door of the Oval Office, Barnes stopped, fumbling for words.

James sensed his frustration. "You don't need to thank me. I was just the messenger. How's Emily?"

"She's doing great, just like her old self. We're so grateful that she's healthy again."

"I rejoice with you. Give her a big hug for me."

"I'll do that."

Entering the Oval Office, the President rose from his desk and met James half way across the room. They shook hands. The President thanked him for coming and told him to sit on a sofa near the massive desk. James noticed the President's puffy eyes. His exhausted appearance didn't match his pleasant words. Without a suit coat, he appeared informal. James was glad for his suit and tie even though it was not his usual attire.

"Would you like coffee?"

"No, thank you, sir. I was served a fine breakfast. I'm all right for now."

The President sat across from him. He noticed the chaplain's glances around the room. "Maybe we should have met in a less formal setting," suggested the President.

"No, this your office. I admit I'm awed. But I was reminded by one of my friends that this belongs to the people of America, and I'm one of those people." Then he added, "Perhaps if I lead us in prayer, it will help both of us relax so we can get on with God's agenda."

The President nodded his approval before bowing his head.

"Our Father in heaven, thank You that we can come into Your Presence and approach Your throne room as two of Your servants. We acknowledge that it is only because of the shed blood of the Lord Jesus Christ that we can approach You. We stand robed in His righteousness and come in the faith He has given us. You know, Lord, how inadequate I feel. You know how my brother here mourns the losses of his father and grandson. I cannot know the weight of responsibility he feels in his position. But, Father, You know our hearts better than we know ourselves. And You know the plans You have for us as individuals and for America as a nation.

"So we humble ourselves before You and ask that
your Holy Spirit supernaturally guide and teach us. I ask
specifically, by the shed blood of the Lord Jesus Christ
and in the power of His Name, that You bind any and all
demonic and evil spirits that may be in or near this room.
Send mighty angels to war, and banish the evil spirits from
our presence so there will be no lies, deception, or confusion
of darkness. Let the light of Jesus the Christ shine in this
room. We now commit ourselves and this time to You. In the
Name of the Lord Jesus Christ, Amen."

The President sighed. He had a look of relief. "I feel
like a weight has been lifted off my shoulders because you
prayed."

"You're probably right. There is a spiritual dimension
just as real as this physical room with all its furnishings.
I asked and believed that the Lord Jesus would clear out
the demonic spirits here trying to hinder us. I have prayer
partners covering us with prayer at this moment. There are
millions of Christians praying about the crisis we're in. I'm
sure many are praying for you. So may I ask some pointed
questions?"

"Yes, I want a man to man, honest talk. I admit that I
was irritated at you after the luncheon. But I've come to
realize you brought a message from God. I can't be angry
with Him. And if He trusted you to bring such a powerful
message, I need to trust that He can give me counsel
through you. I am not ashamed to admit I'm hurting." He
cleared his throat. "I'm also frightened and confused. I feel
as though I'm in an impossible situation. I need answers and
direction."

"Good. Then are you a professing, born again believer in
the Lord Jesus?"

"Yes, I am."

"I also understand that you are a member of The Order
of Bonesmen and participated in satanic rites during your
college years. Is it true that you have not publicly renounced
your membership in that group?"

The President shrugged. "That was during my
college days. It was expected that it would be a life long

commitment. I view it like fraternity rites or a country club membership. The members help each other, but I don't take the spiritual side of it seriously."

"But, sir, the devil and his demons take it very seriously. What you consider to be mere ritual is actually a dangerous spiritual bondage. In the past and now in the present, I suspect this has been putting a curse on your life. I believe it'll continue to hinder you from full obedience to God until you renounce this hold over you. It's a scary area to think about, right?"

The President nodded, looking uncomfortable.

"Let me give you some of my personal experiences with demonic spirits. When I was in Vietnam as an army chaplain, I was placed in combat situations where I had to kill men in self-defense. Several times I was in the middle of deadly battles and, therefore, had to deal with the horrors of war. The Lord later showed me that, when I was wounded and knocked unconscious, the fear of death opened my soul to evil spirits released from the men who had been killed around me. The evidence of this was that I later became depressed, angry, suicidal, and full of hatred toward the enemy. I doubted God.

"Fortunately, before I left Vietnam, I counseled with an older chaplain who told me I was being oppressed by demonic and evil spirits. It wasn't just the flesh or frazzled nerves. He taught me a simple prayer of deliverance that over the next months, well actually years, the Lord used to set me free. Areas of my life that I previously thought were mere problems of the sinful flesh, I discovered were actually motivated and empowered by evil spirits or demons. Since then, I've counseled many veterans with the same problems. I suspect what you consider to be fleshly issues in your life are actually subtle effects of evil spirits."

The President thought for a moment and replied with caution in his voice, "You mean when I lose my temper, curse, and agree to some things I know aren't right in order to get along, I'm doing it because of the influence of evil spirits?"

"Could be. Sometimes it's hard to know whether it's fleshly weakness, temptations, or spiritual influence. But here's the good news. If it is demonic spirits, you can cast them out, drive them away, and be set free if you want to be rid of them."

"Isn't it shirking our responsibly to blame everything on the devil?"

"It can be. Some people do that. Yet the abuse does not negate the reality that we are attacked and sometimes oppressed by demonic and evil spirits or that Jesus wants to free us from them."

"But how do I know what is of the flesh and what is rooted in spiritual activity?"

"You don't have to know. If you aren't sure, ask the Lord Jesus. Let Him handle it."

James reached into his coat pocket and pulled out a 3 X 5 card. He handed it to the President. "Please read this," he suggested.

James prayed silently as the President read a short prayer. When the nation's leader looked up, the chaplain began to explain. "Note the first phrase in the prayer, 'Lord Jesus Christ, I acknowledge that this problem, whatever it is, may be caused by demonic and evil spirits, and if so, I want nothing more to do with it." James stopped to clarify this. "You don't have to know. Lay it before the Lord. He knows.

"Notice, when you pray this, you should use the full title of the Lord Jesus Christ. There are many false lords. Some demons call themselves Jesus. Christians engaged in this type of ministry know there are many false messiahs or deliverers that claim to be from God. But there is only one Lord Jesus Christ Who died on the cross and rose from the dead. He's seated at the right hand of God the Father and has authority over everything in heaven and on earth.

"Next, pray, 'Lord Jesus Christ, I ask that by Your shed blood You bind any and all demonic and evil spirits associated with the specific problem.' Name the specific problem. 'We ask that, You, Lord Jesus Christ, bind them with all their families of active and inactive spirits.' In other words, we're asking our Lord to gather all the spirits that are harassing us in this area. Then we move on to the next request.

" 'Lord Jesus Christ, I ask that You send these spirits to the pit where they can never return to harm, hurt, or harass me or anyone else ever again.' Some theologians may argue that there is no Scripture that directly permits us to pray this, but what it means to me is that we are asking and trusting the Lord Jesus Christ to get rid of them. Where He sends them is no particular concern of mine as long as they don't bother me any more.

"Finally, the logical thing at this time is to give thanks. 'Thank You, Lord Jesus Christ, for hearing our prayer and sending the spirits to the pit, never to return.' Does this make sense to you?"

The President nodded, viewing the card in deep thought. Quickly, his mood changed. James was startled to see the President look at him with glazed eyes. His pupils had narrowed to slits. He had a sneer on his face. James recognized a demon manifesting.

A deep voice spoke, unlike the President's. "You can't have him. He belongs to us by blood covenant. Get out of here before we destroy you."

A cold fear shot through James. Had he not experienced this before, it might have thrown him into confusion. Instead the Spirit of God welled up in him. He forcefully countered, "That covenant was broken and paid in full by the blood of the Lord Jesus Christ. You spirits of darkness and deceit must go. He belongs to Jesus!"

The muscles in the President's neck stood out. His jaw clenched, and a low growl immerged from his throat.

James looked into the President's eyes as he addressed him. "Mr. President, do you want to be free from these demons of hell?"

He watched an intense struggle take place. Fighting for breath, the President gasped, "Yes!"

"In your mind, order them to relinquish control of your life. Fight them!" Speaking to the spirits, James commanded, "In the Name and by the power of the shed blood of the Lord Jesus Christ, leave him. You were defeated at the cross. By the power of His resurrection, release your hold and leave, never to return. Now!"

The growl turned to screams. Throwing the President

backwards, a force knocked the chaplain back, too. The President's body went limp, sliding to the floor. Conscious of a door opening, James saw Agent Barnes burst into the room with a drawn pistol.

James smiled and held up a hand. "It's all right. He's fine."

Barnes stood transfixed. He and James watched as the President opened his eyes, smiled, and pulled himself into a sitting position on the floor. James pointed to the agent.

The President looked at Barnes. "Everything is under control. Thank you for your concern, but please leave us."

The agent holstered his weapon and backed from the room, closing the door behind him as he spoke into a tiny microphone, canceling the alert.

James stood, extended his hand, and helped the President to the sofa. "I was about to say that we needed to command the demons not to manifest themselves or put on a show. But I trust the Lord knew we both needed to see the dominant spirit expelled before we deal with others."

The President rubbed his forehead, marveling, "Why haven't I known about this before?"

"Because you were under tremendous deception. Unfortunately, most churches no longer teach these realities. The demons don't want you to know of their presence or the way they're manipulating you. Now that you know this is real, do you want them running your life?"

The President shook his head and spoke with awe. "No, no, I've never felt such evil fear as I did before it left. For a moment, the darkness became hellish. I smelled an awful presence."

"You mean something like sulfur and rotten garbage?"

"Yes, and my body went limp as though I had no muscles or bones. It's hard to describe."

"All right, I want you to repeat this as I pray. Lord Jesus Christ, thank You for this deliverance. Fill me anew with Your Holy Spirit of power, love, and a sound mind. Strengthen me with might by Your Spirit and continue to cleanse me of all evil influences."

The President repeated the prayer, adding words of thanks and praise to God.

For the next two hours, James took him through a list of areas over which to pray the deliverance prayer. They commanded the demons to leave quietly. The more they prayed, the larger the smile on the President's face. The worry lines softened, and the look of exhaustion was replaced with confidence.

After a long time of prayer, the President walked to the window where he looked at the Washington skyline. James silently prayed for continued wisdom and leading of the Holy Spirit. He reminded himself that, in God's eyes, this was simply another troubled man like hundreds of men he'd counseled in the past. However, his mind screamed that this was different due to the future of entire nations.

The President turned from the window and walked around his desk. He paced back and forth in front of the chaplain as he spoke. "What you need to understand, and I suspect you already know to some degree, is that the men who occupied this office during the last century were to a large degree controlled by the agendas of others, men who were extremely wealthy and powerful. They held no allegiance to any nation. They bought off, corralled, and commanded power-hungry intellectuals, dreamers, and schemers who viewed themselves to be superior to the masses of humanity. They deluded themselves into believing that acquiring vast wealth and power through wars, theft, and any evil necessary was all for the ultimate and greater good of mankind.

"I'm not saying that all those who were allowed to run for this office were merely puppets or actors playing a part. Their personalities and individual leadership capabilities contributed to what they did. The battles for leadership by members of the two major parties were real for those chosen to run. But the men who controlled the winners were mostly foreigners and still are. They dramatically affected the direction of the nation. There has been an unelected power behind the visible government here in Washington. This is not merely the imagination of the so-called right wing fanatics who hold to conspiracy theories.

"When some tried to oppose, or when they displeased the shadow government, they paid for their resistance with their lives or were removed from office. This is the situation I'm in. If I disclose to the American people the real plans these powerful men have for the nation, I'll be taken out. Someone who will cooperate will be put in my place. It's that simple."

James didn't hesitate to answer. "No! It is not that simple! This comes to mind that I trust is from the Spirit of God. You and those who preceded you in this office were not the only ones responsible for the deceit and betrayal that has taken place. Under America's form of civil government, the people are responsible for what happens in the nation. They elected all their representatives in government, from the local commissioners to the men who occupied this office. Granted, from a human standpoint, the elections were manipulated. Only chosen candidates were allowed to run for the higher positions in both parties.

"While most of the people are still blithely ignorant of what is going on behind the scenes, the truth has been widely reported and available to those with the desire to recognize it. Congressmen and a variety of researchers wrote books, spoke out, and warned the nation about the injustices taking place for more than the last century. The media, on the other hand, did a masterful job of making such individuals look like extremist, right wing nuts. Nevertheless, we all share in the guilt of what has occurred.

"You are, before God, the highest representative of the people in this civil government. God will protect your righteous and just actions. It was God Who created billions of galaxies and gave life to inanimate matter. He created the fantastic complexity of the trillions of cells that make up our bodies. Therefore, He is capable of dealing with the elitists of the world. Secretary Howard told me that she believed the timing of Mr. Strafford's death is a vivid illustration of God's power in these developments. I agree with her."

The President listened intently. Sitting down, he motioned for James to continue.

"Here's the biblical rationale for this. The kings of ancient Israel were to rule the people as God's representatives. When these leaders sinned against God, He judged them severely. But on the other hand, if they repented, turned to Him personally, and led the people back to the worship of Yahweh God, He forgave the leaders and the people's past sins and blessed the entire nation.

"King Manasseh is a prime example. He was a wicked king. The Bible says he filled Jerusalem with innocent blood. He even sacrificed his own sons to pagan gods. Because of this, he was led away captive by the Assyrians. In prison, he humbled himself and cried out to God for mercy. God heard him, released him from prison, and brought him back to Jerusalem as the king. He then purged the temple of heathen idols and commanded the people to serve the Lord God.

"How does this apply to your situation? You've sinned against God and the American people. But so have the American people sinned against God. What is needed is an open acknowledgement of our sin and then to ask God's forgiveness for all of us. This is called repentance, turning from our sin to God and His truth. He promises to forgive. But does that mean there are no consequences for our sin? No, not at all. What we have to do is turn from all known injustice and unrighteousness. To the best of our ability, we must begin to alter our lives and our civil affairs according to the truths laid down in the Bible."

The President ventured, "But, Chaplain, we've committed treason. There are severe penalties prescribed in the law."

"Right. But again, who has committed treason against the laws of the land? All of us! Do leaders pay a heavier penalty for their wrongdoings? Yes. However, this must be considered: How do we get back to where God wants us as a nation? It's going to take strong, honest, gutsy leadership. Who is in a better position to do that than those currently in office who are willing to admit their errors and take steps to put things right? If you were to simply resign and go to prison, what would that solve?" James stopped.

In deep thought for a long time, the President finally responded. "You make it sound like it will work. But I find it difficult to even imagine that your reasoning will be accepted by the rest of the leadership in various areas of our society."

James nodded. "True. Also, the masses are not going

to want to accept responsibility for their actions. They've been conditioned to blame their leaders and to think that by punishing the rascals in power, the sins they themselves have committed can be ignored. But God doesn't see it that way. Since we the people were the founders and guardians of this nation, God holds all of us responsible for what happens. So again, we're at the point where as leaders we either trust God completely, or we don't. That's a decision each of us has to make."

The President appeared nervous. "I'm only one man. Frankly, I'm scared. Not just for me, but what about my family? What will Congress do and the entire nation? Don't forget that we've equipped the Russians and the Chinese with better missiles than we have. Plus better missile defenses. What about the terrorists and the hell the international bankers can create if we don't go along with their schemes? Our national debt is astronomical by design and the sheer stupidity of our past leaders. If the foreign banks that hold much of our debt demand payment, it'll cause a depression like the world has never seen before."

The President stood and walked around the room.

"Sir, I don't pretend to understand the ramifications of all these realities," said James. "But again I remind you, who created the Russians and Chinese? Does their power threaten the God Who created the universe? His Word says, 'I am God. There is no other. I formed the light and created darkness. I bring prosperity and create disasters. I Yahweh God do all these things.' To those who oppose His plans for the world, Psalms 2 says, 'God sits in the heavens and laughs' at their pathetic schemes. In Isaiah 40, God tells us that the nations of the earth are as a drop in the bucket. They are counted as small dust on the scale, nothing to Him. In fact, He says they are *less* than nothing and worthless compared to Him and what He's able to do."

The President rubbed his temples with his hands. "Chaplain, I want to believe what you're saying. I really do. But the weight of the decision is pressing on me. These are real issues. People will demand answers that work."

"You're afraid of what men will do, right?"

"Yes."

"Okay, where do you think this fear is coming from, God or Satan?"

"I guess the devil."

"Right. What did I tell you to do when you feel afraid, threatened, or confused?"

"To pray."

"Okay. So get out that prayer. I'm talking with you man to man, one sinner to another. For a moment, forget about being President. You're a frail human who needs God desperately. He's the only One with the answers."

The President grinned. Reaching into his shirt pocket, he removed the card with the prayer on it. Then he bowed his head, reading it aloud. Both men said amen together.

"Here's another truth from the Bible," James said, "that you must keep firmly in mind. The Bible says the fear of man brings a snare. The prophet Isaiah wrote this, I'll paraphrase it: 'Do not fear the reproach of men, nor be afraid of their insults because the men without God are going to be turned into hell. Those who oppose God's plan will be caught in the traps they set for others.' Why should you, a child of the Living God, be afraid of men who are like the grass that soon dies and withers away? You, on the other hand, because you belong to the Lord Jesus Christ, are an eternal being created in the very image of God. There is no power in heaven or on earth that can separate you from the love or presence of God.

"Therefore, your number one concern is to know God and His will for you as the civil leader of this nation. Then you do what is just and right regardless of what others think or threaten to do. From that point, it's God's responsibility to decide what He does with you and the nation. It's really not complicated. You have seen powerful demonstrations of God's actions to indicate He's at work in this situation. If He can command and carry out His threats, why can't He protect you and our nation if you repent? Now you must walk out what He's leading you to do."

The President rose and again began pacing. He asked with a sense of deep contemplation, "But will the people repent? You just pointed out that most of them are not used to accepting responsibility for their actions."

"Good point, but this is not your decision or mine. What it comes down to is our responding to the Spirit's direction as honestly as we can. Obedience is our responsibility. The consequences are God's, which I know from personal experience is scary. But then God never promised that following Him would be easy or without risk. In fact, it's just the opposite. Obedience can lead to downright terror."

James smiled at the look on the President's face that said, "Gee thanks for nothing."

The President glanced at his watch. "It's late morning. Will God strike in judgment if I don't make the decision now?"

"I honestly don't know. I do know, however, from experience that He uses pressure to get me to do what I'm supposed to when I'm hesitant."

"In that case, if I wait, I risk losing my whole family. If I declare the truth, I could lose my life unless He protects me for doing what is right. But the implication of the prophecy you gave is that, if I obey Him, He will honor it. Does He have the power to protect me? Will He protect the nation?"

After a long moment, the President began to nod his head. "Yes! He can, and I trust He will. Would you please pray for me? I've got a lot of work to do."

James bowed his head. The words flowed without conscious effort on his part. He closed with a blessing by Aaron, the priest of Israel: "The LORD bless you and keep you; the LORD make His face shine upon you, and be gracious to you, the LORD lift up His countenance upon you, and give you peace."

McCleen thanked James.

Before leaving, James offered, "Sir, I've got one more thing to say. Would you pass this GPS co-ordinance on to the Secretary of Defense? I know this may sound weird, but one of my prayer partners had a dream night before last and saw a Russian sub lying on the bottom of the ocean next to a sunken ship. He saw these numbers and recognized them as a GPS co-ordinance. The Navy might want to check this out. I've read that the Russians deny they have missile launching subs off our coast."

The President accepted the slip of paper with a peaceful

look on his face. "I'm getting to the place where weird is taking on a whole new definition."

• Calieb was surprised to see that Sam Kirkland's house was in an upscale neighborhood. Sam kept the grass mowed. He had planted flowers so that the house looked like the others in the area. He did not want to draw attention to himself or give reason to suspect anything unusual.

The day after he arrived, Calieb was in the front room when he saw a woman and three children coming up the sidewalk. The young, attractive, white woman wore a dress. The children looked like they were going to a special occasion. His eyes were drawn to the small girl with long dark hair in curls and a bright pink ribbon.

When the doorbell rang, he answered the door. "Good morning. Mr. Kirkland is not here. May I be of help?"

"Hi, I'm Christine Fleming, and these are my children, Bobby, Jonathan, and Lucy. We live across the street. I don't want to appear like a nosy neighbor, but we noticed that Sam is having visitors, so the children wanted to bake cookies to welcome you to our neighborhood."

Calieb was taken back for a moment but then remembered that he was in America. He was supposed to blend into the community. "Oh, I'm Calieb Ashwah, I am an old friend of Mr. Kirkland's stopping by for a visit. This is very kind of you." Accepting the plate of cookies, he asked, "Did the children bake these?"

The three nodded in unison. Lucy announced, "I put in the chocolate chips and my brothers mixed it and mommy put them in the oven. They're real good."

"I'll bet they are. Thank you."

"Are you new in America? I noticed your accent," inquired Christine.

"Yes. I studied at Stanford University in California in the past. There are not many jobs in my home country. Mr. Kirkland and I are trained in the same area, so I have come to see if he can help me find work."

"Oh, I know how hard it is to get a job in these times. My husband lost his position six months ago and had to take a job driving a concrete truck to pay the bills. So we know what it's like to be out of work. Mr. Ah--"

"Ashwah"

"I'm sorry. Mr. Ashwah, would you like to come to our home for dinner this evening? I don't want to appear too forward, but we like to have the children meet people from other cultures. You see I home school my children."

Calieb looked puzzled. "You school them at home? I have not heard of this."

"Yes. Lucy is in preschool, Jon is a second grader, and Bobby is a fifth grader."

Bobby contributed, "We like home school. It gives us more time to play and do things we like to do. We're study other nations and people of the world."

"That is interesting. I do not know what to say. I don't think there are any other plans."

Lucy exclaimed, "Mommy's a good cook!"

"Oh, I'm sure she is."

This took him by surprise. Hospitality is an essential part of the Middle East culture. Besides that, something inside his heart prompted him to accept the invitation. So he said, "If it would not be too much trouble, yes, I would be happy to come."

The children responded with smiles. Christine exclaimed, "Wonderful! Would chicken and vegetables be all right with you?"

"Yes, that would be fine. I noticed Mr. Kirkland has some special bread. May I add that to the meal?"

Christine nodded enthusiastically. "Yes! My husband, Erich, gets home around 5:30, so if you'd come about six o'clock, that'll be great. Well, children, we'd better not take any more of Mr. Ashwah's time."

Calieb smiled. Something tugged at his heart when little Lucy waved goodbye with a big smile on her face. Turning, he closed the door. He hoped they didn't notice the tears. The memory of his younger sister flashed through his mind. He carried a picture of her with him all the time and pictures of his parents and grandparents. An American made bomb had killed them, dropped by an Israeli fighter-bomber. It was the memory of their deaths that kept him on the mission to avenge them.

Chapter Five

The President's Confession

Retired General Mark Leland had received a head's up call from James that President McCleen would be speaking to the nation at 2:00 p.m., Eastern Standard Time. Mark alerted his wife, Florence, and his faithful aid, retired Master Sergeant Ball. They settled with him in his study to watch the newscast on a large screen TV.

The first thing Mark noticed was the change in the appearance of the President. Expecting to see an exhausted looking man, he was pleased with the solemn yet confident face. Mark was not surprised when the President acknowledged his early skepticism of the prophetic word given at the luncheon. As the President admitted the validity of the message, Mark grinned and looked at his wife.

Florence rolled her eyes and whispered, "Don't give me that superior 'I told you so' look."

Mark laughed and winked at Sergeant Ball. Watching television, he heard the President say, "Upon counseling with spiritual leaders and members of my Cabinet, I have come to the conclusion that I must comply with the demands of the message." Mark clinched his fist and shouted, "Yes!"

The President continued, "I know this is going to cause great anguish in the nation. Therefore, I am asking all those who believe in God and who know that God answers prayer, to plead with Him, that He will guide us so we can make things right with Him and with each other.

"I am confessing my sin and asking for God's forgiveness and for yours as well. If God pleases, I want to lead this nation back to God and the true foundations that made her great, which does not mean I want to use government to force any one religion or view of Christianity upon everyone. I believe God is calling all Americans to repent and align

every area of our lives according to the basic truths revealed
in the Bible that this nation was founded upon. I am
quick to remind you that the first and greatest Biblical
commandment is to love God with all your heart, soul, and
mind and your neighbor as yourself. It's based on love, truth,
justice, righteousness, and joy.

"When I accepted this office, I swore an oath to uphold,
defend, and protect the Constitution. This includes the first
ten amendments. I believe it is understood that this includes
the concepts embodied in the Declaration of Independence
where all Americans are guaranteed the rights of life,
liberty, and the pursuit of happiness. The Founding Fathers
understood that the latter right depended upon the right to
the private ownership of property. This country belongs to
all the people, not just a few privileged wealthy or elite."

Mark shook his head in amazement when he heard the
President of the United States admit that he and those
who held the office before him in the past century had been
heavily influenced by a group of world elitists whose goal
was the eventual reduction of America to a third world
status.

"But for most of the past century, the leaders of our
civil government and those who influenced education, the
media, legal system, and other key areas of our national life
have subtly deceived the masses. They successfully turned
this nation from God and from the rule of constitutional
law. They substituted instead a bureaucracy that is slowly
crushing the vital life from our society."

At last, the President spoke of the world leaders' plans to
use United Nations troops in America. Those who resisted
the New World Order would be sent to prison camps located
within the nation.

Mark asked his wife, "Do you believe it, now that it's
coming from the horse's mouth?"

"Some thought it was coming from the other end."

She tried to ignore Mark's reaction as the President said,
"Anyone who resists the concept of a global government
would be labeled a terrorist and, thus, no longer would have
the Constitution to protect his rights. This leads me to the
second point of the prophetic word. There are world leaders

who believe that most Americans will not give in to such
global leadership and the loss of our cherished freedoms.
Therefore, they concluded that it would also be necessary for
the Russians and Chinese to launch a preemptive nuclear
strike to take out America's military.

"Those who have carefully observed international
relations know the West financed and transferred
technology enabling Russia to build better ICBMs. The same
technology was also transferred to China. This is going to be
difficult for most Americans to believe. Leaders in the past
century, as well as most current high officials, have sold
America out. That is exactly what happened.

"I was deceived to believe that all this was necessary
to bring a lasting world peace. As a result, I went along
with the plans because, frankly, I didn't see any way to
fight these powerful individuals. In my spiritual blindness,
I thought it was the necessary price to pay. But through
dramatic intervention by God, my eyes have been opened
to the truth. Now, unless God supernaturally protects me,
I will be killed for revealing these facts. This is why I am
asking for prayer."

Mark turned to the sergeant and explained, "James
told me about his fantastic session with McCleen. Can you
believe the change that's come in that man? Talk about a
miracle of God."

The sergeant held up a hand, indicating that he wanted
to hear the next part of the President's revelations.

"Polls show that between 80 and 90 percent of the
American people say they believe in God and that we all
must answer to Him for our lives. Surveys show that nearly
fifty percent claim to have had a life-changing encounter
with Jesus Christ. Yet you have allowed yourselves to be
deceived by those who manipulate the media, education, and
the courts. The deception is far too deep for me to explain at
this time in a brief message. Please be patient and pray for
those in my administration who agree with me that we are
to undo the sins of the past."

The sergeant looked at the general and said, "He's
asking for prayer. That's the key."

Marked nodded and leaned forward.

"To begin to undo these two specific wrongs, I am rescinding the Executive Order that says our military must absorb a first strike, if attacked, before launching our ICBMs."

"Yes!" Mark exclaimed, practically jumping out of his chair.

"I am ordering the military to prepare to launch our missiles upon proof of any launch against us. I am also ordering the Air Force to arm our bomber fleet with nuclear weapons and have some of them on ready reserve twenty-four hours a day until we have absolute proof that no nation is threatening us. We will also have our missile launching submarines on constant alert.

"Next, I am directing Secretary of Defense Jolene Howard to begin bringing our troops home from areas of the world where there are no direct threats to our well being as a nation. We will not be the policemen of the world or the errand boys for Europe's elitists."

Mark fell back in his chair, raising his hands toward heaven. "Thank God! It's about time!"

The President shifted his voice, pleading with conviction. "I am also asking that you not panic regarding the economy of our nation. The stock market and banks have survived numerous crises in the past. They will continue to provide their services to business and the nation. There are many good things about our nation. In spite of our problems, there's hope for the future. But we must be honest about our shortcomings.

"As to the prison camps, they will be abandoned. Information on their locations will be made public so that people in the immediate areas will be able to see that these camps are closed and, if possible, put to positive use."

The President hesitated before proceeding. "I want to reemphasize that the problems are so great that there are not going to be easy answers or resolutions without pain and suffering. This is a gigantic shift in direction for our nation. Many elected officials here in the nation's capital and the states will oppose the truth being made known. The powerful federal and state bureaucracies will be in opposition to this because it threatens their future. The only way America can be saved from turmoil is by God's direct help. He has promised in His Word that, if we repent, He will protect us. An ancient promise in the Bible, specifically the book of Second Chronicles, chapter seven, verse fourteen, states, 'If My people who are called by My name will humble themselves, and pray and seek My face, and turn from their wicked ways, then I will hear from heaven, and will forgive their sin and heal their land.' "

Mark and Sergeant Ball exchanged glances.

"Notice carefully that this is directed to God's people, those who are in a special relationship to Him. We are the ones who must repent and turn from our sin. This means our personal sin as well as our corporate sins as a society. Then and only then will God forgive us as a nation and heal our land. I am asking that all churches open their doors this coming Saturday and Sunday for two days of humiliation, fasting, and prayer. Presidents through the centuries have called for this many times. It is a time for each of you to realize that this is your nation and your future. Each of you must take responsibility and do what you can."

The President looked directly into the camera. "Thank you for listening. May God have mercy on all of us."

Mark hit the mute button and looked at Sergeant Ball. "James told me that he helped the President write the call for days of humiliation and prayer and pointed out Second Chronicles 7:14. Man oh man, did you ever think you'd hear such things coming from the President of the United States? Praise God! There is hope."

He smiled at his wife. Florence returned the smile. "Okay dear, this confirms what you've been telling everyone for years." She took his hand. Looking into his eyes, she said, "I don't imagine anyone would ever think of me as a prophetess, but I have a feeling this old general is not going to fade away in retirement. I hear in the distance the sound of a bugle."

Mark grinned. He had always thought his retirement was premature.

•   Christine was surprised to hear the garage door open minutes before five. She slipped the chicken into the oven

along with the potatoes before Erich came in and set his
lunch pail on the counter.

He leaned over to kiss her. "I'm kind of dirty. We finished
early."

Christine poured him a glass of ice tea and placed it on
the table where he sat down.

He took a sip before asking, "Did you hear the
President's speech?"

"Yes, and is it ever stirring a storm of controversy. Wait
until you see the expressions of the big three lead reporters.
It was humorous watching them in their attempts to remain
calm while trying to act shocked."

Erich rolled his eyes. "It's a good thing you couldn't hear
the guys I work with. The Rednecks gloated, 'I told you so,'
while the liberals cursed McCleen and everyone in general.
They claim Christians are a bunch of hypocrites. I kept my
mouth shut. The supervisors had to threaten some of the
men to keep them out of fistfights. What's funny is that
guys who hadn't darkened the door of a church in years
were ready to fight anyone who knocked Christianity. It was
chaos."

"Were you able to get your work done?"

"Yes, mixed concrete has to be poured. But what gets
me is that so many people refuse to see that it was God
Who had the original message delivered. God took the lives
of those leaders as an act of judgment just as He said He
would. Why can't they see that?"

"Honey, remember what happened when Jesus raised
Lazarus from the dead? Some who saw it went away,
plotting how they could kill him. Unless God opens men's
eyes, they cannot see the truth."

Erich shook his head and drank the glass of tea. "Man I
don't know what's going to happen in this nation. People are
mad, confused, and scared. The media is blowing everything
out of proportion. Some want the President to resign. Others
think he's a hero for being honest with us."

Christine began rubbing his shoulders. "My prayer
partners believe more and more Christians are giving
themselves to prayer and fasting. We're trusting this is the
right response." She sighed. "You'd better take your shower

so you can spend some time with the children before our guest comes. They're excited about seeing someone from the Middle East. It's going to be a good learning experience for them."

•   Sam was not particularly happy when Calieb explained the dinner invitation. The men had a great deal of work to do in the basement lab. However, he could not object because they needed to maintain a normal front in the neighborhood. His excuse for not inviting guests to his house was his bachelorhood. He said that his house was never in good order nor had he taken the time to have it completely furnished. The truth was that the basement had been converted into a laboratory with equipment he picked up from throwaway items of the lab at his work or pieces he bought in second hand stores. It had taken him two years to assemble the equipment without leaving a paper trail.

After Calieb was introduced to Erich, the children took their guest in tow. They showed him their home school classroom and the projects they were working on. They asked him to point to his country on the world globe. He was surprised to learn that they knew where the Gaza Strip was. Bobby gave a brief overview of the Israel/Palestinian conflict without taking sides. Lucy found a brief picture book on the shelf that had a story about people who lived in the desert. She asked Calieb if he would read it to her to see if it was like his home.

While the children were occupying Mr. Ashwah, Erich and Christine watched television in the kitchen as dinner preparations were finished. Clips from the President's mid afternoon statement to the nation were being played over and over with comments from news reporters, U.S. congressmen, governors, and people on the street.

Erich muted the sound during the ads. "I think it's funny the way the media is still trying to cover themselves for what they released from the White House against the Christians. Yet at the same time, they're attacking the President for lying to the people while not wanting to admit the Christians were right. This afternoon the two-way radio in the truck was hot with guys damning the President and

the Christians, yet saying they didn't believe anything the
media puts out. Some of drivers admitted they're going
to run up bills on their credit cards before the economy
collapses. They were in no mood to listen to me when I
tried to give them financial counsel. They have a different
mentality than the people I used to deal with. But I'm not
sure I'd want to be talking with my previous clientele at this
point. I don't think anyone knows what's going to happen. "

Christine nodded and handed him a tray of items for the
dinner table. She informed him, "Our prayer circle agrees
that this calls for another all night session. I'm planning
to join them as soon as our guest leaves. Have you thought
what you'll say if Mr. Ashwah brings up the subject?"

"No, I'll have to play it by ear because frankly I don't
know what to think of the whole thing. I'll definitely be
praying with you until I fall asleep."

Christine gave him a hug and asked him to turn the
TV off and call the others to the dining room. The children
showed their new friend his place. Lucy took the chair next
to him. Erich asked Bobby to give the prayer of thanks for
the meal.

Bobby solemnly stated, "Please, everyone bow your
head." There was a long moment before he prayed. "Dear
God, we thank You for this good food our mother has
prepared and dad's hard work so we can have it. We thank
You for our new friend. May You bless him as he looks for a
job. And, God, we ask that You be with our President. Show
him how to make things right with You and America. In
Jesus' name, Amen."

Erich and Christine complimented Bobby on his prayer.
Then Christine asked the children to serve their guest first.
They did this with the same politeness they had shown him
earlier. The room was filled with enthusiastic talk.

Calieb found himself enjoying the company, and the
meal tasted delicious. He was pleased that all the family
appreciated the Middle Eastern bread he brought. He
showed them how people in poor countries used bread as a
spoon to eat. The children laughed at their attempts to pick
up food with small pieces of bread.

Later, while the children helped their mother clear the

table, Calieb asked Erich, "How can you be so nice to your President when it was his actions that caused hardship in your nation and to your family? In my country, we would be cursing him, if only in secret. I do not understand."

Erich smiled, mentally asking the Holy Spirit for direction. "I see him as a man like myself. I've made serious mistakes in my life with tasks I was given. The President's position places tremendous responsibilities on him, more than I can imagine. When I gave my life to Jesus Christ, He forgave me for all my mistakes. Jesus teaches that we are to forgive others just as He has forgiven us. Also, I see the President as my brother in the faith, so this is another reason I must extend forgiveness to him as I pray that God will lead him to do the right thing for the nation."

He stopped to see how Calieb would respond to these thoughts. He saw that his guest was thinking it over, so he waited.

Finally Calieb spoke slowly. "Forgiveness, that is not part of Islam. But if it does for you what I see in you and your family, then I must think about it."

Sensing that Calieb had no other comment, Erich added, "I understand from what I know of the conflicts in your homeland how it might be difficult for you to forgive what others have done to your people. We here in America are so blessed to have escaped a lot of that kind of violence. What our leaders have been doing behind our backs disturbs me very much. I can only trust that a just God will enable us as a nation to right these wrongs without falling into the violence experienced by your people."

Calieb appeared hesitant to pursue the subject further. Erich was relieved when Christine returned and invited them into the living room. The conversation was about the children and general topics. Calieb finally excused himself to go home.

He returned to Sam's house where the two men worked late into the night setting up cultures in a controlled environment. Air needed for the growth of some cultures had to be carefully filtered. The exhaust from the containers had to go through ultraviolet rays, ozone, and carbon filters to kill any viruses or bacteria that might come with the air.

One mistake would cause the men to die a quick, horrible death, and their mission would perish with them.

As he worked, Calieb experienced the first twinges of doubt about his mission.

•   Lyman Moore had taken to computers as though they were an extension of his mind. By his teen years, he'd built his own computer and written software that operated and monitored most of the electronic functions around the Moore's suburban home. Home schooled, he was encouraged to pursue his passion while taking the time to round out his knowledge of man and the world he lived in. After a year in a local tech school, he landed a job with NASA and helped to develop software for a Mar's landing craft. He took a lot of teasing from the older men on the team, but everyone respected his abilities. From there, he spent time at the Space Center in Colorado Springs working on software that tracked the numerous satellites, especially the increasing amount of space junk.

Lyman's tendency to get bored with a completed assignment eventually got him in trouble. Once the main challenges were solved, he began to tinker in areas beyond the need of the immediate project. Instead of taking a demotion for unauthorized use of government equipment, he quit and worked for a local Christian organization at the request of a friend.

The software at the International Prayer Center was not a challenge. It just took time to work through the issues. But the realities Lyman was exposed to for the first time in his life were like a time bomb dropped into his conscious mind.

The first thing he noticed was the attitude of the people with whom he worked. Not only did they stand in awe of his abilities, they also expressed genuine appreciation for his help along with a sincere interest in him. It wasn't so much what he could do for them, but he sensed they valued him as a person. His devotion to computers had left some immense gaps in his ability to relate to others.

Being a young bachelor, he was invited to several homes for dinner. This was followed by invitations to join his new friends at church on Sunday morning with the promise of a cookout afterwards. He gladly accepted even though he'd never thought of God, church, or the hereafter. His parents left the subject of religion up to him. It had never interested him before this.

While attending one of the churches, Lyman was invited to a weekend seminar on creationism versus evolution. The seminar blew his mind. The arguments for God creating the universe were compelling. The numbers and size of the galaxies contrasted with the minuteness and complexity of the human cell convinced him there had to be a God Who created all this. The next step logically followed. God had revealed Himself to man through Jesus, the Christ, and people could personally know Him. During the last meeting, Lyman bowed his head and committed his life to Jesus.

The friends he'd made at the Prayer Center were elated. They confessed they had prayed for him and saw this as an answer to their prayers. It made the whole project Lyman worked on take on a new meaning. Prayer indeed worked.

With the computer system at the International Prayer Center working well, Lyman needed a new challenge. He didn't have to wait long for direction. He had heard about the prophesy at the White House luncheon but gave it only a passing thought.

During one of the chats with his geek acquaintances, he heard of the possibility of a preemptive strike on America by Russian missiles. It took on greater meaning when the President of the United States admitted that it was a real possibility. At the same time, Lyman was challenged by a Bible teacher to believe there was nothing impossible with God. The God Who created billions of galaxies and the minuteness of the human cell was capable of doing anything.

While he was reading his Bible one night, a series of ideas raced through his mind. Since computers guide missiles, somewhere there's a computer system that controls the Russian missiles. What if someone broke into that system and planted a virus to throw the missiles off course or send them into outer space? This could save millions of lives. Since there are no limitations for God, and He the Creator knows those computer systems, why not trust Him to show me how to plant the virus?

With childlike faith, Lyman set himself to pray and ask God to show him how to get into the computer systems of the Russian missile complex. He knew the missile systems had their own communication networks, but at some point, it came into contact with the fiber optic telephone system and, thus, the worldwide Internet. If the right codes were used, it might be possible to break into their system.

•   Jolene Howard shook James's hand before sitting across the table from him. "Thank you again for accepting our invitation to counsel with the President. I'm glad you've agreed to spend time here in the White House so more of us can glean from your spiritual insights."

"You are more than welcome. As I told the President, I'm more than a bit overwhelmed by all that God has been doing through me. It is His doing, so I'm resting in that fact."

Jolene smiled at him. "I understand we have a mutual friend in General Leland. I've had two long talks with him in the last two days that were informative."

"Yes, he told me you served on his staff. He speaks highly of your abilities."

"That's good to hear. I just wish now that I'd been open to his insights into the real world of international politics when I served under his command." She looked down. "I was haughty and set on reaching the top, so I didn't want to hear him. I know now that I needed what he said."

"I can understand why you feel that way. But if you'd known the truth then, you probably wouldn't be here. So accept the fact that God moves in mysterious ways to perform His ultimate will. The Bible says He is able to use even our sins to bring about His purposes."

"I think I'm beginning to see that. Your comment brings me to the main reason I wanted to talk to you. I understand the President mentioned that he felt the Lord leading him to ask me to serve as his vice president."

He nodded.

"I must admit I'm flattered. Yet at the same time, I'm terrified. Given the uncertainties of everything, I question whether I'm qualified for the task if called upon to serve as President. I can honestly say I didn't understand all the corrupting influences the powers-that-be placed on our administration. I just saw it as the dynamic of big money and international politics that went along with maintaining peaceful relations with other nations. I was blind to the satanic push to eliminate America and the Christian influence in the world besides the lust of some for total world control. But now that my eyes have been opened, I'm appalled at the way this evil has had so much negative influence on America and our future. I feel overwhelmed with the changes that have to be made if we're to recover and recapture the greatness of America."

"How has this changed your attitude and the assurance you had in your previous responsibilities?" asked James. "If you had the confidence of taking on the position of secretary of defense, why do you hesitate to accept this role?"

Jolene contemplated her answer. "I had decades of experience and preparation for understanding the role of the military to carry out the policies of our political leaders. While the military has an awesome responsibility to ward off or respond to the nuclear threats of Russia and China, it is in some ways a cut and dried situation. We have a variety of weapon systems and the elements of the different branches of the Armed Services that we can employ. Plus, we have a good idea of what our potential enemies are able to do. Based on this, our military leaders can access how best to deal with the situations as they come up.

"But when it comes to the domestic situation in America, the economic, social, political, and spiritual factors, it becomes extremely complicated. There are no clear-cut, easy answers. General Leland helped me see that vast segments of our population have been 'dumbed down,' secularized, and deceived so they have no concept of what the foundations of America actually are. With the loss of Biblical based morality, greed has consumed people at all levels of society. They have also been conditioned to believe the lies of socialism, so they expect the government to meet all their needs and solve all their problems if they just pay their taxes. Many don't even pay taxes and yet expect the welfare system to take care of them regardless of how they live."

She stopped for a minute, shaking her head. "How do we

bring about the radical changes needed without a burden
of pain and suffering which the people will tolerate? That's
why I feel inadequate."

James raised his eyebrows. "There's no question that the
task is daunting. You've identified the root problems. But I
ask this, who would be better qualified for the task? Have
the men who held the office prior to this been particularly
prepared for the position? Or were they placed in the job and
either rose to the challenge or failed?"

He went on before Jolene had a chance to answer. "I
doubt if there's a man or woman in the nation qualified
to fill the position at this point in time. Whoever takes on
the challenge will have to rise to meet it with the help of
God and the good will of those people in the nation mature
enough to know that it's a humanly impossible task.

"What it comes down to is for you to hear from God and
know in your heart what He wants you to do. We have to
trust that He put us in our particular positions for this time
with these challenges. Therefore, He'll give us the grace,
strength, and wisdom to do what He sets before us."

"You make it sound like it will work."

"I don't want to talk you into it. You're going to face some
hard challenges. There are a lot of white people who will find
it difficult to accept a black in this position of authority. Add
to that, those who don't want a woman or someone with a
military background in this position. Then there's the party
affiliations and the petty bickering that will come from those
quarters."

James raised his hand to make the next point. "I think
many people are seeing that the problems we have are
bigger than party politics. But don't forget, you've faced all
the above issues before. You've dealt with them successfully
to this point, so why not in the next phase?"

She smiled. "From what you know of me, do you think I
could rise to the task?"

"Yes. You were the first member of the Cabinet to
recognize God at work. It took guts to advise the President
to seek my counsel and come clean with the American
people. I heard how you stood up to the vice president. You
later understood that his death was a direct act of God. I'm

impressed at how much you have grasped of our situation once you realized that changes needed to be made. So again, trust that, in spite of past failures or wrong motives, God's forgiveness covers the past and gives grace for the future."

James was silent for a brief time before he spoke again. "To be honest with you, I have to tell you something else. I'm an old fashioned person who believes that the Bible has sound instructions for all areas of life. These don't match most of the current politically correct, secular concepts. God created the man to be the leader in the home, the community, church, and social organizations. This has nothing to do with women being inferior to men or less important in God's creation. It's obvious that we wouldn't exist without the female gender.

"The difference between the male and female goes far beyond the physical. It has to do with our essential callings and duties assigned by our Creator. Men are to lead, not dominate or be tyrants. We are the warriors and, thus, the protectors of the female, our families, and communities. The woman was created as man's helpmate with the high calling of bearing and mothering children and nurturing the next generation. Again, this does not make her inferior or less important than the man. In fact, Jesus elevated women by commanding men to love their wives as Christ loved the Church and gave Himself for it."

Jolene's face glowed with happiness. "I'm glad you brought this up. Not long ago I would have exploded in anger and jumped all over you. But there's been a change in my thinking. Frankly, I'm open to serving as vice president because there is a remarkable difference in President McCleen. I didn't know what it was or why it was important until just now. I see him becoming a real man. He's taking responsibility for his actions and exerting positive leadership. He's no longer passive. I like that.

"When he first approached me with his offer, my immediate concern was could I take the tough political battle of running for reelection. But when I began to pray, I asked myself what I wanted for the rest of my life. I realized that I don't want a career in politics or the military. I want to teach, particularly young women. I was frankly shocked by what I learned about myself."

She fought back tears. James waited. Jolene spoke quietly, "What I really want is a husband who loves me and a home full of children. When I visit my brother and his family, I come away envying my sister-in-law. They have their problems, but they're a loving family, and her children are going to shower her with love for the rest of her life."

Jolene hesitated. "It's too late for me to bear children, but I hope it's not too late for a husband and a change in careers when the time is right. Maybe I'm being too optimistic. Our whole administration could be thrown out of office into prison. But I think the President will survive, so I'll not be placed in the position of being President. I can instead be a positive support to him and--"

James broke in, "The President told me he is not going to resign and doesn't feel Congress will get serious about impeachment procedures because they'll have to expose too much of their own dirty laundry if they do. But of course they will make accusations and threats to impress their voters back home that they're taking their jobs seriously. But are you saying you're thinking of stepping down now?"

"No! I believe God has put me here for this time. I should finish what I've started."

"Good!" James's affirmation brought a smile to her face.

He continued, "There are a number of times in history when God raised up women to take leadership because there was no man with the fortitude to do what was required. I meant it when I said I felt God has prepared you for this task. But, I'm also delighted to learn about your future desires. A successful completion of your current responsibilities will no doubt open many choices in the future."

She thought for a moment before replying. "I will consider what you've said about your understanding of God's different roles for men and women."

"I'm glad. I'll leave you with a favorite quote from Scripture: 'There's nothing to hinder the Lord from saving by many or by few.' If America is going to be saved, it will be because of what the Lord God does through those who trust Him."

Chapter Six

God Responds

Madeline Logan barely had enough strength to pull the blanket over her after lying down on the sofa. She wanted to nap in her own bed, but she didn't have the energy to climb the stairs.

Throughout the previous months, friends from her church had brought in meals and cleaned the house regularly, but their presence drained her. Madeline had little energy to spend time with others.

Cancer had spread through most of her body. Not only was the chemotherapy not helping, it had left her bald, puffy, and with pain that even the pain killing drugs didn't help. Tears fell on her pillow as she grappled with conflicting thoughts racing through her troubled mind. Her friends said the right things and showed love and compassion, but could they really understand what she was facing? She didn't think so. How could anyone comprehend the dilemma of being told one had an incurable cancer unless experiencing it firsthand?

The turmoil in the nation added another unwanted stress. Madeline had been active in local politics for years. The recent revelations by the President shocked her. She'd always known about the corruption in the political system but didn't realize the degree of dishonesty. She felt betrayed by those she'd helped place in office, yet was encouraged by the President's confessions and his request for forgiveness. What would these dilemmas mean for the future of her children?

Matthew, her husband, would be home later in the day with their three children. They were always quiet and brought her something to eat, which she swallowed with difficulty. Holding down her food was another problem. She hated being so helpless.

Their faithful friend, Josh Steel, who was a fervent prayer warrior would not give up even when she admitted to him in private that there were times she didn't want to go on living. Her pastor, Reverend Baldwin, also prayed for her as did many at church, but their prayers were nothing like Josh's. He quoted Scripture, pleaded and argued with God, and refused to give up on the idea that God was going to heal and restore her to her family. He believed he had received a promise from God that she would receive a miracle.

Madeline wanted to believe him. She longed to see her daughters, Lisa and Sarah Jane, ages ten and six, marry and have children of their own. She knew eight-year-old Matt Jr. would be lost without her. He had emptied his piggy back and borrowed money from his sisters to buy her a wig. He told her every day that she was beautiful.

She couldn't help but smile at the thought of how much she loved her children. Yet her pain, the nausea from the chemotherapy, and the loss of energy were so constant and dreadful, there was a unending war going on inside her.

In the stillness, she recalled how the Spirit of God had recently revealed that her father, a church elder and officer in one of a local fraternal organizations, had years ago made a pack with the devil to save his business. She gradually came to the conviction that this had given demons the right to oppress her. Because she was afraid to face her father, she made Josh promise that he would not confront him either.

Pondering this, she felt an urge to phone home, but fear instantly shot through her. Memories from her childhood flashed before her of her father's temper and outbursts that caused her to wet her pants. She gasped as the panic inside her grew.

Like a burst of light from a flash camera, a thought pierced the darkness: This fear is not of God. It's from the devil. A verse she had memorized years before came to mind. "There is no fear in love. Perfect love casts out fear."

"Yes!" she cried. "Jesus loves me. He has given me a spirit of power, love and a sound mind. I will not give in to fear. I resist you, Satan, in the Name and by the power of the shed blood of the Lord Jesus Christ. Get out of here!"

Immediately the fear was gone. She relaxed for a moment before reaching for the phone.

"Hi, Daddy. This is Madeline."

The deep, cheerful voice of her wealthy, semi retired father, Clarence Becker, answered, "Hi there. How's my little girl today?"

"Not doing so great, Daddy. Are you by yourself and able to talk for a few minutes?"

"Sure, baby, I always have time for you. I just got home from a lunch meeting at the club. I planned to take a nap before going to the office, but you take all the time you need."

Madeline hesitated. "What I've got to ask you may not be easy to hear. Will you promise you'll listen and not get mad?"

There was a pause before he answered. "Honey, I'm sorry for my temper in the past. I've really been working on it. I've even had a couple of my old associates compliment me on my change of behavior when I'm at the office."

"That's good, Daddy. You know I've been praying with Josh Steel."

"Yes, he's a fine man. I'm afraid I don't have the faith he does, but I'm not too old to learn new things."

"Did you hear the President's speech? He admitted that he's been deceived in the past and was, therefore, delivered from demonic oppression."

"I don't remember that part, but his confessions are what everyone around town has been talking about. We're all wondering how this is going to affect the economy and everything else. I guess I was too shocked when I heard him say that part. I didn't hear anything about demons. Why do you mention this?"

"You remember when you almost lost your business?"

"Yes." She heard the pain in his voice.

"Do you remember telling us you'd make a pact with the devil if he could save your business?" Without waiting for a reply she pressed on. "Did you actually do that?"

All she heard was a gasp.

"Daddy?"

"I'm here. I haven't thought about that for a long time."
Again he was silent.

"Could we talk about it? I think it's important, that it has something to do with my not being healed."

"Oh god, I hope not."

When he didn't continue, she asked, "Daddy, did you?"

"Well, yes, but I forgot about it. Do you really think that could have something to do with your illness?"

"Yes. When Josh, Matt, and I were praying, the memory of you telling Mom and me about it came back as if it happened yesterday. Josh explained how such packs with the devil give him the opportunity to oppress us."

"But my business was not only saved, it has grown to be the largest real estate and financial counseling business in the area."

"I know, Daddy. But has the money really brought happiness to your marriage and us children?"

"Wait a minute, Maddy, don't blame your mom's alcoholism on me. God knows I've spent a small fortune on attempts at rehabilitation. I've got her in one of the best care facilities in the country. Plus, I've covered what your insurance didn't pick up for your cancer treatment. And I haven't told you how much I've spent settling your brother's divorce."

"I know that. I appreciate all you've done. I'm not blaming you. I'm just trying to get down to the root causes. My life is at stake."

A softer voice replied, "I know, baby. I'm sorry I got defensive. I just . . ." His voice trailed off.

Madeline waited for what seemed like a long time before he continued.

"I've been convicted about that in the past. I know it was wrong, but I've been too ashamed to ask anyone for help. I'm not sure many pastors would understand."

She knew he was broken before the Lord, for he wept. She waited to speak until she heard him blow his nose and mumble an apology.

"Daddy, would you confess it as sin to God and ask the Lord Jesus to forgive you and break that curse over our family? Would you do that for me, please?"

"I'm not sure I know how."

"Just talk to God. He knows your heart. If you mean it, the exact words won't matter. Please, Daddy, for me and for yourself and all of us."

She prayed silently. Her spirit leaped with joy when she heard broken sentences interjected with weeping as her father poured out his heart to the Lord. He confessed his involvement in his fraternal organization as sin and pleaded with God to forgive him. Tears of joy fell as Madeline listened, and she said "amen" at the appropriate times. It was the longest time she'd ever heard her father pray.

When he was silent, she quietly added, "Thank you, Daddy. That was a beautiful prayer."

"Will you forgive me, Maddy? I'm so sorry."

"Oh yes, of course. I love you and always will."

"I feel like a great burden has been removed from me. Thank you, Maddy. This is wonderful. But I can't stop crying."

"It's okay. Tears wash away hurt for men just as much as for us gals. I know Josh would love to talk to you and help you understand. He wouldn't think you're weird, okay?"

"Sure, ask him to call me the next time you see him."

"I'll do that. I love you."

"I love you too, honey."

Tears of joy continued to stream down her face as she ended the conversation and hung up the phone.

An unusual warm feeling suddenly flowed through her body. Her automatic reaction was to remove the blanket, but the warmth continued to grow until she realized it was not due to the blanket. She closed her eyes and allowed the healing power of God to move through her. It was so peaceful she drifted into a deep sleep.

• F. B. Markov, head of the Russian Counter Intelligence and a former top KGB official, stood before President Solntsev in his private office declaring, "No! This room has not been and is not being bugged. I have had three different teams check it out. They have the latest detection equipment. The team members were threatened with a death sentence if they missed something another squad would pick up. They all came back with the same report. Comrade, I'm telling you there is absolutely no way anyone could have listened in or recorded what we talked about."

The Russian President took a deep breath and forced himself to relax and speak calmly. "Then tell me, my friend, how did the Americans get this information and place it in their newspapers?" His voice rose with intensity. "How could they know unless you or I leaked this information about our plans to test our new ballistic missile system software in ways not consistent with our treaty with America? Logic says one of us is a traitor."

"No!" Markov shook his head, struggling to find the right words to answer in detail. He wiped sweat off his brow.

Solntsev lowered his voice. "No? Then how?"

Markov dropped into an ornate chair next to the desk, leaned forward, and looked directly at his long time friend. "I have a contact inside an American intelligence agency. Only a handful of our people know about this person. I have no reason to doubt his commitment to us. Neither do I doubt the reliability of the information he is able to pass on. I must add that, by conveying this information, he risks being uncovered. And--"

The President impatiently interrupted, waving his hands, "Yes, yes, get to the point."

"The Americans have a spiritual prophet, a religious seer, or maybe several, who . . ." he gestured in frustration, "who somehow know what we talk about in this room."

The look on the President's face intensified Markov's explanation.

"I know this sounds hard to believe. The American intelligence is as disturbed as we are. They initially scoffed at it. But parts of the information given by these prophets have been confirmed over and over, so the American leaders have come to believe it. They know what can be verified from other sources. I can confirm it because I know what information came from us. Their report of the message is accurate, even the translations of meanings from Russian into English."

The President leaned back in his chair. He too was frustrated but was accepting the explanation. "All right, who are these seers or prophets? Do we know them?"

"Yes, one is the same person, a former Army chaplain, who initially called the American President to task at the luncheon the media reported on. But he is not the only one. There are some previously unknown individuals who have also given accurate predictions and revelations of things to come. Comrade President, our history is full of accounts of such religious people."

"Yes, and most were religious nuts such as the mad priest, Rasputin, who seduced weak willed women and was a drunken psychopath."

"That is true. But the Americans refer to ancient Israel and the prophet Elisha. He was said to know what their enemy's king was saying in his bedroom."

"And you believe this religious quackery?"

"I believe in observable facts. I do not know about the spiritual world, but . . ." He stopped, pointing upwards with his hand for emphasis. "But the facts are forcing me to consider the possibility of a reality that goes beyond the physical. It's something beyond the power of our minds. I remind you of the incidents in the underground missile silo and the weapons storage area. The aberrations or whatever they were scared all the soldiers who witnessed them. In spite of our attempts to discredit their testimonies, the stories have spread throughout the armed forces. Then there is the fact that what was predicted to happen to the American President's family has happened."

"Come on, coincidence or self fulfilling prophesy? One's fears and insecurities cause a person to act out what is feared. You and I have learned not to fear anything, right? Think what we have gone through to reach these positions."

"Ah, my friend, the facts tell me it is more than that. One of the guards in the White House had a little daughter whose back was broken in an automobile accident. Doctors said the spinal cord was severed, that she would never walk again. As the chaplain left the White House, he told the guard his daughter was being healed. When the man called home, his little girl was running around the room, perfectly restored.

"Then there are the reports made by people with no

access to military information, yet they knew where our most secret missile launching subs were located at exact given times and dates. Our subs had evaded detection by the American's underwater devices and their attack submarines until the American Navy was told where and how to find them. We had to withdraw the submarines."

The President sipped his drink, deep in thought. Finally, he looked at his friend. "I want you to know I have not doubted you when I questioned how this information got out. I was simply trying to know how. What I would like now is a full report on this prophet or whatever he is. We will have to take this before the Cabinet and military advisers to see how we can combat these exposures. As you are well aware, while we are close, we are not yet ready for a preemptive strike. Therefore, we must proceed with great caution."

Markov nodded. "We will have an opportunity to find out more about this priest. He has been approved for a visit to our country along with a former defector, Dr. Kampov, who has been invited to read a paper at the upcoming meeting of scientists here in Moscow."

President Solntsev smiled. "Maybe we will be able to see some of his actions up close. This should prove to be very interesting. Yes, very interesting."

•   Calieb was hard at work. It was his shift in the basement with Sam. As he waited for the chemical process to reach its completion before the next procedure, he had time to think. In the days that followed his dinner with the Flemings, he had been in a constant turmoil. When he was not working, he watched the news on television. He was fascinated by the funerals of the government leaders and then the conflicting reports of people's reactions to the President's revelations about his wrong doings. Americans openly opposed the President, and the police did nothing about it. Why did the President allow the media spokesmen to savagely criticize him? How could a society allow such freedoms? America was a mystery, especially those who spoke about forgiveness.

When Calieb was not watching television, his mind kept returning to his visit with the Flemings. He could not put his finger on it, but something had deeply touched him. The love shown among their family members extended also to him. It gnawed at the bitterness and hatred driving his life. Lucy's innocence and sweetness touched a need in his heart. He tried to push these thoughts from his mind, but every idle moment they returned.

Now Calieb sat staring as he remembered the day that had made such a dramatic change in his life. He had been playing outside with his friends when the Israeli jet swooped out of the sky. They all stopped to watch, but their fascination turned to horror when a bomb fell. The explosion knocked everyone to the ground. The noise was deafening. Calieb still felt the fear and shock that occurred when he ran around the corner and saw his home. It was nothing more than a pile of rubble. Later, he watched as neighbors pulled the mangled remains of his little sister from the debris.

A Palestinian Christian family had taken him into their home. After that, his Muslim relatives arranged for his care. But even as a boy, he had noticed something different when he lived in the home of the Christians. Although his hatred for America had been fanned by the Imale's teachings in Muslim schools, memories of the Christians' kindness had never faded. Now those memories, mixed with thoughts of the Flemings, haunted him.

A sharp question from Kirkland brought him back to the moment. "What are you doing? Isn't it time to open the valve?"

Calieb was momentarily taken back. "Yes, yes, I was just thinking of the next process." He busied himself making adjustments to cover his potentially fatal mistake. For the next hour, he was able to focus on the task at hand until their work for the night was completed. But when he retired to his room, thoughts of the little girl pummeled his mind. Her fate and those of untold thousands like the Flemings were the last things he thought about before he succumbed to sleep.

Toward morning, he sat up in bed with sweat pouring from his face. His heart was pounding as he remembered the dream. The prophet Jesus had come to Him and said, "You are being deceived by what you are doing."

"Allah promises I will be rewarded," Calieb had protested.

But Jesus asked, "Do you want to see your reward?"

Intrigued, he answered, "Yes."

"Instantly Calieb was in a room full of beautiful young women clothed scantily in veils. He eagerly approached one who beckoned with alluring gestures. Reaching out to touch her, his hand was burned. The beautiful woman turned into a hideous beast that laughed and tried to rip flesh from his body with fiery claws.

He cried out, "Jesus, save me!" His plea awakened him.

He felt exhausted. His body was tense. When he closed his eyes, the scene returned. Calieb recognized demons from hell. Opening his eyes, he saw Jesus Christ standing at the foot of the bed, holding out his hand to him. Calieb's whole body jumped in fear.

Jesus spoke in His native language. "Come to me, you who are weary and heavy burdened, and I will give you rest. Give yourself to me, and I will give you a true reward, forgiveness, and life eternal."

Calieb didn't know how he knew that it was Jesus Christ, the Son of God. He was overwhelmed with warmth and love that reminded him of his childhood when his mother embraced him after he had awakened from a bad dream. He closed his eyes and heard himself say, "Yes, Lord, I am Yours." Peace enveloped him. The fear and anguish were gone. He felt like he was floating. He had never experienced such joy in his life. When he opened his eyes, Jesus was still there.

"What do you want of me, Master?" he asked in Arabic.

"If anyone harms one of these little ones, it would be better that a millstone was tied around his neck and he was thrown in the deepest sea."

Pain shot through Calieb's entire body. He knew what Jesus was referring to. In the basement, he and Sam were creating enough toxic biological agents that, when delivered to the Washington, D.C., New York, and Boston areas, they could kill millions of men, women, and children. But in his mind, the numbers came down to one sweet little girl. Lucy had insisted on giving him a hug and a kiss on his cheek before he left the Fleming home. It brought tears to his eyes. He felt his heart would burst with anguish.

"Why do you want vengeance?" asked Jesus.

"Because they killed the ones I loved most," retorted Calieb in defiance.

"Will killing Lucy bring back your sister?"

"No, but . . ."

The voice of Jesus was filled with sorrow. "Evil only generates more evil and hurt. It solves nothing. Forgiveness cleanses and heals. Doing what is right creates life."

"Forgiveness? How?"

"As I have forgiven you."

Calieb closed his eyes. His body was shaking, and his breathing, rapid. When he opened his eyes, there was no one in the room. He held his breath for a long moment. The thick curtains blocked most of the morning light. He lay still for a few moments, his mind replaying the dream and vision. He remembered that the Prophet Mohammed had been instructed through dreams and visions.

He got out of bed and opened the door to see if his companions had heard anything. Tiptoeing down the hall to the room where the two drivers were sleeping, he heard the men snoring. He realized that Sam had left for work by now. Breathing easier, Calieb returned to his room and took a shower. Tears of joy fell. He couldn't explain his feelings.

By the time he was dressed, he knew what he had to do. Hurrying to the basement, he checked the sealed bottles and vats that grew the cultures. Everything was in order and would not demand attention until evening. He wanted to destroy that which only hours before he had prized, the accumulation of years of planning and preparation. Now he hated it.

In the rental car, he drove to a shopping center. Finding a pay phone, he parked in front of Starbucks and walked to the phone where he looked up the number for the FBI and made the call. He told them where he was and that, in order to stop a major terrorist act, it was urgent for them to meet him immediately. He had finished his second cup of coffee when two men in suits approached him.

"Are you Calieb?"

"Yes." There were only a couple of people at the tables on the other side of the room, but still Calieb asked, "Could you discreetly show me identification."

The two men sat down and glanced around to see if anyone was looking before pulling out their badges and sliding them over to Calieb.

"Thank you. I have survived this long because I learned to be cautious. May I suggest you order something to drink?"

Agent Will Davis turned to fellow Agent Bradley. "I'll take a double Latté with cinnamon."

When Bradley went to get their order, Calieb slid his green card and international drivers license to Davis. The agent laid a small digital recorder on the table and pressed the record button as he examined the documents.

After Bradley returned to the table, Calieb began to explain the operation at Kirkland's house and their plans to spread biological agents by small planes and vans from the D.C. area up the coast to Boston. He gave the agents details that changed their initial skepticism to enough concern that they ignored their coffee. Davis took out a note pad and began to take notes and then looked around to be sure they were not being overheard. He concluded that one of the best ways to hide was to be in the open where no one would suspect anything serious happening.

When Calieb finished and then had answered a couple of questions about the size of the group he was working with, Agent Davis asked, "Why are you doing this? Why are you turning on your own people at this point in the operation?"

Calieb did not hesitate. "I saw the true God, the Lord Jesus Christ, in the lives of my neighbors. Then early this morning Jesus appeared to me." He described the dream and vision and saw the skeptical looks on the agents' faces. So he asked, "You have heard about the unusual things happening in this nation and your President's confession, haven't you?"

The agents nodded. Calieb asked again, "Are you still surprised by such a spiritual experience as I relate? You must not be true believers."

Davis looked at Bradley and answered, "Well, let's just say we're not all that religious, but we're open. I believe you."

"All right. As a result of my experiences, I gave my life to Jesus. He totally changed me. I don't understand it, but I cannot allow this evil to fall on such good people as the Fleming family or upon a nation that is trying to change for the better."

Tears filled his eyes and his voice broke. "What was meant as evil, I believe God will use to show His love and concern for those who are seeking Him." He struggled to control his emotions.

Davis hesitated before inquiring, "How much money are you expecting?"

Calieb looked puzzled. "What? This has nothing to do with money. This has to do with God's concern for life. A horrible evil must be stopped. Can't you see this?"

Now Davis looked puzzled. It was unusual that an informer would not want payment.

Calieb shrugged the lack of response off and asked for a page from Davis's notebook. He drew a diagram of the basement lab. "These are extremely dangerous biological agents. All the men involved have been highly trained and are expecting to die carrying out this operation. I do not believe they will surrender under any circumstances. If the toxins are released into the air and allowed to spread beyond the house, there will be no way to stop their growth. None!"

He looked around the room uneasily before confiding, "Tonight two more specialists will arrive to help work on the cultures. From this point on, there must be constant care of the vats by technicians who know what they're doing. I'm scheduled to watch during the day, and the other two will work nights. Within forty-eight hours we will have enough to begin the dispersion. I suggest that Mr. Kirkland be picked up at his work, but the rest of the team will remain in the house. I can leave in the evening by visiting the neighbors. The others will not suspect anything."

"What you're saying is that this is not a job for a regular SWAT team. This calls for specialists who know what they're doing, who recognize the dangers."

"Yes, by all means."

"I've got to bump this up to Homeland Security. We'll try to get this set up for tonight. If you get a call from Kirkland's company that he's been detained by a problem at work, you'll know it's set up for tonight. If we can't, meet us at the Flemings'. We'll set up a command post and proceed from there."

After leaving the agents, Calieb drove back and parked the car in Sam's driveway. He went across the street and asked Christine if he could bring the family a pizza dinner that evening. She happily agreed. Calieb then returned and monitored the cultures. He had to fight the urge to destroy them but knew he didn't have the proper way to do so. At 4:30, he received a phone call that Sam had been detained at work. He knew the raid was on.

At five o'clock, the two fellow terrorists they had been expecting arrived at Sam's house. Calieb opened the garage door for them to drive their van inside. When the door closed, they each brought a suitcase into the house. They also had two dispersing units into which the toxins would be loaded. There was another van already in the garage. Both vehicles were to be equipped with fogging equipment to disperse the biological agents outside through another exhaust pipe. The plan had been for the toxins to be sucked into people's cars and carried to places a long way from the freeways before affecting the occupants. By this time, the people in the cars would be carriers, infecting everyone who came in contact with them.

Calieb helped unload the devices and took the men downstairs. There he brought them up to date on the cultures. Both had been trained as microbiologists, so they understood the procedures. They looked over the charts that explained the stage of the cultures. After answering their questions, Calieb explained that he would be at the neighbors' house maintaining the image. The men smiled. As he was leaving, he casually mentioned that Sam would be working late at the office. They didn't appear concerned. Again, it was all part of keeping up appearances.

•   A small group in the White House was the only one to have contact with the President's special guest. James spent most of his time in his room fasting and praying. Agent Barnes either personally escorted him to the exercise room or assigned another agent to take him when no one else was using the facilities.

Early each morning James was asked to join the President in his private quarters or the Oval Office. The President leaned on the chaplain for support during the emotion laden days of the national funerals for his father and Vice President Lynch. James watched the proceedings on television, as did most of the country. The extraordinarily heavy security limited the public's access to the proceedings.

The funeral of President McCleen's grandson was small and private. Since there were no cameras, the President asked James to join the family. It was an emotionally draining occasion for everyone, including James.

Even though the awe of being at the White House and mingling with political celebrities had faded, the sense of responsibility it placed on him was challenging. He alternated between giving thanks for the opportunities before him and asking God why. In fifty years of counseling, he was able to keep marriages together; help young people make decisions about who to marry or where to go to school; and, in a few cases, prevent businesses from going under. Here in Washington he was an unofficial, but nevertheless critical part of a team whose decisions could affect the life or death of literally millions of people and the future of nation states.

His knowledge of the Scriptures, history, and current events, plus his mature faith in the Lord gave him confidence. But at the same time the power and sheer evil of the enemies they were up against shot terror into his heart. The pressure brought nightmares originating from his combat experiences in Vietnam. The demons of hell were opening old wounds in an effort to confuse his ability to respond to current challenges.

After James's meeting with Jolene Howard, Secretary of State Richard Languard arrived at his room. Languard said, "Chaplain, I'm strangely at a loss of words to express my appreciation for what God has done through you."

James raised his hand, but Languard continued. "I know you'll say it's all the Lord's doing, and I'm beginning to understand that. But, I appreciate the struggle it has been for you to come into this high charged place and not be intimidated.

"When you led us in the Eucharist yesterday, it was the most meaningful experience of my life. Your illustration of the grain of wheat was incredible. The simple example of how it has to be buried in the ground and die in order to spring to life to produce more wheat and then grains of wheat being crushed into flour for bread was moving. It was the first time I understood why Jesus was crucified, why He had to be broken and shed His blood in order to pay for my sin. So when we prayed, I gave my life to Him. When we ate the bread and drank the wine, I knew Jesus had changed my life."

Languard's face was wet with tears. He wiped them away with a handkerchief before going on. "I was so emotional I couldn't say a thing. It was wonderful and yet scary. That's why I made excuses about leaving." He smiled. "I've lost control of my emotions more in the last twenty four hours than throughout my entire life, but I'm not ashamed. I'm just afraid that if those who know me well saw me, they'd think I was losing it."

"I knew something important was going on inside you." James exclaimed, "Praise the Lord for what He's done!"

"Amen! What's amazing is that the President of the United States and his wife, two cabinet officers, a secretary, a cook from the White House kitchen, and two secret service agents were in the group. Can you appreciate what it means for a former snob like me to be comfortable and actually feel love for all these people? Woe, this has to be God at work." Languard leaned back, shaking his head.

"That's the power made available to us when gathered at the Lord's Table. While seated before our Creator God, we're of equal value even though we have different functions in life. And when we lift up the bread and the cup, we are participating in the most significant event in the history of mankind. We're not just looking back. We are also proclaiming the future as we join the conquering Jesus Who moves forward to bring the entire creation under His rule.

"I especially want those of you in leadership positions to realize you're not alone in these struggles. The King of all kings and Lord of all lords is with you. Breaking bread together is more than a nice ritual or symbol. It's a tangible way of acting out the reality that we are in Him and He is in us to work out His designs for His creation. When we covenant together with the Lord Jesus and one another, it's the most powerful thing we can do.

Languard spoke quietly, "That's awesome." He glanced at his watch, sighing deeply. "I want to learn more, but I've got to go and put out some potential fires. We have powerful people that want our heads on a platter. But I wanted you to know I'm a new man. I'm on the right side in this conflict."

They shook hands and embraced. James briefly prayed, blessing Languard before he left.

Thinking about what he was experiencing, James realized that these leaders were like many others he had counseled throughout his ministry. While he respected their high offices, he related to them as peers even though they held positions of tremendous authority. What General Leland told him was true. They were ordinary people with extraordinary responsibilities.

When James called his wife and prayer partners or had to take care of ministry related matters with his secretary, Marcie, the origination of the calls were blocked. His wife, Ann, and Marcie were the only ones who knew where he was.

Agent Barnes stopped at James's room for prayer every day before going home. The two men quickly bonded. When James told the younger man that God had warned him of a threat on the President's life, Barnes listened attentively. The threat would come either from a sleeper agent or a "Manchurian candidate," as coined by the famous movie. Whatever, someone had been carefully trained and planted within the existing structure. James was sorry that God had not revealed to him more particulars.

Barnes took the warning seriously and began examining the records of men in the President's detail. He prayed in ways he never had before. All his life, what little religion he observed was private. It had little to do with everyday life and nothing to do with his work.

The healing of Emily radically changed all that. Barnes

gave his life to Christ and experienced a peace and sense
of God's presence never felt before. He read the Bible and
asked about a church that believed God would provide
direction for every area of life through the Holy Spirit.

Going through the records of the agents under his
authority, Barnes had a strong impression to commit
this to God in prayer and ask the Holy Spirit to give
him supernatural insight. It was his task to protect the
President. He knew there were powerful forces wanting the
President destroyed. Barnes bowed his head and began to
cry out to God for direction and help. At first, he was tense
and fearful. Was this real, or was this a psychological game
he was playing? Then he thought of the DVD he'd watched
on the crucifixion of Christ. The debt Jesus paid for him
was real. The changes in his life and family were equally
real. Gradually a sense of peace spread through his mind.
He began to thank the Holy Spirit for being his Teacher,
Comforter, and Helper. Agent Bob Campbell came to mind.
He looked through the stack of files and pulled the man's
folder.

Campbell, a graduate of West Point, had served as
an intelligence officer in the first Gulf War and then had
a tour with the CIA before coming to the Secret Service.
Everything looked in order. He had nothing but high marks
from his past supervisors and ranking officers. But one thing
was missing. What had he done with the CIA? There were
no details, just a glowing letter of recommendation from the
director. He was not married except to his profession. That
was not unusual, but something in his gut instinct troubled
Barnes. Was this the Holy Spirit? He would have to watch
Campbell.

•   Calieb arrived at the Flemings' home with pizzas. He
asked to speak privately to Erich and Christine. He told
them what he had been involved in and about going to
the FBI. Then he shared about his encounter with Jesus.
Their shock turned to smiles. They spoke of a group in the
neighborhood that had felt a strong urge from the Spirit of
God to spend the previous night with Christine in prayer.
Calieb was the central focus. As they began to pray, they felt

a tremendous sense of dread, an evil presence that needed to be pushed back by intense prayer and supplication. It was not until the early hours of dawn that their struggle turned to joy and praise. They sensed God answering their prayers.

Calieb wept as the children were called in and told about his conversion to Jesus. The entire family took turns hugging him. He dropped to his knees as he accepted kisses from little Lucy. He stroked her hair and told through tears about the death of his little sister along with his parents and grandparents. This brought another round of hugs. Finally, Erich and Christine prayed for him and thanked God for bringing him into their lives.

Without a clear explanation to the children, they thanked Calieb for the warning. Then they put the children in their car, took the pizzas with them, and drove away. Calieb stayed behind. He had agreed to work with the Haz Mat team to check the site for dangerous biological cultures. For two blocks around the Kirkland home, people were quietly being sent away. However, everything at the target house appeared normal. If anything went wrong, Calieb would be one of the first to pay with his life for his part in the plot.

•   Federal agents entered the kitchen with guns drawn, using the key for the backdoor that Calieb had given them. They already had looked at an infrared, heat image of the house on a laptop computer and knew exactly where each occupant was located. The picture originated from a small remote controlled spy plane flying overhead. They heard a TV in the front room. Roy Morris, the lead agent, motioned two of the four men with him to watch that room while the others headed down the stairs leading to the basement.

Morris was no ordinary SWAT team agent. He knew the dialect spoken by two of the Iranian terrorists in the basement. As an extra precaution, he wore over his armored vest a robe and headpiece of an Arab sheik. He led the way down the steps with a short-barreled machine gun under his robe. Their tennis shoes made no sound on the carpeted steps. While the agents were familiar with danger, they faced two possible disasters. They had to overcome the terrorists, but if they damaged any of the equipment, they might die from exposure. Plus, it could result in untold numbers of others dying as well. Yet they were not able to risk coming into the house wearing protective suits and oxygen tanks.

When Morris entered the basement, he saw a large table covered with five-gallon glass bottles. Tubes ran from them to vats that looked like fish tanks. One man was seated at the table, another stood behind him. They were intently looking at papers, studying a diagram of a machine that looked like a modified shop vacuum, which sat on the table in front of them. Another man wore rubber gloves and stood next to glass tubes and bottles on the other side of the room. Two armed agents pushed into the room on both sides of Morris.

One of the men at the table sensed their presence and looked up. He was shocked.

Morris spoke to him in Farsi. "We are here to take over the operation."

The three Muslims were momentarily stunned. The one with rubber gloves glanced toward a device sitting on boxes in the middle of the room.

Morris noticed his eye movement and addressed him in Farsi again. "Don't even consider it! We want you to leave."

The agent brought up an automatic weapon that had been under his robe. Seconds seemed like minutes before the man lunged for the device. Morris's machinegun spit out a short burst, and the man's head exploded. His lifeless body dropped to the floor as the two agents' automatic weapons fired three shot bursts into the heads of the two men at the table. Their bullets were designed to break into tiny pieces upon impact and thus not pass through the heads of their enemies and cause damage to glass containers that would release biological agents in the air.

They had been warned that there were enough biological agents in the room to kill half the people on the East Coast, if dispersed. Thousands of practice rounds shot on the firing range paid off. Just as it seemed they had prevented damage to the glass containers, the death kicks of a dying man upset one of the tables. Two glass containers smashed on the concrete floor.

Morris responded immediately. "Go!"

Following the two agents up the stairs, he heard shots. The agents upstairs had taken down the man watching television. As expected, none of the terrorists gave up to save their lives.

Morris yelled a coded command into a mike on his shoulder, "Burn, baby, burn!"

At the top of the stairs, he squeezed between the other agents who had taken canisters from their pockets. They pulled pins, tossed them down the stairs, and whirled, slamming the door to the basement as they raced for the front door behind Morris.

Clearing the front door, they heard muffled explosions of the two fire grenades, which turned the stairwell into a flaming infernal. By the time they were running down the driveway, a large truck slid to a stop. A side door opened for the five men who jumped into the truck. The door closed behind them, and the truck pealed rubber. The men had entered a portable decontamination unit where they would be isolated until it was certain they carried no biological agents from the house.

Two tracked military tanks pulled next to the house. One drove through the neighbor's yard to the back. The other stayed on the street out front. Before they stopped, streams of liquid fire shot from a cannon-like barrel on the turret of each tank. Within seconds, the entire house was ablaze.

The only way to kill the escaping biological agents in the basement was to incinerate them in the hottest fire. While the tanks continued to spray the house with napalm, two fire trucks arrived and began hooking up to hydrants to spray water on those houses nearest the fire.

Calieb watched from across the street, praying that the flames would destroy every molecule. Harmful toxins filled the smoke but were so widely dispersed that there was no danger to anyone downwind. For the first time since his change of heart, he wondered what now? What will happen to me?

•   Calieb informed Will Davis of another team with

a suitcase nuke, but he didn't know where they were
located, just that his group was to co-ordinate the strike
with them. His impression was that they were to explode
it in the capital city as a backup and further disruption
on top of releasing the biological agents. The Homeland
Security detail panicked when they realized they didn't
have information on the terrorist team that was supposed to
take out either the White House or the Capitol. The head of
Homeland Security told the President he didn't know what
to do with this information. Releasing it would only add to
the high tension already existing in the nation. But it could
also put private citizens on the alert and possibly expose the
team.

Sam Kirkland admitted he knew about the team and
that they were to contact him for the final coordination of
the attack. But even if the authorities tried to suppress the
news of his capture, the other team would take precautions
and figure out something was wrong. He assured them that
they knew as much as he did. A committed Muslim, he took
the change of events as something beyond his control and,
therefore, something he simply had to accept.

The President made another command decision. As with
other announcements, he angered some and pleased others.
He told Homeland Security to make public the full details on
the breakup of the terrorist plot to spread deadly biological
agents over the East Coast.

Later the President appeared on television and
announced the news of the intended attack by a dirty
nuclear device. "Millions of Americans have been praying for
God's mercy. This is a clear and startling answer that God is
at work to protect us as we sincerely repent and look to Him.
Although neighbors had no inkling of what was going on in
the house, they were led to specifically pray for the man who
turned on his companions. They had no idea their neighbors
were terrorists. In fact, the Muslims appeared to be good,
hard working people. But God put a burden on several to
pray specifically for the man who had a dramatic encounter
with Jesus Christ."

The President related the specifics of Calieb's dream and
vision as the story had been related to him from the initial

taped conversation with FBI agents. "With a changed heart, the Muslim was led to turn on his friends. This suggests the exact thing we need to do in the case of the other terrorist team that is somewhere on the East Coast. We all need to pray that God will protect us from them. We must seek His leading and directions and trust Him. How and when He chooses to do this is up to Him. He probably won't manifest His deliverance the same way He did with the first group. Our duty is to pray and leave the results with Him."

For many, those new in the faith or with no faith, this was easier said than done. Millions of others accepted the challenge and set themselves to pray and wait upon the Lord.

•   News of Madeline Logan's miraculous healing and Clarence Becker's tearful confessions before the entire congregation raced through the community. Her father's prominent position there and his long time savvy of how to use the media resulted in their stories being quickly reported on radio and television statewide. These were featured along with the news out of Washington about the successful prevention of the terrorist attack. And like that report, there were those who scoffed and ridiculed and others that rejoiced because it strengthened their resolve to turn to the Lord. The identification of the demonic element shocked the Christians more than it did those outside the Church.

His associates informed Clarence that clients were canceling their insurance policies and taking their investment portfolios to other financial institutions. The clients told his associates that they could not trust "a religious fanatic." Clarence smiled and assured then there would be business coming in for exactly the same reason. And he was right.

Her doctors became angry at Madeline's confession. She believed it was sin that she had gone to the medical doctors without first seeking God and waiting for Him to show her how He wanted her to deal with the problem of her cancer. Josh rejoiced.

A spontaneous revival broke out in their suburban

areas as a number of people in old mainline denominational congregations were healed and set free from demonic oppression. The pastors were some of the first to acknowledge their need of cleansing. Those changed by the power of God spread the word to all their relatives, neighbors, and co-workers, and suddenly congregations and their staffs were overwhelmed.

The churches could not hold the crowds showing up for evening prayer, healing and deliverance services. Pastors took the unprecedented action of urging their members to have meetings in their homes on every block of the community. Within a week, 1700 years of tradition had been broken. The Church of the Lord Jesus Christ had returned to its roots, believers meeting in their homes under the leadership of the Holy Spirit.

The dining room or kitchen table became the table of the Lord as neighbors from diverse church traditions laid aside their differences and concentrated on what they held in common. They believed the promise given to the Lord's first disciples applied to them. "I bestow upon you a kingdom, just as My Father bestowed one upon Me, that you may eat and drink at My table in My kingdom, and sit on thrones judging the twelve tribes of Israel." They sensed that the prayers following the celebration of the Lord's Supper were truly anointed with power by the Spirit of God.

It was Clarence who recommended that the ministerial association hold a citywide meeting in the large football stadium. The announcement of the thwarting of the terrorist attack provided added motivation for people to turn to the Lord. Eighty thousand people filled the stands, while another estimated twenty thousand gathered on the artificial turf field. Thousands were turned away and went home to watch on television.

By the time of the gathering, the majority of professing Christians had accepted as fact the prophecies about the threats to the nation. While not all agreed to forgive the President and his administration, there was a growing conviction that prayer and trusting in God were the only hopes for the nation.

Reports that God was bringing a transformation of the

social order across the country electrified the people. This brought great joy and also an awesome respect for God. Songs of praise dwarfed the cheers normally heard for their hometown teams who played in the stadium. The most powerful messages came from ordinary men, women, and young people simply telling what God was doing in their lives. Most of the people stayed to worship and pray all night. Some only left in time to eat breakfast before going to work. Many would take part in noon prayer meetings at their businesses.

In similar ways, but with different triggers, such revival broke out in communities across the nation. God was doing a new work.

• Markov tossed a sheet of paper to the President. "Have you seen the latest from America? They are putting a black female from the Cabinet up for the position of vice president. They must be getting desperate."

Solnstnev shook his head. "I will never understand those people. Are there no real men left in America?"

"It will make no difference. We'll soon be bombing them back into the stone age."

"Ha, if we put them back in the stone age having a direct descendant of stone aged people will serve them well."

Markov laughed, too. "And you will be able to use your great charm with women to negotiate their surrender."

The President rolled his eyes. "Who is going to fill the position of secretary of defense?"

"They are talking of bringing retired General Mark Leland back."

"Oh, Markov, is he not the one who directed the Army Airborne Forces in the Gulf War that proved the superiority of the American's anti-tank forces over our armor?"

"Yes."

Solnstnev stroked his chin. "I don't like the sound of this. He's a real man. Old or not, he's a tiger. We're going to have to watch him closely. Do you agree?"

Markov nodded with a sober look. He was lost in thought.

Chapter Seven

Plans of the Wicked Fail

Another international conference call was put together for select members of the world's elite. When the assistant signaled that all the parties were on the line, Baron Rudolph Steinberg of Germany took control of the meeting and spoke with confidence.

"This call will be short. I want to assure everyone, our plan to send our message to President McCleen has been arranged. We should have results within twenty four hours."

Sir Robert Davies from Great Britain asked, "Baron, what do you think of the appointment of a woman as vice president, a black woman at that?"

Steinberg answered in a straightforward manner. "She was placed in the position of secretary of defense strictly as a politically correct move by the politicians. She has a military mindset that conditions her to accept orders from higher authorities. She's obviously someone seeking power, so we can use her."

"But I hear she's a Christian and backs the President in his revelations to the public."

"So? It merely shows that she is flowing with the requirements of the moment. She'll do the same when she gets the position of President. I say we not harm her when the President is taken out. But I suggest we get to her soon after she's sworn in and remind her that she can be removed as easily as McCleen was. She'll get the point."

A murmur of agreement followed. "Gentlemen, I have a great deal of work to do and assume the same for each of you, so I bid you good day."

•   One morning as James prayed, he had a strong impression that a friend was going to betray the President. When he asked the Lord who it would be, the answer was "an elected official."

James dialed the number for Agent Barnes's cell phone. Barnes answered, heard his explanation, and agreed to get right on it.

Later that morning he met Congressman David Ashby in the hall outside the Oval Office. He asked him to submit to a search.

Ashby objected, "I've already cleared through the screening coming into the White House for my appointment with the President. Isn't that enough?"

"We have orders to search everyone again who comes near the President. That would include the President's mother. Please empty your pockets."

Barnes noticed an old fashioned penholder in the breast pocket of his suit jacket and asked for it. Tiny letters engraved on it stated that it was a historic pen originally used by President Franklin D. Roosevelt to sign a bill in 1938.

The agent asked, "What's this for?"

"I'm going to ask the President to use it to sign this book for one of our party's wealthiest supporters."

Barnes dropped the penholder in a plastic bag and looked directly at Ashby. "Sorry, you'll have to use a pen on the President's desk."

A defiant look appeared in the eyes of the congressman. "Using that pen would be meaningful to this friend of the President. His father was given that pen by President Roosevelt."

Barnes heard tension in Ashby's voice. He said nothing as he watched the man's reactions.

The congressman smiled, shrugged, and replied, "Okay, you're the boss."

"We'll take good care of the pen and get it back to you."

As soon as Ashby was gone, Barnes assigned an agent to take the pen to the FBI lab with instructions to have it immediately examined. Within an hour a lab technician put on rubber gloves before taking it out of the plastic bag. It was an older fountain ink pen that had to be refilled from a bottle. He first tested a sample of the ink and found it to be okay. Then he wrote with it and noticed a clear solution oozing from the side of the pen onto his glove. He tested the substance. It was a rare poison. A minute drop, upon entering the skin, within an hour or so would cause a fatal heart attack. However, it would be difficult to trace in the blood stream.

The lab technician dissembled the pen and discovered a second container with a small amount of the poison under pressure. Just a slight force from writing with the point of the pen would release the poison. By picking it up near the top of the pen, the cap could be replaced and the pen put back into its special case without touching the poison. The individual handling the pen would need a shot of anti venom to negate the poison's effect.

The congressman had already left the White House when the report of the poison reached Barnes. He contacted the agents assigned to follow the legislator. They reported that Ashby had returned to his office and then, within ten minutes, headed for his home in the suburbs. They were ordered to pick him up and take him to the FBI office for interrogation. When the agents entered his home to arrest him, he was packing a suitcase.

As Congressman Ashby was being brought in, teams were sent to search his office and home. Examining his office, they found the antidote for the poison. Ashby's luggage contained an airline ticket to London. Faced with the evidence, he calmly denied everything and asked for an attorney. Then he made a request to go to the bathroom. Two agents escorted him to the men's room and stood outside the stall. Within minutes, they heard him collapse on the floor. The door was locked, so they pulled him from the stall and called for an emergency medical team. It was too late. He had swallowed a poison pill hidden on his person.

No one on Capital Hill connected his fatal heart attack with the events taking place in the nation. The threat to the President's life was not made public.

•   Lyman Moore knew the importance of computer passwords. When he was a teen, he'd enjoyed the challenge of getting through complicated security systems of computer firewalls in large corporations. He had enough respect for those working the systems that he had no desire to damage them. Whenever he succeeded in breaking through, he left messages to let the person in charge know he was there. In some cases, he even left suggestions as to how the system could be improved. It was a game to him. Some were grateful enough to pay him for the insights had he left his address. Others would have taken him to the police.

Now he believed God knew everything. God had created man with the ability to invent and use computers. Therefore, He knew Russian codes and passwords, and if it meant saving millions of lives, why not trust God to give him this information and show him how to use it? Didn't the Bible declare that nothing was impossible for God? At first, the thought made it appear easy. But the more he read the Bible and spent time in prayer, Lyman realized he was up against powerful forces about which he knew little. They had nothing to do with computers.

He spent many hours reading books and talking to mature Christians about spiritual warfare and how to engage and defeat dark forces behind human institutions and organizations opposing God's work in the world. This was already familiar to the men and women loyal to the mission of the International Prayer Center. It was Lyman's ultimate purpose that puzzled some of them. It took awhile for a few to connect the dots. If he saved physical lives, it meant the possibility of seeing their souls delivered from eternal death. Yet two of them struggled with believing this is the way God worked in today's realities.

As Lyman wrestled with God, he came up against what he and others identified as powerful demon spirits. The harassment appeared in the form of nightmares and then a series of unexplained incidents. An angry man rear ended his Jeep at a stoplight and threatened him with bodily harm over minor damage to his vehicle. Only the arrival of a police cruiser cooled the man's anger. Later on, lights in Lyman's apartment burned out, and his refrigerator lost its power, spoiling meat in the freezer and also fresh vegetables.

Computers in the International Prayer Center bombed. They gave their operators fits over minor glitches. This forced Lyman to find a group of more mature Christian friends for prayer support. For a time, they too experienced similar harassment until they corporately saw the real source of the problems and began to exercise spiritual authority over the darkness. The Spirit of God gave them names of specific demon principalities. When they used the authority of the name and blood of the Lord Jesus Christ, they experienced a release from the harassment. Lyman felt a freedom he'd never known before.

Then he wrestled with his pride and personal sins. He was distraught about certain aspects of his thoughts and also with his relationships to others that revealed subtle sins. Sexual lust entered his mind more than usual. He found himself fantasizing about the fame this could bring him. Then he was gripped with fear. How would the Russians respond? Would they find him and send agents to murder him? He spent so much time mulling over these issues that the real mission was pushed from his mind.

Late one night, he was having difficulty going to sleep when he sensed the Spirit of God wanting to communicate with him. He focused on being quiet in the presence of the Creator Sovereign God. During that time, he accepted the fact that he was only an instrument in the hands of God. Lyman renewed his affirmation that he was open to be used by God any way the Master would choose. With that, he committed himself anew to the Lord's service and a deep peace settled over him. He soon fell asleep.

That night the first pieces of information came to him in a dream. He saw a schematic drawing of a computer system and numbers. When he awoke, he wrote the numbers on the pad next to his bed and drew out the system design.

The next piece of information came to him while he was at his computer. Two words appeared in his mind. One was in English and the other, in a language he didn't know but which was revealed so clearly he knew how to spell it. He typed it into a program and ran it through a dictionary that identified it as a Russian word. Lyman experienced cold fear like he never had before. He whispered a prayer of thanks to the Lord Jesus and sensed a feeling of overwhelming insignificance. At the same time, he sensed a power that was not his own.

When he shared the breakthroughs with his intimate prayer partners, some exclaimed praises to God. Others smiled and nodded. They too acknowledged that God was at work.

With a sense of confidence, Lyman retreated to a park at the edge of the Black Forest overlooking Colorado Springs. He found an impressive view of Pikes Peak. Unaware of the families in various spots who were enjoying cookouts, he walked and communed with his Lord. At dusk, he sat on top of a picnic table and watched the last rays of light fade over the mountain.

He was so engrossed in listening for the Lord that he didn't hear the person walk up to him until the stranger coughed, making his presence known. Lyman turned and said, "Beautiful sunset."

"Yes. Only the Creator is able to put on a show like that and be so extravagant. He has no need to keep a record of it either."

Lyman thought for a moment before replying. "Yes. I've never considered it that way. We try to preserve such beauty with a camera, but God can create the same view tomorrow with ease."

They were quiet for a while, soaking in the peace of the moment. When Lyman turned to look at the man, it was too dark to see the features of his face. He sensed that the man was smiling. It was confirmed in his voice when he spoke with quiet assurance. "I have no idea how this fits in with what you have been seeking the Lord about, but I came to give you these two words. They are surprise and Rasputin with the number two as part of the second word."

Lyman repeated the words, and the man said, "Yes." Lyman was so engrossed remembering the words that it took a moment to realize his visitor was leaving.

"Wait! Why did you tell me this?"

The man turned to face him. "I was directed to find you and tell you those words. I have no idea why or what they mean, but I trust that you will. That's all you need to know. Good night." He turned and was immediately lost from sight in the darkness under the trees.

Stunned, Lyman rose from the table and peered through the dark. "Thank you, praise the Lord!" he shouted. He heard no answer. Slowly he made his way back to his Jeep Liberty, repeating the words over and over lest he forget them. The further he walked, the more enthused he became. This sounded like the last two pieces of the puzzle he needed, but he wouldn't know for sure until he could get back to his computer.

Arriving at his apartment, he hurried inside. Within seconds, his MacIntosh was connected to the Internet. Within minutes of following the schematic of web addresses he'd been given in the dream, he bumped up against a page calling for a password. Lyman whispered a prayer and typed in surprise and then hit enter. The page disappeared and another appeared. He could not read what it said, but it too demanded a password. Without hesitating, he typed in Rasputin2 and hit enter. He was in. A chill shot through him. He clinched his fist and shouted, "Yes!"

For the next hour, he navigated through the computer program that was in the language he studied at the space agency. He sensed the presence of the Holy Spirit in the room as he studied and prayed at the same time. His eyes stopped on certain lines that he immediately knew how to alter. In some cases, it was only one character that was changed. In a couple of places, he put in a whole new line of code.

Suddenly he sensed a need to quit the program. Lyman hit save and then the command that took him to the part of the program to show the time and date of his last entry. Making an edit that would not register the time and date of the changes, he backed out of the program and attempted to cover his tracks as best he could.

After going offline and shutting down the computer, he bowed his head. "Lord Jesus, I ask that you blind the eyes of those responsible for the software so they will not discover the changes that have been made. Thank You for guiding me. I trust that You will use this for Your purposes."

Since it was God Who had given him the insights, he was confident that what he had done would also prove to be right. He wanted to rush out and share what he had done with his prayer partners. Instead he went to bed and fell asleep.

•   In God's providence and before receiving the invitation to the White House luncheon, James had agreed to accompany a Russian defector on a speaking tour to his home country. The chaplain's prayer partners confirmed that he should keep his earlier commitment, and the President also encouraged it. After spending time at the White House, James returned home to prepare for the trip.

Years before, he had set out on a quest to learn the truth about what was transpiring in the once occupied countries of the Soviet Union. After a great deal of reading and talking to various people, he met Dr. Zoya Kampov, a renowned physicist, who also held a Ph.D. in Philosophy. Kampov had defected to the West before the collapse of the USSR.

He was a deeply committed Christian. What little press he received in America played up his scientific qualifications but never mentioned his faith in Christ. The media was too embarrassed and prejudiced to admit that such a brilliant scientist could be a committed Christian.

Dr. Kampov was invited back to Russia to speak at a meeting of some of the country's leading scientists on the Anthropic Principle, which is scientific evidence that the entire universe is centered on and exists for mankind. Due to his breakthrough discoveries in astrophysics and chemistry to support the theory, Russian scientists were willing to overlook the fact that he was a committed Christian and Creationist. Therefore, the country's government approved of the visit because it supported the myth that Russia had abandoned its former closed communist system.

Due to the friendship of Dr. Kampov and James, the scientist urged James to travel with him to speak to gatherings of Russian Christians. James eagerly looked forward to this. Even though all the arrangements were made months before, James and some of his prayer partners now questioned the timing of the trip, whether it was indeed the right time to leave America. James knew such details were not to be evaluated in human terms. God had opened

the door, so he would trust the Lord to make whatever use
he could of it. God could protect him in Russia as easily
as in the U.S., maybe even more so. America was not
proving to be the safest place in the world, even with God's
supernatural answers to prayer.

Before leaving, James followed through on a suggestion
from President McCleen. He was asked to appear on a
special nationwide talk show to answer questions about
how God had used him to launch this series of events. He
wrestled with it. His original understanding was that it
would not put him in the national spotlight. However, as he
and others prayed, they had peace about it. Arrangements
were made and announced to the public.

• Teams of snipers from the dark side of the shadow
government were called in to take out Chaplain Parr
before he could make his point on national television. Their
instructions were to produce a takedown that would be
highly dramatic to the public. Another message was to be
delivered to President McCleen. Although he had escaped
attempts to eliminate him, the shadow government wanted
him to know they still had ways of enforcing their desires.
Half the payment to the team was in cash. The other half
would be deposited in numbered accounts at offshore banks
after the mission was completed.

The first two men set up their operations in a vacant
office across the street from the entrance to the TV studio
where the interview was scheduled. The second shooter
was to get into the studio as a backup in case the first team
failed. He came in under cover as a lighting repairman with
an official looking reacquisition stating that studio lights
in the ceiling above the main studio were to be checked.
After being cleared by the studio security office, he dropped
an innocent looking fast food sack into a hall trashcan. It
contained a small explosive devise that he would set off
when he was ready to make his shot.

The sniper climbed the ladder to the walkway where
he opened a large panel that wired numerous overhead
lights. He opened his tool case and took out a flashlight and
several monitoring devices that he hooked up to some of

the wires. Then he brought out a short barreled, automatic machine pistol from the false bottom of his tool case. At this close range, there was no need for a telescope. He screwed a silencer on the end of the barrel. When the weapon was ready, he hung it inside his open coveralls and pretended to check out different circuits in the control panel. He wired in an explosive charge that would throw the studio into darkness and create a fire, distracting everyone while he made his escape. If the task fell to him, he would be in no hurry to take his shot. Let an audience build and get sucked into the discussion before they saw their saintly hero's head explode and splatter all over the talk show host.

James was following his usual approach to an assignment. He and his team were praying, pleading the blood of Christ over him and asking the Holy Spirit to protect him and direct every word. When his limousine pulled up in front of the television station in Denver, a crowd of reporters and cameramen were waiting. James stepped from the car, raised his hand, and shouted, "No comment now. I'll talk to you afterwards, if you still have questions after the interview."

At that moment, the back of his head appeared in the crosshairs of the first sniper's rifle. The sniper's finger closed on the trigger. As he felt the recoil of the rifle, through the scope he saw a pigeon fly into the path of the bullet. The hollow point bullet disintegrated and reduced the pigeon to scattered pieces of flesh and feathers. No one heard the silenced rifle shot. Only a few at the edge of the crowd were annoyed by the pieces of the bird that landed on them out of nowhere.

The spotter muttered, "Geez! Did you see that? A bird flew in the line of fire. Your bullet blew it to bits. I don't think the target has any idea he was under attack."

Bolting another round into the chamber, the shooter asked, "Can I get another shot?"

"No! He's moving into the building. And frankly, I'm not sure we should even try. I have a funny feeling about this. Never have I heard of such a thing that just happened." He shook his head. "I've been keeping up with the news about this so-called prophet. This proves to me the man has connections we don't want to mess with. Pack up! If the backup can get him, fine, but we're out of here! There are safer ways to earn money."

Two policemen helped James move through the crowd of reporters. Inside, a couple of security personnel led him to a dressing room where he was prepped for the show.

•   Randy Chambers, a controversial and popular talk show host, had the nation's first afternoon radio and television talk shows regarding social/political issues that appealed to both conservatives and liberals. He was an incredibly gifted talent with a gracious tact that either attracted or frustrated people on both sides of the issues. Normally Chambers didn't accommodate guests by meeting them for their convenience. However, due to the nature of this opportunity, he made an exception.

James wasn't introduced to the host until he came on stage. As soon as they shook hands, the technicians wired Chambers and him with microphones and checked out the sound levels. The lighting men made last minute adjustments with the lights and cameras to satisfy the control room. It was a live show so there was a scurry to have everything ready by the time the host's musical introduction was heard by the viewing audience.

Chambers took the cue from the floor director and went into his opening statement. With a balanced introduction of his guest, he explained that, since this was a special version of his daily program and not his regular studio, there would be no time for callers. He got right to the point.

"Since the well publicized luncheon in the White House, Americans were deluged with reports of what actually happened. Radio, television, and especially the Internet carried a variety of firsthand reports by those who were present. Jordan Miles, press secretary to the White House, had a different twist. It's an understatement to say this has created tremendous confusion in all segments of the nation. The calls coming into Congress and the White House shut down the phone system and overwhelmed Internet providers. So, Reverend Parr, would you agree it's fair to say that the secular news media has been accused of frantically trying to discount the prophetic words you were reported to have given at the luncheon?"

"Isn't that obvious to everyone since the President has confirmed our version of what was said in his address to the nation?"

"Because the White House has lost the recording of the meeting, there's no way to confirm the exact wording of the message you gave. Isn't that true?"

"Isn't it strange that, when something happens to contradict the official government position on sensitive happenings, the records are conveniently lost? The American people are intelligent enough to know that this is more than accidental. So to speak to the issue of various interpretations of what was actually said, I think it's simply a matter of what happens when different people see a dramatic event. They have a unique perspective and, therefore, give a slightly different version. But there will be common themes."

Chambers asked, "Which were?"

"The President and some of his top advisers were discussing the use of prison camps and a preemptive nuclear strike against the American people. They have known about these matters for some time and have chosen to ride out a nuclear strike in the comfort of their specially prepared bunkers. The President has acknowledged these matters with a different story than was first given by his press secretary. That's what needs to be focused on."

The discussion continued on the differences between what the press secretary released to the public and what the ministry leaders were reporting.

•   Floodlights for the stage held a special part in the job being planned by the sniper. As he looked down through them to the stage, he accepted the fact that the outside team had failed. The task was now up to him. This meant he would get a larger piece of the total payment. He checked the wires to the explosives which were to destroy the wiring panel and cause a fire seconds after the explosion in the wastepaper can downstairs did the same thing. A timer would enable him to get out of the way. In the confusion, he would simply be another person leaving the fire.

He was not paying attention to what was being said, but he knew the two men were having a heated exchange. It was time to take his shot. He raised the gun. Before he could squeeze off the three shot burst, a cameramen on a lift devise rose between the target and him. The director, for reasons only a program director could know, must have decided he needed an elevated view of the two men. The sniper was standing on a small balcony with little room for movement. He leaned to both sides but could not align himself for a clear shot past the camera operator. He put his weapon down and checked to see if anyone below had noticed. It didn't appear they had. Patience was the critical factor in his profession.

•   Personnel of the television station watched the program. The receptionist, Lucy Barren, greeted Lonnie Cleves, the chief electrician for the station. "That was a long luncheon. You're missing out on the big event."

Lonnie waved, heading for his desk. "I'll be sick of it by the time all the reruns and clips are played back."

He began to look through the paperwork on his desk. Examining a pink sheet, he turned to the man at the next desk and asked, "Tony, what's this request to have the overhead lights checked? Did you ask for this?"

"No, I thought you did. Western Electric must have hired a new guy. I called the supervisor he had on his card and checked it out. He okayed him."

"Who'd you call?"

"I don't remember. They're a big outfit. Wait a minute. You didn't request this work?"

Lonnie didn't answer. He punched the number on his phone for security.

•   "Reverend Parr, would it not be the right thing to do for you to reveal to the public who leaked this information in the first place."

The expression on James's face revealed his dismay at the question. "There was no leak. It's been widely reported that the Holy Spirit of God revealed this to me during the luncheon. It's what we call a prophetic word. How it actually comes to one is difficult to explain because I'm not sure it's the same for everyone who experiences it."

Chamber's face showed he didn't like the answer. "But how are we supposed to know this comes from God? There are constant reports of supposed men of God getting a divine word that never come true. Or they are so vague it's difficult to deny or confirm their predictions."

James retorted, "The Bible is clear that from the beginning of recorded history there have always been both false and true prophets. But the Bible has a simple, foolproof way of knowing who is real. If what the prophet prophesies comes true, it is assumed that God has sent it. If it doesn't, the prophet in ancient Israel was to be put to death as a false prophet."

Chambers jumped on the last statement with a smirk on his face. "Wow, if that were still practiced today, there would be a lot of dead preachers and TV evangelists!"

"Yes, I agree. One of the things I've had to fight myself is that I have never wanted to be identified as a prophet for that very reason. But in what area of life do we not experience the same problem? Try to think of one profession where the good and the bad do not exist, the true and the false or counterfeit. It's certainly not unique to the Church."

Chambers paused, looking down at his "cheat sheet." He said, "Okay, but the Church leaders I've read say that God no longer declares His will through men as He did in Biblical times. And that's not just from those in the liberal churches. Many orthodox theologians say the same thing, don't they?"

"I'm aware of that. The Bible also says that God does not change. He is the same yesterday, today, and forever. His methods, however, are not always the same. There are more supernatural activities at different periods in history, but there's no solid evidence that God has stopped using supernatural means to intervene in history or occasionally in our personal lives. What the Church has largely agreed on is that there will be no more revelations added to what is already in the Bible. The Bible is complete. But the application of these revealed truths to current events is another matter."

Chambers started to interrupt, but James held up his hand and persisted. "Wait, let me make two points. There is a natural fear, in all mankind, of God bursting into our lives in a dramatic way. That goes for the believer as well as the nonbeliever. Second, we have a spiritual enemy who knows how to counterfeit God's methods in order to confuse us. God allows these deceptions to blind those condemned to death and to mature those who are called to follow Him.

"Therefore, what the Bible says to do with prophesies or interpretations of Scripture is to test them by His Spirit. Do they align with what is already revealed in Scripture? Do they have a ring of truth?"

"So you're saying that your prophecy was from God because the President admitted publicly that it pointed out truth?"

"And look at what happened. Because he didn't tell the truth to those at the luncheon, two members of his family and a key member of his administration died. Whether you choose to believe these were acts of God's judgments or not, the fact is that the President has confessed to our government leaders being in on one gigantic fraud perpetrated against the American people. In this case, God chose to use a dramatic way of getting the truth out. So regardless of the fact that there are false prophets, in this case, I stand by what came forth from me while taking no credit for it myself."

"So you're saying that God doesn't like government?"

"No!" James shook his head with obvious disgust. "He doesn't approve of civil governments that are in rebellion against him. As I see it, here's a fundamental problem with people like you. You believe big government is the answer to all our problems. Yet the fact is that it's been full of self centered, greedy liars who consistently get caught pulling off underhanded deals."

"Yes, we value government leadership, but we also demand acceptable levels of honesty. Our current leadership has been shown to not live up to that standard. Therefore, they should be held accountable for their actions. That's why I'm with those calling for the impeachment of the President."

Raising his eyebrows, James asked, "Acceptable levels? Who defines what's acceptable? But an even more important question is what's the foundational problem in our nation? Looking at all the crises we're having, where do you lay the biggest guilt for causing the moral decay in the nation?"

Chambers shrugged. "You tell me. You obviously have a prepared answer."

"Yes, I do, but I'd like you to commit yourself. Hasn't the media taught people to respond to every conceivable problem that comes up -- whether it's streets needing repairs or the war on terrorism -- with the mantra, 'The government ought to do something?' " James paused to force an answer, knowing a good reporter hates dead air time.

"Yes, I suppose you're right. We've come to expect a lot from government."

"But the governments in Washington or state capitals aren't the main problem, and neither are they the solution to our most basic needs for reform in the nation. They are merely a symptom of the cause of our difficulties. God had it right in the book of Second Chronicles where He says, 'If my people, who are called by my name will humble themselves, and pray, and seek my face and turn from their wicked ways, then I will hear from heaven, forgive their sin and heal their land.' The foundational issue needing to be faced is the fact that in the true American system of government, it is the people who are responsible before God for what happens to the nation. To be more specific, because America was founded as a Christian nation, it's the Christians who are to guard the nation and solve any life-threatening problem that comes before us as a people.

Chambers glanced at the clock. They had run out of time, so he asked the obvious. "Why Christians?"

"Because God commands His people to transform all areas of life according to the rules He's laid down in the Bible. It's that simple. I came here today for one reason, and that is to call upon Christians to get on your knees and cry out to God for mercy. Plead with Him to spare our nation and do whatever He has to, whatever He knows is best, to purge the evil and restore justice, righteousness, and truth to our nation. He's our only hope."

"What if they don't take your counsel?"

"The judgment of God will come on the entire nation. What the terrorists were going to do with those biological agents will be child's play compared to what God can do through nature, war, and plagues. Those are the three main instruments He has used throughout history to express His wrath. But again, if people repent and turn to Him, He will deliver them, which does not mean that some will not die for the gross sins of the nation."

Chambers turned to the camera. "I don't pretend to fully understand what Pastor Parr is saying. But I have to admit, he does not lack in intelligence or intensity in what he believes. As a former reporter speaking for journalists, we are supposed to remain unbiased in our reporting. That's a noble goal few of us actually practice. Therefore, I leave to you, the listener, to come to your own conclusion. Thank you for tuning in to this special feature of Randy Chambers's National Briefing. As always, we welcome your civil and reasoned responses."

Chambers closed the program, and the director went to advertisers. In the lighting racks above, the sniper saw his opportunity. He planned to take a shot either when Chambers and James stood to shake hands or when the camera operator lowered the equipment toward the floor. Ready to close on the radio-controlled devise that would set off the distracting explosion downstairs, he felt a nudge on his leg.

"Mister, hand me that weapon real slow. Don't try anything funny, or I'll send a charge of buckshot up your hind end with this shotgun."

The sniper looked down to see the barrel of a shotgun pointed at his crotch. A serious looking security officer stood at the bottom of the ladder. Another uniformed man had a large caliber pistol aimed at him. The sniper remembered that he'd recently thought nothing else could go wrong. Wrong again.

•   Russian Major Sasha Bagrii was intent on running a computer test of the updated software programmed in the ICBM warhead in his silo. Through the grapevine, he learned that the missile test launch had gone badly, and no one knew why. With time on his hands, he planned to do some testing of his own. A copy of the program was put into a separate computer system in their underground control center. Sasha would give additional training to his crews. One of his greatest challenges was keeping up the morale of the crew and their focus on the grave responsibility they had. After years of sitting around, running drills, cleaning up their spaces, and rereading old books and magazines, it was easy for apathy to set in. If word did come to make a launch, the sudden change in the midst of dull minds might produce undesirable results.

Sasha made it a point to take his men a step further than their standing orders demanded. He challenged them to come up with a computerized launch, something on the order of a video game. It took them into areas of programming that his commanders might think was unnecessary for enlisted men or even himself, but he was willing to take the risk. Plus, just maybe, he could find what some smart mouthed computer programmer had missed.

Using updated software, his crew went through a simulated launch. The computer faithfully replicated the rocket blasting off on its mission. But as it escaped the earth's atmosphere, instead of arching over the North Pole, it simply continued into outer space. The crew worked frantically to alter the missile's course, but nothing could be done. Everyone was shaken. They concluded they must have done something wrong.

The crew reloaded the software and ran the test again with the same results. When the next shift came on duty, Sasha didn't mention the problem but set them running the same test. They got the exact same results. He did not sleep for the next 24 hours as he and the crew attempted to find the flaw in the program. When the next crew returned, he stopped the routine and went home to get some sleep, thinking, maybe resting will help me figure out what my men are doing wrong. But when he awoke, Sasha admitted what he had refused to face before. Perhaps there was something wrong with the software itself. What if someone higher in the command structure had made a mistake? After dressing and saying goodbye to his family, he headed for his commander's office and requested an immediate conference.

•   General Borisov was the supreme commander of all Russian missile forces. In his hand was a top-secret report on a test launching of one of their most advanced intercontinental missiles. Before him stood Damen Vollokh, the lead scientist in charge of the team that developed the software for the missile program.

The general's hands trembled as he laid the report on his desk. Removing his reading glasses before speaking to the man standing before him, he asked, "Are you telling me, what this test indicates is that, if we launched our missiles now, there is a good possibility they would all fly off into space?"

Vollokh gulped, yet without hesitation answered, "Yes, sir."

"And this includes the missiles on our submarines and our mobile systems?"

"Yes, sir. They are all tied into the same central control system to prevent unauthorized launches. The virus was planted in that system and transmitted to all the missiles' launching controls before we knew it existed. It was so well hidden that it was only accidentally discovered by one of our missile launch commanders. We are trying to trace and verify the source, but it is extremely difficult to know for sure how this could have happened."

"These systems are all protected by passwords. It had to be a person with access to the system, did it not?"

"It would appear to be so, comrade, but who could that be? There are only a few who know the final passwords. Most of these people are not computer experts with the ability to alter the system. Once someone entered the password, the software developer would not know what it was. Each step from then on would be double-checked by others who did not know who the original computer specialists were or the passwords. It is very troubling. But, there is one other possibility."

The general's face lit up. "Yes, go on."

"It seems ridiculous, but we traced a possible link back to

America--"

General Borisov interrupted, "To the CIA?"

"No, no. It seems to be a personal computer in Colorado, to a man registered under the name of Lyman Moore. Our agents checked him out. He did work for the American space agency, but now he works for something called the International Prayer Center. He is a private citizen with no connection to the government that our sources could discern."

"But how could he break through all our security? The intelligence agencies of the world have tried and failed time and again."

"We don't know, sir. We are continuing to work on understanding that, while at the same time checking possibilities of internal sabotage. Which again is highly unlikely because of the complexity of the process."

Borisov contemplated the situation. Vollokh nervously glanced around the room. After a long time, the general leaned forward and put his hands on the edge of the desk.

"How long will it take to fix this, comrade? Can't you simply reprogram the software?"

"Yes, sir, we can find and correct the errors, but it'll take . . . well, no one knows for sure how long it will take. We'll have to write new software and test it to be sure of no other viruses. I'm sorry, sir, but it's impossible to put a time frame around it now."

"Are you talking about days, weeks, or months?"

"Months at the very least and possibly a year by the time it's tested."

"A year or more!" Borisov's face registered unbelief.

"I'm afraid so."

The general slumped and buried his head in his hands with a loud groan. Speaking to no one in particular, he exclaimed his frustration and consternation, his voice rising as he spoke, "Billions and billions of rubles and millions of man hours and you're telling me it may have all been stopped by one man with a home computer half way around the world? Amazing! Truly amazing!"

•   The Flemings returned to their home with a renewed

realization of the depth of the spiritual warfare they were
engaged in. Looking across the street, they saw the burned
out basement. The houses on both sides were charred black
from the heat. The trees in their own front yard had wilted.

They understood better how their naiveté had enabled
them to enter into realms of evil they knew little about.
Yet in God's grace, they had been spared and used by
Him to accomplish His purposes. Like so many American
Christians, they saw this as an opportunity to enter
deeper into the mysteries of prayer and God's sovereign
interruptions in man's affairs.

Even the President of the United States had admitted
in public that he'd been deceived by demonic spirits and set
free from their power through prayer. While not mentioning
them by name, he used the Flemings' experience as an
example for others to trust God. His call for renewed efforts
and dedication in prayer was heard loud and clear by
millions of Christians. When local churches couldn't hold the
crowds who went to pray, many gathered in homes where it
was easier to share childcare, enabling others to be released
for prayer.

In spite of the spiritual awakening of many, it appeared
to the Flemings that the nation was on the verge of a
civil war. The news was full of government and business
leaders accusing the President and others on his Cabinet
of becoming religious Iotolyas. Even those who professed
to be Christians were divided. Some were supportive of
the President's personal religious convictions but felt they
should not interfere with his civil responsibilities. They
were raising the cry of the separation of Church and state.
Others pointed out the historical evidence that the Bible
and the Christian faith were part and parcel of America's
early history and that there was no conflict over the states'
obligations to abide by just laws that originated in Judeo
Christian tradition. Nor was it wrong for any leader to apply
his faith in carrying out constitutionally defined duties.

Erich learned when he was obedient to the quiet urging
of the Spirit of God to stay up late into the night and pray
with the neighborhood group, he needed less sleep and still
had the energy to handle his concrete truck. He also had

more peace and contentment about his job. Inwardly he had fought against having to associate with the crude elements of society. His MBA from an Ivy League university was seen as an advantage but not as a reason that God had to bless him materially to maintain a privileged position in society.

Christine sensed another area where the Lord was challenging his core values. "Erich, what do you think about having a black woman appointed as vice president?"

"I'm not sure. I don't think we're ready to have a woman as President, especially in such a crisis time."

"Your prejudice is showing. With your Southern background, don't you think her being black has something to do with it?"

"No, I honestly don't."

Christine grinned. "Honestly?"

Erich rolled his eyes. "Well, maybe a little bit. Okay, logically I'll admit she's in that position because she has leadership qualities. My concern is more in the area of the way men and women deal emotionally with tough issues. If the Russians launch their ICBMs, will she panic under pressure?"

"Oh, a man wouldn't panic?"

"All right. I guess the bottom line is, I don't want to see everything changing all at once. There's so much happening, it's difficult to keep up. This is something we need to study the Bible about to see what it actually teaches and then pray about current applications. What the Lord wants is the key issue."

Christine smiled. "Remember, it was Jesus Who raised the standards for women."

Erich grabbed her and hugged her. "Yes, but He also teaches in His Word that we men are still the head honchos of the family."

She returned his embrace, kissed him, and murmured with a coy smile, "Yes, Exalted Master. Would His Highness like his dinner hot or cold?"

•   "Chaplain Parr, I'm glad we were able to reach you. Newly confirmed, Vice President Jolene Howard and Secretary Richard Languard are here with me in the Oval

Office. We want to let you know how pleased we are that
God protected you at the television studio. Also, thank you
for going public and defending our cause. Another thing we
called about is to tell you we're concerned about your safety
during your trip to Russia."

"Thank you, Mr. President. Our enemies must be
desperate if they think taking me out is going to help their
public image."

Jolene hastened to say, "Pastor, I think you're more
important than you give yourself credit. We thank God for
the wisdom He has given you and how you've helped all of us
to find a deeper relationship with Him."

"I'll second that," affirmed Languard. "That's saying a
lot for a liberal Unitarian, a former Unitarian. There are so
many things changing in my life that I won't be surprised if
I end up changing my party affiliation as well."

They laughed heartily.

James acknowledged, "Again, I thank all of you for your
affirmation of God's mission in my life. But, I remind you,
I'm just a backwoods preacher that God tapped for this
mission."

"Chaplain," said the President, "I have to remind you
of what you told me, that we all have to keep a proper
perspective on the position God places us in. You also said
we should not fall to the human temptation of pride due to
our positions. We are all everyday people whom God has
chosen to elevate in the eyes of others."

"Agreed. A preacher loves having portions of his sermons
quoted back to him. It shows the message got through."
Changing the subject, he asked, "How are you folks
weathering the storm? From what I hear on the news, you're
still in the midst of extreme controversy. Jolene, if I'd been
in those Senate hearings, I may have punched out a few of
those bigots." Pausing, he added, "Please forgive me for not
addressing you as Madam Vice President. I think of you as a
friend."

"I'm pleased to have you address me informally as a
sister in Christ and friend. And I was only able to maintain
my composure during the confirmation hearings by God's
wonderful grace." The hurt in her voice was evident.

"Frankly, I think the rudeness helped swing many to my side. I must admit, however, it left scars that I cried about in private. But I wasn't about to let them know how much it hurt."

The President agreed. "She's right about the reaction to the bigots. They hurt themselves and their position far more than they hurt Jolene or the reforms we are trying to bring."

James said with emphasis, "Mr. President, this illustrates something I've been thinking and praying about that I want to share with all of you. There is no question you're fighting a fierce uphill battle against members of Congress, the media, those in government agencies, and a certain percentage of the general population. But as I've tried to tell you before, your real battle is against demonic spiritual forces that hate God and all He wants to do in this nation.

"Here's something you have to know about demons. By their very nature, they are full of hate, anger, fear, and, therefore, pride, which means they don't trust each other or their master, Satan. Thus, they are not a harmonious group of beings. So it's reasonable to assume that the people they are working through have the same problems.

"Think of some of the world leaders we discussed. They hate and mistrust each other. They are leading different factions who, for the time being, work together in attempts to control the entire world. The reality is that, in their pride, greed, and jealousy, they end up stabbing each other in the back. They think they can take over the world by dividing it up among themselves. But they have an impossible task. Not only will they be unable to agree on the use of the power God gives them, they have to administer their kingdom through faceless bureaucrats. Such individuals are also full of greed, pride, and fear that others will take what they have. So we think we have a rough road to walk, but it's nothing compared to their difficulties."

The three listening were quiet for a moment as they digested these thoughts.

Lanquard was the first to speak. "This probably reveals my ignorance of the Bible and God's ways, but why does God allow all this in the first place? Why doesn't He just wipe the rich, arrogant elitists out and let His people build the kind of world He wants?"

"Good question. Jolene, we talked about this. You tell him."

"James, you sound like a politician trying to dodge a hard question. No, I take that back. You're just being a good teacher. You pointed out that God has set up His kingdom so we grow and mature in our knowledge and relationship with Him through our struggle against evil. In this warfare, He shows us His ultimate power when we trust Him to fight the battles for us. Besides that, if He were too quick in executing His wrath, none of us would last long. He is patient, giving us and also those opposing us ample opportunity to repent."

"That's close enough," said James. "It's why I have peace about going to Russia. God has opened the door to go into the very heartland of one of our enemies, so I trust the Lord to protect me and manifest His glory in whatever ways He chooses. This doesn't mean I haven't had second thoughts or that all will be well from a human standpoint. The same is true for you. You've got to fight the battle as best you can on a moment by moment basis with the wisdom the Lord gives you--"

The President interrupted. "Which reminds me, we have important leaders waiting to see us so we'd better say goodbye and take on our next challenge. But before we do, would you lead us in prayer, Chaplain?"

"Yes. Our God and Heavenly Father, we again commit ourselves to Your care. Give us wisdom to carry out the tasks You've put before us. Lead us through the dangerous times ahead. We trust You to keep each of us safe so we can complete the work You've given us. In Jesus's Name, Amen."

Chapter Eight

A Visit to Russia

On a bright sunny morning, James and Dr. Kampov arrived in Moscow. After adjusting to jetlag in their hotel room, James had visitors. Three pastors arrived to speak to him, so he invited them to be his guests at dinner. Meanwhile, Kampov had commitments with friends whom he hadn't seen in years.

At the hotel restaurant that night, James and his guests had just been served their meal when two well-dressed men approached. They asked if they could have a private word with James.

"What you have to say can be said in front of these men."

"All right. The office of President Solntsev has sent us. He would like to meet with you. But because of the way the media has been handling your visit, he requests that it be kept quiet. He hopes you can appreciate this request for privacy."

James tried not to appear surprised. "I can understand that. Let me talk it over with my friends. I'll give you an answer as soon as I finish my meal, okay?"

The men nodded. "We'll be in the lobby. It is imperative that the President meets you as soon as possible. He is available now."

James smiled and said, "Yes, I understand."

After the men were out of earshot, James turned to the pastors who were looking at each other in amazement.

"What do you think?" asked James. "Is this on the up and up? Can I trust them?"

The older pastor didn't hesitate. "If they wanted to, they could have broken into your room tonight or simply picked you up off the street. Since they are being polite and extending the invitation in public, I'd think you should go with confidence. Remember, this is Russia. You really don't have a choice in this matter."

The younger man remarked somberly, "I've never heard of our President wanting to talk to any of us. I see this as an open door for you to witness."

The others nodded in agreement.

James prayed quietly, "Holy Spirit, give me Your peace if this is of You."

The others added, "Amen."

He picked up his fork and said, "I'm not going to let this good food go uneaten. Let him wait."

The others eagerly began their meal. They were not used to eating so well.

•   James indicated that he was ready to meet with the Soviet President and was asked to follow the two men who led him to a black Mercedes. Another car with a flashing light took them through the streets to the Kremlin where they hurried through the gate and came to a stop in front of an imposing looking building with armed guards at the entrance.

Mr. Markov stood waiting on the steps and introduced himself to James, asking him to follow. He led to a richly furnished room where President Solntsev met them. After introductions, James was invited to take a seat in front of the fireplace with a crackling fire.

The President's English was easy to understand. "Thank you for coming. May I first ask how you would like to be addressed? Is it Reverend Parr or Chaplain? I understand you served with distinction as an army chaplain, is that true?"

James answered confidently, "Suit yourself. I'm not into titles, but since you asked, I like Chaplain. Reverend seems a bit stuffy, and I really don't fit the stereotype of the typical pastor or priest."

"Very good, Chaplain Parr. I suppose you are wondering why we have asked you to meet with us."

James chuckled. "That, sir, is an understatement. But then with what has happened in my life recently, I'm learning not to be surprised by anything. So what may I do for you?"

Solntsev's seriousness changed. He almost jokingly admitted, "You Americans have a way of getting right to the point. I like that." Pointing to the other man in the room, he continued, "Mr. Markov is responsible for our intelligence gathering and the security of our state secrets. He has presented strong evidence that you and some of your spiritually minded friends seem to have, well, shall we say, an inside track with the supernatural. You, or some of your friends, were able to tap into our most tightly guarded secrets. We would like to verify this. If it is true, we are up against something we know little about. But, if this is not the case, we must find the leaks or the undercover agents in our midst."

"What are you specifically referring to?"

"The location of a top secret, missile launching submarine and the fact that Markov and I had secretly discussed breaking a missile treaty with your country. Our conversation was reported in your newspapers. There is also other disturbing and costly interference with our internal matters."

"If you already know what my friends and I have revealed, what more is there for me to do to convince you?"

"Perhaps you could give us a demonstration of this kind of ability."

James laughed. "Look, I'm no trickster or magician. It's not for me to conjure up some miracle to impress you or anyone else."

The President shrugged. "All we want is to verify what we've heard, to have some proof of this phenomenon."

James thought for a long time while the men waited for him to speak. "First, God has revealed the basic truth of His existence in the marvel of His creation, something anyone can see. The size and complexity of the universe speaks loudly of a Creator. Our bodies give evidence of a Designer. It's far too complex to have just happened. Second, God has revealed in the Bible how men are to live and relate to Him. If you reject those fundamental sources, creation and the inspired Word of God, He's not obligated to bow to your unbelief by cheap magic tricks. If you don't believe these sources, you wouldn't believe if someone were raised from the dead.

"So why are you doubting? The facts are these: With no way of knowing where your submarines were located, the Spirit of God gave ordinary people insight as to their location. This was a way of getting the attention of government and military leaders so they, and others, would see their need to turn to God for direction concerning our nation's safety. If you think you can hide from the God Who created and controls every molecule of this creation, you're spiritually blind. Evidently, God wants to use these little demonstrations to get your attention as well."

The Russian leaders exchanged glances. At last, the President spoke slowly. "We have staked our lives on the conviction that religion is a crutch for the weak. We only believe in what we can touch, see, and hear. It is difficult for us to conceive of anything beyond the mind of man."

"How do you know that's all there is?" asked James.

President Solntsev raised his hands in a pleading gesture and struggled with the answer. "This is all science can show us."

"But what's your evidence? Science is wonderful for the limited realm in which it operates. But it's limited to the material world. There's another area of existence known as the spiritual dimension. You can't put that in a test tube or examine it under a microscope. So let me ask a question. What would you accept as evidence that you're wrong and that the spiritual realm is real?"

The Russians hesitated. James was quiet, looking from one to the other.

After a long silence, Markov answered. "This takes us back to our original reason for inviting you here. We hoped to see a demonstration, something that would show us one way or the other."

James bowed his head toward Markov and replied, "All right, what I hear you saying is that you're open to be shown. I will, therefore, spend time in prayer, waiting upon the Lord to see if He is willing to give you something to convince you that this is not hocus pocus or accidental." He raised his finger to make a point. "But I warn you'll be seeing the hand of God. If you don't begin to believe

His directions, you'd better start wearing an enormous lightening rod."

Their puzzled looks caused James to realize that he had been using slang. "Okay, I mean if you don't accept His guidance or revelations, He may strike you with lightening. God, after all, has a limit to His patience."

The two leaders looked at each other and nodded.

President Solntsev agreed, "That sounds reasonable." At a loss for words, he asked, "May we offer you a drink?"

"No thanks. I had wine with my meal before coming here. I appreciate your hospitality though. I'm looking forward to meeting your people and seeing your country."

The President thanked him for coming. James asked for a way to contact them if and when the Lord gave him a message for them. Markov produced an email address.

Escorted to his hotel, James told Dr. Kampov about his experience. The older man was amazed. They concluded that this would turn out to be a gratifying visit.

•   Jack Warren, U.S. Secretary of the Treasury, responded to a conference call with leaders of the world's shadow government. There was urgency and impatience in his voice when the operator made contact with the key leaders of banking and global economics.

"I'm assuming you have all heard about the discovery of viruses in the Russian missile software and how this set back their portion of our plans?"

Lord Davies answered, "Yes, it's a setback, but keep in mind, they can fix the bloody software. They still have Yamantau Mountain and their entire underground military complex with all its missiles. The leadership has been shaken. However, with a few more loans, we can stabilize that situation. I believe what most of us are concerned about is why your President has not received the messages we've been sending. What do we have to do to convince him? Or must we replace him?"

Theodore Bernhart of Belgum asked, "I'd like to know why we didn't take advantage of the exposure of the President and his family during the funerals to take him out? I think that would have gotten the message loud and clear to the American people as to who is really in charge."

Davies suggested, "But it's the economic situation. That's where we can send the loudest message. When it comes down to their bank accounts, that's when they'll be willing to yell Uncle."

Warren reasoned, "But I haven't been able to get any kind of consensus as to what you want to do. The fed is throwing in all kinds of emergency patches to keep the dollar from sinking, while some of you in Europe are using the Euro to sabotage the dollar. The evasive Orientals are driving the gold market up, so what the hell are we in the U.S. supposed to do?"

The calmer voice of Baron Steinberg was heard. "Gentlemen, this is precisely why we've called for the international meeting, which, I trust, all of you are planning to attend. Any one of us, or we as an economic committee, cannot make these kinds of momentous decisions. We all know there are different opinions and some with alternate goals that have to be taken into consideration. As to getting our message to President McCleen, it's my understanding that one of our key assets will be soon activated, so we should have results within the next few days. We know the Americans are a historically resilient people. That's why we have had to plan such strong measures to bend their wills to the global community. We must not panic but employ all our resources to counter the attacks of our ultimate enemy."

He stopped to allow the others to voice their affirmations. No one wanted to openly oppose this powerful man even though in their hearts some hated him. They remained quiet to allow him the floor.

"Mr. Warren, will you and your key staff be at the meeting?"

"Yes, of course. I was hoping I could get some counsel on what to do in the meantime. While there are many who are loudly protesting the actions of the President and his religious followers, nevertheless events such as the termination of terrorist cells are bringing more and more people to his side. America is in the grips of a spiritual revival that frankly many of our people are frightened of. I hope you can appreciate what it's like to be here in the midst of it."

"Yes, friend," Steinberg assured. "I believe we can sympathize with you. But remember, our forefathers faced such trials in the past. What history shows is that emotional phenomenon tends to dissipate quickly. Therefore, we will keep up the pressure on all fronts. I'm confident that, when we all gather, our spirit guides will show us solutions which none of us have been able to discover alone. I suggest we continue doing what has been given us. We must wait until we meet together to learn what to do as a united front. We have also arranged a meeting of the United Nations at the same time of our meeting, so we can have them immediately affirm and put into action the decisions we make.

"Gentlemen, as a closing thought, we can be thankful for this challenge because I see it pulling previous warring factions together. We will come out of this more united and stronger. So until we meet, let us bid each other a good day."

No one protested the end of the conference call.

•   James accompanied Dr. Kampov to his meeting with the Russian scientists. The whole event was conducted in the Russian language, and there was no one available to translate the lecture or the questions that followed. James tuned out the lecture and spent the time in prayer for Dr. Kampov. He sensed a great amount of spiritual opposition in the large auditorium in the form of angry demons whispering hatred into the minds of the men and women who nevertheless were listening intently to the lecture. Almost everyone took notes even though printed copies of the lecture were to be made available later.

It was during the question and answer period that James felt the tension in the room rise to a boiling level. He didn't have to understand the native tongue of those in attendance to read their body language. Also, the tone of voice used by those asking the questions was obvious. Dr. Kampov's voice remained gentle yet forceful with his answers. James and the doctor had previously discussed in detail the lecture points. At the heart of his lecture was strong, scientific evidence that refuted, in fact devastated, the theory of evolution.

James decided it was the innate curiosity of the Russian scientists and the quality and profound insights of Kampov's work that had presented this opportunity. The points Kampov made in his lecture were clear. Many of the scientists became quite angry. It was amusing to James. These learned men and women, who were supposedly devoted to the objective search for truth, were reacting like children who had just been told Santa Clause did not exist and there would be no Christmas this year.

In an adjoining dining facility, a hearty luncheon was served following the lecture. Seated next to Dr. Kampov, James learned the key points of the scientists' objections. While Dr. Kampov kept his outward appearance as a cool, confident man of science, James detected deep sorrow.

Two reporters interviewed Dr. Kampov following the luncheon. They also interviewed many who had attended the lecture. What appeared in newspaper and television news was a collection of comments by intellects, politicians, and particularly Russian Orthodox leaders who had unanimously turned against humble Dr. Kampov, denouncing him. Dr. Kampov's only comment to James was that they had heard the truth. What they did with it was their responsibility before God.

The next morning they were invited to speak at a gathering of Moscow pastors, a small number of educators, and others who wanted to hear Kampov's Christian testimony. Dr. Kampov was also to present arguments for God being the Creator of the universe in six literal days.

What amazed James and Dr. Kampov was the appearance of a television news camera crew in the dingy lecture hall. They came to record his speech and James's testimony. James brought greetings to the Russian Christians from those who loved God in America. On behalf of all Americans, he thanked the ones who had faithfully prayed for a spiritual revival in his country. He assured them that God was answering their prayers and encouraged them to continue their efforts because there were powerful enemies trying to stop what God was doing.

James had never seen Dr. Kampov so animated as he spoke. He didn't read from a science paper. He spoke from his heart, and the longer he took, the more tears of joy James saw on the smiling, and, in some cases, scarred faces of pastors.

James took a seat in the audience after speaking. A young pastor next to him discerned that he didn't understand Russian, so he whispered bits and pieces of Dr. Kampov's message to him.

As Kampov made strong points on the theory of evolution, that it was a tool of Satan, several men from the back of the auditorium shouted obscenities and cursed him. Kampov paused to wait for the opposition to stop. Several pastors rose, calling for silence.

Chaos ensued. Several protesters rushed into the aisles to the front, yelling at the top of their voices. Before anyone could stop them, they had reached Dr. Kampov. A screaming man hit the doctor, knocking him against the wooden chairs. James and several others surged forward to pull the intruders off Kampov. In the process, James was hit on the side of his head and knocked to the floor. He crawled through the scuffling crowd toward Dr. Kampov. In the process, he was stepped on and kicked. His hand was badly crushed.

When he reached Dr. Kampov, an elderly pastor was cradling the scientist in his arms. James noticed an unnatural angle of his friend's head. His face was peaceful, but his eyes stared upward. James waved his hand over his friend's face. His eyes didn't move. Then James felt under his chin and was unable to detect a heartbeat. He groaned, ignoring the ongoing yelling and struggle around him. Looking at the pastor, he saw tears in the man's eyes. The pain of James's own injuries could not keep him from being overwhelmed by grief. "Why God, why?" was all he could say.

The event was captured on video and made the evening news. Since Dr. Kampov was an American citizen, the press in America came to his defense by reporting the story. This in turn gave him and his message more press in the Russian morning news. It also made Russia's political leaders more angry and frustrated. They wanted to keep up the appearance that all was peaceful between America and

Russia, but this event eradicated that.

By noon, James, with a bruised face and bandaged hand, was invited to appear on a Russian television program to air throughout the nation that evening. The motivation of the TV producer was ratings. The way to get it was to ask James to debate two leading Russian scientists. The subject would be the pros and cons of scientific evolution.

• Christine's original Bible study and prayer group had divided twice due to the increased interest of her neighbors. Members of the original small group were now leaders in their own homes. New believers were being instructed and encouraged to get into deeper issues of the faith. Through the Internet and national TV programs, Christians sensed they were part of a mighty movement of God that was including every segment of the American society.

Hostile discussions in offices, coffee shops, and restaurants became prayer meetings as conversation shifted from national issues to personal relationships with the Lord Jesus. Even the media was seeing the shift in the public attitude and began to give more time to the positive nature of the spiritual revival.

In Erich and Christine's home, the people who gathered represented different races, educational backgrounds, and political persuasions. Children were included in the prayer and study time. As the Scripture taught, "From the mouth of babes, God would speak." And He did.

The attempts on the lives of the President and James Parr, the latter of whom God had used to initiate this series of events, made a deep impression on the Flemings. They determined to join other Americans to stand guard in prayer over the leaders of the nation and the revival occurring across the country.

When word of the attack on James in Russia and the tragic death of Dr. Kampov reached the Flemings, their prayer groups were called to an extended time of fasting, prayer, and waiting before the Lord. They were determined that God show Himself powerful to stop the intentions of evil men worldwide. More people had begun to realize the threat to their ultimate safety occurred because of the actions of men and women from many different parts of the world who had been empowered by Satan.

The core of the Christians' pleas came from the imprecatory prayers of the Psalms. "Let them, the enemies of God, be confounded and dismayed forever. Yes, let them be put to shame and perish, that they may know that You, Whose name alone is Yahweh, are the Most High over all the earth." They also called on God to use His host of mighty angels to aid and back them in their quest for righteousness.

·   Agent Barnes could not trust his suspicion of Todd Campbell to anyone but James. With the chaplain's absence, Barnes decided to assign Campbell to duties that would keep him away from the President. Yet this was only a temporary fix.

The funerals of the President's father and grandson, as well as the vice president, had been close to nightmares for Barnes and his detail. The opportunities for assassination were staggering. Increased security measures introduced after 911 proved to be a blessing for Barnes's job. Of course, one of the assassins could have been planted among the thousands of police and soldiers brought in for additional protection. His team breathed a sigh of relief when the President and his wife were back safely in the White House.

The attempt by a member of Congress to kill the President had a lasting effect on Barnes and his men. Who were these power hungry elitists of the world that had invested the amount of time and effort to put such a man in Congress and then used him in an assassination attempt? What kind of evil were the President and his staff up against?

It was not normal protocol for the President to ask Barnes for his opinion on any issue, but it had become normal for Barnes to be asked to come to the President's office.

"How's Emily?" the President inquired.

"She's doing great, sir. It's a boost to one's faith to be hugged by a walking, talking miracle."

The President smiled broadly. "That's great! When things quiet down, bring her to the White House so I can give her a hug as well."

"She'd love that, sir."

The smile on the President's face turned to a look of concern. "I've received disturbing news. Dr. Kampov has been killed. A group of ruffians broke up his presentation to Russian pastors, and one of the thugs killed him. James was with Kampov but escaped with minor injuries."

"I'm sorry to hear that, sir. It seems like the chaplain keeps getting into scrapes. I haven't had an opportunity to tell you this, but a news cameraman reviewing the tape of James's arrival at the TV station in Denver noticed something unusual. He sent it to us. Under examination, it appears a sniper shot at James outside the station, but the bullet hit a pigeon. The Lord protected him outside the studio as well as inside."

"That confirms the convictions I've had. I'm going to send an Air Force plane to pick up Dr. Kampov's body and bring him home. I want the chaplain to get out of Russia and come home where we can give him protection. I know your agents are being overworked now, but I think he deserves our help."

Barnes nodded in agreement.

The President continued. "I know you're not going to like this, but I believe I need to go to the airport and meet the plane when it lands at McClure."

Barnes winced. "Sir, I appreciate you sending the plane and all, but I have to protest. It puts you at too much risk."

"I knew you'd say that. However, this is an opportunity to snub the Russians and let the powers that-be-know we're not going to cower to their threats. I don't know if they were behind Kampov's death, but I know they are out to get me. I'm not going to let them make me a prisoner here in the White House."

"Do we have to announce that you'll be there ahead of time? If we could just let a few newsmen know, that would make our job a lot easier. We'd pick them up at the last minute and not even let them know what was up until we got there. You'd still have lots of publicity afterwards."

"Sure, that would be all right." The President extended his hand as Barnes rose. "I want you to know that I have a new appreciation for what you and your staff do. Check it out, and let me know if it's feasible. If you conclude it's not right, we'll see what else we can do."

Barnes knew if he pushed it, he might be able to persuade the President to stay in the safety of the White House. Then he remembered to pray about it, as James had impressed on him: "Ask the Holy Spirit to tell you what to do." Barnes did and felt peace to go ahead with the President's request. Then Todd Campbell came to mind.

• James was escorted to the television station where the program producer, who simply introduced himself as Alex, explained in broken English that this was an independent station. Thus, he was not under the control of the government as long as he used discretion in the choice of his programs. He was confident they would have a large audience tonight since Drs. Tosh and Romanofski were widely known scientists. Both lectured at Moscow University and were published in science journals around the world.

"Chaplain Parr, we want to show the Russian people as well as the international community that we treat our guests with kindness. We want the world to know that what the ruffians did to Dr. Kampov was not representative of the Russian people or our government."

"Thank you for being able to present our views to the Russian people."

James was placed in a small room where a young woman applied makeup to cover the black eye and cuts on his face. Looking in the mirror, he wasn't sure which made him look worse, the bruises or the makeup. Eventually he was escorted to a plain television set with no scenery. It merely consisted of two tables set at ninety-degree angles to each other against a black curtain. Seated between James and the two scientists at the intersection of the tables was an interpreter to translate James's statements into Russian.

Before everyone was seated, introductions were made, James to Drs. Tosh and Romanofski. After microphones were tested and the levels set, an off-camera announcer made an opening statement and introduced the participants. As he did so, the interrupter whispered the English translation in James's ear.

The announcer reached the end of his introduction. Matter-of-factly he stated, "The title of the debate tonight is 'Evolution Versus the Christian Belief in Creation By a Supreme Being.' We will allow our guest from America to make his opening statement and ask the first question. Former Army Chaplain James Parr."

James spoke slowly so the interpreter could translate. "Thank you. I count it a privilege to have this opportunity to speak to you. I am deeply sorry that my friend Dr. Kampov could not be here. He loved his native country and you, the Russian people. He was happy to be able to return here and share his discoveries with his scientist friends for whom he had great respect and admiration.

"He was a man dedicated to the search for truth even when it led to discoveries that caused him to reverse previous held positions. Dr. Kampov was not afraid or too proud to admit that he had been wrong when he discovered truth. It is sad that those afraid of truth could not just have used their intellect to oppose Dr. Kampov. Although they used brute force to silence him, there is a truth stated in the Holy Bible that will haunt those villains. 'He being dead, continues to speak.'" James stopped until the translation was complete.

"My first question is what do you mean by the term evolution especially as it relates to science and religion?"

The two scientists showed surprise.

Dr. Tosh answered, "Evolution is a term used to express the scientific proof that all life evolved from lower forms, and, therefore, there is no God involved in the process. Religion is something that primitive man invented to explain what they could not know from observation. The priests used superstitions to control the ignorant and weak. When man became wise enough to develop scientific proofs which dispelled the myths of religion, we threw it aside because it impeded our progress."

"How do you know that what you're saying is true?" asked James.

Dr. Romanoffshi had a condescending look on his face when he answered. "We use science to establish our proofs, and our intellectual knowledge and reason to draw conclusions. We do not need religious myths to establish what is best for the future of mankind."

"But what are your proofs that there is no God?"

The two scientists shrugged as if it were a ridiculous question needing no answer.

James continued quickly, "Well, if it's so obvious, surely you can give us scientific proof."

Tosh's voice reverberated with impatience. He began his answer indignantly. "What has religion given man? Poverty, senseless wars, ignorance, and superstitions that hindered man's freedom to evolve to his full potential--"

James interrupted, "Wait a minute! Stop! Religion causes poverty? Has science done away with poverty or war? It seems to me that science has only increased man's ability to kill his fellow man with more efficiency. Ignorance? I find it astounding to blame religion, especially Christianity for perpetuating ignorance. Western Christian nations were the pioneers of education and built great centers of learning. Sincere Christians founded all the oldest universities in America to further man's knowledge and search for truth. The greatest scientists have been Christians, or at least they operated in the freedom of a Christian based society. They made the greatest advancements in all areas of science. And where have ordinary people of all races and stations in life enjoyed the greatest personal freedoms but in a nation founded by self declared Christians, my home nation, America! So I ask again, what are your proofs that there is no God, and especially that God did not create what is?"

Tosh bowed in mock humility toward James. "You are a very clever debater. Most of our audience will not know that using logic, you cannot prove a negative. So we cannot prove there is no God. What we can provide is evidence that, to understand life as having evolved from the basic elements of nature is a superior way to view life and achieve what is best in life--"

James interrupted again. "So, has science been able to produce life from inanimate particles?"

"No, not yet. But we have proved that we can live without religion."

"But what if you're wrong, and when you die, you

discover there is a God Who holds you accountable for the way you have lived your life?"

Romanoffski blurted, "But we are not wrong!"

Just as quickly, James countered, "How do you know?"

Tosh beat his partner to the answer. "I know because of my superior intellect. I have three earned Ph.D.s. Dr. Romanoffski and I have the respect of men of superior minds around the world who--"

Again interrupting, James said, "I don't doubt or disrespect your intellectual abilities. You are intelligent men. But how do you explain a universe that contains billions of galaxies of immense size that even your great minds cannot comprehend? How do you explain the trillions of cells that make up our bodies? Those cells are too small to see, and yet each has a DNA molecule, a blueprint for a person's entire body. Powerful microscopes now disclose that a single cell has billions of what can only be described as complex machines. These cells reproduce themselves by the billions while we are speaking. All this speaks powerfully of a Designer, a Master Mind of fantastic power--"

Tosh angrily broke in as the translator tried to keep up with James. "No! Our mind is all there is! We are our own gods."

"How do you know? You've never died and come back to life," shouted James.

"And neither have you!" Romanoffski shouted in return.

James said, "Ah, but I know someone who has. The Lord Jesus Christ died and was resurrected--"

At the mention of the Name of Jesus, Tosh clenched his fist, bared his teeth in a hissing sound, and glared at his American opponent while pounding on the table. James recognized this as a manifestation of a demonic spirit and paid no attention to the translation of what came from the man's mouth.

Pointing his finger at Tosh, James cried out, "Lord Jesus Christ, I ask you to bind that spirit of rebellion and pride. By Your shed blood, leave this man. Set him free through the powerful Name of the Lord Jesus Christ now!"

Tosh jerked about, his face twisting in an ugly fashion. He was in a struggle of magnanimous proportions with an unseen force. Romanoffski, looking horrified, shoved his chair away from Tosh.

James commanded, "In the name of Jesus, be gone, you foul spirit!"

Tosh's arms flew up. His body fell limp, and he toppled against the table, knocking over the microphone. The translator, momentarily stunned, translated James's command.

James had been aware that Tosh's left arm was short and withered. Gently, he spoke, "Sit up."

Tosh did as he was told. He looked stunned.

"Dr. Tosh, stretch out your left arm. Jesus is healing it."

The scientist looked at his arm and obeyed. The translator spoke a few words in Russian and then gasped and shouted the final part of the translation. Tosh stared at his arm as it grew to normal length. He held his breath in amazement. Then he slowly rotated his hand and flexed his fingers as if he'd never seen a hand with fingers before.

James heard shouts and exclamations from the dark areas of the studio. Romanoffski jumped up, nearly falling backwards in the process as he retreated into the darkness where he collided with a camera. James caught a glimpse of terror on the man's face when the cameraman cursed him. Then James looked at Tosh who appeared dazed. Both men smiled when Tosh spoke in Russian. It took a couple of seconds for James to realize there was no translation coming forth, so he turned to the translator who was staring trance-like at Tosh's arm.

James elbowed the translator. "What's he saying?"

The interpreter began, "He says he's free, he's free. He is thanking you. He's, he's--"

James grabbed his arm. "Yes, what? Come on!"

"He's saying that Jesus has set him free and healed him."

James turned to look at Dr. Tosh's face. Joyous laughter erupted from the chaplain.

Tears of joy and a smile lit up the scientist's entire being. He began to speak in English. "I have been wrong. I was blinded by pride, fear, and hatred."

The interpreter was taken back for a moment but then

switched to speaking his words in Russian for the viewing audience.

Tosh raised his hand to his mouth. The next words were emitted while he wept. "As a child, my mother told me about Jesus and read the Bible to me. Deep in my heart, I always knew she was right, but I chose the way of the world. I did not want to suffer as a follower of Jesus." He reached toward James. "My brother, will He forgive me?"

James nodded enthusiastically. "Yes, God has forgiven you. He proved it by setting you free from the devil's grip. He healed your arm. Now give your life to Him. Surrender your all to Jesus."

Tosh looked up and began to pray in Russian. James's mouth fell open in surprise as he waited for the translation.

"Forgive me, Jesus. I give You what is left of my miserable life. I am sorry for my rebellion. Forgive me. Forgive me. Oh, thank You, Lord Jesus. Thank You for setting me free. Thank You for this honest brother who faced me with the truth."

• Alex, the producer, was extremely happy as he worked in the production booth. Shouting directions to the camera operators, he believed this was a fantastic break for him. He had on tape a dramatic healing and the religious conversion of one of the nation's leading evolutionists. This would make Alex famous. Hollywood could not top it. He would be sought after internationally after this was sold to the major networks. He had a gut feeling that this was going to be something special. He would not allow his crew to screw this up. "Keep the tape rolling!" he yelled. "The hell with breaks for advertisers! They'll beg for time in the future."

• Dr. Tosh ended his prayer with "amen." He rose from his chair, ignoring the lights and the camera, and embraced James who had risen and stepped around the translator. He kissed James on both cheeks and hugged him, Russian style. Then he held James at arm's length and spoke to him in English.

"You must tell the people that evolution is a lie. It is a stupid, religious fraud."

"No," James insisted, "you tell them."

"I have been so steeped in the lies, I don't know if I can tell the truth," he replied.

"Okay, let's both do it."

"Yes, very good." Tosh impulsively embraced James again and kissed his cheeks.

They returned to their seats.

James looked toward the camera with the red light. "You have just seen a demonstration of the love and power of God. The Lord Jesus Christ who walked the earth two thousand years ago healing the sick and setting free those oppressed by demonic spirits is with us in Spirit today. As Dr. Tosh told you, evolution is the real myth, not Christianity. It's a lie invented by men who refused to acknowledge God. And why do they reject God? For one simple reason, they want to be free to indulge in the sins of the flesh. They want the praises of men. Their pride stands in the way of acknowledging obvious truth."

The translator, struggling to keep up with James, tapped his arm to remind him to slow down.

"There are no scientific facts to back the ridiculous theory that life evolved from inanimate objects. None! The geological record shows there are no transitional fossils, not even one in the millions of known fossils. On the other hand, there is a great deal wrong with the religions of man and the churches that have turned into mere organizations instead of instruments of God to love and serve people who have been created in the image of God. The reality of the Lord Jesus Christ and His love for all those who turn to Him in simple trust cannot be denied by the corruption in man-centered churches and the religions of men.

"I challenge the Christians of Russia to repent and begin to seek and pray to God day and night for Him to change your communities and nation. I encourage you to pray the imprecatory prayers from the book of Psalms against the enemies of Christ. Ask God to bring them to their senses just as Dr. Tosh has been delivered from his blindness."

Tosh was nodding and punctuating James's remarks with his healed hand.

James persisted, "I admit that most of America's

leaders are as pagan as those in Russia. But I want you to understand that a group of wealthy, power hungry people plan to destroy the Church of the Lord Jesus Christ. These people control Russia and America at the human level. They resent the freedoms and prosperity America once offered the world. But God will destroy them if they don't repent. We Christians represent the real power in this world, and that is God Almighty. Yet we are not to manifest our power with guns or through buying off others. We show the power of God by living the truth and facing down America and Russia's enemies on our knees.

"I was up most of last night and today praying for God's leading and strength before coming to the studio. Others who knew about it were also fasting and praying. I believe this is why God moved so powerfully tonight. It was not the result of my goodness or abilities. It was the power of God using me as a vessel in His service.

"Cry out to God for His mercy to be shown to your nation and the other nations around you. His heart is broken over the corruption, over the threat of worldwide war. Pray that your leaders will literally turn your weapons of war into farming instruments so that you may enjoy peace. That's what we little people want. If we cry out to God, repent of our sins, and seek Him, He promises to forgive our sins and heal our land.

"I'd like the director to turn the camera on Dr. Tosh. Let the people recognize the contrast from what he looked like at the beginning of the program and the peace and joy radiating from his face now."

• Alex was totally engrossed in the live program before him. He had an American on Russian television debunking all the garbage the Russian people had been fed for decades. It was happening on his program. What a break! It took his assistant's frantic grip on his arm inflicting pain to get his attention.

"Alex, you idiot, the station's owner is phoning!"

"What? No! Tell him I'll call him back."

"No! He says you are to pull the plug on the program. Now!"

"What?"

"Here, you talk to him!"

Alex grabbed the phone. "This is Alex."

The station owner shouted, "Go to music. Get that bastard off the air, now!"

"But this is dynamic. I'll bet our viewers have doubled in the last half hour."

"You idiot, do you want to get us killed? The authorities are not going to appreciate this."

Alex argued, "But this is not about politics or even religion. I don't give a damn about what they're saying or believe. You know that. This is about ratings, exposure. This is what television was made for."

"You fool, do you forget where you are? You're in Russia, you stupid idiot! Now cut them off the air. Say it's technical problems and destroy the tapes. Do it now, or you're fired! You hear me? If you don't, you won't have a future, period."

Alex's mind was only half listening. At first he was sick to even think of losing such a winning program. But then a deeper realization came to mind. Yes. I'll go to music and declare technical problems. And what would the people know? That the station buckled to political pressure. They got too close to the truth. This will only add to the people's hunger to know more. Destroy the tapes? Not on your life! I'll edit them and make a killing on the black market, and, if need be, smuggle them out to the West where I'll sell them for a mint.

He spoke quietly, "All right, you're the boss. I'm sorry I questioned your authority. I just got carried away."

"No more excuses or apologies. Just do it. Now!"

Alex got off the phone. Turning to the key operator on the main board, he said, "On the count of three, go to black on the broadcast signal and get ready to throw up the technical difficulty sign. Then bring up background music. One, two, three! Yes! All right, keep the cameras rolling. No! Don't turn off the recorders. Go find me some old, worthless cassettes. When I stop the interview, get me all the master tapes. As far as you're concerned, this program never existed. Got it?"

His operator threw him a puzzled look.

Alex grinned and winked. "I'll give you a cut under the table. Remember, this is Russia." He laughed and then watched the cameras as they continued to tape the American speaking through the interrupter. Ah yes, this is Russia. As the man said, there is a God, and He has just shined down on a poor, struggling TV producer.

In about twenty minutes, Alex sensed that James and Tosh were beginning to repeat themselves. He went into the studio. Staying out of the line of the camera, he got James's attention, held up four fingers, pointed to his watch, and then drew his forefinger across his throat. James got the point. Four minutes to wrap it up.

• Cameras were off. James assured Tosh, "Dr. Kampov would have gladly given his life to see what happened here tonight."

"Yes, I can now understand that. I also realize it may not be long before I join Dr. Kampov. Despite the theoretical openness, the reality is that in Russia evil rules. I suppose I could attempt to flee to the West, but I doubt I would be allowed. Perhaps my death can free others." Tears filled his eyes. "Do not judge these tears as coming from fear or regret. For the first time in my life, I have a peace I have never known before. I'm not afraid of death. These are tears of great joy. I have spent a lifetime trying to explain away and run from my own demise, but now, with God as my witness, I have no concern."

"Don't sell your life cheap or underestimate the power of God to protect you until His purposes have been accomplished. Satan's followers are trying to kill my President and me. Each time they've been stopped in miraculous ways. I pray that the Lord Jesus will do the same for you. Remember, He is still the true God of Russia."

"Yes, thank you, my brother. I have so much to learn and so much to repent from. May God give me the time to do what must be done."

• James received an urgent message the next morning to bring his luggage to the U.S. embassy. He was to be flown home on an American military plane, along with the body of Dr. Kampov. He'd been scheduled to speak in Red Square that day at a large rally sponsored by evangelical pastors. However, Russian authorities canceled it. Their excuse was that they were concerned it would create a riot. The Russian people were not fooled. This only added credibility to the message they'd heard by television.

Alex interviewed the converted scientist and James after the program and slipped part of that interview into a news program later that night. His picture showed Dr. Tosh's healed arm and the peace and joy on his face. The news reporter said nothing about the healing. The picture told the story.

Enterprising businessmen began producing copies of the TV program and selling them on the black market, along with pirated video copies of The Passion and The Life of Jesus from the gospel of John. The truth would get out to the people who wanted to know it.

Alex was closer to being converted to Christ than he realized, but for now, he was simply doing his job. He produced follow up programs on the criticisms by the other scientists. They sounded stupid in light of what had happened to Dr. Tosh.

The initial result of all of this was a fresh outbreak of persecution of Christians by the Russian Orthodox Church and the government. However, this only resulted in more people wanting to purchase Bibles and increased numbers of Christians meeting in secret to worship God the Father. God was answering the desperate prayers of His people.

Chapter Nine

God Shakes Things Up

In preparation for their trip to the airport, Barnes called together the President's immediate detail for a weapons check. He had seldom done this, but the agents accepted his explanation.

"I have to admit that, with all the tension of the last days, I've grown slack in the basic care of my weapon, and I suspect some of you may have done the same. It's my duty to see that we are ready to meet any emergency. So let's start with the most basic weapon we have, our side arms."

Walking down the line of men, Barnes accepted each pistol, ejected the clip, cleared the chamber, and checked for cleanliness. A couple of times, he turned away from the agent and held the weapon up to the light so he could look through the barrel. When he came to Todd Campbell, he did the same, only this time it appeared to the men that he almost dropped the clip as it slid from the butt of the pistol.

He grinned and looked at them. "How to make a great impression as a leader of men."

Several snickered. Barnes turned, held the weapon up, and then slid a clip back into the butt of the pistol. He handed it to Campbell. Proceeding down the line, he finished the inspection of each man's weapon. Then Barnes left them to check the weapons of the snipers, traveling with the motorcade and all the assortment of weaponry carried by the full team.

•   The President's motorcade had no trouble reaching McClure Air Force Base outside the capital. The timing was perfect. The giant C5 aircraft was taxiing to the meeting spot when they escorted the nation's leader from his limousine. This was the first the media knew of President McCleen's decision to be there.

Part of the Secret Service detail was already facing toward the small group of Dr. Kampov's family and friends, waiting behind low barricades. Agent Campbell stood near the President but faced the crowd. Barnes's attention was drawn to a cell phone ringing. He turned toward the sound and saw Campbell pull a phone from his pocket, place it to his ear, and listen for only a couple of seconds. He closed the phone and slipped it back into his pocket without taking his eyes off the crowd.

Slowly Campbell turned and looked directly at the President. Barnes was close enough to see his eyes narrow. A chill shot through him. It felt like the hair on the back of his neck was standing. Barnes watched Campbell turn his head to face the crowd. He moved toward the President, all the while watching Campbell as discreetly as possible. He suspected the phone call had activated a deep psychological trigger just as a well-trained dog leaps at his master's command to attack. Barnes expected the same behavior from Campbell.

The senior agent had only taken a couple of steps when he saw Campbell turn and focus on the President. Campbell walked toward the nation's leader who was not facing him at the time. The agent's hand moved suddenly. Reaching under his coat, he pulled out his pistol and thrust it toward the President's head. Another agent became aware of what was happening and reacted with Barnes who was standing closer to the President. Barnes saw the trigger finger squeeze. Only the senior agent knew that nothing would happen because, during his weapons inspection, he had slipped another clip into the pistol with bullets that had dud caps in them.

Barnes leaped toward Campbell who was ejecting the bullet and preparing to again draw down on the President. Barnes's tackle knocked Campbell to the ground. The other agent had his weapon out but held his fire for fear of hitting his boss. Barnes was surprised at how easy it was to throw Campbell's body down and jerk his two hands behind him. Two other agents were there to assist.

By this time, the scuffle had attracted the attention of the President and those standing around him.

Barnes looked up. "The situation is in hand, sir. Proceed with what you planned."

The agent bodyguard next to the President was ready to grab him and hustle him away.

Barnes caught his eye. Shaking his head, he held up his hand. "It's all right. We've got things under control."

The noise of the plane's engines winding down drowned out further conversation. The two agents pulled Campbell to his feet.

Barnes whispered to them, "Take him away. Keep him bound until you can strip him of every item of clothing on him. Remember what happened to the congressman."

They nodded and led him off. Campbell made no effort to resist or protest.

In the past, Barnes had wondered if there really was something to the idea that men could be preprogrammed to carry out a suicide mission. He didn't doubt it any longer and silently thanked the Lord for warning him and showing him how to protect his President.

•   "Comrade Toschoff." President Solntsev spoke with enthusiasm. "I have you on speaker phone with the other members of the Central Committee. We all want to congratulate you on the excellent work you have done preparing the Yamantau Mountain Complex."

"Thank you, Mr. President. Everything is proceeding according to plan. Your request to speed things up has motivated my whole team to work harder."

This was a tongue in cheek comment. Actually it had brought a lot of complaining and slowdowns by numerous workers who resented being confined to the underground world.

The President responded, "We have your reports in front of us, but given the nature of the strange things that have been happening to some of our operations, we wanted to see how everything is going with your projects."

"It is all is going well, comrades. Food purchased from the Americans, with their own money, I might add, has been placed in special air-dried storage bins that are climate controlled and free of any possible contamination by mice

or insects. Our mill is already grinding some of the grain
for our maintenance crew, and our bakery is turning out
breads and pastries that will make your mouth water just to
imagine them. We are doing this as a trial run to be doubly
sure we are ready.

"Our hatcheries and chicken farm will supply fresh
eggs and meat. Our dairy will produce fresh milk. The
green houses, artificially lighted and fertilized with manure
from the chickens and cows, will turn out fresh vegetables.
The nuclear reactor supplies all the electricity needed for
artificial sunlight and the numerous other electrical needs.
The thousands of feet of granite provide all the protection
necessary from any nuclear missiles that the Americans or
their puny allies can possibly launch. If, of course, they can
get them past our superior missile defense system."

"Yes, yes, comrade, we appreciate your pride and
enthusiasm for the facilities. Is everything working well in
the production of the new model of ICBMs?"

"The operation is going well. After what happened to
the software in the launching codes, we have physically
separated our computers from any outside source. We will
continue to turn out weapons of mass destruction, spare
parts, and munitions for tanks and other weapons, which
have also been protected from direct counter nuclear
attacks."

Toschoff wanted to add that, by the time Russian tanks
rolled across Europe and the Middle East, it would be too
late for anyone to do anything about it. Without America's
military, the Europeans would give up without serious
opposition. Much of this future success would be because of
the gigantic underground city he had designed and built.
But Toschoff knew that would be too boastful, so he merely
added, "We are making the last minor finishing touches, and
we are fully stocked. As far as we are concerned, as soon as
your computer experts repair the software and test it, we
will be ready. Nothing can stop us now."

Immediately after this statement, Toschoff's massive
desk began to shake. The glass in the chandelier tinkled,
causing Toschoff to catch his breath. "What the hell?"

"What is it, Toschoff?"

The desk stopped shaking. Toschoff held his breath.
"I don't know. There were vibrations, probably from the
blasting in one of the tunnels that has not been--" Before he
could say the word finished, his world collapsed around him.
Ceiling tiles and the chandelier crashed to the heaving floor.
He toppled unceremoniously to the carpet with eyes and
mouth wide open. Fear surged through him as he had never
experienced before.

The seconds crawled by. Screams of terrified office
workers pierced the deafening rumbles of crashing rock,
snapping steel girders, and other falling debris. The
earthquake lasted only seven seconds. It took only a few
seconds for the falling stones to settle and for sagging steel
beams to snap under the overwhelming weight of rock that
fell from the ceilings of the massive tunnels.

This was followed by a brief period of silence. It only
seemed that way due to the sudden contrast caused by the
absence of the deafening roar. The moans of injured people
and screams of terrified men and women who had been
plunged into darkness rose amidst the hiss of escaping
gasses and water sprayed from broken pipes.

If Toschoff could have been honest, he would have
admitted the terror in his pounding heart. With trembling
hands, he reached for a support of some kind that would
help him off the floor and from under the sheets of ceiling
tile partially covering him.

He automatically felt his face, wondering if his eyes had
been injured. Then he knew what had happened. Broken
electrical wires had shut off the lights. Being inside a cave,
the darkness was total, which only added to everyone's fear.

Then he remembered, the emergency battery powered
lights were there that he'd wanted to exclude because of
the added cost. Now his automatic response was a heartfelt
"Thank God!" He rose with great effort above his solid oak
desk. Through the smashed office door, he saw light in the
hallway.

Rising shakily to his feet, his head bumped against
braces which moments before held the ceiling supports.
He attempted deep breaths to calm his nerves, but when
he tried, he was immediately made aware of the dust that

filled the air. Thoughts raced through his mind. No smoke yet. But how long do we have to get out before fires fill the air with poison gasses? Wait a minute. We planned for fires. Not only did we build automatic fire suppression, there are ex navy firefighters trained and on round-the-clock duty. They're ready to challenge such a possibility.

This brought a momentary sense of comfort. Stumbling toward the outer office, he became aware of his secretary's moan. She was pleading for help. Before reaching her, he thought, If my office is an indication of the total damage, the water pipes and the means to get to any fire or fuel spillage will prevent the fire crews from . . . Oh my God! This can't be! His mind recoiled with the reality of the situation. He didn't stop to consider why he, a declared atheist, was automatically referring to the God he had denied all of his life.

Toschoff stepped to the mangled doorway of his office. Peering through darkness to a shaft of light, he realized the light came from a battery powered emergency lamp. Reaching into his pocket, he removed a handkerchief to cover his mouth and nose. Making a mask, he tied it behind his neck.

A high-pitched, piercing scream jarred his senses, echoing off the walls of the tunnel. It was followed by increased noise. People were calling for help while others shouted words of encouragement or curses. Once again he heard a moan and a plea for help. It brought him back to an action mode. He banged his legs against a sharp object that caused enough pain to make him swear. Another plea rose from Tanya. She was moaning louder now.

Enough light was available for him to see his secretary struggling to rise from the rubble. He shoved objects off her body. Then he placed his hands under her arms to help her rise.

"What happened?"

"We must have been hit by an earthquake. Are you all right?"

"I don't know. My head hurts. Oh, my ankle!"

"Let me help you. Let's see if we can walk to the light. We have to get out of here."

Even as he said the words, a conflict emerged in his mind. The hell with her! I have to get out of here. My expertise is needed to save this facility. Secretaries can easily be replaced. Yet, how can I be so cold hearted? She was one of the women that gave me sexual satisfaction and creature comforts in the long hours demanded of me by this project. I owe some human kindness to her.

The two struggled through the debris to get to the hallway and the precious light source. He thought, I will see that the man who insisted on these lights being installed gets some kind of medal, a reward for his foresight.

When Toschoff and Tanya arrived at the light, they brushed aside the tiles that partly covered it. He used his jacket to remove dirt from the lenses of the lamp and felt elated as the light drove away the cursed darkness. However, what the light revealed brought a groan. He saw total destruction.

A giant, black hole yawned where his prized computer room had once been. He automatically turned the light up to reveal a gapping concave hole in the ceiling of the cave. Hundreds of tons of rock had collapsed and smashed the computer room to the lowest level of the cavern three stories below. He couldn't bring himself to shine the light into the hole. His mind calculated that up to a dozen highly skilled technicians and millions of dollars worth of equipment and programs were buried, along with whatever and whoever were on the floors below.

Stunned by the gravity of the situation, he was brought to action by Tanya's whimpers of pain and fear.

"Look at my face," she agonized. "I must be bleeding. There is blood all over my blouse."

He turned the light toward her and saw a piece of skin with hair hanging from the left side of her forehead. Blood flowed down her once attractive face.

"Here, hold the light. I'll tear a strip from my shirt and use it as a bandage to stop the bleeding." Pulling his shirt from his trousers, he tried to tear a strip with no luck. The tightly woven fabric resisted. "Damn!" cried the engineer.

He reached into his pocket and pulled out a small knife. Opening the blade, he cut through a seam, ripping off a three or four inch strip from the bottom of his shirt. He then cut it from the other side, closed his knife, and put it back into his pocket. He placed Tanya's hanging skin on her forehead and wrapped the cloth around her head, tying it in a knot at the back. She flinched and complained about the pain the entire time.

At last they were able to make their way toward the stairwell only to discover it had collapsed. To the side stood a steel girder with angled crosspieces they could use as a ladder. Tanya cried with more pain as she used her damaged ankle, but the fear of being left alone drove her on. By the time they reached the bottom floor, they saw small groups of individuals working their way through the debris. The couple gravitated toward the lights being used by others to move toward the exit.

The exit was over a quarter of a mile away. There were no tramways or electrical carts to whisk them to fresh air and sunlight. Instead, there were blocked tunnels, mountains of rubble, shattered equipment, and equally broken bodies. The air was full of dust. Offensive odors assaulted their noses.

The distinctions of rank and privilege were forgotten. There was only one common concern, to get out of this tomb before flooding water, broken gas mains, or storage tanks turned it into an infernal and made the air unbearable. Some made the effort to help the less fortunate, while others who could either walk or crawl ignored everyone else and put all their energies toward reaching safety.

Fortunately, the giant blast doors had not been able to close. This allowed a growing number of people to settle on the railroad tracks, the main method of travel into and out of the mountain complex.

There were several carefully concealed helicopter pads that were to have enabled the elite to be transported in during an emergency. People of high rank entered the complex through special tunnels. However, most of these had collapsed, as had the airshafts. Even if the giant fans had not been crushed and too damaged to function, it made little difference because there was no power to keep a steady flow of fresh air in the deep caverns.

Toschoff made it to fresh air just as the sun was setting behind the mountain. He hoped the safety mechanisms had worked to protect the core in the nuclear generating plant deep inside the mountain. A coded message had already been sent to alert the leaders in Moscow of the disaster and call for medical help. However, not all the survivors were concerned about secure communications. A nearby cell phone transmitter, powered by solar, had survived. Soon several open cell phone conversations were aired to family members. These were picked up by listening satellites and relayed to Echelon, America's gigantic intelligence collection facility in England, then on to intelligence agencies in the U.S.

•   Markov sat staring into space for a moment before beginning to talk out his feelings. "I remember reading the Bible as part of my university studies in classic literature. I read the story of the Israelites being delivered by their God from slavery in Egypt. What struck me was the frustration the Egyptian Pharaoh must have felt when God destroyed his army in the Red Sea. I think I understand. How do you fight against such a force? The only answer is you cannot. Let's face it, comrade. We were defeated before we even went to war."

Solntsev objected half-heartedly. "But we still have our underground bunkers in the Moscow area. We can repair the software in our missiles and build others to replace those lost in the mountain. Our anti ship, supersonic cruise missiles are still better than those of the West's. We have our armed forces."

"Oh, so you want to tempt God to strike us, using something similar to the Muslim terrorists who wanted to unleash biological agents to kill millions of Americans? Or perhaps He will turn the Chinese against us. I never trusted those little yellow men. We have too much of their blood in us, you know."

The President threw up his hands in despair.

Markov sighed deeply. "Old friend, I think we need to get drunk and then enjoy a vacation at one of our estates. We can spend the rest of our days talking big and playing the

European elite against the rich Americans. We will enjoy the comforts our positions grant us. The hell with taking over the world! Let others carry the burden. After all, who will care when we are dead? Huh?"

Solntsev smiled. "I will drink to that. As you say, who will care? In fact, who put such a ridiculous goal in our minds to start with? Maybe we need to invite that American prophet to visit us again. Perhaps he can convince us to convert." He grinned and suggested, "You would make a good bishop, Markov."

Markov frowned. "Let's not get too carried away, comrade."

Both men laughed. They got up and walked toward the liquor cabinet.

Official news sources inside Russia would know little and report nothing of the true nature of the tragedy at the Yamantau Mountain Complex. A mighty earthquake, registering 8.1 on the Rickter scale, was reported to have hit in the area, but there was little damage since it was sparsely populated.

The underground Christian network spread a different story. Relatives of those working at the secret project began to spread bits and pieces of the truth, which caused many to turn to Christ and His Church.

Intelligence agencies in the U.S. were able to gather information about the size and importance of the event through intercepted phone calls and the number of transmissions between leaders in Russia and their satellite countries. Clearly something dramatic had occurred in Russia. Only brief news bits were shared with the world. However, it was enough to let the Christians know that God had heard their prayers and answered. He moved indeed in a dramatic way that only He was capable of doing.

At the same time, Internet transmissions revealed the Lord was giving peace to millions in America involved in prayer and fasting for the safety of the nation. All the nuclear weapons possessed by the West could not have done as much damage to the Russian mountain as God did in a matter of seconds. To top it off, it was done without any direct cost to the taxpayers. The message of those accepted as prophets admonished the faithful to press for total victory. The battle in prayer for a safer world was not over yet. There were still one or more suitcase nuclear devices in the hands of men determined to use them.

•   Solntsev and Markov were killing off another round of drinks when Markov's assistant, an Army colonel, knocked on the door and entered.

"Sir, you asked me to notify you if we received any communication from the American prophet. I'm sorry, but the operator did not draw this to my attention sooner. Here is a brief email." He handed it to Markov who read it to the President.

> "Dear Mr. Markov:
> As you requested, I am passing on something that may give you the evidence you asked for. Please relay to your President that today at 15:32 hours, there will be a great shaking in your nation to demonstrate God's power. I don't know what it will be. Let me know if this makes sense."
> Chaplain James Parr

Solntsev chuckled. "Great, after it happens, he wants to take credit for predicting it. I told you that people like that are worse fakes than we are." He laughed. In a drunken stupor he added, "And that's pretty bad."

Markov's assistant hesitated and then said, "Sirs, I draw your attention to the time the email was posted."

Markov looked at it. "The thing isn't in military time. What time would that be?"

The assistant had already calculated the time difference. "It comes out to 10:12 our time, over five hours prior to the earthquake, which hit exactly at 15:32 hours our time."

Both men sobered. They looked at each other a long time before Markov sighed deeply and said, "Well I'll be damned!

How did he know that? How did he know that?" His voice trailed off.

Solntsev let out a hearty laugh and threw his glass toward the liquor cabinet where it shattered loudly. "Yes, you drunken son-of-a-whore! You are damned! In fact, we are all damned! Right, Colonel?"

The third man in the room stood stone faced, his eyes darting from one man to the other. The President sobered a bit, remembering something.

"Say, Markov, were we not supposed to be at the big meeting of all the world's rich, famous, and powerful leaders tomorrow?"

Markov groaned. "Oh yes. The unfortunate incident at Yamantau caused me to forget. All the arrangements have been made. But you know what, Mr. President, sir? I think we should tell them to go to hell. No! Given all the disasters we have experienced lately, we should ask them for a big loan. Yes! That's what we need to do. But instead of wasting our precious time, I say we send our bankers. They're good at asking for money. Do you agree, Mr. President?"

Solntsev smiled. "Mr. Markov, if you will kindly hand me another glass of Russia's best vodka, I will drink a toast to such a presidential decree." Pointing his finger at the colonel, he spoke dramatically, "Colonel, send out the orders. The bankers shall go in our stead. We have other important matters to attend to, like getting drunk, right?"

Markov nodded and headed for the liquor cabinet while the colonel saluted, turned on his heels, and left the room. He would pass the word on to the bankers. It was clear that the President and his security chief were in no condition to be in a public meeting watched by the world's elite.

Later a reply email was sent.

> To Chaplain Parr:
> The President asked me to inform you that he is impressed with the information you sent. As you may have heard, there was a mighty earthquake in the mountains at the exact time

you predicted. It was another
unwelcome event for us.

If you ever return to Russia,
the President asks you to visit
him. Until then, we desire
your friendship and your kind
thoughts.

F. B. Markov,
Office of the President

Chapter Ten

The Remaining Threats

When Erich walked in the door, Christine allowed the children time to hug him and tell him about their day's activity. But after fifteen minutes, she served him a hot drink and suggested that the children give her time with their father. They ran off to finish their Monopoly game.

Christine eagerly began to relate the latest news. "You heard about the big earthquake in Russia, didn't you?"

Erich nodded.

"Look what I got off the Internet. Pastor James Parr, who just got back from Russia, emailed the Russian President's office and told him God was going to demonstrate His power at 15:32 hours. That's military time. And guess what? It was the precise time of the earthquake. The word leaked from America's intelligence is that the quake destroyed the huge, secret, underground city we've read about."

Erich looked at the email. "Did James Parr get that word from the Lord?"

"I don't think so. It came from someone he trusted, so he passed it on to the Russians. Erich, this is a fantastic answer to prayer. Not only was a virus planted in the Russian missiles so they can't launch them, but one of their main sources of protection and the production of ICBMs has been destroyed. And, too, there seems to be a great revival of faith sweeping across Russia just as it is in this country. Isn't it great?"

"Yes, it is. But I see here that they are reminding us to keep praying because there's still that terrorist bunch with the suitcase nuke they haven't been able to locate." Erich yawned. "I'm going to have to leave most of the praying up to you ladies for awhile. The demand for concrete is down with all the turmoil in the economic sectors, but I got a call from one of the fellows at the old firm. They may need me. They're getting more calls from people wanting help salvaging their portfolios. It seems that some are beginning to see a light at the end of the economic tunnel."

Christine dropped the papers on the table and gave him an enthusiastic hug. "I knew if we didn't panic, God would lead us to something better. I believe He's prepared you to give people the help they need."

He returned her hug and said, "I'll accept that."

•   Jolene Howard was experiencing her first conflict with the President. With the support of Richard Languard, she continued to press her point.

"Mr. President, I understand why Jack Warren has to go to the European Summit along with the chairman of the Federal Reserve and some of the key representatives from both houses of Congress. But they are all members who are opposed to you and your new policies. Surely we should balance the delegation with some of your strongest supporters."

The President showed no emotion when he replied. "Beyond those required to go because of their positions in the Cabinet, the banking community, and Congress, the rest have all volunteered to go." He shrugged and continued, "Which is their privilege."

Richard added, "I have to agree with Jolene. Every one of them has expressed opposition to you, some vocally. Nearly all the leading politicians and those in the banking community from around the world that are attending the conference have come out against you. Don't you think we need some strong supporters? There is still time for one of us to make arrangements to go."

The President leaned forward. "I appreciate the fact that you don't hesitate to disagree with me. You know I respect your counsel. Neither do I think your assessment of who is for us and who's against us is wrong, but . . ." He raised his forefinger to make a point.

"I remind you of what you said when you convinced me I needed Chaplain Parr's counsel. You admonished me to exercise the authority of my office as the leader of the

American people. You were right about the power of this office, and that's what I'm attempting to exercise now. I don't give . . ." He caught himself. "I was going to express my opinion in a colorful way, but my wife has encouraged me to keep my language clean. I don't care one bit what those pompous, stuffed shirts say, care, or do, which includes the delegates from America.

"Their actions have no lawful authority over the American people or the Constitution of the United States of America. Granted, what they do can hurt us economically. But I've come to the decision that I must do what is lawfully right and best for the American people. We don't need those who are for us to face the criticism they would if you were to go. I'm convinced our fate is in the hands of God. So let our enemies rant and rave while our friends worship, pray, and look to our Lord Jesus Christ about the future."

Smiles appeared on Jolene and Richard's faces as they glanced at each other and then looked at the President.

Jolene turned her attention to the folder in her hands. "What's next on the agenda, Mr. President?

•   CIA Agent Tom Holman headed a special office. It provided safety for foreign personnel from oppressive regimes who sought refuge in America and provided valuable information to the U.S. government. Holman established safe houses in suburban areas where such foreign personnel lived without drawing attention to themselves. He had prepared a study of the types of neighborhoods that were best. Once a house had been purchased under a fictitious name or corporation, it was rental property. Neighbors ignored renters.

Those who worked for Holman, handling the books or transporting the personnel, had the same attitude. These foreign personnel simply became faces that no one cared to remember. Thus it was that, years before, someone in the structure of the shadow government recruited Tom Holman. He proved reliable to shelter certain people without inquiring who they were or why they needed a safe place to hide.

In the confusion of the massive Washington bureaucracy,

there were committees that had been established as far
back as World War II. Still on the pay roll, these supposedly
took care of matters for a war that had ended decades ago.
Thus, it was not unusual that Holman's budget remained
unquestioned as long as there were examples of men such
as the former Dr. Kampov who had defected to America,
bringing valuable scientific knowledge that saved the nation
untold billions in the development of the space program.

As time passed, a group of Palestinian men asked for
protection from Israel. The four were housed in a suburb
outside the District of Columbia. Their neighborhood paid
no attention to a large shipping container delivered to the
house. With some difficulty, the four men slid it into the
garage and closed the door. The container held pieces of
machines that made metal dyes. If the container had been
X-rayed or opened for inspection when it was removed
from the ship, nothing particularly suspicious about the
contents would have been found. A base for one of the pieces
of equipment was a metal box. Lead lined, it contained a
suitcase nuclear device hooked to a portable power supply.

Hamal Mohammed was the leader of the four-man team.
He and another fellow had received intensive training on
the maintenance and care of the suitcase. They also knew
how to set it off. The other two men were fellow soldiers
committed to dying for the cause.

They were to coordinate their attack on the capital
city with Kirkland's team. When that team had been
eliminated, they continued to prepare. Waiting for the
signal to launch their assault, Hamal had time to watch a
news report on television. It told about the UN bickering
over sending troops to guarantee the safety of the newly
formed Palestinian state. This infuriated Hamal. He made
his decision. He would not listen to those giving the order to
strike the White House instead of the Capitol.

Hamal blurted to the others, "The UN is holding a
meeting of political leaders in conjunction with world leaders
in Luxembourg. This is the place and the time to strike!"

The others appeared confused. Hamal, sensing their
hesitation, stated emphatically, "It's our lives that are on the
line. I'm tired of the UN's attitude toward our homeland."

Abdul spoke with caution. "We were originally assigned to take out the U.S. Capitol and as many of the members of Congress as possible. The latest orders were to prepare to take the White House when the President is there. Isn't that more important?"

Hamal exhorted, "No, I've suspected all along that the Jews are behind the UN. This is just one more confirmation." He switched off the TV and gave his full attention to his team members.

"I was given the responsibility of leading this attack. I've always followed orders, but you know how many times our leaders have been wrong. Again, it's our lives that are being sacrificed. I'll tell you what I will do. I will pray to Allah again. He will show us."

After a great deal of discussion, the men agreed to follow Hamal's directions. The next morning he told them he was confident that it was Allah's will to strike the UN. After breakfast, they sprang into action.

Money was no problem. The team had cash and credit cards with large lines of credit. So Hamal moved his operation to a New York hotel. He registered as Shiek Hamal Mohammed, in town for the UN meeting. The suitcase bomb in the lead lined protective box was placed in a four-wheel drive Suburban. They rented a stretch limousine and hired off duty New York motorcycle cops to provide an escort on the morning of the first meeting.

•   Luxembourg's meeting was billed as an emergency for world leaders. The subject would be the global economic crisis. All the super wealthy heads of ruling families, corporate leaders, Counsel on Foreign Relations, Trilateral Commission, and the various old fraternal groups along with their advisers, security teams, and spiritual gurus were in attendance. Secretary of the Treasury Jack Warren led the delegation from the United States.

•   The member of a small terrorist group, Abu Duba, had worked himself into the position as head of security for a sheik in one of the Middle Eastern oil kingdoms. This gave him access to the entire hotel complex that housed the

Luxembourg delegations. Security consisted of many layers
of the military and police with the inner circle composed of
select security personnel for individuals or national groups.
Guards with heat seeking, ground to air missiles had been
stationed on the roofs of the highest buildings. Stopping
limousines and screening delegates and luggage became
routine in order to gain entrance to the grounds. Vans took
delegates to the hotel.

Personal bodyguards kept their side arms for good
reason. Should any of them act traitorously, there would be
many others with weapons. The "criminal" would have little
opportunity to commit his heinous acts before being gunned
down.

Duba had been originally trained and assigned the task
of destroying Middle Eastern leaders who did not accept the
goal of driving Westerners from Muslim nations. He knew
a non-Muslim, wealthy member of the Western powers
financed his group. But he didn't know who the man was
or why he funded their missions. Thus, he was puzzled
when the decision came to strike Western leaders. Why
kill the source of their finances? Was it a matter of revenge
against those paying to have Muslim leaders killed? He
could only assume this would be a better use of the limited
resources his Muslim leaders had for achieving worldwide
goals. Whatever the reason, the mission was something he
considered worthy to give his life for.

Lethal biological agents were given to Duba to carry
out his new mission. He smuggled the toxic agents into the
hotel complex hidden in deodorant bottles. Two things were
accomplished. He found the central heating and cooling
fans that distributed air to the entire hotel complex. Under
the guise of inspecting all areas of the hotel security for
his master, he got past the security guards for each area
and poured several ounces of biological agents into the
fans. It was odorless and slowly vaporized, sending spores
throughout the buildings. The toxins were slow acting and
would not cause noticeable damage for ten to twelve hours.

Walking to the kitchen where the opening banquet
was being prepared, Duba made a fuss over the purity
of the meats, soups, and drinks to be served. He had

devised a special dispenser in the heels of his shoes so that everywhere he walked, minute amounts of spores spread on carpets and the kitchen floor. These were picked up by others and carried throughout the complex.

•   Robert Lanford Davies came to the meeting of the world leaders accompanied by his son, Robert Daniel Davies, Jr., and his twelve year old son, Robert L. Davies, III. After they checked through security and their luggage had been delivered to their luxurious suite of rooms, the elder Mr. Davies escorted his son and grandson to the banquet hall. Leading them to the podium, he explained why he wanted both of them there.

"In this room will gather the most powerful, influential men the world has ever seen in one place. The wealth represented here is staggering. There's no group or nation that can compare to or compete with them. I want you to meet more of the key leaders and their sons. Young Robert, these will be the men you will be trained to work with so that you can carry our mission to its completion."

The youth smiled at his grandfather, acknowledging his life mission. He listened as his grandfather went on, "I'm disappointed that Baron Von Steinberg and his son, Peter, may not be here."

Robert Jr. responded in shock. "He's not coming? Why? He's one of the most powerful leaders in our group."

"I received a call from his personal assistant that he had suffered chest pains. His physicians were insisting he get it checked immediately. The Baron might have to spend the night in the hospital."

"Serves the bloody bastard right! We'd all be better off if it proves to be fatal," said Robert Jr., venom in his voice.

The older man said, "Robert, while it's true he's pulled some dirty tricks under the table on us, he's still been one of our strongest leaders to keep the factions in our group together."

Placing his hand on his grandson's shoulder, he spoke directly to him. "I want you to develop a friendship with Peter. He's your age. While he doesn't yet show the characteristics of his father, the mantle will someday pass to him."

"But, Grandfather, if his father isn't trustworthy, why should I be his friend?"

"You must learn that you have to be close to your enemies lest they take advantage of you. It's part of the craft you need as a leader in our global cause.

As they conversed, workers added final touches to table decorations. Duba entered the large banquet facility through a servant's entrance and hurried toward the front. He merely nodded to the three as he passed them. When he turned and began working his way through the tables, the youngest Davies asked, "Grandfather, why are such men allowed in this meeting?"

The elder man patted his grandson's shoulder. "We have to allow some of the leaders of the inferior races in the group so they can be used to control their parts of the world. This man is probably one of their security personnel. You must realize that part of your learning process will be to understand those types of people and how best to make use of them in the overall plan. That's why you are learning several foreign languages--"

The boy's father interrupted, cautioning, "While you will make friends with some of them, you must always keep a sense of distance lest you begin to think of them as equals. You will find a few to be quite likeable and intelligent. But ultimately they will never be allowed to rise to the rank that your family name gives you. This can become quite a burden. Is that not true, Father?"

"Yes, but that's simply one of the encumbrances you learn to bear if you fulfill your duty to us and those of our kind. However, the privileges far outweigh the obligations. My forefathers earned our right to enjoy these responsibilities and privileges of leadership. While some acquired their wealth and proved their leadership through past wars, my generation understood there were better ways to bring the world into subjection.

"Through our control of the education of the masses, modern communication, and psychological techniques, we learned how to accomplish our goals without resorting to outward force. Do you remember, I explained that we used large loans to third world nations for gigantic, impressive projects?"

"Yes, Grandfather. You knew they would never be able to repay the loans, so this put them in financial bondage to you and the others. Also, the money never actually went to their country. It went to large corporations owned by our class."

The older man spoke again, "Yes, that way we haven't had to use force in those cases. It was cheaper, well actually more profitable to buy the nation than it was to send an army to conquer the people. In the case of what is planned for the independent, stubborn people of America, we are requiring them to spend their money to be the policemen of the world. At the same time, we're using a great influx of immigrants to break up the harmony of their culture. These and other subtle pressures break their will to resist our plans for global control. As hard as we try to use education, economics, and medicine to bring about control, sometimes we still have to resort to force. But due to setbacks, as with the recent events in Russia, those efforts usually take longer than originally planned."

The youngest Davies, impeccable in his suit and tie, looked up at his grandfather. "Thank you for allowing me to be a part of this gathering. I will do my best to make you both proud of me."

"I'm sure you will. We need to go to our rooms and put on our tuxedos before we have drinks in the lounge."

The three paid no attention to the workers who looked down at the floor when the Davies passed them.

•   Guests throughout the Luxembourg hotel complex awoke in the early morning hours feeling ill. They had sore throats, runny noses, and coughs. Vomiting and bloody bowels followed. Available medical people were pressed into action. Antidotes used by the doctors had no effect.

As the sun rose, panic spread through the complex. The doctors themselves also became ill and knew they were helpless. A few of the leaders were rushed to nearby hospitals. The doctors in those medical buildings ordered the area quarantined. Security personnel and people living downwind from the hotel reported the same symptoms.

By mid morning, people dropped dead of heart attacks, or their lungs filled and they drowned in their own fluids. The doctors and lab technicians who rushed in wearing protective covering soon discovered the biological agents. They declared there were no cures and that wherever infected people went for treatment, they would spread the agents to unprotected persons exposed to them. The only good news was that sunlight and time would kill most of the spores. The destruction would not spread forever if those infected were contained.

Although great pressure was put on those responsible for the health and welfare of surrounding nations to do something special for the world leaders, the matter was totally out of their hands. Surviving troops were ordered to shoot to kill anyone attempting to leave the area. Fortunately the weather service predicted that the event would be followed by sunny weather. However, the cleanup would take days of round-the-clock effort and endanger everyone who came near the site. Therefore, the ultimate, drastic decision was for men in airtight protective suits to place all the dead inside the complex and burn it to the ground, along with their personal effects.

•   On the same morning at the opening session of the United Nations, an official looking limousine led by a Suburban full of security personnel passed through security after the driver in the Suburban waved papers and complained that his Sheik was late for the morning session. The two vehicles pulled up in front of the UN world headquarters. Before guards could stop it, the Suburban drove down the walkway and crashed through the entrance. In a blinding flash, the UN building became a pile of radioactive rubble that served as the tomb for UN leaders from around the world.

The area would be contaminated for decades to come from the effects of the dirty nuclear device. It would also serve as a dramatic monument to the failure of the United Nations to bring peace to the world through their subtle grab for global control. The building that once looked like a giant tombstone had become just that for man's grandiose schemes.

Those responsible for training and guiding the team were mystified. Why did they not follow orders and strike the U.S. Capitol? No one would ever know what went through the minds of the terrorists. But most Christians saw this as an answer to their prayers. The Capitol and the masses on the East Coast had been protected. A huge thorn in America had been removed.

For years, a few Americans, considered extreme, rightwing radicals by most, had been calling for the U.S. to get out of the UN. Instead, God got the UN out of the U.S. It was seen as poetic justice.

• James and his friend, General Leland, now serving as Secretary of Defense, were on a conference call with President McCleen and Vice President Howard. The President requested, "Chaplain Parr, we'd like your spiritual assessment of recent events."

"I think we all agree that the actions at the UN building and in Luxembourg were the hand of God in answer to prayer. I see these as God's judgments against evildoers. Many people will find this conclusion shocking and cold hearted, but as I understand God's ways, this is my best call.

"I see it as His way of giving His people here in America a greater opportunity to carry out their responsibility, that of returning this nation to her true roots. Of course, these events have not destroyed all those men who dream of world domination and the occult forces behind them. The age old spiritual battle will continue and--"

General Leland interrupted with his observations, "But it did greatly reduce their numbers and slowed them. It's going to take a long time for the survivors of the powers-that-be to put their act back together. In spite of economic turmoil which their demise is causing in world markets, I believe, when the dust settles, all nations will be better off."

The President added, "Speaking of reducing the number of our powerful enemies, you won't see this in the news. My intelligence briefing this morning had an interesting side note. It seems that Baron Rudolph Steinberg deliberately opted out of attending the Luxembourg meeting by faking a heart attack."

"Isn't he the big shot among the European elitists?" asked General Leland.

"Yes, he was. So our intelligence wanted to know why he missed such an important meeting. From information gathered, we learned that his physicians faked his heart attack."

James asked, "How in the world do these guys learn this stuff?"

"Well, it turns out they put the Baron in the hospital to make it look legit. But when they prescribed a sedative to help him sleep, a nurse gave him the wrong drug. Steinberg had a bad reaction to it. When they tried to correct the reaction by giving him another drug, it put him into a real cardiac arrest. Things went from bad to worse, the medical staff lost control, and the guy died.

"We learned this by tapping into the phone conversations of the doctors and hospital personnel who are all trying to shift the blame on each other. In their case, they're not worrying about being sued. They're concerned about keeping their heads attached to their bodies. You don't make a mistake like that with one of the wealthiest and most politically powerful men in the world and just say you're sorry."

General Leland asked, "Did the Intel boys come up with any possibilities as to why he skipped the meetings? Do you think he had an inside track about what was coming?"

"No, they didn't receive anything specific on that. All they've got to go on is the fact that the Baron faked the heart attack. There is evidence that his money supported some terrorist groups. It would be hard to prove in a court of law, however. His money may have been behind the UN explosion as well as the act in Luxembourg."

James noted, "This is consistent with the kind of power plays demonically controlled men like Steinberg try to pull off. With all his supposed buddies gone, it would have placed him in a strong position to be at the top of the totem pole."

"So God let him know who the real boss is." Leland spoke with lightness in his voice.

President McCleen went on, "Before we move from

that situation, there is one other piece of information our intelligence received. Steinberg's heir, his only legal son, Peter, has been strongly influenced by one of his riding instructors, a committed Christian. Peter became angry at his father for having the instructor sent out of the country to keep the man from having any further contact with Peter. God was working on more than one angle of the problem."

"One less future problem for us to worry about," the general concluded.

"Yes, but only one of many, I'm afraid. Getting back to what James said earlier, a couple of huge thorns were removed, but this doesn't mean all the problems in America have been solved by any means. My major concern now is getting across to the American public that it's not going to be easy or painless for us to recover from the results of decades of economic madness, greed, and corruption in all segments of our society.

"I think I've convinced most of them that we are not setting up a religious dictatorship. The threats of impeachment have died in Congress. The leaders there and the public know it would be nonstop if everyone were thrown out for past mistakes. Of course, losing some of our most vocal opponents in Luxembourg has not hurt us either. So for the most part, the people are stuck with those of us in office, at least until the next election. I'm hoping they will see that, as Americans, we still have our land, homes, factories, roads, computers, a fantastic power distribution system, and communication mediums. We can again become productive. We have a lot going for us."

"Right on, Mr. President," James agreed. "I'm no politician, but while we're making changes, the sizes of the federal and state governments are going to have to be reduced so legitimate taxes can be lowered. Instead of all that money going for wasteful government projects, it should go into new businesses and the rebuilding of the basic infrastructures of cities, such as sewage systems, bridges, and water systems."

Vice President Howard had a lilt in her voice when she commented. "Chaplain, I do believe you'd better run for a seat in the U.S. Senate. We need your kind of thinking here in Washington."

"Thank you for your confidence, but I believe the Lord wants me to stick closer to home. On the other hand, I might do some writing on these issues."

"Listen, James," said General Leland with enthusiasm, "you talked me into getting back in the saddle. Don't think we're going to let you go back to a lazy retirement."

The President agreed. "I think you're right, General. We've not eliminated the threat of terrorism. One of the best ways to stop that is to assimilate the numerous aliens in our culture who have come into America legally. I've pledged a greater effort to remove those who entered our country illegally. Plus, we're using troops to close the borders so that others cannot come in. But the ones here legally need to be educated and led into a spiritual transformation, which will enable them to appreciate and conform to the American traditions of faith in God, hard work, and self reliance as they learn to speak and write English. We need someone to lead this effort at the national level." The President asked, "General, do you know someone highly qualified for that Cabinet level job?"

"Yes, sir, I think I do. I also know he'll say he's too old, along with a string of other excuses a mile long. But I've never seen him back down from a call to duty."

Jolene reminded, "I recall someone making a strong argument for the government welfare system to be replaced by personal charity through churches and local, private organizations. He pointed out that it wouldn't be an easy or painless process but believed it could be done. I think he'd be the man to lead that kind of effort."

There was laughter before James asked, "Do I sense an attempt to railroad someone into a position he hasn't asked for?"

The only answer was from the general. "Toot, toot!" It was followed by more laughter from everyone.

No final decisions were made during the lively interchange between new friends. They did all agree, however, that in spite of the challenges, there was hope because, by the grace and mercy of God, Americans had again triumphed. Ω

Help Spread the Message
of *America's Choice.*

If you appreciate the message in these two novels, please help us get the book to others.

All profits from this novel will be put into efforts to call Christians to repent and pray for the reclaiming of America for Christ and His purposes.

We are doing what we can to make it as easy as possible for you to help. Do not underestimate the power of personal referrals.

Also, please check out our websites for Biblically based teachings and prayer aids.

Here's how you can help.

Order copies for friends.

Email friends a FREE e-copy.
Go to www.freedom-loving-books.com
for details.

For those not on the Internet
or who want printed copies,
buy a whole case -- huge discount.

Phone or write for details:
(970) 323-5202
P.O. Box 412, Olathe, CO 81425

"Those who say it cannot be done should not interfere with those of us who are doing it." S. Hickman

"...it does not require a majority to prevail, but rather an irate, tireless minority keen to set brush fires in people's minds.." Samuel Adams

Check out our website:
www.freedom-loving-books.com
for other listings and how to contact the author.

Deep in the heart of every person is the desire to be free. Whether it's emotional freedom to break the inner bars of your own self imposed prison or the yearning for a social order that provides the liberty to pursue your dreams in your own unique way, the quest involves common elements.

You need knowledge, inspiration, and encouragement to press for your highest and best. The Internet is a fantastic tool in man's current struggle to find the means of achieving this foundational longing of the human spirit.

It provides the free flow of information and the basis for gaining knowledge and inspiration. The challenge is learning how to separate the truth from the flood of lies, disinformation, and deceptions.

Freedom-loving-books seeks to provide practical, focused information in a variety of formats that will inspire, enlighten, and aid you in your search for being all that you can be. You're invited to stop by for a visit.

About the author

Frank Meyer writes from a wide variety of life experiences. These include growing up on a Southern Illinois farm, serving as a radio intercept operator in the USAFSS during the Korean War era, graduating from Princeton Theological Seminary, and being ordained as a Presbyterian pastor.

After ten years, he left the pastoral ministry in 1976 to spend the next thirty years seeking to apply Biblical Christianity to the critical social, economic, and political issues of this era. He writes with a passion, using the power of drama in fiction and documented history in nonfiction to call Americans back to the foundations that made this nation a magnet for freedom loving people around the world.

Frank and his wife Judith have been married since 1962. They have two married sons and three grandchildren and currently reside in Colorado.

Other Novels by Frank Meyer
The Clark Evans Trilogy

Like it or not, guns are a controversial issue as our society becomes more violent every day.

Whether you are for or against guns, *Gun Rites* helps you understand why personally owned weapons play a necessary role in keeping America free.

The very existence of Western civilization is threatened by today's social and political realities.

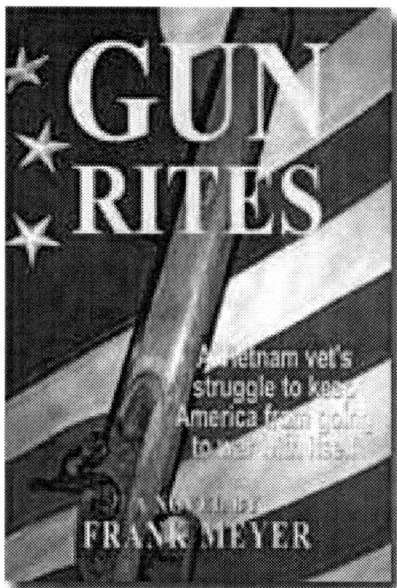

This adventure novel shows how your rights under the Second Amendment are in jeopardy and why guns are part of the *rite* of being an American.

Please accept this offer for a free chapter. Visit our website http://www.freedom-loving-books.com and click on *Gun Rites*. Type your name and email address in the request box. Chapter One will automatically arrive by email.

The book retails for $15.95, plus shipping and handling. Purchase information is on the website. Or phone Infinity Publishing at 1-866-289-2665.

See readers' comments in the front of this book.

If you enjoyed *Gun Rites*, here's the next adventure in the Clark Evans trilogy.

There is a great deal of evidence that some of our soldiers were left behind after the Vietnam War.

Clark Evans agrees to help a friend find out what happened to his only son declared MIA in Vietnam. In the process, he becomes a victim of the government's betrayal of one of their own, a U.S. senator. Again he is forced to fight for survival against unseen enemies who use the power of government to cloak their evil.

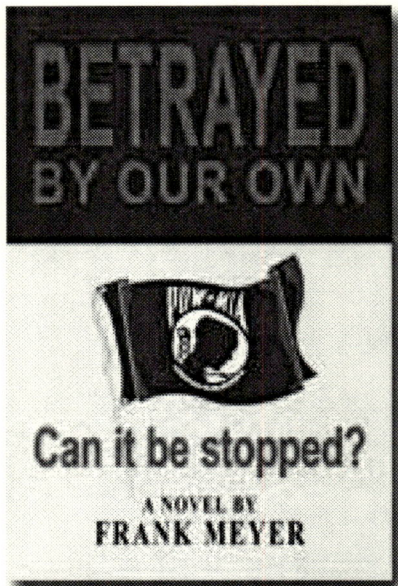

BETRAYED BY OUR OWN

Can it be stopped?

A NOVEL BY
FRANK MEYER

Experience the challenge of dealing with political power gone amuck. Fight back with our characters when everything seems to be going wrong but human compassion refuses to give up. The drama will take you from the jungles of Southeast Asia to the battlefields of Europe and from the beauty of the South Pacific Islands to the back streets of Washington, D.C.

Please accept this offer for a free chapter. Visit our website http://www.freedom-loving-books.com and click on *Betrayed*. Type your name and email address in the request box. Chapter One will automatically arrive by email.

The book retails for $15.95, plus shipping and handling. Purchase information is on our website. Or phone Infinity Publishing at 1-866-289-2665.

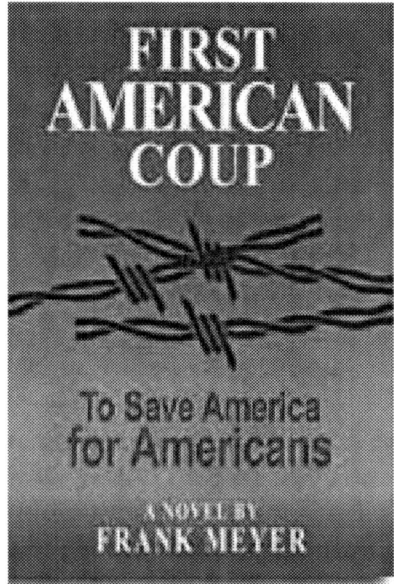

A final word from the Word

"The word which came to Jeremiah from the LORD, saying: 'Arise and go down to the potter's house, and there I will cause you to hear My words.'

"Then I went down to the potter's house, and there he was, making something at the wheel. And the vessel that he made of clay was marred in the hand of the potter; so he made it again into another vessel, as it seemed good to the potter to make.

"Then the word of the LORD came to me, saying; 'O house of Israel, can I not do with you as this potter?' says the LORD.

" 'Look, as the clay is in the potter's hand, so are you in My hand, O house of Israel! The instant I speak concerning a nation and concerning a kingdom, to pluck up, to pull down, and to destroy it, if that nation against whom I have spoken turns from its evil, I will relent of the disaster that I thought to bring upon it.

" 'And the instant I speak concerning a nation and concerning a kingdom, to build and to plant it, if it does evil in My sight so that it does not obey My voice, then I will relent concerning the good with which I said I would benefit it.

" 'Now therefore, speak to the men of Judah and to the inhabitants of Jerusalem, saying, "Thus says the LORD: 'Behold, I am fashioning a disaster and devising a plan against you. Return now every one from his evil way, and make your ways and your doings good.' " ' "

"And they said, 'That is hopeless! So we will walk according to our own plans, and we will every one obey the dictates of his evil heart.' "

Jeremiah 18:1-12 NKJV

In 586 B.C., Solomon's temple was destroyed, and the people were either murdered or carried away into captivity.

Printed in the United States
70259LV00002B/478-510

9 780978 547615

Frank Meyer